Leaning the gun up against the side of the car, he picked J.J. up, opened the rear door, and placed him in the backseat. Looking at the blood on his hands, he picked up the gun and went back to the cabin. After cleaning himself up, he returned to the car. The keys were still in the ignition where J.J. had left them. The man started the car and drove back down the road to an access road that led to the electric company service road. Once on the service road, he drove another three miles until he found the exact spot he was looking for. He drove the car to the very edge of the precipice He got out and removed J.J.'s body from the backseat and positioned him in the driver's seat. After placing the car in neutral he walked behind the car and shoved it toward the edge. It took one good push to get the car moving. It teetered on the edge for a moment, then heaved forward and started its descent into the deep ravine hundreds of feet below. The man stood and watched as the heavy Cadillac sheared off small trees and branches as it moved downwards. At one point he saw J.J.'s arm as it flopped out the window. As it hit a huge rock, the car did a complete somersault and disappeared into the bowels of the ravine. Even though the car was out of his sight, he could still hear the sound of metal against wood and rock until there was an eerie silence.

ECHOES OF DEATH

THE SMOKY MOUNTAINS MURDERS

MARLENE GARY
MITCHELL YEAGLE

a BlackWyrm book
Louisville, Kentucky

ECHOES OF DEATH: THE SMOKY MOUNTAINS MURDERS

A BlackWyrm Book
BlackWyrm Publishing
10307 Chimney Ridge Ct, Louisville, KY 40299

Printed in the United States of America.

ISBN: 978-1-61318-127-0
LCCN: 2012940295

First edition: July 2012
Second edition: October 2013

CHAPTER ONE

THREE DAYS AFTER THANKSGIVING Conrad Pearl was laid to rest in the Bethel Cemetery in Townsend, Tennessee. Beneath a grey overcast sky, six pallbearers carried his coffin from the hearse to the gravesite.

Grant Denlinger exited the long, black limousine and helped his wife, Dana Beth and his mother-in-law, Ruth, from the backseat. He put his arms around both of them as they climbed the small grassy slope, surrounded by tall pine trees. He hadn't recalled much about the funeral service at the church, except he was amazed at the great number of people who had attended. Previous to Conrad's death, he had no idea how popular his new father-in-law had been. For the last three days his mind had been filled with the circumstances of the man's death. Dealing with the grief of Dana Beth and Ruth hadn't made things any easier. He could understand the way they felt; Ruth losing her husband, Dana Beth, her father. He felt guilty for not sharing the same level of grief they were experiencing. He was still torn over his decision regarding the truth he discovered about Conrad.

Passing a large oak tree at the crest of the slope, he noticed an older man standing next to the tree. He was dressed in black loose fitting clothes with a black knit cap pulled down over his ears. The man seemed out of place as everyone else was congregating down by the gravesite. Grant couldn't make out the man's face, but at the moment he really didn't care. Maybe the man was one of the grave diggers or a curious passerby.

At the bottom of the slope, Grant looked around at the people gathering under the canopy by the open grave. Some were sitting, others stood. They were Conrad's neighbors and friends, his students and fellow professors, people from the church he attended, business people from Blount County and the Knoxville area, his beloved wife and daughter. Just like at the church service, there wasn't a single person at the gravesite who had not held Conrad Pearl in the highest esteem. The accolades continued as Grant overheard various comments:

"He was such a generous man."

"He was the best professor I ever had."

"He really cared about his students."

"Conrad will be deeply missed."

Many of the same people living in Townsend and the surrounding area were still dealing with the fact that a serial killer, an unknown individual who was responsible for four murders in the past year, was still on the loose and waiting to strike again. Grant knew a different side of Conrad Pearl—a dark side no one else would ever know. It had been only four days ago he had accidentally discovered clues in his wife's parents' garage that led him to believe Conrad might be the killer they were seeking. Later, that day, on the front porch, he and Conrad had a very uncomfortable conversation. Conrad not only admitted to the killings, but also shared two different stories with him. Reasons, according to Conrad, that were justification for the four murders.

Conrad revealed to him that four decades ago he and his brother had witnessed the brutal murders of not only their parents, but also their horse, three dogs, and two pet fawns they had been raising. They were unable to identify the killers. The murders were never solved. He and his brother were sent to a state-run home and eventually adopted by a family in Knoxville. Conrad told him he never forgot what he witnessed that day when the animals on their farm were gunned down. He vowed that someday he would get his revenge. As the years passed, he had tried to put that terrible day behind him, but the horrid memory of not only his parents, but especially their animals that had been shot to death, festered in his mind. All those years, he had been waiting for that one single event in his life that would trigger his revenge. Then, two years ago, he had been diagnosed with cancer. With special treatment he could beat or possibly delay his death for a few more years, but he kept his ailment secret from his family, refused treatment, and decided to set his sights on getting his long awaited revenge. He had to get even and set things right for animals who were mistreated.

That day on the porch, Conrad explained he had only a few months to live, if that. Along with his cancer, he had developed serious problems with his heart. Now that Grant knew the truth, he had a choice to make. Grant, being an officer of the law, could turn Conrad in, the murders would be solved, and Grant would wind up a hero. But, there was a downside to turning Conrad in to the authorities. Dana Beth and Ruth would be exposed to the fact that their father and husband was a serial killer, and what about the baby Dana Beth was carrying? How would the ugly truth about her father affect the birth of the child, not to mention the child's future? Was Grant ready to destroy the lives of Ruth, Dana Beth and his new baby? On the other hand, if he didn't turn Conrad in, who would no doubt soon die, the murders would stop and remain unsolved and the lives of his wife, daughter, and grandchild would be salvaged. Either way, it was a tough decision to make. If he decided not to reveal Conrad as the killer he would be jeopardizing his very integrity; going against the oath he had taken as an officer of the law. He had to decide what was right and then live with the consequences. Not even a week had passed since he had left Conrad's house, completely baffled, not sure of what decision to make.

The next morning, on his way to the Townsend Police Station, he had still been undecided. He arrived at the station early and had taken a short walk in the rain while trying to clear his mind and come up with a rational reason why he should turn his father-in-law over to the authorities. Sitting in his Jeep, soaking wet, he finally decided he was going to do what was right despite the fact the truth would hurt his mother-in-law and his wife. After all, he hadn't committed the murders—Conrad had.

Why should he carry the burden around for the rest of his life, maybe even jeopardize his career because of something someone else had done? He decided to turn Conrad in—but not to Axel Brody, the Chief of Police in Townsend. Brody was an ass and would never let him forget that he had married the daughter of a brutal killer, a man who had killed four people, one of which was Axel's own cousin, Butch Miller. Miller had been on the Townsend police force.

Grant walked one block up the street to the temporary FBI headquarters. He felt more comfortable turning Conrad into the Feds rather than Brody. His hand was no sooner on the doorknob when his cell phone rang. It was Dana Beth telling him her father had died in his sleep. She needed him to come home. He realized that Conrad's death changed everything. There didn't seem to be much sense in turning him in now that he was dead. The murders would stop, although remain unsolved. In time, the people of Townsend and Blount County would forget about the murders, everything would get back to normal and Ruth and Dana Beth would never know the truth.

His daydreaming was interrupted by the sound of the minister's voice, "Amen." The funeral was over, most of those in attendance started toward their cars while others stood and talked with each other. Hugging Dana Beth, Grant guided his wife and Ruth back up the hill. As they approached the tree, Grant noticed the man who had been standing there earlier was walking away. Suddenly, an odd sensation gripped Grant as they passed the tree; the aroma of Peach Brandy tobacco floated in the air. He hesitated as he stared at the back of the man who was now ten yards in front of him. Dana Beth noticed Grant's odd behavior. Dabbing at her eyes with a handkerchief, she asked, "Are you all right? Is there something wrong?"

Nodding in the direction of the limo, he answered, "No, nothing's wrong. I guess it's just the funeral and everything. Come on, let's go home."

Two weeks later, on a Monday morning in the second week of December, Grant sat in the kitchen at his grandfather's farm, where he and Dana Beth were temporarily living. Grant sipped his coffee as he glanced at the clock above the stove. It was just after five in the morning; far too early for his mother or Dana Beth to be up and around.

Dalton, his grandfather, joined him at the table as he offered to refill Grant's cup, "Warm 'er up?"

Grant pushed his cup across the table and answered, "Yeah, guess I'll have another before I take off for work."

Dalton set the pot on a hot pad on the table and pulled out a chair. "How is Ruth doing? I suppose she is still having a hard time with Conrad's death."

"Not all that well. I guess that's to be expected. She was married to the man for almost twenty-five years. Dana Beth and I dropped by yesterday to see how she was getting along. She told us she was considering moving to Chattanooga. She has a sister who lives there. She was widowed a few years back. With the insurance from her husband's death, her sister opened a small gift shop. Ruth says it keeps her busy and she does pretty well. Ruth claims that it feels odd to be in the house alone without Conrad even though she refused our offer to come stay with us. Besides that, she says she can't keep the place up herself, although she needs to stay busy. If she decides to move in with her sister, well, then she won't be alone and she can work at the gift shop. It's not like she's moving out of state or across the country. Chattanooga's only a few hours away."

"I can understand the way she must feel," said Dalton, as he gestured with his cup. "When your grandmother died, there was no way I wanted to stay here on the farm by myself. If it wouldn't have been for your mother moving in, I'd have pulled up stakes just like Ruth is talking about. Then, after you and Dana Beth got hitched and moved in, the ol' farm seemed full of life. Looking back, I'm glad I stayed put."

Grant got up from the table and walked to the sink and began rinsing out his cup. "I got a call from Agent Gephart last night. We're starting the profiling process this morning at the FBI Headquarters in Townsend. He said it might take a week to ten days."

Dalton fingered the rim of his cup. "That's right, I remember when you got back from Charley Droxler's place you said that a couple of weeks following Thanksgiving you'd be getting together. Who's all going to be involved in the profiling?"

Grant turned as he answered, "Well, there were four of us on the original investigative team. Gephart, Chief Blue from Cherokee, and me. We included Doug Eland from Louisville who took most of the photos of the crime scenes and places of interest. Gephart invited Sheriff Grimes from Maryville. I suppose that's because three of the four murders took place right here in Blount County. Since he's the County Sheriff, I guess he should be involved."

"What about Brody?"

"You know how Axel reacts to this kind of stuff. If he can't be in control of the entire shooting match or if he's not the center of attention, he doesn't want to be involved. He's made it pretty clear he doesn't approve of Chief Blue getting involved in a case that's not in his jurisdiction. You'd think with Butch Miller, being one of the murder victims, he'd want to be right in the middle of the investigation. He made it a point over at Charley's, that if we were not going to listen to him, then he wanted no part of it."

"Chief Blue is one of the best, if not *the best* profiler I've ever met," remarked Dalton. "Brody isn't even in the same ballpark as Chief Blue. To tell you the truth, folks around town don't have much faith in Brody anymore, especially since the murders this past year. Of course, I never had to deal with what Brody has been facing when I was the sheriff. People are really on edge; citizens and business owners as well. This last murder over at Charley Droxler's place has gained national attention. If we don't get this thing solved quickly the tourist trade will start to drop off. It's one thing for people to feel unsafe, but when you add the fact that fewer tourists means less money in their pockets, Brody will be the one who suffers. If, and I say if, there is another murder, Brody could lose his job. I can tell you from past experience that being the Chief of Police here in Townsend for the most part is a rather uneventful job, however when something does happen, people in these parts expect action. Brody is running right on the edge of the cliff and I think he knows it."

Grant walked to the kitchen door. "I best be getting ready. Gephart said our first meeting is at seven."

Dalton stood at the sink pouring the remainder of his coffee down the drain. "How does ol' Brody feel about you being out of the office for a week?"

"Gephart said he was pissed as hell, but what choice does he have? The Feds swing more weight than Axel does. He'll just have to deal with it." Hesitating at the doorway, Grant turned, "It'll be nice not to be around Brody for a week or so, but when I get back I'll have to listen to his line of crap. I'm not looking forward to that. There'll be hell to pay."

Grant drove one block beyond the Townsend Police Department to the temporary FBI headquarters that had been set up in town to investigate the ongoing murders. Pulling into the front lot, Grant noticed Gephart's green sedan, Doug Eland's Land Rover, and a dark blue cruiser marked on the side with bold lettering: **CHEROKEE POLICE.** It appeared that everyone was present except Sheriff Grimes.

Grant no sooner entered the small building when he was greeted by a pleasant looking receptionist who politely asked, "May I help you, Sir?"

"Yes," responded Grant. "Agent Gephart is expecting me. The name is Denlinger."

"Of course, Officer Denlinger, everyone is in the backroom. You can hang your coat up over there by the filing cabinets. There's coffee and donuts when you get back there." Looking at the clock on the wall, she went on, "The meeting will be getting underway in about ten minutes."

As he hung up his coat, Grant commented, "Coffee sounds good. Thank you." He walked down a short hallway and past a four-foot Christmas tree decorated with multi-colored lights, and ornaments. He entered the backroom where everyone stood talking.

Gephart was the first to see Grant. "Grant, grab a cup of coffee. We're just about to get started."

As Grant poured coffee into a Styrofoam cup, Doug approached him and extended his hand. "It seems every time I come back to Townsend there is another murder. I hear it was Charley Droxler this time."

Pouring himself another cupful he asked, "Wasn't Charley friends with Asa Pittman, the first victim?"

"That he was," answered Grant. "Actually, Asa and Charley hung out with three other old cronies from Townsend. They meet every Monday, Wednesday, and Friday over at the Parkway Grocery for coffee and local gossip. They've been meeting there for years."

Gephart walked over as he interrupted their conversation. "That's right. Asa and Charley were old friends. Out of the original five, two are dead. Seems kind of strange...don't you think?"

"Yeah, that does seem odd," said Doug.

With that, Gephart gestured toward some folding chairs in the corner of the room. "If everyone would please be seated we'll begin discussing not only the relationship of Asa and Charley with the other three men, but many other topics."

As everyone took a seat, Chief Blue shook Grant's hand. "I'm sorry to hear about the death of your father-in-law. I was out of town and couldn't attend the funeral or the viewing. How is your family getting along?"

Grant sat down as he answered the question, "Conrad's wife, Ruth, is having a lot of difficulty accepting the fact he's gone and well, my wife is doing her best to get her mother through this tough time while she deals with her own grief."

Gephart got the meeting started as he stood in front of the group. "First of all, I think you all know Harold Green, my associate. Even though Harold was not directly involved when we visited all of the crime scenes, he has been kept up to date on what we have discovered. He has worked hard to accumulate and organize all of the evidence you see scattered around the room. So, at this point Harold is a member of the team. I invited Sheriff Grimes to attend but he won't be here until tomorrow. He has some pressing issues in Maryville he needs to clear up."

Grabbing a pointer from a desktop, Gephart continued, "Before we get started I'd like to familiarize all of you with the evidence we have so far." He walked to a large map tacked to a framed section of corkboard and stated, "Here we have a map of not only Blount County, but Sevier County as well. You will notice four blue stickpins, which indicate the location of the four murder scenes:

Thunderhead Trail where Asa Pittman was murdered, the Southeast side of Laurel Lake where Mildred Henks was found, J.J.'s Junk Emporium where Butch Miller was located and finally Charley Droxler's farm where we discovered Charley. The yellow stickpins indicate the probable points of abduction: Asa Pittman's farm, Mildred Henks' home, the north side of Laurel Lake and Charley's farm. It is thought that three of the victims were murdered in Blount County; two in the Townsend area, one over in Alcoa, and one in Sevierville in Sevier County."

Moving further down the wall, he aimed the pointer at a four by eight section of corkboard covered with photographs lined up in neat rows beneath the location where they had been taken. "Next, we organized all of the pictures we have on the crime scenes and places of interest."

He walked to a table next to the far wall and motioned with his right hand. "Here we have all the physical evidence we have collected over the past year." Gesturing at a window above the table he went on, "Out back behind the building we have Miller's truck and boat that were found abandoned up at Laurel Lake."

Gephart handed the pointer to Harold and stood directly in front of the others. "As we cover each area, Harold will point out locations, photos, and items pertaining to that particular murder. Agreed?"

Everyone nodded in agreement, then Gephart began as Harold pointed to the first blue stickpin on the map. "The first murder took place in early April up on Thunderhead Trail in The Great Smoky Mountains National Park. The victim's name was Asa Pittman." Harold pointed to an old mug shot of Asa then at a photograph of his dismembered and mangled, bloody body as Gephart explained, "Doug, who happened to be in the vicinity taking wildlife photographs was the first to come upon the body. Here we see the photos he first took, then more photos upon our return. As you can see the second set of photos indicate the position of the body had changed and the condition of the body had deteriorated from the first photos taken. This, more than likely was caused by the return of the local wildlife, especially the coyotes, Doug originally ran off."

Walking back to the table, Gephart continued his rundown of the first murder as Harold continued to point at the items mentioned. "The county coroner reported that there were traces of novocaine or some sort of drug that causes a numbing effect to the body. From what we have been able to determine Asa Pittman also had traces of some form of chloroform in his blood. He was then secured to a tree with duct tape. We found small sections of duct tape at the scene. The coroner also reported that the victim's fingers were amputated via the use of some sort of tool. Only two of the fingers were located. They were stuck to a shred of duct tape. The other fingers were no doubt eaten by the wildlife drawn to the scene by the smell of blood. From all indications, the victim bled out while secured to the tree. He was more than likely dead before the animals had a go at him."

Picking up a mason jar filled with formaldehyde, Gephart held it up for all those in the room to see. "Inside this jar we have the two fingers found at the murder scene. As you can see the fingers are cleanly cut away from the victim's hands."

He put the jar back down onto the table and picked up a two foot section of a tree branch. "The coroner has substantiated that this branch was cut from the tree with the same tool that was utilized to amputate all ten fingers. The blood on the branch and the hair samples match the DNA of Asa Pittman. The branch was used to hit Pittman over the head. The coroner discovered fragments of bark from the branch on the remains of the victim's scalp. This, however was not the main cause of death."

Next, Gephart picked up a blood-stained belt and buckle. "This was also located at the scene. The initials AP on the buckle indicate that Pittman was the owner." Pointing the belt and buckle at Grant he went on, "Grant told the coroner that just three days prior to the murder he was at the Parkway Grocery when Asa was telling Charley Droxler and the other three he hung with that he had just purchased the belt and buckle over in Cherokee."

Gesturing, Gephart continued as Harold aimed the pointer at the first yellow stick pin. "Before we move on to Asa Pittman's farm, the location where we believe he was abducted, are there any questions on the Thunderhead Trail murder scene?"

Doug raised his hand and asked, "What about the hair sample Chief Blue found in that low hanging tree out by the actual trail? How did that pan out?"

Snapping his fingers, Gephart apologized, "I'm glad you mentioned that, Doug. I'd forgotten all about that." He reached down and picked up a small clear bag containing some strands of hair. "The DNA on the sample did not match up with Asa Pittman just as Chief Blue said when he first discovered the hair sample. It might belong to the killer or any number of people who have hiked the trail. So, at this point the sample still remains as evidence, but it may turn out to be nothing." Turning back to the map he asked, "Before we get into our investigation at the Pittman farm, are there any more questions about the Thunderhead Trail murder?"

Everyone seemed to be satisfied and remained quiet. Gephart looked at the map again as he explained, "There were two major clues that were discovered at the Pittman farm. The first clue found by Grant when he visited the farm shortly after the murder was traces of a substance in the kitchen that turned out to be tobacco, which later was described as a Peach Brandy flavor. The tobacco became a clue only after we found traces of the same type of tobacco at Mildred Henks' home and then at Charley Droxler's place. The fact that Asa Pittman didn't smoke, Mildred Henks did, but not a pipe, and Charley did not smoke, leads us to believe the tobacco was left by the killer at all three locations. Our killer smokes a pipe and his chosen brand is Peach Brandy."

Walking to the photographs on the corkboard, Gephart pointed out that the second clue was the photo of the spices that were organized in alphabetical order in Pittman's kitchen. "The organization of these items sticks out like a sore thumb when you consider the rest of Asa's house was filthy and disorganized. There is a strong possibility the killer, who we believe is very organized, sat at the kitchen table, smoked his pipe, and at some point organized the spices from A to Z."

A few hours later, after examining the evidence again, Gephart took a drink of his coffee. "Gentlemen, it's almost eleven. We've been at it now for just about four hours. I think we should break for lunch. Originally, I was going to have lunch catered in, but I decided against that since over the next few days we're going to be spending quite a bit of time in this room. It's important we remain attentive and fresh during our investigation, so I think we'll take a two hour lunch break each day. You are all on your own for lunch." Checking his watch again, he remarked, "Everyone needs to be back here by one o'clock."

Doug stood and stretched as he looked at Grant. "Okay, where's lunch?"

"How about Lily's," said Grant. "They always have great soup and a large sandwich selection." Putting on his coat, he gestured at Chief Blue. "How about it Chief...you in?"

Chief Blue smiled. "Yeah, a big bowl of soup sounds good."

"See you boys at one," said Gephart. "Harold and I are going to order in. We've got some paperwork that's long overdue."

Walking down the hall, Doug held up his keys. "I'll drive."

Doug cut into his hot roast beef sandwich as he commented, "Lily's is the perfect place for lunch when you consider what we're going to be doing the next few days."

Grant removed a lemon slice from his iced tea and asked, "How's that?"

"Well, I was just thinking, this is where I had breakfast the morning before I found Asa Pittman up on Thunderhead back in April. I remember that day. I was really looking forward to getting up there in the woods and getting some great wildlife shots. I don't think I'll ever forget the way the body looked. Those coyotes and whatever else got to Pittman really did a job on him. Whenever I come down to the Smokies, I always enjoy my time here. I never look forward to driving back to Louisville. But, that week was different. Finding Asa Pittman's body out there in the woods marred what normally for me is a great week. The mountains, the woods, the wildlife, the flowers; all the things I enjoy about coming down here were replaced with a ghastly murder. Later that week when I finally headed north, little did I know, or did any of us realize that Pittman's murder was just the beginning. Here it is almost a year later and even though you guys have found some pretty significant clues you're no closer to catching the individual responsible for the deaths of four people than when we were standing around up on Thunderhead staring down at the mangled body of Asa Pittman."

Chief Blue buttered a slice of bread and commented, "Doug, you and I have been friends for a long time, but I have to disagree with you on that fact. We now know a lot of things about this person we didn't know back then. Like most people, you can't see much progress in our investigation unless we handcuff a suspect and bring them in. In a case like this there are a lot of behind the scenes things going on that will eventually lead us to the killer." Picking up his spoon, Chief Blue continued, "Don't get me wrong, Doug. I think you're a very talented photographer, one of the best I've ever seen. I'm amazed at the talents other people have that I don't. For instance, I could never do what you do for a living. I simply just don't have the talent, nor do I have the ability to write a book, paint a picture, or build a house. The point is everyone is good at something. When Grant and I chose to be officers of the law we knew we would be faced with many situations. Some as simple as giving a parking ticket to a situation as complicated as the one we have now."

"Look, I get it Chief," said Doug. "But I don't see what any of this has to do with bringing this killer in."

Chief Blue looked at Grant as he shook his head signifying that Doug wasn't getting his point. Turning back to Doug, he pointed out, "It's like this, Doug, profiling is like putting together a thousand piece puzzle. Everything has to fit together exactly right before you can see the whole picture. Take you for instance. You take wildlife photos. I've seen some of your work. The end result is always your amazing photographs. But I'm sure there are a number of things you do before creating the actual pictures. Finding the right location, making sure your camera is in working condition, waiting patiently for a good shot, developing film and on and on it goes and only after you have accomplished these things can your wonderful photos come to life. It's the same thing with us. There is a process: visiting crime scenes, collecting clues, interviewing people, asking questions, all of which will enable us to catch our killer."

"Okay, okay, I get it," said Doug as he raised his hands in defense. "When it comes to this profiling business, I'll admit, I'm way out of my league. Tell me about the mental picture which your department has on this killer."

Grant remained quiet as Chief Blue explained, "If Gephart were here he would no doubt say we're getting ahead of ourselves. This is just our first day and we'll probably get no further than the Pittman murder by the end of the afternoon. As the week continues we'll get into the murders of Mildred Henks, Butch Miller, and Charley Droxler. Personally myself, I don't think we're going to discover anything about the killer other than what we already know, but that's part of the process. You never know."

Swallowing a bite of his lunch, Doug remarked, "I'm going to refer to the killer as a man for two reasons: the killer has to be relatively strong when you consider that Pittman and Henks had to be carried or dragged to where they were discovered. You also found traces of pipe tobacco at three of the four murder locations, which eliminates most women."

"That's correct," agreed Chief Blue. "The fact that he smokes a pipe tells us something about him. Pipes are not as popular as they were years ago and as a general rule younger men do not smoke a pipe. So, I'd say our killer is older; thirties, forties...possibly older."

"I think I'm starting to get the hang of this now," said Doug.

"Our killer, if I remember correctly from our investigation a couple of months back was thought to be an animal lover."

"Right again," said the Chief. "Pittman shot at anything that came near his house. He trapped and hunted illegally and sometimes skinned animals before they were even completely dead. Henks ran a puppy mill and treated her dogs horribly. Miller stole neighborhood dogs and turned them over to a dog fighting ring where they were torn apart in training sessions and finally, Droxler had a herd of horses he practically starved to death. Our killer has made it clear, not only to us, but to the public, that he will not stand by and allow animals to be mistreated. In the eyes of many people in the area, our killer is looked at as a hero. He is simply doing what a lot of people feel is justified. They could never do what he has done, but they are not overly sympathetic to those he has killed."

That evening, Grant pulled his Jeep into the driveway of his grandfather's farm, turned off the ignition and sat for a few moments as he thought about the day's events. Chief Blue had been right. They had gotten no further than the Pittman case. Just before they wrapped things up for the day, Gephart said the Henks' murder would be discussed on Tuesday.

Grant was not looking forward to the next few days; hour after hour of pouring over clues that hopefully, at least in the eyes of everyone else involved would lead them to the killer. Grant knew it was a waste of time. He already knew who the killer was and that he was buried in the Bethel Cemetery. He was the only one who knew the truth; a truth he could not reveal. He was going to have to be careful and act as if he was genuinely interested in catching the killer. He had managed to get through the first day shielding the fact that he knew who the killer was. But as the week passed he was going to have to become more involved. He just couldn't sit around and not be involved, especially with Chief Blue in the meetings. Blue was more perceptive than the average person. He had already picked up on Grant's lack of interest the very first day. Blue had asked him when they were ready to leave if he was all right and commented that he just didn't seem to be himself. Grant had lied to him saying he was still dealing with the death of his father-in-law and he was concerned about his wife and mother-in-law.

Conrad had been right. He had told him he was going to have to make a decision and right or wrong—live with it. The days and months that lay ahead were going to be difficult as he would continue to question his concealment of the truth about Conrad Pearl.

CHAPTER TWO

GRANT SLID THREE QUARTERS into the metal slot of the stand alone air machine at the end of the Parkway Grocery parking lot. Unscrewing the cap from his left side front tire, he placed the air hose over the tire stem. After a few seconds he put the air gauge on the stem. *Perfect, thirty-four pounds.*

He shivered as he moved to the driver's side rear tire and repeated the process. The weather for the past week had been exceptionally cold. The temperature was in the mid-thirties with a stiff breeze driving the wind chill down into the teens. As he moved around to the other rear tire, light snow began to fall. Checking the air pressure, his concentration was interrupted by a familiar voice, "Morning Grant."

Looking back over his shoulder, Grant saw the lanky frame of Zeb Gilling standing next to the Jeep. He was wearing a camouflage jacket and bright orange hunting cap and held two cups of steaming coffee in his gloved hands.

Satisfied with the air pressure, Grant moved to the last tire, then spoke, "Morning Zeb." Then he remembered. "That's right it's Monday. Guess you're waiting for Luke and Buddie?"

"Yeah, I got here a little early today. I was sitting at our regular table by the front window when I saw you pull in, thought you might like a cup of coffee." Setting the large coffee on the ground next to Grant, Zeb kept right on talking, "Besides that, I've been wanting to talk to you about something."

Finished with the last tire, Grant stood as he picked up the coffee and set it on the Jeep's hood. "Thanks for the coffee. What's on your mind?"

"Well...it's not...just me," stammered Zeb. "Me, Luke and Buddie have been talking quite a bit about the murders. Hell, that's all we've been talking about...it's what everyone is talking about." Taking a swig of coffee, he pulled the collar of his jacket up around his neck. "After Asa was killed, and then Mildred, we were pretty nervous and then when the other murders happened, well...it sure has put us all on edge. Man, we ain't had a murder around here in more years than I can count. I can't imagine why a killer would pick our area."

Cutting Zeb off in mid sentence, Grant walked around the front of the Jeep and replaced the hose back on the air machine. "So what is it you want to talk to me about?"

"I'm getting there, just hold on for a minute." Walking around the back of the Jeep, he joined Grant by the air machine. "What I'm saying is that's all anybody has been doing...talking. Everybody knows that's what you, Gephart, Chief Blue, that fella from Louisville and whoever else is involved have been doing this last week. I mean, hell, Grant, this killer, whoever he is, has been running around these parts knocking somebody off every season this past year. When is it going to stop? Everyone is interested in what you guys came up with this past week?"

Taking a drink of his coffee, Grant answered, "Zeb, you know darn well I can't go around talking about what we discussed."

Zeb, frustrated, spoke again, "Well, if you're not going to tell anybody what was discussed, I sure as hell hope you've figured out when you're going to nail this killer. There's been enough talking. We need some action around here! Out of the five of us who meet here at the Parkway, two are dead, Asa and Charley! Which one of us is going to be next?" Looking back toward the store Zeb shook his head then turned back to Grant. "Remember when you came to us right here at the Parkway earlier in the year for help about the dog fighting ring? You said if anybody knew what was going on around here it would be us. You're right. There isn't too much that goes on in and around Townsend we're not up on, but this one's got us stumped. I've got to tell you Grant, folks in town are beyond upset. Your boss, Axel, better get on the stick or he might lose his job. That's all I'm saying. When you think about it shouldn't he be right in the middle of this investigation? I mean, for crying out loud, his own cousin was killed, one of our own police officers. It's like he doesn't care. Well, he better start getting involved...and quick. The people here in Townsend are fed up. Brody is an elected official and that can be changed next election. Spring is right around the corner and if things go the way they have this last year, come April, we'll be faced with yet another murder." Looking back at the store, Zeb spotted Buddie's truck as it pulled in. "Look, I gotta go. The other guys are here. Just think about what I said."

Grant watched Zeb walk across the lot to meet Buddie as he climbed out of his truck. Buddie waved at Grant, then he and Zeb entered the store. Grant let out a long breath, the warm air escaping his lungs vaporized in the cold air. Getting into the Jeep, he turned on the ignition and sat back in the seat sipping his coffee. He would have liked nothing better than to have told Zeb that Conrad Pearl was the killer they were looking for. He was getting upset with people who kept reminding him about the murders. He wondered if this is what every day was going to be like until spring came.

Pulling out of the lot, he thought about what Zeb said. Most everyone in town was upset not only about the fact that they couldn't seem to catch the killer, but with Chief Brody as well.

Looking back, it seemed like it would have been much easier to turn Conrad in. First of all he wouldn't have had to sit through a week of going over clues that he, and he alone knew were never going to pan out, and secondly, he wouldn't have to continue lying to everyone he met when the topic of the murders came up. It was too late for that now. He had made his decision and he was going to have to go with it until at least next April when everyone was expecting the killer to strike again. When that didn't happen, things would start to ease up and by this time next year the whole matter would be history.

Turning onto the Alexander Parkway, Grant noticed the electronic message being flashed across the bank's marquee, which read: ONLY SIX SHOPPING DAYS LEFT 'TIL CHRISTMAS. A large blue spruce sat at the corner of the bank's parking lot. It was decorated just the same as it was every Christmas season for as far back as he could remember. In the adjacent lot stood the manger that was supplied each year by the local lumberyard. Later in the evening, volunteers from several of the churches in Townsend would show up in handmade Biblical costumes, along with some farm animals from outlying farms to re-enact the nativity. That reminded him that tonight he and Dana Beth were portraying Joseph and Mary.

Ever since he was a youngster, his mother had brought him into town to see the enormous blue spruce, but more importantly, the nativity scene. For years, Conrad acted as one of the three wise men and Dana Beth felt it was only proper out of respect for her father that she and Grant participated this year. She contacted the church and they were more than glad to have Grant and her volunteer. Tonight it was their turn to portray the Holy Family.

Driving up the street, he thought about how cold it was going to be as they huddled together in the makeshift wooden manger. Stopping at an intersection, he saw Lewis Sutton, in his ancient, sky blue Cadillac make a right turn. Just like every Christmas

Lewis had attached a Christmas wreath to the front grill of his car. An old rusted out pickup truck followed Lewis through the intersection just inches from the Cadillac's bumper. The driver of the truck laid on the horn as he angrily waved his fist out the window. Apparently, Lewis was not driving fast enough for the man in the truck. As Grant watched the moment of impatient driving, he recognized the driver of the truck; Ambrose Stroud. He and his brother, Cletus were not exactly what one would call model citizens. The entire Stroud clan, who lived on the outskirts of town, had been a pain in the ass to the Townsend Police Department for years. Usually it was Axel who dealt with the Stroud family since they seemed to be a little bit afraid of him. Between occasional bouts of public drunkenness, their kids missing school on a regular basis and visits out to their place due to domestic violence, Brody always said that the town, the county, the state, the world would be better off without the Strouds.

Farther up the street he noticed Christmas decorations in shop windows and yard ornaments in front of various businesses. He always enjoyed the Christmas Season, but this year it seemed like the holidays had been anything but joyful.

Pulling into the Townsend Police Station, he noticed Marge's yellow Volkswagen, Kenny Jacks' compact Ford and Brody's truck parked in the lot. Everyone was at work. As he got out of his Jeep, he reminded himself that he had to get over to Pigeon Forge and get his Christmas shopping done. He had to get gifts for his mother, Dalton, Ruth and Dana Beth. What could he possibly purchase for his mother-in-law and his wife that would ease the pain of losing their husband and father? He'd worry about that later. Right now, within the next few seconds he was going to be face to face with Chief Axel Brody and he had no doubt that it was not going to be pleasant.

His hand wasn't even on the door to the station when he heard a loud voice coming from inside. "Axel Brody, if I wasn't a Christian and a woman, I'd take you out behind this station and give you an old fashioned ass kickin'."

Rolling his eyes, Grant pushed open the door, his thoughts of an unpleasant morning at the office seemingly coming to fruition.

Marge, the station secretary, slammed the office phonebook down on the top of her desk, and then with her hands on her hips stared out the back window. "Morning, Marge," Grant said jokingly, as he tried to make light of things. "Should I come back at a more convenient time?"

Turning, Marge trying to compose herself answered, "You picked a bad day to return to work. It seems our Chief has gone over the edge."

From down the hall, Grant could hear arguing:

"Look, I've been here for nearly eight months. This was only supposed to be temporary," Kenny Jacks growled.

"I don't care if it's been eight hours, eight days or eight months. If it takes *eight years* to solve these murders then, by God, you're gonna stay right here in Townsend and remain on the Townsend Police Force."

"That's bullshit and you know it!"

As the argument down the hall continued, Grant walked to the office coffee machine to refill his empty cup. "What the hell's that all about?"

Marge sat behind her desk as she took a deep breath. "Kenny wants to go back to Maryville. Brody doesn't see it that way. He thinks, no, he is demanding that Kenny stay until we have these murders in hand."

"Well, based on what we and the Feds accomplished this week, it might just be eight years," remarked Grant.

"Not a good week I take it?"

"We didn't learn anything new or enlightening. Just rehashed everything we already know."

From down the hall came another round of aggressive bantering: "Jacks! For your information I'm the Chief of Police here in Townsend and as long as you're assigned here you'll treat me with the respect I deserve."

"Oh, I see. We're all supposed to just sit around here and listen to your line of crap because you're wearing a badge on your chest that states you're the Chief of Police. By the way, where did you come by that badge, a cereal box!"

"Jacks, that's enough. Get your ass out of my office and back out there on the streets, now!"

"You don't have to tell me twice. I'm outta here!"

Seconds later, Kenny stormed down the hall, grabbed his hat from a hook on the wall, and started for the door when he saw Grant standing by the coffee machine. "Don't envy you much. He's been bitchin' all week about how you haven't been here."

Brody walked into the front office. "Jacks, what are you still doin' here?" Kenny gave Brody a dirty look then exited the building.

An equally dirty look came across Brody's face as he leaned on Marge's desk, picked up the receiver of her phone and remarked sarcastically, "Are you goin' to get that ad called in to the paper or do I have to do it myself?"

Marge stood defiantly as she raised her hand to her neck. "Don't push it, Axel. I'm a patient woman, but I've had it up to here with your lack of people skills. One more word out of you this morning and you're going to be looking for not only an officer to replace Butch, but you're going to need a new secretary. Understand?"

Axle shook his head in frustration as he turned and looked at Grant. "Denlinger! My office, now!"

As Brody stomped back down the hall Grant hesitated for a moment and addressed Marge. "You really wouldn't quit, would you?"

"Normally, I'd say no. I guess I've grown used to the Chief's mood swings, but this past week he hasn't let up. To tell you the truth, if he doesn't calm down, I'll be looking for some new scenery."

Setting his coffee on her desk, Grant smiled as he commented, "Well, here I go into the lion's den!"

Walking into Brody's office, Grant sat across from the Chief's desk and waited for him to speak. Brody, searching for something in his top desk drawer, slammed the drawer shut and opened another as he muttered to himself, "I can't find nothin' around this damn place!" Giving up, he looked at the doorway and shouted down the hall, "Dammit Marge, where's my black notepad!"

Marge responded as she yelled back, "It's *your* notepad, not *mine!* I don't ask you where my lipstick is, so don't ask me where your damn notepad is."

Brody sat back in his chair as he stared up at the ceiling out of frustration.

Grant, realizing that their conversation had to start at some point, made the first move. "Ya know Chief, you really should back off Marge. If it wasn't for her this whole place would fall apart."

Giving Grant an icy stare, Brody pointed his finger across the desk. "In case you haven't noticed it, Denlinger, this place is fallin' apart *and* you're one of the main reasons!"

"Me? What did I do wrong? Hell, I just walked in the door."

"That's exactly right, Wonder Boy, *you* just walked in the door. Maybe things would be runnin' a little smoother around this place if you would have walked in the door last week."

"I had no choice in that decision," argued Grant. "Since I was part of the original investigative team on the killings, Gephart wanted me in on the meetings." In an effort to avoid Brody controlling the conversation, Grant blew the past week's meetings off as unimportant as he remarked, "If it's any consolation, we walked away without uncovering anything new." Grant, revealing what he knew to be the truth went on, "Personally I feel the murders are over. Come next April things will start to get back to normal."

Brody, still searching his desk for his notepad was only half listening as he continued to complain about the way things were going at the station. "Do you even have the slightest idea how frustratin' it's been here this last week? I've been workin' my ass off tryin' to get someone to replace Butch. I've placed ads in the local papers, even up in Knoxville. I've contacted other cities in the area to see if they have anyone that would be willin' to work here in Townsend. Nothin'! Not a single applicant. Kenny Jacks wants to go back to Maryville. Grimes said he could send someone back over here to replace Jacks but that still leaves us an officer short. I mean, what the hell is wrong with people? I'm offerin' a full time position with benefits, decent pay, a job where they will never be laid off."

Grant shrugged. "Hey, if I wasn't already on the force here in Townsend I'm not too sure how quickly I'd be to jump in the boat. I can see where potential applicants would tend to tread lightly."

Snapping his fingers, trying his best to steer the conversation away from the fact that he had not been at the office for the last week, Grant suggested, "What about Lee Griner?"

Brody frowned as he responded, "Back when I hired Butch, I considered Griner. Lookin' back now I can see with the way things turned out, I probably should have hired Lee instead of Butch."

"Ya know, I've always wondered about that," said Grant. "I went to school with both Butch and Lee. Butch was a troublemaker all through high school. I just figured you hired Butch over Lee because he was your cousin. I mean, when you think about it, Lee was more qualified for the job as an officer: four years in the Marines on the military police, a crack shot, not to mention his military discipline."

"Discipline!" exclaimed Brody. "That's exactly why I didn't put him on the force. Don't get me wrong, there has to be a certain level of discipline in police work, but when Lee came back home from the service it was as if he had never left the Marines. His yes sir everythin' by the book attitude just didn't fit in with our small town way of life. Now, I'm no Sheriff Andy Taylor and this isn't

Mayberry, but still, as an officer you have to tone things down some in these parts."

"I think you should give Lee a call," Grant said. "I run into him once in a while around town. He's working over at the lumberyard, driving a forklift. He's got a wife and two little girls and quite frankly in talking with him on occasion, I think his gung ho Marine attitude has gone by the wayside. He's a good man and has all the qualifications to get the job done."

"Hmm," muttered Brody. "Maybe I will give Lee a call."

From down the hall came loud voices.

"We wanna see the Chief!"

"Yeah, we need to talk with Brody!"

Then came Marge's voice, "You can't just go back there. Hold on!"

"Hey, we're taxpayers. We put him in office and if we wanna see him, then by God we will!"

Within the next few seconds, Zeb Gilling, Luke Pardee, and Buddie Knapp stood just inside Brody's office door, followed by Marge who tried her best to apologize. "Chief, I'm sorry. I told them they just couldn't come back here."

Brody eyed his three visitors then calmly excused Marge, "It'll be all right Marge. You can go back out front. I'll handle this."

Grant retreated to the far corner as the three men moved toward the desk. Before they could say a word, Brody smiled as if he couldn't believe what he was seeing. "What do you three bozos want?"

Zeb, who at the moment seemed to be assuming the role as leader of the trio, sat in one of two chairs facing Brody's desk. Buddie remained standing by the door while Luke slowly lowered himself into the other chair.

Brody looked directly at Zeb as he suggested, "I wouldn't get too comfortable if I were you. I've got a lot on my to-do list today and it doesn't include sittin' here talkin' with the three stooges."

Zeb leaned forward in an effort to display the fact that he was not intimidated. "I reckon we'll get as comfortable as we please, Axel. If it wasn't for regular folks like us who voted you in as Chief, well…your ass wouldn't be sitting in that chair."

Buddie took a step closer to the desk. "Yeah, Brody, we got a bone to pick with you."

Luke chimed in realizing that there was power in numbers. "You might as well make *yourself* comfortable, Axel, because you're gonna sit right there and listen to what we have to say."

Brody sat back in his chair and folded his hands across his rotund stomach as he looked at the clock on the wall. "All right. You boys have five minutes. What's your beef?"

Zeb blew off Brody's remark about their allotted time to speak as he stated, "You never liked any of us," as he gestured at Buddie and Luke, "and that includes Asa and Charley. Let's face it. You're not on our Christmas card list either, but that doesn't make any difference. We all want the same thing; to bring this killer to justice. Like I was telling Grant just this morning over at the Parkway, there's been enough talking. We need action."

Brody shot Grant a hard look as he held up his hand for Zeb to stop talking. "So these three clowns showin' up here at the office this mornin' was your idea?"

"Now just hold on, Axel," argued Grant. "I just ran into Zeb by accident over at the Parkway. He told me everyone in town was frustrated with the lack of progress we're making. I never said anything or even suggested that Zeb and his pals come barging in here to give you a piece of their mind. I'm just as surprised as you they're here this morning."

Not allowing Brody to get a word in, Luke spoke up, "Like Zeb was saying...we need some action...and we need it now. Me, Zeb, and Buddie have more at stake and more to worry about when it comes to these unsolved murders."

"What in the hell are you talkin' about?" snapped Brody.

Buddie jumped in on the conversation as he held up one of his index fingers to make a point. "Out of the five of us who meet at the Parkway Grocery, two have been killed. Hell, Axel, one of us could be the next victim."

"Buddie's right," added Zeb. "Three of the murders are connected to us. In case you haven't been informed Axel, Asa had a thing for Mildred Henks. She made it pretty clear she didn't want anything to do with ol' Asa. That little piece of information was never even discussed until Mildred was killed *and* in a similar fashion. We all started to think that just maybe somebody who was seeing, or at least was interested in Mildred, took both of them out and—"

Brody interrupted Zeb as he explained patiently, "Grant and I have already discussed that possibility and the Feds as well have that information. The motive for the murders has leaned heavily toward Asa and Mildred's lack of respect for animals, not a love triangle."

Grant sat on the edge of the desk and asked Zeb, "You said three of the murders were connected to you fellows. Asa and Mildred count for two. Which one of the other two murders are linked to you guys? I don't understand."

Zeb seemed more relaxed now that he had their attention. "Charley and I go way back. We met in the third grade. Over the years we remained friends. He was like a brother to me. There wasn't anything we couldn't confide in each other about. Here's the thing. Asa wasn't the only one who had interest in Mildred Henks. Charley took a shining to her also, but never planned on doing anything about it until Mildred approached him one evening while he was eating at Hooter's. This happened after Asa was murdered.

"She just walked right up and joined him at his table. She sat down, ordered a pitcher of beer and a round of wings. They talked for hours. She left, inviting him for dinner over at her place. Poor ol' Charley thought he had a shot at her. Turns out the only interest Mildred had in Charley was the large pasture he had on his farm. She presented him with a business proposal. She had an opportunity to purchase a small herd of horses, thirty-one to be exact, at a well below market price. What she needed from Charley was a place to keep the horses for a few weeks until she could sell them to local riding stables. She claimed that she was going to make a sizable profit and agreed to split it with Charley. The deal fell through; the horses were not the quality the stables were looking for. Charley continued to contact Mildred about the horses because he wanted them off his property. Mildred was supposed to supply him with food for the herd but she never did. Then, Mildred was murdered and Charley is stuck with a herd of horses he had no bill of sale for. Three of the horses died from weakness for lack of food and the rest of the herd was heading in the same direction."

Brody sat up straight in his chair. "Well, that clears up where those damn horses came from. We figured Charley was murdered because of the poor condition of the horses, which falls right in line with the killer's motive of the other three. They were all unkind to animals. Unless you're beatin' the hell out of your dog or doin' somethin' that's considered cruelty to animals then why on earth would you feel in any danger of bein' the next victim?"

Zeb stood, his anger once again on the rise. "Look, Brody, you better get your ass in gear on these murders. The people in this town are pissed to say the least. Now, if you can't get the job done...then we will!"

"And just what does that mean?" Brody laughed. "Don't stand there and tell me you three ol' farts are going to grab your huntin' rifles and head out to the woods or the surroundin' neighborhoods and track down our killer." Brody stood as he reached for his coat.

"Tell ya what. Why don't you three old fellas head on back down to the Parkway and sit by the window and bullshit each other like you always do. Because that's what you're good at. Now, get out of my office before I really get pissed!"

As the three men exited the office, Zeb hesitated at the doorway and turned back. "Do your job, Axel. If this situation doesn't start to turn around...and fast, we'll get someone to come here to Townsend, somebody that can and will find this killer."

Once again, alone in the office, Brody turned to Grant. "What the hell was Zeb talkin' about? Do you know anythin' about this person Zeb knows he can contact?"

"I don't have a clue what he meant. He probably made the whole thing up," answered Grant. Walking toward the office door he half saluted. "I'm gonna hit the streets and start patrolling unless you have something else you want to bitch about." He hurriedly close the door before Axel could answer him.

Grant placed his arm around Dana Beth at the manger scene as she cradled the doll in her arms. Normally, those who organized the nativity scene each year at Christmas utilized an actual live child but considering the colder than usual weather, they had opted for using a doll. Aside from the Christ Child façade, everything else in or around the manger scene was in fact real; the three wise men and the shepherd were portrayed by local citizens, a cow, two sheep, and a donkey were donated by Mr. Pike who owned a local farm. Surprisingly a neighborhood dog had wandered into the manger and curled up in the hay in the corner. A split rail fence had been placed on all three open sides of the eight by twelve manger to keep overly interested children from entering and the animals from exiting.

Grant sniffled and huddled close to Dana Beth as he spoke softly, "Think I'm trying to come down with something; maybe a cold. This might not have been the best idea to be out here in this weather. How cold do you think it is?"

One of the wise men, Drake Clemmons, overheard the conversation. Leaning toward Grant he answered the question. "If this were actual Biblical times, we'd just have to take a stab at the temperature but seeing how we're in modern-day Townsend,

Tennessee all we need to do is look at the bank sign to get the answer." Looking toward the bank he smiled as he announced, "Twenty-eight degrees."

Grant looked out at the line of people who surrounded the manger, cups of hot chocolate and donuts donated by local churches clutched in their hands as they viewed and explained the manger scene to their young children. One little girl pointed at the cow as she asked her mother, "Are the animals real?"

Before the woman could answer, the donkey, which was tethered to the fence near the back of the manger, let out a loud bray and then proceeded to urinate on the straw. This caused laughter from the audience as the woman answered the child, "Yes, most definitely...the animals are real."

Grant pulled his robe closer to his neck as he looked at the donkey and remarked, "Can't get more realistic than that." He looked out at the growing crowd as they moved in closer to view the nativity scene. Suddenly, the aroma of fresh hay and pine needles was disturbed by a familiar smell wafting from a curl of white smoke: *Peach Brandy pipe tobacco*! Grant's eyes darted around the crowd. Standing at the very edge of the fencing stood a man wearing a dark knit cap, a pipe held in his mouth. The man reminded him of the man he had seen standing by the tree at Conrad's funeral.

Out of curiosity, Grant stood and began to move toward the man but just then Dana Beth placed the baby in the small wooden cradle as she commented, "I need to stand for a minute. I'm getting a cramp in my side."

Grant, whispered, "Are you sure you're okay?"

"Yes, I'll be fine. I just need to stand here for a minute or so."

Grant looked for the man again, but he was gone. Craning his neck, he searched the crowd from the left to the right then looked off into the distance. Dana Beth, noticing his odd behavior bumped him on his arm, asking, "Who, or what on earth are you looking for?"

Changing the subject, Grant bent down and picked up the doll as he jokingly stated, "Actually this is kind of amusing when you think about it. You're supposed to be Mary, the mother of the Christ Child, a newborn, and here you are three months pregnant."

Looking down at her stomach which was completely covered by her long robe she whispered back, "Do you think they can tell?"

"No, and besides that it really doesn't make any difference."

Kneeling back down on the straw, Dana Beth mentioned Conrad. "My father always loved this time of the year. He was always one of the wise men. He was such a good man and not just during the holidays. He gave generously to the church, not to mention he was an usher and he sang in the choir, and he loved animals. He was always donating money to the local ASPCA. He kept the bird feeders in our backyard filled and making sure there were peanuts out for the squirrels." Clutching the doll to her breast she sobbed slightly, "I really miss him. It saddens me to think he won't be around to see his grandchildren."

Grant pulled the hood of Dana Beth's robe closer to her face as he tried his best to console her. "It'll be all right. It's just going to take some time." Looking at the clock on the bank sign he commented, "Just after nine o'clock. We've only got about an hour to go. Are we still going to your mother's house tonight?"

Wiping a tear from her eye, Dana Beth answered softly, "Yes, she's expecting us."

An hour later, Grant guided the Jeep from the nativity scene parking lot and headed for his mother-in-law's house. Dana Beth closed her eyes as she rested peacefully. Grant's thoughts drifted back to the man with the pipe back at the manger: *Who was he? I'm sure he was the same man I saw at Conrad's funeral. Peach Brandy pipe tobacco. The same aroma that I discovered in the van in Ruth's garage.*

His train of thought was interrupted as Dana Beth nudged him on his arm. "You okay? You seem to be daydreaming. Every time you're deep in thought, you drive really slow."

Reaching over he took Dana Beth's hand in his. "I'm just tired and cold. I'll be glad to get to your mother's place."

Grant placed an armload of logs in the log rack then placed his hands near the warming fire. "Boy does that ever feel good. I thought I was going to freeze to death at the manger scene tonight."

Dana Beth was cuddled up on the couch, wrapped in a woolen afghan, sipping on a mug of hot chocolate. Ruth placed a small tray of assorted cheese and crackers on an end table then took a seat next to the fire as she poured herself a glass of wine. "I'm glad you stopped by tonight. There's something I want to discuss with both of you. I know I haven't exactly handled Conrad's death very well. I'm sorry that it's been so hard for me to talk about it."

Dana Beth sat up on the couch. "Mom, it's only been three weeks since we buried dad. No one expects you to be acting any differently than what you are. It's perfectly normal. I've done a lot of thinking over the past three weeks. At first, I didn't think I was going to be able to move forward. I know I don't have to like it, but I have to accept the fact he is gone. If dad were here...that's exactly what he'd tell us to do. Move on with our lives."

"I know what you're saying is true. It's just so hard to believe he kept his illness from us," said Ruth. "If he had just said something, we could have gotten treatment for him. It's like he just allowed himself to slip away. I don't understand. We had such a solid relationship for all those years. I just don't understand."

Grant, jabbing the fire with a poker, remained quiet. Staring into the flames, he realized once again that he had done the right thing by not turning Conrad in as the killer. Ruth was having enough problems as it was without knowing the truth about her husband and Dana Beth, according to what she had just said, appeared to be moving on. He'd keep the truth from Ruth and Dana Beth. He'd rather feel the pain than expose the truth to them.

Ruth cleared her throat and took another sip of wine as she straightened up in her chair. "Listen...I have something to say. Part of the reason I'm having such a difficult time with Conrad's death is not having him around the house. It's just so difficult to deal with. Everywhere I look in this house there are memories of him." Setting her wine glass down she went on, "I've decided to sell the house and move in with my sister over in Chattanooga. This shouldn't come as any great surprise to you. We talked about this last week."

Dana Beth was about to speak but Ruth raised her hand. "Please...let me finish. I've already talked with my sister. She's got more than enough room at her place. I can help out at the gift shop. She told me she needs the help. Her shop is located in a strip mall and the store next to her just went out of business. She has decided to expand her shop. The owner of the mall said if she wanted to rent the empty store next to hers he would knock out the wall and she can expand. From what she tells me her business is doing quite well."

Dana Beth, finally able to get a word in, spoke. "But what about the house? The market right now is not all that great. Why, you might not sell the place for a year. Someone would have to take care of it until it sold."

"I've thought of all those things and I've come up with a solution." She looked at Dana Beth then to Grant. "You two can buy the house."

Dana Beth stared at Grant with a look of disbelief on her face then spoke as if she were unsure of what she was saying. "Mom...I don't know. I mean, Grant and I have only been married for a few months. We don't have that much money saved and we don't have any furniture. This is just so sudden. We planned on staying at Dalton's farm for a couple of years so we could save up and then maybe consider getting a place of our own. What do you think, Grant?"

"If it's just a matter of your being alone here in the house, Ruth, we could always move in with you. We could help you keep the place up. That way you wouldn't be alone."

"I've considered that, but I still think it would be best if I move in with my sister. She's all alone over there in Chattanooga. It'll be good for both of us. Besides that, just think. If you two buy the house it can remain in the family. Your new baby can sleep in the room where you slept, Dana Beth. You can eat meals in the house you grew up in, cook in the kitchen you're used to. I can visit from time to time. It's perfect. I'm not worried about the money. We can work that out and if necessary we can arrange owner financing.

"I'm leaving the bulk of the furniture right here so you don't have to be concerned with that expense. I've already discussed my plans with Mr. Potts over at the bank. Conrad and I have dealt with him for years. He said he didn't think there would be a problem with you getting a loan. Now, if you're not interested... fine. I'll just put the place on the market, however I really wish you kids would consider my offer."

Grant took a seat next to Dana Beth on the couch. "I agree with your mother. This is a good thing for us...and for Ruth. It's a win win situation. What do you think?"

"Okay," exclaimed Dana Beth. "Next week we go see Mr. Potts at the bank."

CHAPTER THREE

HE WAS TOTALLY OUT OF HIS ELEMENT, devoid of everything that was familiar to him. Fast food restaurants and stores selling tee shirts took the place of tall pines and meandering trails. The smell of pizza and barbecue replaced the scent of fresh earth after a rainy night or pinecones basking in the sun. Yet, when he shielded his eyes he could see the mountains behind him and he knew he was only minutes from returning to what he considered familiar surroundings.

Wearing a knit cap pulled down over his ears, a black wool jacket and his feet shoved into size thirteen boots, he slowly walked down Parkway Boulevard. Passing Ripley's Believe It or Not Museum, he tilted his head to study the crooked building and then continued on down the street. Not really focusing on anything in particular, he passed shop windows filled with colors and shapes. Taking his hands out of his coat pockets, he opened the door to the Flapjacks Pancake Cabin and stepped inside. He walked over to a small table near the front window, which he had occupied everyday for the last two weeks and removed his coat and hat.

The waitress nodded a friendly greeting, "I'll be right with you, Hon." After delivering a tray of food to another table, she approached him, placed a glass of water on his table, and took a pencil from behind her ear. "What's it gonna be today, the cabin breakfast again?"

"Yes, thank you," he said.

Walking toward the kitchen entrance the waitress spoke back over her shoulder, "Be right back with your coffee."

Sitting back in the seat, he made himself comfortable as he looked around the restaurant. There were two customers seated at the counter and a couple at the other end of the eatery. *Good,* he thought. He really didn't like being around a lot of people. The waitress was back in what seemed like no time at all and she poured him a cup of hot coffee. "I remembered; no sugar, no cream. You like it straight up, don't you, Hon?" He nodded and smiled, then looked out the front window as he watched the parade of cars slowly moving down the Parkway.

His breakfast arrived and he delved into the three plates of food. He liked the biscuits the best. They reminded him of the biscuits back home; big, soft biscuits, which he slathered with butter. He ate slowly, savoring the food. There was no reason to hurry. He had nowhere to go today. He had yet to wrap his thoughts around why he should stay in Gatlinburg. Maybe he should just get in his truck and drive back home. Then again, if he stuck around maybe he'd get some answers to the questions swimming around in his head.

After paying his bill and leaving a generous tip, he walked outside and looked up and down the street. Instead of going left and walking back to his motel, he decided to walk in the opposite direction further down the Parkway. He had grown tired of watching television most of the day. A good long walk would do him good.

There were mostly shops and tourist attractions lining the sidewalk. Occasionally, he would sidestep a group of tourists shopping for souvenirs. A large neon sign caught his attention. Flashing in bright red and blue lights was the name: **_J.J. Pickler's Bear Emporium._** The display window was filled with statues and pictures of bears of all shapes and sizes. There were carved black bears wearing straw hats and holding welcome signs, bears with their paws in honey pots and a large wooden bear wearing coveralls and smoking a corncob pipe. Lined up across the front of the store there was an assortment of concrete and wooden bears. On the left of the building he noticed a partially rusted wire cage. He walked over and stood in front of the cage. There was a black bear sitting in the far corner of the cage rocking back and forth. The bear's nose was raw and red, probably from rubbing up against the wire. What he was looking at disturbed him. He turned and entered the shop.

Walking down a narrow aisle filled with souvenirs, he heard someone yell, "If I can help you with anything just let me know." On the other side of the store, J.J. Pickler was reading a newspaper, his feet propped up on the sales counter.

Approaching the counter, he addressed Pickler, "How much you want for that bear outside?"

At the prospect of a potential sale J.J. stood up as he answered, "Which one, hell, there must be two dozen out front?"

"The one in the cage."

Leaning on the counter, J.J. gave his latest customer an odd look. "You're kidding right? You want to buy the live bear?" J.J. let out a loud chuckle, "That bear ain't for sale. I just bought her a few months back. She's a real moneymaker."

"She don't look right. Her coat's dull and she's thin. I'll give you twice what you paid for her."

"Look, she's fine. I feed her every day. She brings in lots of customers. Like I said...she ain't for sale."

J.J. went back to reading his paper and the man just stood there looking from side to side as if he were getting frustrated.

"Where'd you get her from?" he asked.

Throwing the paper to the floor, J.J. was getting annoyed. "Well, that ain't none of your damn business, but if you must know, I bought her off a farmer from over in the next county. He got her when she was a cub, but she got too big for him to take care of. She ain't mean, but she's a handful. Any more questions?"

The man just stood there staring at him. J.J. moved as close to the counter as he could get and leaned toward the customer. "If you're not gonna buy something just go on and git!"

Walking slowly out of the store, the man stood in front of the bear cage for a few seconds then moved on down the street. One block down the Parkway he went into the Food Mart and came out carrying a sack containing four chicken legs and three sliced apples. The only thing on his mind was the bear down the street in the cage.

Sitting on a nearby bench for half an hour, he figured enough time had passed. The owner of the store had probably forgotten about him. Getting up, he walked back up the street and waited until a small group of tourists entered the store. *The owner should be occupied and he would be free to visit the bear once again.* Walking casually up to the cage, he removed a chicken leg from the sack and pushed it through the wiring. The bear instantly raised her head, but did not move. She sniffed the air. It took her a moment, but she finally got to her feet and made her way across the cage. She sniffed the piece of chicken, pushed it around with her nose, and then downed it in one gulp. Smiling, the man dropped two more legs through the welded wire fencing. The way she tore into the chicken made it obvious she was hungry and whatever the owner was feeding her was not enough.

He didn't hear the door of the shop open and slam shut until J.J. Pickler was almost next to him. "Hey! Get away from my bear! What the hell are you feeding her?"

The man quickly stuffed the remaining chicken leg and the apple slices through the fencing as Pickler continued to yell, "What's the matter with you? You hard of hearing? I oughta call the law on you. That's my bear and you ain't got no right messing with her."

An angry glare covered the man's face as he pointed to the bear and yelled back, "She's hungry. Look at her! She's way underweight. I know a lot about bears. Look at her coat. It's all dull and matted and she doesn't have any life in her eyes. You're not treating her right. That cage is too small."

J.J. thought about getting right in the man's face, but the intensity in the man's eyes combined with his large body frame warned Pickler to keep his distance as he tried to reason with him. "Well, that don't make you no expert. She's fine. You feed her too much and she ain't gonna do nothing I tell her to. I spent a lot of time training her so you better leave her be."

The man glared at J.J. as he demanded, "You got a license to keep this bear? Let me see your license!"

Suddenly J.J. had enough regardless of how big the man was. "I ain't showing you nothing, Dumb Ass. Now get the hell away from my property. You're nuts, ya know it? Now, git out of here. You come around here again and I'll kick your ass!"

The man just stood there staring at J.J. who was praying that his bluff would scare the man off. Finally, clearly irritated, the man turned and walked up the street mumbling to himself. A few pedestrians who had witnessed the confrontation moved on up the street as they shook their heads in amazement.

Back at the motel, the man paced back and forth across the small room. He had to figure out a way to help the bear, but at the moment he couldn't think of anything. His head hurt. Placing his hands on his head, he flopped down on the bed and closed his eyes. It would take some time for him to figure out what to do about the bear.

It was dark when he awoke. The alarm clock next to the bed read: 10:07 P.M. Realizing he hadn't eaten anything since breakfast, he decided to find a place to have a nice meal. Someplace that served home cooking and big portions. After passing several restaurants that were already closed, he saw a sign pointing down a side street. GATLINBURG GRILL HOME COOKING AND GOOD EATS. He was ready for a good home cooked hot meal. As he entered the door, he stopped, trying to adjust his eyes to the dim lighting. There were people everywhere; standing and sitting at round tables as they laughed and drank bottles of beer and mixed drinks. Four men in the corner were engaged in a rowdy game of pool, two other men just down from the men's room were playing darts. Loud country music blared from a jukebox next to the bar. Aside from the loud music, a thick layer of cigarette smoke hung in the air. Backing toward the door he thought, *Don't like it here. Too many people...too loud.*

Bumping into a waitress carrying a tray of empty beer glasses, he turned to look at the girl. Humbly, he apologized, "Sorry."

The girl flashed him a wide grin as she responded, "Saw you when you came in. We're pretty full up right now, but I think there's a seat over at the end of the bar." Taking him by the arm she offered, "Come on, right over here."

Not wishing to be impolite he followed without saying a word. He plodded across the room and took a seat where the girl indicated, trying not to bump into the man sitting next to him. The girl motioned to the bartender and yelled at the same time, "Hank...customer down on the end!"

The bartender, a towel draped over his shoulder, approached, "What's your pleasure, Pal?"

The man, feeling confused, just stared back and remained quiet.

Repeating his request in a different manner, the bartender asked, "What are you drinking?"

Looking at the large assortment of beer, wine and whiskey bottles displayed behind the bar, the man raised his hands almost as if he were helpless, then answered, "Just a Coke please." The bartender rolled his eyes, grabbed a glass, and proceeded to fill it with Coke from a soda dispenser. Sliding the drink in front of the man the bartender said, "There ya go, Pal."

The man looked at the drink and then at the bartender, as he spoke slowly, "Can I get something to eat?"

"Sure, Janis will be right with ya."

After a few minutes the waitress came back to him as she remarked, "Sorry I took so long. Hank said you wanted to order something to eat. What can I get you?"

The man looked around in a confused fashion. "Uh...I don't see a menu. Can I have roast beef, mashed potatoes, and lots of gravy?"

The girl gave him a big smile as she explained, "Sorry, but our kitchen closes at six. Well, at least as far as dinners are concerned.

At this time of night all we have to offer is pizza, burgers, hot wings, and nachos. Our cheeseburgers are the best in Gatlinburg. They're really good and they come with cottage fries and slaw."

Disappointed at the choices, he wanted to get up and leave, but the waitress was being so nice to him. "Okay...give me a cheeseburger and the rest of the stuff you said."

"It's happy hour. All alcoholic beverages are two for one. What can I get you to drink?" she asked.

"I don't drink. Alcohol makes me sick. Nobody should drink. It can make a person really mean. I'll just have another Coke. Is that okay?"

"Sure," she said. "I'll be right back with your drink."

He watched her walk down to the other end of the bar where she said something to two men who were sitting in front of her. They turned and looked at the man as they laughed at something the waitress said.

He ate his burger and fries, pushed the slaw to the side, and downed the last swallow of his Coke. Looking at the ticket the waitress had brought along with his meal, he pulled a large roll of bills out of his pocket and slowly counted out ten ones and laid them on the bar. The man who was sitting next to him got up and left, but the empty stool was quickly taken by one of the two men who had been at the other end of the bar. The other man stood close, on the other side of him. The man who had seated himself on the empty stool asked, "Where ya from?" then added, "My name's Big Joe and my friend on the other side of ya is Bobby."

Pulling his knit cap down closer to his eyes, he answered, "Do you mean me?"

"Hell yeah, I mean you!" said Joe "Ya look like a tourist. I thought maybe ya needed some directions or somethin'. Where ya from?"

"North," came the short answer.

Bobby spoke up, "North. Where in the north?"

He was getting nervous as he tried to answer the question, "Just north."

Joe took offense as he remarked sarcastically, "North and just north don't sound like the name of no town I ever heard of."

"Me neither," said Bobby. They both laughed

The man, getting nervous, stood as he pushed himself past Bobby. "I gotta go."

Joe placed his hand on the man's chest as he suggested, "Hold on friend. You're not bein' very friendly. We just wanted to talk to ya some."

"No, I'm leaving. I just have to walk five blocks up the street to my motel." Pulling his knit cap down even tighter on his head, he tried to head for the door, but was stopped by Bobby blocking his way.

"Well, since you're not from around here I've got ta warn ya. You gotta be careful walkin' around the streets at night. I reckon ya don't know this, but they done had four murders in this neck of the woods this past year. Yes sir, four bad ones. Some maniac has been killin' off people who mistreat animals. Butchered them up real good. They sure would like ta catch that bastard but ya don't look like somebody that would hurt no animal, so I guess you're safe." Letting out a loud laugh, Bobby thumped him on the back.

He was getting irritated. He just wanted to leave. There were too many people near him. The smoke and the loud music was bothering him. He just wanted to get outside. Looking at Bobby, he spoke up in an almost cocky fashion, "Well, maybe those people deserved to die. It ain't right to kill animals. Animals don't hurt anybody if you leave them alone."

Joe, mimicking the man's attitude pointed out, "Whoa, well lookee here...we got us one of them tree huggers." Joe placed his hand on the man's shoulder as he addressed Bobby, "Ya hear that Bobby? He said them people deserved ta die!"

"I need to go," the man said. "I don't want to talk no more." He pushed his way past the two men and walked toward the door. He heard loud laughing behind him. Outside at last, he took a deep breath of air glad he was away from the two men and the crowded bar. He was upset and sweating profusely. Maybe a walk in the cold night air would calm him down. He had walked two blocks when a blue pickup pulled up next to him. Bobby stuck his head out the window and yelled, "Hey, Big Fella, get in. We'll give ya a lift." Shoving his hands into his pockets, he kept walking trying his best to mind his own business. The truck kept slowly moving right next to him. "Hey," yelled Bobby. "Mr. from the north, did ya hear me? You some kind of nut?"

The man stopped and looked over at the truck. He noticed Bobby's hand, his knuckles covered with tattoos. He wondered why the man had called him a nut. Why was he being so mean? He just wanted to get back to his motel room where he would be safe and away from mean people. "I don't want a ride. I'll just walk."

Joe, who was driving, leaned over and looked past Bobby out the passenger side window. "Well hell, I guess we'll just have ta pull over and walk ya home, Big Fella."

The man felt like running, but between his large boots and clumsy gait he knew he couldn't run very far. Moving closer to the buildings along the street, he started to walk faster. He heard the truck behind him pull over, then the sound of their footsteps as they took long strides to catch up with him. He could hear their voices as they talked with each other, laughing and joking about killing raccoons and possums. "Yeah, somebody oughta kill all those damn varmints! Who needs those little bastards anyways?"

Before he realized it, Joe was at his side. Bobby stepped in front of him preventing him from going any farther.

Joe draped his arm around his shoulder as he asked smartly, "What do ya think about that, Pal?"

Bobby looked at a passageway between two buildings. "I gotta take a leak. Come on, let's go back in there for a second." Reaching out, Bobby touched the man on his arm.

The man objected as he jerked away at the same time twisting away from Bobby. "Don't touch me! Why do you keep touching me?"

Bobby held up his hands. "Hey take it easy there, big guy. I just gotta take a leak." He took three steps into the dark passageway, Joe was still at the man's side.

The man seemed to be getting nervous. "No...you go. I'm fine. I know my way back to the motel."

Without warning, Joe pulled a knife out of his pocket and skillfully turned it over in his hand. "Sure, no problem, but before ya walk to your motel ya can give me your wallet and that roll of money ya got in your front pocket!"

The man stared at Joe, but kept his eye on Bobby who was trying to circle around him. Backing up against the wall of a building, he was now facing both men. "No, you can't have my money...it's mine! Just get away from me and let me walk to my motel."

"Don't think so," said Bobby, as the smile on his face turned to a nasty stare. "Just give us the money then ya can leave."

For his size the man was as quick as a mountain cat as he swung his left arm out, his fist catching Bobby square on the right jaw, then turning quickly, his right foot connecting with Joe's crouch. Joe doubled over and fell to the ground as the knife in his hand clattered on the pavement. Bobby leaped for the knife and then lunged at the man who had stepped to the side. The man's huge hands reached out and grabbed Bobby by the neck, pulling him off the ground with little effort. He slammed Bobby's head into the brick wall, Bobby's body went limp. Joe screamed when he heard the sickening crunch of bone meeting brick. Bobby slid to the ground, a trail of blood ran down the wall. The man picked up the knife with his right hand and stood over Joe, looking down at him as he clenched his left fist.

"Please don't kill me," pleaded Joe. "Please...we were just foolin' around. Please...God...don't kill me!"

The man dropped the knife, turned and started up the street talking to himself, "They should have let me be. They wanted to hurt me. They're not nice men. They should have left me alone."

At seven the next morning, the man entered the Flapjack Cabin. "Morning," said the waitress as he took his familiar seat. "You look tired today, Hon. Have a rough night?"

He looked at the waitress. He liked her...she was nice. "I had a bad dream."

"Aw, that's a shame. I bet a big ol' breakfast will fix you right up." Pouring him a cup of coffee, she commented, "I'll have your regular breakfast out here in a few minutes. Drink your coffee. That'll perk you up."

Looking out the front widow, the man wondered what happened to those two men who had threatened him the previous night. He kept wondering why they hadn't left him alone. He wondered what happened after he left them in between those two buildings.

He sat in silence for five minutes when the waitress returned with his breakfast. "There you go. Enjoy." She refilled his coffee and moved off to another table.

The waitress had been right. The early morning meal was making him feel better but his mind was still a jumble as he relived the events of the previous night.

Ten minutes passed when the waitress laid the bill next to his empty plate. "Well, you sure made quick work of that," she said as she stacked his plates on top of one another. "You feel better?"

Rather than answering her question, he asked a question of his own. "Can I ask you something?"

"Sure, Hon, what is it?"

"I want to find someplace to stay. Not a motel. I want a cabin, but not one of those with other cabins around. I want something by itself. I've been up into the Smokies twice this past week and there were all kinds of people roaming around out there. I saw tents, big RV's and cars everywhere—"

The waitress interrupted him as she stated, "Oh, those few people. In a few months those trails will be bumper to bumper with folks coming in here. Now, getting back to the cabins. Most people like the real cozy cabins. I sure do. Give me one with a hot tub and a wet bar and I'll be fine." Setting the plates back down on the table she put her hands on her waist as she continued, "Let's see, the only person I know around here who rents secluded cabins is Walt Lansing. He lives over in Townsend and he has some cabins way back in the woods. Reason I know that is because my sister's husband likes to spend time up there alone. He's a health nut and goes up there to find roots and herbs. That sound like what you're looking for?"

The man nodded, as he said, "Yeah...way back in the woods. That's what I want."

Ripping a sheet from her menu pad she took a pencil from behind her ear as she explained, "Here, let me write down some directions. Drive down to Pigeon Forge and pick up Route 321 to Townsend. When you get to Townsend, take a right on the Lamar Alexander Parkway. Walt's about a half mile up the road. Can't miss his house. He's got a giant windmill in his front yard next to a large sign that reads **Cabin Rentals**. You tell him Irene sent you to see him. Now, be sure and come back here and see me again, okay?"

Smiling, he said, "I will. I know where Townsend is." As usual, he left her a nice tip. She always treated him nice.

CHAPTER FOUR

THE MAN HAD NO PROBLEM locating Walt Lansing's place. Irene's directions had been easy to follow. Pulling into the front yard he was met by two black labs. They stood by his truck and waited patiently until he got out. They greeted him with wagging tails. Petting both of their heads, he was interrupted by a friendly voice from the other side of the truck, "Hi, can I help you?"

Walking around the front of the truck, the man asked, "You, Mr. Lansing?"

"That would be me."

"Irene from the Flapjack Cabin sent me to see you. I want to rent a cabin. She said you had some way back in the mountains. That's what I want."

Rubbing his hand across his face Walt remarked, "Yeah, I know Irene, she's a nice lady. To tell you the truth, I usually don't rent my cabins out in the off season. They have running water and electricity, but no central heat." Looking back over his shoulder at the mountains, he went on, "It can get mighty nippy back up in there. Course, there's a buck stove and a fireplace in each one of my cabins, but I don't have any wood stacked up there right now. Most people don't like being isolated during the winter months, especially if the weather turns bad. Sure you wouldn't want something closer to town? I know most everyone around these parts who rent cabins. I could give one of them a call for you."

The man shook his head as he lied, "I've been sick. I need to get away for a while. Doctor said it would be good for me to go somewhere where it is quiet and peaceful."

Resting his foot on the bumper of the truck, Walt explained, "Ain't really that much up there right now. Probably a couple of blankets, some sheets and a few towels, but that's about all. Might be a few dishes in the cupboard. There's a toaster and an electric skillet and a few other utensils. Stuff like that."

The man smiled. "That would be okay. Don't need much."

"How long you want to stay up there; week, two weeks?" Walt asked.

"I'd like to rent one until spring."

Walt was surprised. "Well, I've already got all the cabins rented starting in May. So, I can only rent you one up through April."

Pulling a thick wad of bills from his pocket, the man asked, "How much would it be from now to the end of April?"

The sight of the money caused Walt to smile. "Tell you what. I normally rent the cabins for twelve hundred a month during the tourist season, but since it's the off season and if you really want to rough it out up there, I'll let you have one for, let's say three hundred a month. How's that sound?"

The man didn't even hesitate at the price. "That's fine."

Walt grinned, then said, "Here's what I'll do. January is almost shot. That leaves just three months. We'll call it nine hundred, but you have to be out at the end of April."

The man peeled off nine one hundred dollar bills as he asked, "When can I move in?"

"Today, if you want or you can wait until next week."

"I'd like to get up there today if it's okay."

"Shouldn't be a problem. I normally have people who rent from me fill out an application, but you seem like a nice sort of fella and besides that, you paid me cash money up front so that really won't be necessary." Walt smiled. "Cash makes my bookkeeping a lot easier."

The man smiled and nodded.

Walt turned and started for the house. "Just let me get you some directions up to the cabin and I'll be right back."

The man knelt down as the two labs circled him, each one fighting for his attention as they pawed at him and licked his hands. He loved dogs. Looking in the direction of the mountains, he smiled realizing that soon he would be alone where he felt comfortable.

Walt returned, handing him the keys to the cabin. "Now when you get up there be sure and check the flue before you light a fire. Sometimes our local critters have a tendency to build nests in there. Make sure you keep the trash bin chained and locked. The black bears up there are craftier than a safecracker when there's garbage around, especially leftover food. Don't leave any food out on the porch. I had to have the screens replaced twice last year. Bears go right through it. Another thing, don't be wondering around outside after dark. I guess that just about covers it. Nobody will bother you up there. The trash company comes by on

Wednesdays. Other than that, you probably won't see a soul. Oh, and one other thing. You're not a hunter are you? I don't allow hunting on my property, but those damn poachers sneak up there and hunt anyways."

The man answered, "No, I don't hunt."

"All right then," said Walt as he removed a small notebook and a hand drawn map from his back pocket. You can write down your name and address in this notebook and give me a couple of telephone numbers I can reach in case of an emergency." He handed the man a pen and then spread the map out on the hood of the truck. "Okay, you go down the Parkway, that's the road in front of the house, then go about a mile, take this road and turn left." He continued with his directions covering every turn and curve to the cabin. "My phone number is right here on the bottom of the map. I'm also going to leave you my brother's number. Me and the missus are leaving for Florida in a few days. Weather gets too cold for her around here this time of year. As the years have gone by we've turned into snowbirds. We won't be back until mid-April, so if you have any problems just give my brother a call. He's part owner, so he's familiar with the cabins. One other thing... hold on a minute."

Walt ran to the house and returned a minute later holding a brown bag. "The wife made pumpkin bread yesterday. Put a loaf in there for you. Hope you enjoy the cabin. I reckon I'll see you in April."

The man reached and shook Walt's hand as he replied, "Thanks, I'm looking forward to getting up there, and I'll take good care of your cabin."

Walt stood in the yard watching the truck pull out onto the road. He picked the notebook up from the hood of the truck and realized the man had not written anything in it. *Darn, he must have forgot since I was showing him the map. Oh well, he seemed like a decent fellow.*

After leaving Walt's, the man drove back to Gatlinburg and checked out of his motel. Next, he stopped at the Food Mart where he loaded two carts brimming with food and drinks and piled them into the back of his truck. Heading down the Parkway he had one last stop before driving back to Townsend. He wanted to check on the bear. As usual, the bear was sitting in the corner of the cage with her head down. After pushing a handful of strawberries and some chicken through the wire fencing, he stood back and watched her eat. He still had it in his mind to help the bear. He just wasn't sure how he was going to go about it.

At the intersection of Route 321 and the Parkway in Pigeon Forge, he stopped for gas. Standing at the pump, he heard a man at the adjacent pump talking on his cell phone. "Yeah, they said some busboy went out to empty the trash and he found the body. He ran back inside and got the manager. Sure enough, the man was deader than a doornail. They said his head was smashed in." There was a pause then the man started to talk again, "I don't know. They aren't saying anything about the way he died, only that it looks like a homicide. The victim was some guy from North Carolina. Okay, I'll call you later."

His hand tightened around the handle of the gas pump as he thought, *Was the man talking about Bobby? Was Bobby the man they had found?* Placing the nozzle back on the pump he was glad he was leaving the area and going to a secluded cabin over in Townsend.

The cabin was well off the beaten path, obscured by tall trees and bushes on three sides, the fourth side had an attached porch on the second level facing an amazing view of a deep valley that disappeared into the distance. It was situated at the end of a dirt road, the nearest neighboring cabin he had passed was a half mile back down the road. It was perfect. As he unloaded the groceries, a sense of peace fell over him. The seclusion reminded him of back home.

The interior was rustic with log walls that were tastefully decorated with paintings by local artists. The kitchen, main bath, and master bedroom were situated on the upper floor, a rec room, second bedroom, laundry room and half bath on the lower level. A set of patio doors on the upper floor led to a screened in porch complete with an outdoor hot tub and three rocking chairs.

After stocking the shelves and the refrigerator with groceries, he placed two duffle bags that contained his clothing, along with two rifle cases and ammunition in the bedroom. He hung the new red ball cap he had purchased at the grocery store on a hook by the door then went to work following Walt's instructions. He checked the flue and then went outside and made sure the lock on the trash bin was secure. He found a large plastic bag of bedding in the bedroom closet and made the upstairs bed. Stepping out onto the porch, he felt a stiff wind blow up from the valley and across the porch. It was going to be a cold night. He decided to gather some wood for the fireplace before it got any later.

At the end of the dirt road where it butted into a small, grass covered side yard, he entered the trees and found that the cabin was on the edge of a gradual ravine. Walking down the side of the slope, he picked up twigs and branches then went back two more times to gather small logs. On his last trip back to the cabin, he stopped and took in a deep breath of mountain air. He liked this place. He liked it a lot. It was quiet and smelled of the outdoors. No people around, no cigarette smoke, no loud irritating music— just the wind and the trees and the unseen wildlife. It wasn't home, but it was as close as he was going to get.

Stacking the wood next to the fireplace, he started a fire with some old newspaper someone had left behind. Once he had a roaring fire going he filled a skillet with water then dropped in three hotdogs.

After he ate and cleaned up the dishes, he relaxed in front of the fireplace and he took a pouch of tobacco from his shirt pocket and placed a few pinches in his well-used mahogany pipe. Reclining in an easy chair, he took a few deep draws on the pipe, the pleasant aroma of Peach Brandy filled the room. He closed his eyes as he thought about the upcoming day. He could sleep late if he wanted to, then get up, have some bacon and eggs then head into Gatlinburg. The plan for saving the bear was starting to come together in his mind.

By eleven o'clock the next morning, he was standing across the street from J.J.'s Bear Emporium. Two couples, standing by the cage, stared at the bear who remained at the rear of the cage. After a few minutes one of the couples headed up the street while the other went into the shop. Walking quickly across the street, he went to the side of the enclosure and spoke softly to bear. "Hello there, old friend. Are you hungry today?" Opening a sack he had with him, he extracted some berries and a chicken breast.

Associating him with food, the bear got up and approached. As he stood there watching her eat he realized that feeding her was only one way he could help the captive bear. He had to come up with another idea. A way that would ensure her freedom.

He had been standing there for nearly ten minutes when he heard the familiar voice of none other than J.J. Pickler. "Got dammit, all to hell! I told you to stop feeding her!" His loud screaming startled not only the man but the bear as well who retreated to the back of the cage. "I'm gonna call the police right now if you don't step away from that cage and head on up the street."

"I'm going," said the man, "and I ain't coming back no more."

As the man started up the street, J.J. followed him for a few steps as he yelled at him, " Good, don't come back! Mess with my bear, will ya. You just better not. Now, go on...git!"

For the next two weeks the man sat across the street at different times of the day watching every move J.J. Pickler made. He knew what time he opened and what time he closed. Each and every day he'd wait until someone entered the shop then he would cross the street to feed the bear.

On Sunday afternoon as he stuffed some chicken through the cage, he gently spoke to the bear. "I'll be back tonight. Got a surprise for you."

Getting into his truck he drove down the Parkway, an open map with a drawn line running from Gatlinburg to Sevierville, lying on the seat next to him. He drove northeast on the Parkway and finally turned onto the Tn-71 Scenic Parkway. Following the signs, he drove thirteen miles until he slowed down and turned onto Allensville Road and into the parking lot of Home Depot.

Parking his truck in the huge parking lot, he entered the store and stopped at the customer service desk where a young girl greeted him, "Can I help you, Sir?"

The man looked around the large store in confusion then spoke, "I want to rent one of those trailers you got out front."

"Okay," said the girl. "Let me call one of our Lawn and Garden employees up here and we'll get you fixed right up."

A few minutes later, an older gentleman approached the desk and was directed by the girl to the man standing next to the desk.

Reaching for the man's hand the employee introduced himself, "My name's Harold. Are you interested in renting one of our trailers?"

"Yes," answered the man. "I need one for a day, maybe two."

After filling out some minor paperwork and hooking up the taillights, the employee waved good bye to the man as he pulled out of the lot with an eight by ten cargo trailer hitched to his truck. On the seat next to him laid a set of heavy duty bolt cutters he had also purchased. He had no idea what time it was. He never wore a watch. He needed to find out what time it was since J.J. always closed early on Sundays.

Turning on the truck radio, he hit the scan button until he heard a smooth talking voice: *This is radio station WSEV bringing you the best in contemporary music from Gatlinburg, Tennessee. And now for the noonday news. Gatlinburg police are still searching for a suspect in the killing of Bobby Mackinaw of Saulters Path, North Carolina. Numerous people have been questioned but there are still no definite leads. Mr. Mackinaw was employed by a construction company from North Carolina that has been working in the area for the past two months. Another employee, a Mr. Joseph Winfield, who was seen with Mackinaw just hours prior to the murder, has disappeared. Anyone knowing the whereabouts of Winfield, who is believed to be traveling in a blue Ford Ranger pickup with North Carolina plates, is asked to contact local authorities.*

He turned off the radio. They hadn't said anything about him. *Why should they,* he thought. He only did what he had to, to protect himself.

By the time he got back to Gatlinburg, it had started to rain; a slow cold drizzle that would turn to sleet if the temperature dropped much lower. After listening to the noonday news he figured it was around one o'clock. J.J.'s closed on Sundays at six. He'd wait for an hour after J.J. closed up for the day. It would be dark by then. He had six hours to wait before he made his move. He decided to park the truck and trailer in the far corner of the Food Mart. He would walk over to the Flapjack Cabin, have lunch and visit with Irene, then take a nap in his truck and wait for seven o'clock to roll around.

The loud beating of the rain on the roof of the truck brought him out of a relaxing nap. Looking at the clock on a bank sign next to the Food Mart, he noted the time at 5:25. J.J. would be closing up in a little over a half hour then he had another hour to wait.

Getting out of the truck, he entered the Food Mart and purchased a package of fresh fish fillets and a large coffee. Back in the truck he placed the fish on the passenger seat and sat back, enjoying the hot coffee while going over his plan to rescue the bear. Pulling the collar of his coat up around his neck, he adjusted the heater up a notch as he felt a chill from the cold rain.

At exactly six o'clock, J.J. Pickler rolled a two-wheel dolly out the door and loaded up all of the bear statues in front of his store and he took them inside, turned off the lights, and locked the front door. Finally, he threw a large tarp over the top of the cage, climbed in his car and pulled out onto the street. From across the street the man sat in his truck and watched. Everything so far was going according to his simple plan.

The bank clock on the corner read 6:58. *Close enough,* thought the man. He started the truck, pulled across the street, and backed the cargo trailer into the empty lot next to the shop. He got out, opened the trailer doors, then got back in. Putting his truck in reverse, he maneuvered the trailer up against the padlocked cage gate leaving a one-foot space in between the cage and the rear of the trailer. Getting out of the truck, the man realized the rain was going to make his task easier than he thought. All of the nearby shops were closed. It was dark and the rain was keeping most people inside. He checked the surrounding area. Except for an occasional passing car, no one was in sight. He quickly pulled the tarp from the cage. The bear was lying in the corner. She raised her head, but made no move to get up. Using the bolt cutters he made quick work of the metal hinges as he slid the door to the side. The bear was clearly disturbed at the noise he was making and stood up. Next, he tossed a fillet at her feet. She sniffed at it, then devoured it quickly. He placed three more fillets in the back of the trailer then threw two more into the cage, one in the middle and the other near the opening. The bear walked slowly to the piece in the middle, keeping her eye on the man. She looked at the open door, then at the fish as she moved to the piece near the door. She was just inches away from walking into the back of the trailer when she sat down and stared into the black abyss. She could smell the fish that was just a few feet away. Her massive head moved toward the direction of the wonderful aroma, but she refused to get up. Looking up and down the street, he knew he couldn't wait long for her to enter the trailer. He had a frightening thought. What if the bear didn't move? He couldn't wait all night. Someone would soon walk by and wonder what was going on. If he had to leave without the bear there was no way he could reattach the cage door. She might wander out onto the street. Maybe she'd make it to the mountains or she might be seen roaming the streets and be shot. If that happened he would be very upset.

Suddenly, the bear stood and walked into the trailer, the scent of the fish too much for her to resist. Now, came the tricky part. He quickly jumped in the truck, gently pulled forward, got back out, and closed the rear doors. The bear was too busy eating to notice the trailer had moved. Climbing back into the driver's seat, he felt a sense of exhilaration knowing the first part of his plan had gone smoothly.

Pulling out onto the street, he wondered if he was really doing the right thing. He knew the bear had been miserable in the cage, but how would she survive in the wild? Would she try to find humans that would feed her or would she wander into the territory of another bear? He knew she wasn't going to be strong enough to defend herself, yet, he had always heard that for a wild animal one day of freedom was equal to a thousand days in captivity. He was going to give her that chance and hope for the best.

It was nine-thirty by the time he arrived back at the cabin. He waited a few minutes before opening the back of the trailer, hoping she had settled down from the long, uncomfortable ride. Opening the back of the trailer, he quickly ran back to the safety of the truck. The porch light illuminated the entire side yard. A few minutes had passed when he felt a thump as she jumped from the back of the trailer. Opening the door slightly, he looked back to see what she was doing. At first she just sniffed the air, moving her head back and forth. He imagined she was confused, but the feeling of the rain on her back and dirt beneath her feet rather than the metal bottom of the cage felt good to her. After a few minutes of standing near the truck, she slowly walked to the trees by the side yard and disappeared in the rain. The man remained in the truck for another fifteen minutes before entering the cabin.

The next morning, J.J. Pickler pulled into the empty lot next to his shop. Getting out of his truck, he first noticed the tarp was not covering the cage. His thought that the wind probably blew it back was quickly erased when he noticed the cage door leaning up against the side of the cage and his bear nowhere in sight. Standing in front of his shop, his hands on his hips, he looked up and down the street. "I'll be damned. That sum bitch stole my bear!" Unlocking the shop, he entered, slammed the door, and immediately went to the phone to call the police.

Pacing back and forth in front of his shop, mumbling beneath his breath, J.J. waited for the police to arrive. Finally a cruiser pulled up in front of the shop, an officer got out as he pulled a report pad from his shirt pocket. The officer greeted J.J., "Good morning, Mr. Pickler, I'm Officer..."

Before he could finish the sentence, J.J. interrupted him. "Good morning, my ass! Somebody done stole my bear and I want her back! Put out an APB or whatever the hell you people do when something like this happens!"

The officer, already aware of Pickler's reputation as a man with a short fuse, flipped open his pad as he asked his first question, "When was the last time the bear was here?"

"Last night when I locked up. Just like always, I checked on her just before I left."

"Is the cage locked at night?"

"Of course it's locked. There's usually a damn bear in there. What do you think I am...an idiot? It's always locked." Walking over to the cage he pointed to the cage door. "Look, somebody cut the door right off its hinges."

"What does the bear look like?" asked the officer.

Sarcastically J.J. answered the question, "What does any bear look like?"

The officer corrected himself, "I meant what kind of bear is it?"

"She's a black bear...female...goes about 250 pounds."

"She have a name?"

"No, she doesn't have a name," J.J. yelled out of frustration. "She's a bear!"

The officer was about to ask his next question, but was cut off again by J.J. "I already know who stole my bear. Write this down. Big guy, kind of on the clumsy side, dark clothes, knit cap pulled down over his ears. Never saw him around here before. Couple of weeks back he was feeding the bear. I told him to stop and he gave me a rash of crap about how she wasn't being treated right, how she didn't have any life in her eyes, how she was hungry. He was a weirdo. I know he was the one who stole her."

Flipping the pad shut the officer spoke professionally, "All right, we'll get back to you."

"That's it?" shouted J.J. "You're not going to take some fingerprints, pictures...something?"

"Look, Mr. Pickler. We're right in the middle of a murder investigation. I realize you're upset about your bear, but that's not our number one priority right now. We'll do everything we can to find your bear."

Realizing that was all the cooperation he was going to get from the police, J.J. followed the officer out the door. "I'll find the Got damn bear myself and when I do somebody is going to have an ass full of buckshot!"

The officer turned and addressed J.J. "Taking the law into your own hands can be dangerous and besides that, it's a criminal offense."

"I ain't done nothing wrong and you can't charge me with anything. This is my business, my shop. Now, go find my bear or I will!"

The officer shook his head in wonder, climbed in his cruiser and pulled away from the shop.

J.J., frustrated at the police went back inside the shop, locked the door, and stomped up the street. He needed a drink.

Two blocks later he headed down a side street to the Gatlinburg Grill, flung open the door and went to the bar. A waitress was setting up the tables for the lunch crowd. Looking at her watch, she got a strange look on her face. "J.J., it's not even nine o'clock yet. You're three hours early for lunch."

"Not here for lunch Janis," snapped J.J. "Give me a damn beer!"

"Bartender's not in for another half hour."

"Well, then I'll pour one for myself."

"Geez, J.J., what got your goat this morning?"

Plopping down on one of the bar stools, J.J. slammed his fist on the bar. "Somebody stole my bear, that's what! Took her right out of the cage."

Janis, now behind the bar, took a beer glass from a stack at the end of the bar and drew a cold glassful from the tap. Placing a coaster on the bar she handed J.J. the beer. "That's a shame. You call the police?"

"Damn right, I did, but hell they ain't gonna do nothing! They're too worried about some construction bum they found dead up the street." He took a long drink and wiped the froth from his mouth with his sleeve.

"Yeah, I know all about the murder," said Janis. "The police were in first thing this morning questioning me again. I told them everything I knew about the guy."

J.J. was curious, "You knew the guy?"

"Not really. He and a pal of his named Joe came in here every night for the past two months. They're from North Carolina. Been working on that new hotel they're building over in Pigeon Forge. They'd come in here after work, have dinner, then drink the rest of the night. We kidded around some but that was it. Then, the night Bobby got killed some fellow came in here. I remember him because he seemed confused. Said he wanted something to eat so we set him up at the bar. He had a burger and a couple of Cokes.

"He was a strange bird. Well, Bobby and Joe get to talking with this stranger, one thing led to another and before long they're hassling this guy. I could see he just wanted to be left alone, but they wouldn't let up. Finally he walks out of the place. Wasn't ten seconds later that Bobby and Joe left. I didn't think anything of it. That was the last time I saw them. Now, I gotta tell ya. Bobby and Joe were kind of on the rough side, but that stranger, well he looked meaner than they did: big man he was, dark coat, knit cap pulled down over his ears. He never even took it off while he was eating."

"Wait a minute," said J.J. "You said a big guy...acting kinda weird?"

"Yeah, why you know him?"

"I'll be damned. That sounds like the same idiot that was messing with my bear. I'll bet you a dime to a dollar he's the one who stole her." Getting off of the stool, J.J. swallowed the last of the beer, threw two dollars on the bar, and headed for the door. "I'm gonna call the police again. I already told them I know who the guy is, but they just blew it off. I'm gonna tell them what you said. It all adds up. Thanks, Janis."

"Hey, don't go getting me mixed up in this," Janis yelled, but J.J was already out the door.

Sitting on the screened in porch at the cabin, the man lit his pipe as he reclined in one of the rocking chairs. Looking out across the valley, he saw the mist that covered the tops of the mountains. He took a sip of his morning coffee as he thought about the bear. He wondered if he'd ever see her again. It really didn't make any difference—she was free—free as God had intended. He decided that after he took the trailer back he'd stay away from town for a while. With the murder of the man who had attacked him combined with the theft of the bear, he thought it best to lay low. Besides that, he didn't need anything the town had to offer. He had everything he needed right there at the cabin. The thing he cherished the most was the solitude, the sound of the birds and the wind. He smiled as he drew in a deep breath of mountain air and puffed on his pipe.

CHAPTER FIVE

WHEN HE AWOKE, a drift of snow was banked against the bottom of the door. The surrounding brown mountains and gray sky had turned to crystal white. He smiled to himself. He loved the snow and the cold air against his face. He was glad he had decided to gather extra wood the night before and it only took him minutes to get a roaring blaze in the fireplace. He plugged in the coffeepot and turned on a radio he had found tucked away in the spare bedroom closet. The sound of fiddles and banjos filled the cabin as The Wabash Cannonball came rolling in. Today he would have to eat oatmeal again. The eggs and bacon were all gone and he had forgotten to buy pancake mix the last time he was at the Food Mart.

Since taking J.J. Pickler's bear and returning the trailer, he hadn't been to town in over two weeks. He had set up a daily routine for himself that filled each day and allowed him to sleep soundly each night. Every morning after eating breakfast, he'd put on his heavy coat, knit cap and his boots and venture into the woods for a walk. Marking his way with bent twigs and notched tree trunks he ventured into the mountain thickets until he figured he traveled at least five miles from the cabin. Going in a different direction each day, he always found his way back with ease.

On one of his daily hikes, he discovered a waterfall cascading into a stone-filled stream and a number of small caves. Yet, another day he stumbled onto an abandoned shack that at one time had been used by local moonshiners. The ramshackle shack was hidden away beneath a vine covered outcrop. The small building intrigued him. An old rusted still, or what was left of it, sat in the corner. Various sizes of filthy plastic jugs were strewn about. Three large 50# empty sugar sacks lay near the still. There were broken glass jars scattered around, a rusted iron bed frame opposite the still and two wooden stools pushed against the wall next to the remains of a pot-bellied stove. He wondered how long the still had been out of business.

On another one of his walks, about two miles from the cabin, he came across a cleared electric company service road. He followed the road for another four miles. He enjoyed walking up the road, which was far easier than trampling through the wet, thick undergrowth after a heavy rain. The trees had been cut down to make room for the man-made poles and electrical wires that carried electricity to the surrounding area. At one point, the rutted weed-infested road was bordered on one side by the mountain, the other side of the remote landscape falling off into a deep ravine. He couldn't see the bottom from where he stood.

He loved the deep forest. He was a denizen of the woods. It was his domain. It was where he felt most comfortable: no loud noises, no people, and most of all, no one telling him what he could or could not do. It had been over thirty years since he had decided to leave the crowded city behind and live the simple life of a woodsman. He was as comfortable in the woods as most people were in the comfort of their homes. He knew the call of the native birds and the habitat of every creature that lived in the forest. He knew which roots and berries were edible and how to construct a warm bed and shelter out of pine boughs. He was familiar with plants that could be used for medicine and to heal wounds. Even though he was on the clumsy side, when he was in the woods he could move about like a mountain cat, making his way across the forest floor without the slightest sound. He could stand perfectly still while woodland creatures moved around him. It was the smell of humans that caused animals to panic and flee. He knew they had good reason. Most people brought them nothing but grief and pain. If he remained in the area for any length of time, the forest animals would begin to trust him.

Returning to the cabin every day, he'd eat lunch, take a nap, gather some firewood, and then take a late afternoon walk. Aside from his walks in the forest, he found the best part of the day to be just after supper. He'd drag one of the rockers from the porch and place it in front of the fireplace. While the radio played country music, he would whittle small animals out of pine or ash or sometimes he'd play solitaire, keeping score on a small pad of yellow paper.

After two weeks of daily walks in the woods, he returned to the cabin and found the black bear he had rescued from Pickler sunning herself on the top deck of the cabin. He slowly moved around to the front door and slipped inside. He watched her from the window. She looked calm and peaceful, her coat looked a little better, and her nose had started to heal. His first instinct was to feed her, but he knew if he did, she would keep returning for food or start seeking out other humans. That might be what would end her life of freedom. Rather than feeding her, he grabbed a metal pot and a large mixing spoon, opened the door a crack, and banged on the pot. Startled, she jumped up and ran down the stairs into the woods. He hated scaring her, but he knew it was for her own good. He saw her several more times in the following weeks, but she stayed clear of the cabin.

J.J. Pickler was still raising a fuss over his missing bear. He had placed a sign on the now empty cage that read: *Where's my bear?* Of course, anyone entering his shop would ask what the sign was all about and he would reveal to them how his bear had been stolen. After weeks, the Mountain Press finally picked up on the story and on the very back page of the local news section they printed a small one paragraph segment which was entitled in a bold heading: **Where's Pickler's Bear?** J.J. felt like he was beginning to be a celebrity of sorts.

The police, on the other hand, were not amused with his constant haranguing about his missing bear. They were also angry about his telling everyone he met that the local police refused to assist him and they should all be fired. He told everyone that he had informed the police about the man who stole his bear. He also told people he was positive it was the same man that had been seen at the Gatlinburg Grill talking with Joe Winfield and Bobby Mackinaw the night Mackinaw was killed.

Even though the police felt Pickler was grasping at straws they decided to revisit the people who had been interviewed about the murder to see if they remembered anything else about that night. The police had nothing to lose. The trail of Bobby Mackinaw's killer was growing colder by the day. Janis, the waitress at the Gatlinburg Grill, gave them the same detailed description of the man that she had before. It was identical to the description Pickler had given them as the man he said thought took his bear.

The police called in a sketch artist from Knoxville, and from the description given by Janis and J.J. they came up with a composite picture that appeared to be on the ominous side, looking like a character from a B-Grade monster movie. The picture displayed a man with a long narrow face, with deep-set eyes that seemed to stare right through whoever was looking at the drawing. His head was covered with a knit cap pulled down to just above bushy eyebrows, his face covered with an outgrowth of short, dark whiskers. The composite drawing was placed in the paper the following morning.

The normal stack of morning papers arrived at the Flapjack Cabin just after 6:00 a.m., the same time Irene was starting her shift. Cutting the string securing the stack, Irene began to place the papers at the end of the counter. Resting on one elbow, she flipped through the paper as she drank her morning coffee. Suddenly she stopped, "Well, I'll be darn." Signaling the other morning waitress to the counter, she pointed out, "Thelma, look here, there's a picture of our favorite customer right here in the paper."

Looking over her shoulder, Thelma read the short article. "Says here the police are looking for him. They want to question him about the murder of Bobby Mackinaw and the disappearance of J.J.'s missing bear. Can you beat that?"

Taking off her apron, Irene tucked the paper under her arm and grabbed her purse from behind the counter. "Tell Larry I've got to run uptown. I should be back in less than an hour. Watch my tables will you?" She was out the door before Thelma could ask her why she was in such a rush.

Backing out of the parking lot, it took only a few minutes for her to drive to the Gatlinburg Police Station. Inside, she went to the front desk and spoke with the officer on duty who she knew. "Morning Carl, I was wondering if there is someone I could talk to about this?" Placing the paper on the desk she pointed to the picture.

Carl seemed surprised. "You know this man, Irene?"

"Well, I don't know him personally, but if this picture is who I think it is, I might know a couple of things about him."

Carl stood up. "Wait right here. I'll get the Chief."

Minutes later, Carl returned with Police Chief Allan Blake and another officer by the name of Williams. Blake asked her to step into a small office where she was seated. Williams offered her coffee but she declined. She felt a bit uncomfortable and hoped she was doing the right thing.

"Okay, Miss Whorl," said Allan. "Tell me what you know about this man."

Fumbling with her purse she began, "He started to come to the Flapjack Cabin right after Thanksgiving. He always sat at the same table right next to the front window. He seemed like a nice man. The picture in the paper doesn't do him justice. He wasn't as mean as this picture displays. He was shy and not much of a talker. He was polite, never caused any trouble, and always left me a big tip. He didn't strike me as a troublemaker or someone who would kill somebody."

"When was the last time you saw him, Miss Whorl?" asked Williams.

"Let's see, the last time I saw him was around the end of January. So, I guess it's been about a month. The last time he had breakfast, he asked me if I knew anyone around here who rented cabins. Said he wanted something way back in the woods. I gave him Walt Lansing's name over in Townsend. I know he has a few cabins." Tapping the paper with her hand she went on, "I think this man is sick, kind of in his head. Maybe he's just slow, or he's real sad about something, you know, like when somebody really is down. He just had that kind of lost look. Anyway, that's the last time I saw him." Snapping her fingers, she remembered something else. "You know it's strange, the last time he stopped by for breakfast, he looked really tired. I asked him if he was okay and he said he had a bad dream. Now, here's the strange part: that was the morning after Bobby Mackinaw's murder. Do you really think if he killed somebody the night before, he would come back to the restaurant for a casual breakfast? I sure don't think so. Aside from the fact that he looked tired he didn't act any different than he did any other time."

Allan turned to Williams as he ordered, "Get Walt Lansing on the horn."

Williams nodded, stood up, but then hesitated. "Wait a minute. I just thought of something. Walt's in Florida. Won't be back until April. He and his wife go down there every year in the off season."

Allan gave Williams a strange look. "And you know this how?"

"We bowl together in a winter league. He's never here for the last few weeks that we bowl. Something else, he said he doesn't like to rent his cabins out in the winter. We can try and call him down in Florida if you want."

"No, not yet," said Allan. "I don't really see the connection here." Holding up the paper to make his point he explained, "This guy, as far as we know, was in town a few weeks prior to the Mackinaw killing, then, weeks later Pickler's bear shows up missing. Why would this guy, if he indeed did kill Mackinaw, hang around town for a couple of weeks then steal the bear? It just doesn't add up. Irene says he seemed like a mild mannered sort, and another thing; you can't believe anything Pickler says. He's not the most reliable person. Remember last year after Butch Miller was found murdered over at Pickler's junkyard. He disappeared for weeks. Let's just wait and see if anyone else comes forward with information on this man."

Allan stood. "Thanks for coming in, Miss Whorl. If we need you for any further questioning we'll give you a ring."

Irene smiled and left. She had done her civic duty and in her own mind had probably saved an innocent man from being accused of something he didn't do just because he was a bit peculiar looking.

Coincidences are defined as twists of fate, accidents or even sometimes as luck. The idea that the man from the cabin over in Townsend and J.J. Pickler would decide to do their grocery shopping on the same day and at a store where they had never shopped before was a coincidence they both would have avoided if they had any idea how the day would turn out.

The man, since moving to the Townsend area, decided he would never return to Gatlinburg. He had killed the man they called Bobby and had stolen Pickler's bear. He couldn't be sure he hadn't been seen and he liked the laid back way of life Townsend offered: less people, less noise, the hustle and bustle of Gatlinburg nearly a half hour drive away.

Pickler was in Townsend that morning planning to visit an old codger who carved bears from tree stumps. With the upcoming tourist season just around the corner, he needed to increase his inventory. As J.J. drove past the Townsend IGA, he noticed an advertisement on the front of the store: BUY ONE GET ONE FREE *ON ALL CANNED GOODS!* Pickler, a cheap bastard who couldn't resist the idea of saving a few pennies, pulled into the lot, grabbed a cart and entered the store. It was only seven in the morning and J.J.'s appointment with the woodcarver wasn't until eight o'clock. He had plenty of time to stock up on non perishables and still get to his appointment. Looking around the store, he didn't see many customers. *Good,* thought J.J. *I can get what I want before everything gets picked over.*

Neither the man nor J.J. realized they were just two aisles away from each other. The man put the last few items he needed in his cart. Standing back and reviewing what he had bought, he scanned the cart: bacon, eggs, coffee, pancake mix, TV dinners. He only needed two more items; toilet paper and bread. J.J. was grabbing cans of corn, green beans, hash, and soup off the shelf as the man walked directly behind him bumping into his cart. "Sorry" said the man.

J.J., busy grabbing every can of noodle soup he could get his hands on glanced over his shoulder at the customer wearing a bright red ball cap and swore beneath his breath, "Dumb ass!"

The man finished his shopping first and headed for the checkout. J.J. hopped in the same line, two customers separated the two men. J.J. was busy reading the front cover of the Enquirer. He looked up momentarily as the man in the red hat received his change and walked to the exit doors. J.J recognized the man as the customer who had bumped into him. Under his breath he swore again, "Damn hillbilly!"

J.J. was beginning to get impatient. The customer in front of him had a number of coupons. Gazing out the front window, he noticed the man in the red hat loading his groceries in the back of a pickup truck. There was something oddly familiar about the man. J.J. continued to watch him and just before he climbed in the truck, the man removed the red hat and placed a knit hat on his head pulling it down over his ears. It was then that J.J. recognized him. "Well, I'll be damned!" Pushing past the customer in front of him, he yelled, "Let me by...move!" Leaving his cart in line, he pushed another man to the side and bolted for the exit door all the while yelling, "That sum bitch stole my bear!" The customers in the immediate area just stared at J.J. as if he was nuts.

By the time J.J. made it out the front door, the truck was pulling out of the lot and onto the Parkway. J.J. yelled again, shaking is fist in the air, leaving customers in the lot startled by his loud outburst. Running across the lot, he jumped into his Cadillac. As he placed the key in the ignition, the car sputtered. J.J. yelled, "Come on...come on!" He turned the key a second time and the engine came to life. Flooring the gas pedal, he backed into a row of shopping carts sending them in every direction. Profanity spewed from his mouth as he circled the parking lot and headed for the entrance, all the while keeping his eye on the truck that was heading up the street. As he turned onto the Parkway, he ran over a low concrete abutment. His car bounced into the air, one of his hubcaps came loose and careened off of the curb coming to rest in the grass at the side of the road. "Got damn," he bellowed as he saw the truck stop at a red light just up the block. J.J. beat on the orange, shag covered steering wheel and yelled, "You ain't getting away you thieving bastard! I'm coming after you. I gotcha now!"

There were two cars in between J.J. and the pickup. As the light changed he veered around the two vehicles. He followed the truck down the Parkway and out past the town limits.

Ten minutes passed before the truck made a left hand turn onto a side road that led out into the country. A short distance later the truck turned onto a dirt road. J.J. kept his distance. There was a light covering of snow on the road that made it easy to follow the tire tracks.

Following carefully, he paid attention as the curvy road led up into the mountains. The truck made two left hand turns and then a right over the next four miles. J.J. hesitated at each turn making sure the driver of the truck was not aware he was being followed. Another half mile passed and J.J. started to wonder where in the hell the man was going. *Did the man know he was being tailed? Naw, he was too dumb for that.* Taking a left turn up a steep, gravel covered road, J.J. had to step on the gas. The loose gravel made it hard for the Cadillac to get any traction, the wheels spitting rocks off to the side of the road. The car bounced through a number of small ditches where the road had washed away. Then, there it was! A rustic cabin tucked away in a grouping of tall pines. The truck was parked on the side of the gravel road in front of the cabin. Looking around, J.J. realized how far up into the mountains they had driven.

Now what? he thought. Taking his revolver out of the glove compartment, he checked to make sure he had a full load. He thought again, *This guy's a nut. Should I get out and go knock on the door or just stay in the car and honk?* Putting the gun on the seat next to him, he laid on the horn, then rolled down the window. Beating on the side of his car, he yelled toward the cabin, "Hey you inside, come on out!" He waited. Nothing. Putting both of his hands on the horn he let it blare for a good five seconds. Slowly the door opened and he could see the man's frame filling the doorway. He stood there for a moment, and then stepped out onto the porch.

"You're the guy who took my bear, ain't ya?" yelled J.J. "I want her back and I want her back now! You understand?" There was no response.

J.J. stuck his head out the window. "Hey, Dumb Ass! I'm talking to you. Where's my bear?"

The man seemed nervous as he answered, "She ain't your bear no more. I set her free. She's living in the woods now."

Slamming his hand on the side of the car door, J.J. cursed, "Well, I'll be a son of a—"

The man cut him off before he could finish, "You don't call me dumb no more. You're the dumb one. You don't know how to treat animals."

J.J. was livid. His eyes narrowed as he spit out the window. "Is that a fact? Well, here's a fact for ya." Grabbing his gun he leveled it at the man as he spoke strongly, "You're a thief. You stole my bear. I have every right to shoot you right where you stand. Now, you're going to show me where my bear is. Understand?"

The man held his hands up in front of himself as he spoke humbly, "Okay...just let me get my coat and hat and I'll take you to where she is."

The man slipped back inside the door. J.J. grinned as he thought to himself, *Hell that was easier than I thought. Dumb shit's gonna lead me right to her.* Getting out of the car, he closed the door, but kept the gun pointed toward the porch. *Once he shows me where the bear is I'll head back down the mountain to where I can get cell phone reception then I'll call the police. I can come back and get the bear after this creep is arrested.*

A few seconds later, the man stepped back out onto the porch in a heavy-duty coat and his red hat. J.J. smiled to himself as he knew that he held the upper hand. Before he could utter a word, the man brought a 22 caliber rifle from behind his back, aimed and fired two bullets, ripping through J.J.'s chest, knocking him back against the door of his car, the echo of the gunfire resonated across the valley.

J.J.'s body slid down the side of the Cadillac to the ground where he slumped over sideways. The man kept the rifle trained on J.J. as he approached carefully. J.J.'s eyes were still open, a look of surprise and horror covering his face. His chest was heaving in and out. He was still alive. The man kicked the side of one of J.J.'s legs as he scolded him, "I told you, you weren't getting that bear. You shouldn't have called me dumb." Pointing the rifle at J.J.'s head, he squeezed off another shot; a steam of blood ran down J.J.'s face from the perfect hole in his forehead. The man repeated himself, "You shouldn't have called me dumb."

Leaning the gun up against the side of the car, he picked J.J. up, opened the rear door, and placed him in the backseat. Looking at the blood on his hands, he picked up the gun and went back to the cabin. After cleaning himself up, he returned to the car. The keys were still in the ignition where J.J. had left them. The man started the car and drove back down the road to an access road that led to the electric company service road. Once on the service road, he drove another three miles until he found the exact spot he was looking for. He drove the car to the very edge of the precipice He got out and removed J.J.'s body from the backseat and positioned him in the driver's seat. After placing the car in neutral he walked behind the car and shoved it toward the edge. It took one good push to get the car moving. It teetered on the edge for a moment, then heaved forward and started its descent into the deep ravine hundreds of feet below. The man stood and watched as the heavy Cadillac sheared off small trees and branches as it moved downwards. At one point he saw J.J.'s arm as it flopped out the window. As it hit a huge rock, the car did a complete somersault and disappeared into the bowels of the ravine. Even though the car was out of his sight, he could still hear the sound of metal against wood and rock until there was an eerie silence.

Starting toward the cabin, he stopped dead in his tracks as J.J.'s bear stood near the side of the road. She sniffed at the air, pawed at the ground and slowly walked back into the forest. J.J. would never bother her again. Looking up at the sky, he saw two bald eagles circle high above. He smiled. They were such beautiful birds. He was hungry. It had to be getting close to lunchtime. He was looking forward to eating some of the bean soup he bought at the grocery store. They said it was homemade. He hoped they were right.

CHAPTER SIX

DANA BETH HANDED the ink pen to Grant as she sat back in the cushioned chair, rubbing her hands gently over her protruding belly. She let out a long sigh. Veronica Styles, the real estate agent smiled at Dana Beth, asking, "How far along are you now?"

Dana Beth returned a wide grin. "Almost six months. The baby is really getting active. For the first two months of my pregnancy I thought I'd never start showing but as you can see, I've packed on the pounds these past few months. The doctor says she's gonna be a big baby."

"So, it's a girl?"

"That's what the doctor says."

Grant signed the last form. The closing for the sale of Ruth's house was finally at an end. Grant stretched his hands over his head. He never realized how complicated the paperwork process was for purchasing a home. Rubbing his wrist he commented, "Glad I'm not famous. Signing autographs all the time, everywhere you go. We've only been here for an hour signing papers and my right hand is worn out."

Thurmond Potts, who represented the bank, stood and reached for Grant's hand, "Congratulations, you are now the proud owner of Ruth's home. I can't tell you how pleased I am that the house is staying in the family."

Dana Beth rose slowly using the table for support. She stood behind her mother, her hands on Ruth's shoulders. "These past couple of months have been difficult, with the death of my father, then Mom deciding to move to Chattanooga." Looking at Ruth, who was still seated, she smiled. "But, if that's what makes mom happy then I'm all for the move. I never thought Grant and I would have our own home so shortly after getting married, but the thought of raising our children in the home where I grew up is very comforting."

Veronica asked, "So when are you actually moving to Chattanooga?"

"Tomorrow," Ruth said. "Dana Beth and I have been going through stuff for the past week. We have to decide what we're going to do with some of Conrad's belongings. I've got a lot of things I'm going to donate to the church for their mission drive. There are some things I'm going to pitch. I'm not taking all that much with me, mostly clothing, personal items and a few mementos. I'm leaving most of the furniture at the house. I'll have everything I need at my sister's place. Besides that, the kids have told me I can come back here and visit whenever I want."

Outside the bank parking lot, Grant hugged Ruth and then kissed Dana Beth. Opening the door of Dana Beth's small compact car, he helped Ruth inside then turned to his wife. "I'll meet you and Ruth back at the house later this afternoon. I shouldn't be more than a couple of hours in Gatlinburg." Walking her around to the driver's side, he gently ordered her, "And don't be doing a lot of lifting. Remember what the doctor said. Don't push yourself too hard."

Climbing in the car, Dana Beth smiled. "Don't worry, I'll be fine."

Watching her pull out of the lot, he walked to his Jeep, which was parked next to Veronica Styles' car. Veronica was placing her briefcase in the backseat when she noticed Grant approaching. Closing the trunk she addressed him before he could get in the Jeep. "You worked on the Mildred Henks case didn't you?"

"Yes, I did," responded Grant.

Veronica leaned up against her car as she folded her arms across her chest. "Mildred and I worked together. She's the one who trained me when I first got started in real estate years ago. If she hadn't been murdered she would have been at your closing today. She handled most of the transactions here in Townsend. Mildred was a topnotch agent. I remember right after she was murdered how the word got out about how she treated those dogs she had on her place. I, for one, just couldn't believe it." Looking directly at Grant, she asked, "Was it really as bad as they said...I mean the condition of the dogs and where they were kept?"

"I'm afraid so," Grant replied.

Veronica went on to explain, "We have three dogs. My husband is a big dog lover and when the news broke about Mildred, he said she deserved what she got. Myself, well I feel what she did was wrong, but to be killed the way she was...that's just horrible. Were you over at the golf course when they found her?"

"Yes, I was the first one on the scene."

"It must have been a horrible sight with her stuffed in that cage, all her fingers and toes cut off—"

Grant, not interested in reliving the afternoon of Mildred Henks' murder, cut Veronica off, "Listen I've really got to run. Thank you for the work you did at the closing."

Climbing in the Jeep, he watched as Veronica pulled out of the lot. He sat back in the seat and shook his head in wonder. It seemed like the memory of the year's past murders were never going to leave him. Pulling out of the bank parking lot, he headed up the Parkway. Turning onto Route 321 he turned on the radio, hoping some music would intervene and take his mind off of the Henks' murder.

He gazed at the passing countryside. A fresh one inch layer of snow coated the ground. It was the beginning of March and winter had lingered longer than usual in the Smoky Mountains. January and February were traditionally months that left everyone in the doldrums: cold weather, Christmas bills to pay off, leafless trees, not many tourists in town. Each year when March finally rolled around, everyone was getting into the spirit of the upcoming tourist season which normally kicked in right after Easter. But this year it was different. Business and shop owners who normally would be hiring seasonal help, taking inventory of their stock and making needed repairs to their buildings were still dealing with below average temperatures, stiff winds, and snow.

Grant was dealing with his own pre-spring season depression. Ever since that afternoon on Conrad's porch he felt like a silver ball in a pin ball machine: bouncing here and there, never sure of where he was going to land. Who was he going to have to lie to next? The only thought that brought him any relief was that April was only a month off, and unlike everyone else who expected another spring murder, he knew the murders were over.

He thought about the most recent murder of Bobby Mackinaw over in Gatlinburg. Some folks were trying to say the local killer had struck again, but he knew different. Mackinaw's murder had been for lack of a better phrase a "run of the mill" murder.

As he passed through Pigeon Forge, it was just as dead as Townsend with very few tourists in town. The only sign of life were the locals who were out grocery shopping, visiting the dentist, the post office, or any number of things that go on in people's everyday lives.

Thinking once again about how everything in Townsend had ground to a halt, he thought about Axel Brody. Normally when everyone else in town was in a good mood, Brody displayed a foul mood, but for the past month it had been the opposite. Brody seemed happier than he had been in quite some time. Everything seemed to be going his way for a change.

Lee Griner had accepted Brody's offer for a position as an officer on the Townsend Police. Sheriff Grimes had called Brody and told him he was keeping Kenny Jacks on the Townsend force until May. Then, if it looked like the murders had stopped he would transfer Kenny back to Maryville. Marge was even in good spirits now that Brody had calmed down.

Ten minutes later, Grant entered the Gatlinburg town limits. The town was equally as dead as Pigeon Forge, *the calm before the storm,* he thought. When the end of April hit there would be an unending influx of tourists, from every corner of the country, flooding the streets and shops. Stopping for a red light, he looked at the long row of shops on his right: Smoky Mountain Leather Goods, Gatlinburg Gifts and Novelties, Franklin Candy, and J.J Pickler's Bear Emporium.

The light changed and he pulled out as he stared at the sign above Pickler's shop. He wasn't aware that Pickler owned a shop in Gatlinburg as well as the junkyard in Sevierville. Passing the shop, he noticed a large sign posted on a cage next to the building: **Where's my bear?** *What the hell is that all about?* thought Grant. Minutes later, he pulled into Buzzy's Auto Repair. Parking the Jeep, he walked into one of three open bays and looked for his old friend. Buzzy, who was talking with a customer, noticed Grant as he entered and waved continuing his conversation with the customer. Leaning against a windshield wiper display, Grant looked around the large garage. The place was a madhouse. All three lifts were occupied with autos in some state of repair. One employee was rolling a tire across the greasy floor, while another was checking a diagnostic machine, still another was pushing a roll around tool chest beneath one of the elevated cars.

Buzzy, finally finished with his customer, approached Grant with his usually friendly smile plastered across his face. "Grant! Where in the hell have you been, buddy? The last time you brought your Jeep in was what...last July? That's been eight, nine months. Unless you're doing business with someone else your poor ol' Jeep is way overdue for an oil change."

"I know, I know," said Grant. "That's the reason I'm here. You can put your mind at ease. I haven't taken my business anyplace else. I've just been busy. Since I last saw you, I got married and we're expecting a little girl, not to mention that there's been three more murders which I'm sure you're aware of." Before Buzzy could say anything, Grant produced an envelope from his coat pocket. "My grandfather gave me a gift for Christmas; a complete auto detailing for my Jeep. And while I'm at it I do need an oil change."

"Yeah," said Buzzy. "I remember when Dalton was in here just before Thanksgiving. Didn't have much of a chance to speak with him. He said he was in a hurry, but that he wanted to get you a detailing gift certificate for your Jeep." Turning and displaying all of the activity in the garage, Buzzy went on, "We ran a special for detailing, and the response was more than we expected. That's why we're so damn busy." Taking the envelope from Grant, Buzzy opened it then stated, "Good news, bad news, pal. The good news is that we're giving a free oil change when somebody brings one of these in. The bad news is I'm booked all the way through next Saturday."

"That's all right," remarked Grant. "Slot me in."

"Consider it done." Wiping his hands on a rag he took from his back pocket, Buzzy glanced at a clock in the corner of the shop. "It's almost lunchtime. If you have time to eat, I'm buyin'."

Mimicking Buzzy, Grant laughed, "Consider it done!"

Taking a set of keys from his pants pocket, Buzzy suggested, "I'll drive." As he pulled out onto the main street, Buzzy looked both ways and asked, "Burgers sound okay? The Gatlinburg Grill has the best in town."

"I'm just along for the ride," said Grant. "A burger sounds good."

Two blocks down the street they passed J.J. Pickler's place. Grant's curiosity got the best of him. "Don't tell me that's the same J.J. Pickler that owns the junkyard over in Sevierville?"

"One and the same," answered Buzzy. "He sold the junkyard after the murder. He stayed away for a few months and then he settled here in Gatlinburg. The word around town is after he got back, he cleared himself of any suspicion that he had anything to do with the murder. Can't say I blame him for not wanting to keep the junkyard. Guess J.J. was the first one on the scene. It must have been horrible seeing Miller's body ripped to shreds. On top of that the note he found with those severed bloody fingers duct taped to it that said *Pickler you're next!* I don't think I would have hung around either."

Making a left hand turn onto a side street, Buzzy motioned up the block to a large sign. "The Gatlinburg Grill is just up the street. Looks like it's busy." Pulling over to the curb, he lit up a cigarette and climbed out.

Walking up the street, Buzzy pointed to a passageway between two buildings. "Speaking of murder scenes, right there in that passageway is where Bobby Mackinaw had his head bashed in. Wanna have a look see?"

Grant looked at Buzzy in amazement. "God no! I saw enough spilled blood last year."

Continuing up the street, Buzzy took another drag on his cigarette as he waved at someone he knew. He turned his attention back to Grant. "I just thought you might be interested in seeing the crime scene. I mean, what the hell, that makes five people this killer has taken out."

As Buzzy reached for the Gatlinburg Grill's front door, Grant corrected him, "Where did you come up with five murders? Bobby Mackinaw's murder has nothing to do with the four from last year. Mackinaw's murder is totally unrelated."

Buzzy was about to respond when he was interrupted by a waitress. "Buzzy! Who's your friend?"

Buzzy made quick introductions, "Janis, this is Grant. He's an officer from over in Townsend. Grant, this is Janis, the best waitress in Gatlinburg."

Placing two beers down on a nearby table, she then asked, "You two here for lunch or just a cool one?"

"Yep," said Buzzy. "Burgers and maybe even a beer or two."

"A couple of gents just got up from a booth over there by the front window next to the jukebox. Have a seat and I'll be right back to clear it off and take your order."

Sitting at the booth, Buzzy commented, "Janis is a doll. We used to date back in high school. She's married now and has a couple of kids."

Janis came back to the booth, handed them two menus, and asked them what they wanted to drink. Buzzy ordered a beer and Grant a Coke. When she returned with their drinks, they ordered their burgers.

Taking a long sip of beer, Buzzy picked up on their previous conversation at the front door. Pointing his bottle at Grant he asked, "Why would you say that Mackinaw's murder was not committed by the same killer who committed the other four murders?"

"First of all the profile doesn't fit," said Grant. "No duct tape, no missing fingers. Secondly, unless you have some sort of proof Bobby Mackinaw was mistreating animals there would be no reason for the killer to take him out."

"I guess you're right, but there is something weird going on here in Gatlinburg," Buzzy said as he took another swig of his drink. "My brother-in-law is an officer on the Gatlinburg Police Force. He was just at the shop yesterday. According to him, J.J. Pickler has disappeared again. Been gone for almost two weeks now."

"What do you mean gone?"

"Gone...disappeared, that's what I mean. The owner of Franklin Candy, which is located next to J.J.'s place, noticed that J.J.'s store wasn't open for two days. The man calls Pickler at home to see if he's all right, no answer. Not sure what to do, he waits another day and calls Pickler again...still no answer. He starts to get worried about the situation. He knows how J.J. is about making money and so he calls the police. They go to the shop and bang on the door. The shop is all-dark inside, but when they look through the windows, nothing seems to be disturbed. Then, they make a trip out to his trailer and he's not there. They ask around the trailer park and everyone they talk to says they haven't seen Pickler for almost a week. Then, they break in his trailer. There was food in the refrigerator, a pack of cigarettes on the table. No signs of anything out of the ordinary. His pickup truck was there but his Cadillac was gone. Everything appeared to be in order at his store, too. There were no signs of a struggle. So, at this point nobody knows where Pickler is or what happened to him. He's been gone for two weeks now."

Grant was about to say something when Janis returned with their lunch. "There you go, boys. If you need anything else just let me know. Enjoy those burgers."

Grabbing a ketchup bottle, Grant commented, "Look, Pickler is a weird sort of character and I might add not one to be completely trusted. He's not what you would call a model citizen." Taking a bite out of the burger, he explained, "Before Miller was killed, we got a tip that dog fights were being held at Pickler's junkyard. Pickler must have been tipped as well. When the police showed up, the only evidence, if you want to call it that, was a lot of scattered beer bottles and a couple of empty dog cages in one of his warehouses near the back of the junkyard. It was obvious that dogfights had been conducted on his property. Pickler explained it all away by saying that he had a bunch of friends over one night for a party and that's why the beer bottles were there. He said he had found the dog cages in an old truck that he picked up for salvage. He was planning on selling them. So the police really didn't have any solid proof to go on, so Pickler merely got a slap on the wrist."

"There's more to it than just that," said Buzzy as he bit into a French fry. "Two weeks after Mackinaw was killed, Pickler called the police over to his shop. He reported to them that someone had stolen his bear—"

Grant interrupted, "His bear?"

"Yeah, he had a bear he kept in a cage next to the shop. The bear did some tricks and customers could get their picture taken with it."

"Is that legal, I mean to have a bear in a cage like that?"

Picking up another fry, Buzzy answered, "Yeah, he had a permit to keep it, but I heard that there were a few complaints from the local animal activists, but there wasn't much they could do. Pickler fed and watered the bear and as far as I know he never mistreated the animal."

Grant had a puzzled look on his face. "You said that he reported the bear stolen. Did the activists steal the bear?"

"Not according to Pickler. When the police showed up at his place, he informed them that a couple of weeks prior to Mackinaw's murder, he had a strange customer come into his shop complaining and asking questions about his bear. He finally left after saying that someone needed to rescue the bear. Later, the man returned and Pickler caught him feeding the animal. Pickler ran him off, but two weeks later the bear was missing."

"So that's the reason for the sign on the cage?" asked Grant.

"That's right. Pickler gave the man's description to the police, but they just kind of blew him off. The Mackinaw murder was still fresh on everyone's mind. A missing bear was not at the top of their priority list, so Pickler made it known that the police were worthless and he would find the bear on his own."

Grant held up one of his hands, "But I still don't see what any of this has to do with the murder of Bobby Mackinaw."

Janis was walking by their table with an empty tray as Buzzy stopped her. "Janis, can you come here for a sec?"

She stopped and asked, "Is there something else you'd like? Maybe another beer?"

Buzzy leaned forward. "Remember that strange dude that was in here the night of Mackinaw's murder."

"Sure, why?"

"I was wondering if you could explain to my friend here what happened that night?"

Looking around the tavern she nodded, "Looks like I can take a couple of minutes." Gesturing to Grant she ordered him in a friendly manner. "Shove over."

Grant slid across the vinyl booth seat as Janis seated herself. "I remember that night like it was yesterday. This big fellow comes walking in here: dark clothes, knit cap pulled down over his ears..." Two minutes later, Janis finished up with her rundown on the night of the murder, "...didn't think anymore about it until the next morning when they said they found Bobby murdered." She stood as the bartender signaled her to a booth at the other end of the tavern. "Gotta go, guys."

Buzzy watched as she walked away from their booth then turned his attention back to Grant. "What Janis didn't get to tell you is what happened when the police showed up here to ask some questions. When they asked if anything unusual happened prior to the murder, Janis told them about the strange man who had come to the tavern and had been confronted by Joe and Bobby. The description she gave the police of the stranger matched the same identical description that Pickler gave to the police about the man he thought stole his bear."

Grant shrugged his shoulders. "Look this all sounds on the strange side but it still doesn't mean that this stranger killed Mackinaw or that he's the killer we've been looking for this last year."

Buzzy shook his head as if Grant didn't know what he was talking about. "There's still more to this story. Joe Winfield disappeared the night Mackinaw was killed and wasn't located until last week when the authorities ran him down in Florida. They brought him back here for questioning and what he told the police leaves no doubt that this odd stranger is the killer. Joe told the police after they left here that night, they ran into the man down the street. They started to talk to him but he went crazy without any warning and grabbed Bobby and smashed his head into a wall. He kicked Joe and down he went. Joe thought for sure the guy was going to kill him, but he just stomped off talking to himself. Joe said he checked Bobby and when he discovered he was dead he panicked, and got out of town. The point is the police have

Joe Winfield in custody, since he is an eyewitness who claims the knit cap man killed Bobby. They're holding Winfield on some trumped up charge until they're sure he wasn't involved in Mackinaw's murder. Now whether this man is responsible for the disappearance of Pickler is anyone's guess. But think about this. The killer we've been plagued with for the last year has killed four people who mistreated animals. We already know Pickler had a run in with this guy at his shop over the bear and the man said the bear needed to be set free."

"So after this man killed Mackinaw and supposedly stole Pickler's bear, he up and disappeared?" stated Grant.

"Yep, and I know if the police find him, I bet he knows what happened to Pickler." He continued on with his story while he ate his lunch.

Pushing the last of his fries to the side, Buzzy waved his hand in the air, "Enough talk about who's missing and murders. You said something about how you got married last year. What's that all about?"

Grant sat back on the seat as he explained, "Married my high school sweetheart last September and we're expecting our first child in three months. Doctor says it's going to be a little girl. Her father passed away just before Christmas and her mother is moving to Chattanooga. She sold me and the wife her house. As a matter of fact, I just signed all the paperwork before I drove over here this morning."

Buzzy laughed then commented, "Why you're just becoming a regular citizen aren't you? The next thing you know you'll be wearing one of those sweaters with patches on the sleeves, sitting in a rocking chair on your porch reading the paper, an Irish setter at your feet."

Thirty minutes later, Grant was turning onto Route 321 headed back to Townsend. Buzzy had driven him back to the garage and reminded him about the appointment for his Jeep next Saturday. Stopping behind a school bus that was picking up a group of children, he thought about his lunch discussion with Buzzy. There had been yet another murder in the vacation Mecca of the Smoky Mountains. He and he alone knew it had absolutely nothing to do with the four murders of the past year, but, nonetheless, another person had lost his life in an area of the country where murder was practically unheard of. A place where people came to get away from the everyday frustrations of their job, the economy, or any number of problems they were facing. It was a haven of great restaurants, gift shops, and a relaxing environment with plenty of enjoyable places to go and things to do, a place to get away from it all, and now a place to be murdered!

Passing the school bus further up the road, he recalled what Buzzy had said about the police not going to see Walt Lansing or even going up to the cabin where the man who had been identified as the killer of Bobby Mackinaw had stayed. He didn't quite understand why they hadn't followed up on that kind of a lead, but it really wasn't any of his business. He also thought about the disappearance of Pickler and the fact that once again, following a local murder, he up and vanished. Conrad never mentioned that he had left the note on the fence for Pickler. Maybe he did and maybe he didn't, but even if he did, what did any of that have to do with Pickler disappearing again?

His thoughts about J.J. Pickler were interrupted as he noticed the entrance to the Stroud's place. Just like always Otis and Maude Stroud sat on their old lawn chairs next to a pop-up tent. Today they were selling tomatoes, canned peaches and an array of junk their sons picked up at yard sales. Grant thought that the old couple would have made a great Norman Rockwell painting; Otis always dressed the same: baseball hat, long sleeved flannel shirt buttoned up to the neck, sweat pants, and western boots. His overweight wife, Maude, always donned one of her homemade, baggy, flowered dresses with her feet encased in high top sneakers. Her nylon stockings were rolled down around her ankles. Grant must have seen them sitting in this same spot hundreds of times over the years. Both of them with a cigarette and a can of beer held in their nicotine stained hands. It was just last week that Brody had been called up to their place. Cletus, their youngest son had been beating on his wife Ruby once again. Grant smiled. He knew how much Axel hated dealing with the Strouds.

Parking the Jeep in the driveway behind Dana Beth's car, he saw his wife carrying a basket of clothing into the garage. The small moving truck they rented sat next to the garage, its backdoor open. Ruth exited the kitchen door with a box of shoes cradled in her arms. Setting the box on the back of the truck, she noticed Grant as he approached. "Grant, you're just in time. We ordered a pizza for lunch. We've been working our tails off."

Just then Dana Beth walked back out of the garage. Seeing her husband, she smiled as she wiped her brow with the back of her hand. "Whew! My father had a lot of clothes, plus mom is getting rid of a lot of her old stuff. We're donating them to the church. They said they've got plenty of families who could use them."

Gesturing toward the house, she let out a long breath. "The pizza guy was just here. Let's eat before it gets cold."

Following Ruth and Dana Beth inside the house, Grant leaned up against the kitchen counter. Taking a slice of pizza from the box, Dana Beth put it onto a plate then reached for a two-liter bottle of soda. "Come on Grant, get in on this."

"I'd love to, but I just had lunch with Buzzy over in Gatlinburg. I'm stuffed." Looking around the kitchen he asked, "What else needs to be done? There's no sense in me standing around while you two eat. I can be getting something done."

Taking a bite of pizza, Ruth pointed toward the kitchen door. "Well, there's a lot of work that needs to be finished up in the garage. I'm sure you can use most of the tools that are out there: mower, leaf blower, weed trimmer, and a bunch of other stuff. You need to go through the items in the garage and decide what you want to keep. Whatever you don't want or can't use needs to be stacked in one of the corners for a yard sale Dana Beth and I decided to have when the weather breaks."

Grant, removing a piece of pepperoni from the top of the pizza asked, "What about that old van out there?"

"God, I forgot about that old thing," said Ruth. "I haven't ridden in that van for years. I don't know why Conrad kept it around. I guess I've forgotten about it because he kept it behind that black tarp. If you want to keep it fine, otherwise you can see what you can get for it. I have no idea where the title is. Probably in the glove compartment."

Walking toward the kitchen door, Grant asked, "Are you sure there's nothing in here you need help with?"

"Absolutely," said Ruth. "The only thing left to do is carry the rest of my clothes to the moving truck. We can handle that if you'll concentrate on the garage."

"Okay, the garage it is."

Grant felt a sense of relief that the van was now going to be completely in his control. He thought about the evidence in the back of the vehicle. For the past four months he had been concerned that Ruth might go out to the garage and possibly discover what he had found. The fear of that happening passed when he and Dana Beth bought the house. As he entered the garage, he stared at the long, black tarp that concealed the van.

Grabbing the flashlight from the workbench, he ducked beneath the tarp. He opened the van door and climbed into the driver's seat. Aiming the light into the back of the van he saw the black gym bag that was still where he had left it. He sat back in the seat and thought that after April passed and there were no more murders things would begin to calm down. He would then sell the van after hiding the gym bag and its contents up in the overhead garage storage area and at some point he would dispose of them as well.

Taking a deep breath to relax himself, he smelled the aroma of Peach Brandy pipe tobacco that seemed to linger inside the confines of the van. Looking down at the console, he saw the pipe and the pouch of tobacco. Then it hit him! *Peach Brandy tobacco. A man wearing dark clothes with a knit cap pulled down over his ears.* He suddenly recalled the man at Conrad's funeral who had stood off at a distance; the same man he thought he had seen at the nativity scene. He had been wearing dark clothes and was wearing a knit cap. Grant remembered how, when the man had walked away from them when they had left the cemetery he thought he had picked up the aroma of Peach Brandy, the same identical aroma he had smelled at the nativity. *Could it be?* Could it be the same man the Gatlinburg Police were searching for—the man accused of killing Bobby Mackinaw—a man who might just have possibly stolen J.J. Pickler's bear *and now* Pickler winds up missing again. *Who was the man?* He had thought after discovering Conrad as the killer, the unsolved puzzle had been completed. Now it appeared a piece was missing and it was all centered on the man in the dark knit cap. *Who was he and why was he in the area?*

CHAPTER SEVEN

THE FIRST TEASING DAYS of warm weather turned into another cold snap as Mother Nature proved that she was still in charge. A few scattered crocuses had stuck their yellow heads out and now bowed from the early morning frost. The man shivered as he placed the last of his possessions in the back of his truck. Walking back inside the cabin, he put on his coat and knit cap and took one last look around at what had been his home for the past few months. He was satisfied that he was leaving the cabin cleaner then when he first arrived. He wished he could stay longer. It had been a time of solitude he sorely needed, but he promised Walt Lansing he would be out by the end of April. He always kept his promises.

Looking out across the valley he saw wisps of blue mist, the Smokies were famous for. They weaved their way through the vast forest, the tops of the mountains still not visible. He had time for one last walk on one of the wooded trails he had created. Maybe he'd see the bear one last time. During the past months he had seen her on occasion. She seemed to be doing well in her new environment. He was glad she found her niche in the forest. He was sad he was leaving her behind, but he was also proud of what he had done for her.

An hour down the trail, he stopped for a moment, a familiar scent filled his nostrils. He recognized the smell immediately; smoke! Someone was in the woods invading his space. Turning in a complete circle, he raised his head as he drew in a deep breath of crisp mountain air tainted with the smell of something burning. His keen sense of smell quickly identified the burning of damp wood and leaves. He searched the surrounding trees for any sign of the smoke, but found none. Proceeding down the trail, he determined that the smoke was somewhere nearby. He picked up his pace, carefully as the scent grew stronger with each step.

A few minutes later, he heard movement; the distinct sound of someone stepping on leaves and twigs. Twenty yards ahead, off to the left of the trail he saw the smoke as it rose lazily upwards and drifted off into the trees. He crept forward until he had a clear vision of the fire. He camouflaged himself behind a small grove of tall pine trees and watched a short, thin man dressed in heavy duty hiking boots, dark green pants, and a brown flannel shirt. He wore an old ball hat, worn backwards, centered on his head. The intruder was walking around a fire he had started in a small clearing. He was picking up twigs and small branches and placing them on the fire. The reddish-yellow flames licked at the cold morning air as a trail of smoke rose up through the trees. He knelt down next to the fire and holding his hands over the flames, he rubbed them together. Wrapping his arms around himself, he moved closer to the fire.

Still hidden behind the pines, the man surveyed the scene. There were two, large brown burlap sacks lying on the ground, along with a shovel and a bucket. There was no sign of a rifle or any other type of weapon. Stepping out from the cover of the trees, the man asked, "What are you doing out here?"

The trespasser, taken by surprise, jumped back from the fire, falling to the ground. He quickly turned around and seeing the man standing next to the pines, he responded loudly, "Got damn! You scared the crap out of me. What the hell do you mean by sneakin' up on me like that? I nearly pissed myself!"

The man didn't answer his question, but instead pointed out, "You're not supposed to start a fire without the proper pit, especially this far back in the woods. It's dangerous to start a fire on the ground near dry leaves and twigs. Those flames can travel faster than you can run. You could cause a big forest fire."

The intruder stood up, wiping off the back of his pants as he continued to stare at the man. "You some kind of park ranger or somethin'? Because if you are, well this ain't park property. You have no jurisdiction here. Besides that, I'm watchin' the fire ain't I?"

Not liking the intruder's attitude, the man shook his head as he stepped forward. "I'm not a ranger, but this is my property, at least for a couple more hours so you better put out that fire and git."

"Hold on a minute," said the intruder. "What do you mean...this is your property for a couple more hours? That doesn't make sense. You either own this land or you don't."

The man remained silent. He didn't know how to explain what he had said.

The intruder, realizing that the man who walked up on him was not too sure what he was talking about, commented, "Just give me a few minutes to warm up, then I'll leave." Crouching once again in front of the warming fire, the intruder went on, "I forgot my heavy coat this mornin' and I'm half frozen." Rubbing his arms he stated, "Sure didn't expect it to turn so cold." Looking up at the man, he asked, "You cold?" He could tell the man was irritated by his presence. Maybe some small talk would settle him down. He didn't want any trouble. He looked at the man who had moved even closer: large and unkempt, dark clothing, knit cap pulled down over his ears, strange eyes, light, untrimmed beard. He didn't look like the law. Maybe the man was up to something. Maybe he was a local moonshiner or had a stash of weed further back in the woods.

Finally, the man smiled as he stepped closer to the fire. "No, I'm not cold. You have to know how to dress for this kind of weather." Looking up at the sky, he remarked, "It's changeable this time of year. When you're ready to leave I'll show you the proper way to put out a fire. Most people just kick dirt over the flames and leave. You can't do that. The ashes smolder underneath and sometimes break through. You have to spread the ashes out, cover them with dirt, and then wait ten minutes to make sure it's completely out."

The intruder grinned. "You must've been in the Boy Scouts...right?"

There was no response from the man, just a deadpan stare.

The intruder extended his hand. "I'm Danny Bock. Just up here doin' a little turtle huntin'. Didn't mean to cause any problem. What's your name?"

Thinking for a moment, the man lied, "Bud, you can call me Bud." He looked at the burlap sacks and asked, "Why are you hunting turtles? You got kids who want a pet turtle?"

"Nah, I collect them for money."

"Is that what's in those bags?" asked the man.

"Yep. Wanted a few more today before I left this area, but it got too damn cold. I'm gonna call it a day."

Staring at the moving sacks on the ground, the man asked his next question, "What do you do with those turtles?"

"Well," said Danny. "The small ones I sell to pet shops. I get three to four dollars apiece for them. The big ones I ship down to Miami. I've got a connection who put me in touch with this doctor down there that makes some kind of crazy Chinese medicine out of them. He'll pay me a pretty penny for whatever I send down there. Yep, ain't a bad way to make some travelin' money."

The man got a strange look on his face. "Turtles don't make good medicine. Why would anyone kill a turtle? I don't understand. They don't hurt anybody."

"That's where you're wrong," pointed out Danny. "This doctor claims that ground up turtle cures everythin' from athlete's foot to a limp dick. Don't really make much of a difference to me long as I get paid. I don't care what he does with them. They can make ashtrays out of their shells for all I care." Danny gave Bud a sideways look, then asked, "What did you mean when you said this was your property for a couple more hours?"

The man hesitated nervously, but then answered, "I have to move. I was staying at a cabin back up the mountain, but my time is up. I gotta leave before the people who rented it for the summer show up."

"So, you're not from around these parts?"

"No, not from here."

"Where are you from?"

"Up north."

"You sound like a drifter...like me. I've been driftin' for the past ten years. Ain't a bad life. I spent some time in the army, but I made sure I got booted out before they sent me off to Iraq. Had no desire to go over there. I ain't one much for a regular job. Don't like people tellin' me what to do or when to do it. I'm my own man. You won't find ol' Danny Bock punchin' a time clock." Huddling down closer to the fire he explained, "I can always find a way to make money. I was out in Nebraska last fall. Was shootin' coyotes for ten bucks a pelt. The farmers out west hate those varmints 'cause they kill off their sheep and young steers. Made me a nice wad of cash, but the weather got cold so I got the hell outta there. Been layin' up at a place in Indiana just before I come down this way. Was doin' a little gamblin', smokin' some good weed, but then it was time to move on, so I wound up here. Turtle money will get me to Miami. I guess after I get down there I'll hunt up some sea turtle eggs. Now, that's some good money. I can get as much as ten bucks an egg." Tossing a nearby stick onto the fire he commented, "You don't talk much...do you?"

Looking at the sacks the man answered, "How many turtles you got in those sacks?"

"Oh, I reckon about fifteen or twenty, but I got a whole mess more back at my motel room. I've been pickin' them up for almost a week now. Easy pickin's. Turtles are pretty stupid. Most hibernate on the south side of hills under old logs and bushes. They're comin' out this time of year so it don't take much effort to find them if you know where to look." Danny continued to talk, "Findin' them is easy. Now, the hard part is gettin' them ready to travel. Gotta make sure I pack them so that if the police stop me for some reason they won't discover what I've got in my van." Looking at his watch, Danny turned to Bud. "Listen I'm plannin' on bein' out of my room by this evenin'. You wouldn't want to make a few extra bucks would you? Maybe you can use the money. Tell you what, you help me pack the turtles up I'll pay you twenty bucks then I'll treat you to a pizza and a couple of beers. How's that sound?"

The man glanced at the burlap sacks then back to Danny, "Okay...I'll help you."

Danny started to stomp out the fire as he pointed south. "My van is parked down there on an old electric company road. You have a car?"

"Yes, back at my cabin. I've got a truck."

Pushing dirt onto the glowing embers, Danny took control of the conversation. "Here's what we'll do then. I'm stayin' at a bedbug joint just on the edge of Townsend. It's a rundown place. Sets just down the road from the corner of Route 321. The Mountain Vista, that's what they call the place. I think I'm the only one stayin' there right now. Doesn't surprise me none. It's a real hole in the wall. Only cost me $29.99 a night. They don't even change the sheets. Hell, I haven't seen the owner all week. I'll meet you there in an hour or so then we'll get started packin' these turtles up."

"Okay," said the man. "Meet you at the motel."

Danny slung one sack over each of his shoulders and headed down through the forest as he spoke back over his shoulder, "See ya there."

The man walked to the fire, noticing that Danny had done a horrible job of putting it out; a few embers were still glowing red hot. Using his boot, he covered the embers as he watched Danny disappear into the trees. As he clenched his fists he thought to himself, *I hate that man. Turtles don't hurt anyone.* He waited a few minutes until he was sure the fire was completely out, then turned and headed back to the cabin.

When the man reached The Mountain Vista it was just the way Danny had described the place. The man pulled into the macadam parking lot that was filled with ruts and potholes. The motel itself consisted of ten units, five on either side of a small structure with a handwritten cardboard sign on the door that read: *Office*. A road sign that was suspended by one of two hinges dangled awkwardly from a rusted post next to the road: **$29.99 PER NIGHT-VACANCIES**. The only vehicle parked in the lot was a beat up, faded red van, Danny stood next to it waiting for Bud to arrive. Danny commented on the row of units as the man got out of his truck. "I told you the place was a dump." He fumbled for the room key in his pocket as he ordered, "Bud, you can go ahead and get those bags out of the van. I'll get the door."

The man opened the back of the van and carefully pulled the sacks to the edge of the rear door, making sure he placed his hands beneath the sacks so the turtles would not be jostled about. He walked slowly toward the door; both sacks cradled in his large arms. He no sooner stepped inside the motel room when the acrid odor of urine and feces overwhelmed him. Walking to the center of the room, he was stunned at what he saw. There were turtles everywhere: in boxes, in Styrofoam coolers, in the bathtub and crawling around on the bathroom floor. Putting the sacks down, he stepped over a few turtles that were loose in the bedroom. He turned over several that had flipped onto their backs. Sitting on the edge of the bed, he noticed more coolers, a number of cardboard boxes and a large stack of old books near the headboard.

Danny closed the door as he checked the setting on the air conditioner. "Ain't a pretty sight, is it? Smells awful, but you get used to it." He sat forward on the chair as he picked up a large shopping bag and removed four rolls of silver duct tape. He rubbed his hands together, speaking as if he were an expert. "Okay, here's what we need to do. First, we need to separate any of the turtles smaller than a coffee cup and put them into the coolers." Picking up one of the larger turtles he explained, "Now watch me. What you do is take one strip of tape and place it long ways across their head and wrap it around their butt. Then you take two more strips and tape down their legs inside the shell. Then, you simply place them in one of those cardboard boxes. You can put about three or four layers of turtles in each box, then cover them with newspaper and then place a layer of books on top. After that, you just close the box and tie it shut with the rope over there on the dresser. Shouldn't take us more than a couple of hours to get them all boxed up and ready to go."

With a look of sadness on his face, the man asked, "Won't they suffocate if you tape them up inside their shells?"

"Naw," joked Danny. "If you leave a small slit they'll get enough air to survive. I'll probably lose some, but it's no big deal as long as most of them survive the trip." Danny stood up and checked his wallet, then reached for the door. "Look, you go ahead and get started. I'm gonna run up town and get us a pizza and a six-pack. I should be back in about thirty minutes. Are you sure you understand what to do?"

"Yes," said the man. "I understand."

"Good then," said Danny as he left, the door closing behind him.

The man sat down on the bed. He was overwhelmed. Tears filled his eyes. He'd never seen anything like this in his life. These poor, harmless creatures were stunned and scared, taken from their natural environment. They were probably hungry and thirsty. He noticed one turtle in the corner that appeared to have died. He slammed his fist down on the dresser. How could anyone be so cruel? He carefully picked up the turtle Danny had used as an example and started to carefully remove the tape from its shell.

Placing the turtle in a cardboard box he began to gather others as he thought to himself, *He said he'd be back in about thirty minutes.* He was about to carry the fifth box of live turtles out to his truck when he saw Danny pulling into the lot. Ducking quickly back inside, he put the box on the bed. He grabbed the rope from the dresser and wrapped it around his hands three times, leaving the rest dangling between his hands. He turned off the light and stepped next to the wall by the air conditioner. He waited patiently in the darkness until he heard the slamming of Danny's van door.

A few seconds later, Danny opened the door and walked into the dark room. "What the hell!" Just as he reached for the light switch a length of rope was pulled over his head and yanked down to his waist, tightening his arms to his sides. The six-pack fell to the floor along with the pizza box. "Got damn...what the hell!" he yelled as he tried to keep his balance.

The man quickly closed the door and turned on the light. Danny, realizing that Bud thought he was an intruder ordered, "Hey it's me! Take this damn rope off."

The man wrapped the rope around Danny's body two more times and shoved him down on the chair. Danny began to kick his legs and wiggle around as he tried to loosen the rope. "What the hell are you doin'? Let me loose! If you want my money...take it. Ain't much, but if that's what you're after, then take it and leave."

Securing the rope tightly around Danny, the man reached for a roll of duct tape as he spoke softly, "Don't want your money."

"Then what do you want?" Trying to relax, Danny gave the man he had called Bud a disturbing look. "You sure don't strike me as no robber. You're not one of those perverts...are you?"

Pulling a pocket knife from his pants pocket, the man cut off a small six inch strip of tape and placed it firmly across Danny's mouth just as he started to scream. Danny was jerked to his feet and thrown on the bed where his feet and hands were taped. Reaching for the second roll, the man began to tape his waist and stomach. Using a third roll, he taped up his shoulders and neck until the only part of Danny's body that was not wrapped in the tape was his head. The man took a break as he pulled back the curtain to make sure no one was around.

He walked to the bathroom and splashed some water across his face then took a short drink, cupping the water in his hands. Returning to the bed, he smiled to himself as Danny tried to free his cocooned body as he rocked back and forth helplessly. Picking up the roll of tape, the man continued putting tape on Danny's head leaving only his ears, eyes, and nose exposed. He positioned Danny's body up against the headboard. The man straddled Danny's body as he spoke sternly, "Now, you pretend you're a turtle and you're on your way to Miami to have your legs and head cut off." He looked into Danny's fear-filled eyes one last time before he placed a strip across his eyes. "Like you said. It's no big deal if some of them suffocate." Placing a strip over one of Danny's ears he spoke again, "If you hold your breath you might live for a couple minutes." He taped the other ear and then the nose. Looking down at Danny, he said, "There now. You'll never kill another coyote or hurt a turtle ever again." He began to gather up the rest of the turtles as he watched Danny's body move slightly as he struggled for air.

Turning his attention to the turtles, he put as many as he could in the remaining boxes. When he ran out of boxes, he placed the last few turtles in the bed of his truck hoping they had enough strength to make it back to the forest. Walking back into the room he checked one last time for any live turtles he might have missed. He ignored Danny's taped up torso and switched off the light after checking the time on the nightstand clock. It was just after one o'clock in the afternoon. He would take the turtles back to where he first met Danny and release them. It might be hard on them at first, but he hoped they would all survive. After the turtles were safely back in the woods he knew exactly where he was going.

CHAPTER EIGHT

TED ATWATER PULLED INTO The Mountain Vista Motel, guiding his Lincoln Continental across the rugged parking lot. Parking sideways in front of the office, he opened the door and emptied his overflowing ashtray onto the pavement, the collection of cigar and cigarette butts mixed with grey ashes falling to the ground in a small dusty cloud. Ted climbed out, sidestepped a large pothole, and looked down at the end of the units on the right where he saw Danny Bock's red van. Bock had paid for a week, which ended three days ago. He told him he was going to be out of the room by Friday and here it was the following Monday and he was still a guest; three days longer than what he had paid for.

Removing a pack of cigarettes from his shirt pocket, Ted shook a smoke out of the pack and removed it with his lips. Enjoying his twelfth cigarette of the day, he sucked in a deep shot of nicotine, then blew it out through his nose as he opened the backdoor of the car and removed a worn briefcase. He looked across the street. The parking lots of The Valley View Lodge and The Highland Manor Inn were filled to capacity even though it was early in the season. They were both larger operations than his rundown, ten unit fleabag, but he had no one to blame but himself for the lack of business.

Three years ago when his grandmother died, she willed The Mountain Vista to him. At that time it had been a prospering business. When he first took over the business, he had two employees, an older retired couple that had been employed by his grandmother for years. The wife took care of cleaning the ten rooms on a daily basis and her husband mowed the lawn, maintained the small swimming pool, and did whatever maintenance was required throughout the year. Even though The Mountain Vista was one of the smallest motels in Townsend it had a reputation for over twenty years as one of the best run and cleanest places to get a room for the night or a week at an inexpensive price. The high standards of cleanliness and customer service his grandmother had established over the years began to deteriorate the moment Ted took the reins.

The Mountain Vista began its downward spiral in less than six months. In order to fund his gambling debts, he decided to fire the retired couple, assigning the room cleaning to his drug addict girlfriend and the maintenance and lawn mowing to her twenty-two year old son who had just been released from prison and never held a job for more than a week.

Along with the musty odor of leaking roofs and the mold on the bathroom floors from leaking toilets, there were numerous bugs. Many of the windows no longer operated and the pealing siding and drooping gutters which were created from Ted's cutback on business expenses, made the Mountain Vista as no longer being part of his regular customers' vacation plans in Townsend. Even the customers who had previously stayed at the motel would turn out of the parking lot the moment they saw the deplorable condition of the place. His customer base had been reduced to an occasional couple looking for a one night stand or people like Danny Bock who were on the shady side to say the least.

Entering the cluttered office, Ted threw his briefcase on a chair as he made his way through the filthy room littered with piles of lamps, alarm clocks, chairs, and wall mirrors. Over the past week he had cleaned out everything that could be salvaged from the units except for Number Eight where Bock was staying. As soon as Bock checked out, he would strip Number Eight as well. He was in the final stage of going through the foreclosure process and he wanted to get everything saleable out of the place before the bank showed up and slapped a lock on the place.

Fumbling through the top drawer of the office desk, he located the master key, tapped his cigarette ashes into an overflowing ashtray on the edge of the desk, and headed out the door. Walking across the front of the units to Number Eight, he had a strange feeling about this Danny Bock character. A week ago when he had checked in there had just been something odd about the man. But, as usual, Ted had little concern over what a guest did after they checked in as long as he got paid. He received his payment, which covered Bock's stay up until Friday. It was obvious, from the presence of his old van that Bock had not left. Ted could have cared less if the man decided to stay a few more days, but Bock owed him money and he was determined to collect before he skipped out.

Peering in the window of Number Eight, he noticed that the curtains were slightly open in the middle. The inside of the room was dark. Bock was either still in bed or had walked up town for some reason. Ted banged on the door, waited a few seconds, then looked into the darkness of the room once again. No answer. Banging on the door again, he shouted, "Bock, this is the owner, answer the door. You owe me for three days!" Banging on the door again, he continued to yell, "Bock, if you don't answer the door I'm coming in!" There was still no answer.

He took the room key from his pocket and inserted it into the lock and slowly pushed the door open as he shouted into the darkness, "Bock, you in here?" The stench coming from inside the room caused him to back up as he covered his mouth and almost gagged. Wiping his eyes with a handkerchief he swore, "Damn!" Reaching around the corner of the doorjamb, he flipped on the light switch and pushed the door open with his foot as he covered his nose with the handkerchief. He forced himself to enter, the first thing he saw was a large form on the bed that appeared to be wrapped in silver tape. He stared at it for a few moments trying to figure out what it was. Noticing a shovel leaning up against the wall he picked it up and nudged the form. It remained lifeless. A trickle of foul smelling liquid seeped out from between the strips of tape. He started to gag and ran toward the bathroom, but the smell in the room was overwhelming. Still gagging as he ran out the door, he slipped on some sort of black matter that was smeared across the floor.

Back outside, he took three long, deep breaths as he moved away from the doorway and leaned on the van. His hands shook as he placed another cigarette between his thin lips, *What the hell was on the bed? What was that awful smell? What was that stuff all over the floor?* Taking the first drag on his smoke, it hit him. *My God. Was that Bock on the bed? How will I be able to explain this? I'm in enough trouble with the bank. I don't need the police coming down on me for a murder at my place.*

Walking toward the office, he stopped and returned to the van as he considered hiding the body or whatever it was. *No,* he thought. *I'm not going back in there and touching whatever the hell's on the bed. I haven't done anything wrong.*

He flicked his cigarette to the ground and ran to his Lincoln, opened the driver's side door and grabbed his cell phone from the dash. Nervously, he punched in the number for the Townsend Police Department and waited for someone to pick up. After three rings a pleasant voice answered, "Townsend Police Department."

"Thank God!" exclaimed Ted. "Listen, this is Ted Atwater over at the Mountain Vista Motel. I'm not sure, but I might have a dead body in one of my rooms. It's horrible! You need to get someone over here right now!"

Marge grabbed her pen and pad as she waited for Ted to stop talking. "Let me get this straight. Ted Atwater...Mountain Vista Motel...dead body. Where are you now, Mr. Atwater?"

"I'm at the motel office. I'm not going back down to that room without the police. I haven't touched anything. Tell Brody to get someone down here quick. I'll be waiting in front of my office."

"All right," said Marge. "Stay put. An officer will be there in a few minutes."

Brody was just coming out of the office bathroom as Marge was walking back to his office. Opening the door, Brody adjusting his trousers almost ran into Marge. "Excuse me, Marge. Those tacos we had for lunch are runnin' right through me."

She pushed the slip of paper with Atwater's info written on it towards Brody's oversized gut and ordered, "Hitch up your pants, Chief. We just got a call from Ted Atwater over at The Mountain Vista. Says he thinks there might be a dead body in one of his rooms. Sounded like he was scared out of his wits!"

Brody, grabbing his hat off of a hook looked at the duty roster hanging on the wall. "Who's on duty today?"

Marge, responded, "Lee and Grant."

Brody half joked as he pushed open the door leading to the parking lot. "Got damn! Sounds like the Civil War. Get both of them on the horn. Have them meet me over there." Hopping into his pickup, he backed up, jammed the gearshift down into first, and turned on the flashing lights and siren as he sped out onto the street.

Turning onto the Parkway, he thought about Ted Atwater. He was a no good gamblin' son of a bitch if there ever was one. He had a nasty reputation around town as a man who couldn't be trusted.

Slowing down for a red light he then sped through the intersection, just as two cars pulled to the side of the road. Making a left hand turn just past the intersection of 321, Brody's pickup bounced across the rough parking lot of The Mountain Vista. As he stopped next to Atwater's Lincoln, he saw Ted standing at the front door of the office. "Marge said you've got a dead body in one of your rooms."

Atwater took a long draw from his cigarette and then threw it on the ground. "That's right, Chief. In Number Eight. It looks like a dead body, but I'm not a hundred percent sure."

Brody placed his hands on his protruding hips. "Looks like a body!" he repeated sarcastically, "It's either a body or it ain't, Atwater."

"Well," Atwater shot back, "I can't tell if it is or not. It's all wrapped up in some sort of tape or something."

Giving Ted an odd stare, Brody motioned for him to follow. "Come on, let's take a look."

"I'm not going in there again," objected Ted. "It smells like hell. Made me sick to my stomach."

Getting directly in Ted's face, Brody said, "Look, I don't care what it smells like. You're goin' down there with me. Probably smells like crap because you don't keep the place up." Grabbing Ted by the arm, he ushered him down the cracked sidewalk that ran in front of the units as he continued to berate Atwater, "It's a wonder anybody could survive a night in this dump."

From up the street came the sound of another siren as Lee Griner approached The Mountain Vista. He made a wild turn into the lot and pulled next to the van as Brody and Atwater stopped in front of Number Eight. Hopping out of the cruiser, Lee placed his hat over top of his G.I. hair cut and approached, "What we got, Sir?"

"Not sure yet," answered Brody, as he pointed his thumb toward Number Eight. "Ted here claims there's a body in there."

Geez, let's hope he's wrong, thought Brody.

Snapping on a pair of white plastic gloves, Lee looked Ted up and down then walked to the front of the van. "Have you been in there yet, Chief?"

"No, just walked down here from the office."

Looking back up the street, Lee asked, "Do you think we should wait for Grant?"

"Hell no!," barked Brody. "You and I can handle this just fine. Wonder Boy will be here soon enough with all his book learnin' and crime scene investigation crap he learned in college." Placing Ted next to the van, he ordered, "Atwater, I want you to stay right here and don't move until I say so."

Taking his pack of cigarettes from his pocket he asked, "That's just fine with me. Okay if I smoke?"

Brody gave Ted a disgusting look as he answered, "Atwater, when don't you smoke? Personally, I don't give a shit if you die of lung cancer right here in front of your shithole business and furthermore, stop blowin' that damn smoke in my face!"

Brody withdrew his revolver and nodded to Lee, "Let's go, I'll go in first, you follow, but not too close. We don't know what or who's in there."

"There isn't anybody alive in that place," said Atwater. "I can guarantee you that. Nobody can stand it in there with that stink."

Hesitating at the doorway, Brody backed off as he waved his hand in front of his face. "The stench comin' out of there is awful." Pulling a hanky out of his pocket, he placed it over his nose and mouth then entered. Lee followed, his face wrinkled in a disgusting frown, his revolver in his right hand, his left hand covering his nose and mouth.

Stopping next to the bed, Brody looked down at the duct-taped form. Lee joined him as he spoke through the fingers over his mouth. "Looks like a body to me, Chief."

Brody picked up the shovel next to the door and poked the body, then remarked, "Yeah, but it looks like a damn mummy." Gesturing with his head he ordered Lee, "Check the bathroom."

Seconds later, Lee walked back into the main room. "Nothing in there but three dead turtles and a pile of coolers." Pointing to the floor he continued to speak, "There's two more dead turtles over here by the dresser and a whole lot of turtle crap."

Brody signaled for Lee to follow him back outside where they both took long deep breaths. "Is it a body?" asked Ted.

"Looks like one, but we can't be sure until we get some of that tape off." Looking at Lee, Brody apologized, "Sorry, Lee, I didn't bring any gloves with me. We're gonna have to go back in there and peal some of the tape off so we can determine what or who we're dealin' with."

"Yes, Sir," said Lee. "Ready whenever you are."

Another siren sounded up the street. Brody motioned for Lee to enter. "That's Denlinger now. Let's get in there before he shows up here with his stupid ass camera and blue notebook."

Lee nodded as he headed for the door. "Listen, let's make this quick. I can only hold my breath for about two minutes."

Following Lee into the room, Brody joined him at the edge of the bed. Pointing with his revolver, he ordered Lee, "There, on the head it looks like a small piece of duct tape over where the mouth should be. Try and peel that back."

Lee reached out and tried to grab the edge of the tape, but the gloves made it too awkward to get at the edge. He reached into his pants and removed a small pocket knife, opened it and slid the blade beneath the edge of the tape, slowly pulling it back. What he saw made him wince as he held up the backside of the tape for Brody's inspection. Between the smell and the appearance of skin that had been ripped away from the victim's lips, Brody ordered Lee, "Put the tape back. I've seen enough. It's a body."

Brody didn't wait for Lee, but stumbled back out the door gagging and coughing. Seconds later Lee followed, shaking his head in disgust. Grant's cruiser pulled up next to where Lee's vehicle was parked. Noticing the Chief bending over trying his best to keep from vomiting, Grant asked Lee, "Guess you found a body in there? Must be pretty bad."

Walking toward his cruiser, Lee answered, "Pretty bad isn't the phrase I would choose to describe the condition of the body in that room. Downright disgusting would be a better way to put it."

Opening the cruiser door, he grabbed a bottle of water, unscrewed the top and took a long drink. He walked back to Brody and offered him the bottle, "Here, Chief, better take a drink."

Grant walked to the door and looked in, but remained outside because of the strong odor. "I assume the victim is inside that duct tape."

"That's the way it looks," confirmed Lee. "We pulled back a small section of the tape and the skin came right off. I've never seen anything like that before."

Brody, clearing his throat took another drink, then ordered, "We have to get this area cordoned off. There's a couple of rolls of caution tape behind the seat of my truck. Tape off the entire perimeter of this place."

As Grant and Lee walked to the truck, Ted lit up another cigarette. "Guess you won't be needing me for anything else. Think I'll just head on home. I need a stiff drink...maybe two or three."

Brody finished off the water. "You're not goin' anywhere, Atwater. I've got a lot of questions and you better have a lot of answers."

Ted was amazed. "You can't possibly suspect me. I had nothing to do with this nightmare."

"I didn't say you were a suspect, only that you have to answer some questions." He hesitated and yelled at Grant and Lee who were starting across the lot. "Denlinger! Before you get started call Sheriff Grimes and the county coroner. We need them over here ASAP!" Turning back to Ted, Brody started his questioning, "I assume that you had a guest stayin' here in the room?"

Ted nervously fingered his cigarette as he answered, "Yeah, I did."

"When did he or she or whoever the hell it was check in?"

"Danny Bock is his name. He checked in last week and was supposed to be out by last Friday. I came in this morning and saw his van was still here."

"Where is this Bock from?"

"I don't know."

Brody repeated, "I don't know! What the hell does that mean?"

"Just what it sounds like...I don't know."

Brody stepped closer to Ted as he asked, "You didn't notice where he was from when you checked his driver's license?"

"Didn't ask for any ID."

"Why the hell not?"

"Look, Chief, I'm on the verge of being foreclosed on. I'm going out of business. Why should I care were this Bock is from?"

"Why! I'll tell you why. Because now we have a body in one of your rooms and we don't have a clue as to who it is or who this Bock is or where he's from."

Ted was getting cocky as he responded, "So you're assuming that the body in there is Bock."

"Until we have proof that it's not, yeah, we have to assume that it's your customer, who by the way we know nothin' about thanks to your lack of business savvy."

Ted shrugged off Brody's dissatisfaction with how he conducted business and said, "I'm outta here."

"You're not goin' anywhere until we get some answers around here," stated Brody once again. "First off, you're goin' to go back in that room, open the window and turn up the air conditioner."

Ted objected, "I'm not going back in there. You can't make me. I don't work for you. If you want that window open and the air turned up, you or one of your officers will have to do it. Besides that, I don't want my fingerprints on anything in there."

Grant and Lee were just returning with the caution tape as Brody went off on Ted, "Look, Atwater, you don't decide what goes on here...*I do!* You're right. I can't make you go back in there, but I can hold you for questionin'. I can detain you as a possible suspect and that's exactly what I'm gonna do." Turning to Griner, he ordered, "Lee, take Mr. Atwater here down to his office and lock him in. If he gives you any crap...cuff him!"

Lee took Ted by the arm. "Yes, Sir."

All the way down the sidewalk to the office, Ted spewed out an unending series of objections, "You can't lock me in my own office. I haven't done anything wrong. I don't have anything to do with what happened back there in that room. This is still my property. Brody can't shove me around like this. I want to call my lawyer. I know my rights!"

Grant approached the doorway to the room as Brody shook his head. Looking in the room Grant asked, "You don't really think Atwater had anything to do with this, do you?"

"Aside from bein' a poor businessman, a loudmouth and a scumbag...no," answered Brody. "Dependin' on how things pan out here, we'll probably ask him a few more questions and then let him go."

Motioning toward the room, Grant probed, "Mind if I go have a look?"

"Be my guest, but do me a favor. When you get in there open the window all the way and turn up the air."

"No problem," said Grant, slipping on a pair of plastic gloves as he entered the room. He wrinkled his face as the strong odor hit him. Quickly, he unlocked the window and raised it then turned the air conditioner on High. Going to the bed, he noticed that the edge of the tape had been raised. Carefully he peeled back the tape, the blood red skin adhering to the sticky side. Leaning forward he smelled the ripped lips of the victim and quickly pulled his head back and reapplied the tape. Walking to the bath, he looked in the tub then back out in the main room. He bent down and looked under the bed, where two turtles lay dead, their eyes sunken into their heads. He searched the drawers in both the dresser and nightstand locating a set of keys next to the alarm clock. Taking the keys, he exited the room and walked a few yards out into the lot to escape the horrid smell. Tossing the keys to Brody he spoke, "Here, these might be the keys to that van." Looking back at the open door, he gave his opinion of what he had discovered. "There are three different smells in there. First, beneath the bed, there is a musty odor as if the place hasn't been cleaned in some time. Secondly, there is an odor coming from the body especially when you peel back the tape that indicates that the body has been taped up for a while. How long I don't know. The third odor we are predominately smelling is turtle urine and feces. I found two dead turtles under the bed, three in the bath and two more over by the dresser. When you consider all of the coolers, cardboard boxes and dead turtles it's obvious that somebody, maybe the person on the bed was poaching turtles."

"Well," said Brody as he tossed the keys from his right hand to his left, "let's see what we can find in the van." Walking to the driver's side door he unlocked the van as he ordered Grant, "Check out the front. I'll have a look in the back."

Grant slid into the driver's seat, leaving the door open. The same nasty odor that was in the room was present in the confines of the van. Brody unlocked the rear doors as he turned his head at the smell. "Smells like a shithouse on a tuna boat." Using a small shovel that was near the back, he began to move items around. "Looks like three more coolers, a stack of cardboard boxes, a pile of old books, a couple of burlap sacks and a suitcase." Dragging the battered suitcase to the edge of the van he allowed it to fall to the ground. He flipped the latch open and inspected the contents.

"We've got two pair of work pants, three tee-shirts, socks, underwear, pair of deck shoes, a razor and some shavin' cream and some other stuff. That's about it. Looks like he may have been gettin' ready to leave this place when he got an unexpected visitor." Closing the top of the suitcase with his foot, he yelled up through the van, "Find anythin' interestin' up front?"

Grant, shut the cover on the console and answered back over the seat, "Not yet. There's nothing in the console except some loose change and a few old cigars. I'm looking in the glove box now. Let's see, we've got what looks like a new map of Tennessee, a well-used map of Nebraska, two very old candy bars, pack of gum, bottle of aspirins and well what do you know, a vehicle registration."

By this time Brody had opened the passenger side door. "Who owns this rig?"

Unfolding the official document, Grant read, "The van is registered in the state of Nebraska to a Mr. Daniel P. Bock of Des Moines, Iowa. The registration expired two months ago." Flipping down both sun visors, Grant continued talking, "Nothing up here except some gas receipts for the Parkway Grocery. All dated this past week. Our Mr. Bock sure has been doing a lot of driving. Looks like he filled up four times." Looking at Brody who was standing just outside the door Grant asked, "Did you happen to see what state the plates are from?"

As he walked to the back of the van, Brody answered Grant's question, "No, but I'll check." Seconds later came the answer, "Nebraska tags...expired."

Lee returned from placing Atwater in the office. Brody wasted little time in getting things in motion. "Lee, I need you to take the registration that Grant found, plus this plate number back to the office. Have Marge call the police in Des Moines and see what they can tell us about this Daniel Bock. Then I want you to have her call the state police and run these tags."

Walking to the van, Lee took the registration from Grant then went to the rear of the vehicle as he wrote down the plate number.

As Lee was pulling out of the lot, Sheriff Grime's cruiser followed by the Blount County Coroner's van pulled in.

As he climbed out of the cruiser, Grimes placed his hat on his head and approached Brody. "Can't believe it. Another murder."

Brody shook Grimes' hand as he responded, "At this point we don't know if we're lookin' at a murder, but it's leanin' in that direction. The body is completely wrapped in duct tape. Smells like hell in there. There are a few dead turtles in there also. Grant here, thinks somebody is poachin' turtles."

Bookman, carrying his black medical bag joined the group. "Good afternoon, Chief Brody." Looking off toward the mountains he commented, "This reminds me of last year, April wasn't it, when we came over here and went up to Thunderhead Trail where Asa Pittman was murdered. When the first of April hit this year and no one was murdered around here I felt such a sense of relief. When the second week of April rolled by without an incident, I just figured it was over. Now, here we are in mid-April and we've got another murder on our hands."

Grant climbed out of the van and jumped in on the conversation. "I don't think this murder has anything to do with what went on last year."

Brody disagreed with Grant as he pointed out, "That surprises me. You feelin' that way especially with what we've already learned about that body in there."

Grimes gave Brody a strange look. "What are you driving at, Axel?"

"Simple," said Brody. "Grant worked on the FBI's investigative team. He probably knows more about our killer than anyone here. He helped to create a profile of the killer and I think there are some similarities with the body in the room and with the murders we had last year."

"In what way?" asked Grimes.

Bookman interrupted as he suggested, "Speaking of the body, I've got to get in there and get to work."

As he walked toward the room, Brody gave him a warning, "It smells like hell in there. If you're gonna be in there for any length of time you better strap on one of those protective breathin' masks."

Bookman didn't respond, but gave Brody a thumbs up as he entered the room. Brody, Grimes and Grant trailed Bookman to the door, but did not enter. Brody answered Grimes' previous question as he pointed at the taped up body. "The similarities I was talkin' about are that duct tape was used in this case. If you'll recall, duct tape was used in each one of the four murders last year. Also, last year each one of the victims was left where they would be discovered, almost as if the killer wanted us to find them. Same thing here. The body is left propped up on the bed where it would be found. And another thing: the dead turtles in the room along with the coolers and cardboard boxes substantiate what Grant said about someone poachin' turtles. It's illegal to take turtles out of their natural habitat in Tennessee. I've read about these turtle poachers. They capture them, then ship them off where they are eventually killed and used for makin' soup or medicine. One of the main things Grant has stated about our killer is that he is an animal lover and will not put up with any form of animal cruelty. He has and still may be makin' his point. A possible turtle poacher bein' his latest victim."

"There's one important fact you're leaving out, Chief," said Grant. "All four of the victims last year had their fingers cut off with some sort of a tool and were drugged with chloroform. Two of the victims, the first two, were shot up with some sort of novocaine. I didn't notice any bloodstains on that body in there in the area where the hands and feet are located—"

Bookman interrupted the conversation, "Gentlemen, you can talk until you're blue in the face but until we get this body over to the lab in Maryville and get it examined it's just all speculation. Now, if you'll excuse me, I've got to get to work."

Grimes, looking up and down the front of the units remarked, "Looks pretty desolate around here. Is this place actually open for business?"

Brody removed a pack of gum from his jacket pocket, placed a stick in his mouth. "The owner is a man by the name of Atwater. I got him locked up down at the motel office. This place is close to bein' in foreclosure. By all rights he probably shouldn't be open, but that's none of my business."

"Do we know the identity of the victim in the room?" Grimes asked.

"We're not sure yet. Might be the owner of that van. A man named Daniel Bock from Iowa. The van is registered to Bock, but the registration is expired. The plates on the van are from

Nebraska, also expired. The van smells just as bad as the room, which means Bock was probably transportin' turtles back here to the motel."

Looking back into the room, Grimes suggested, "While Jeff is doing his job, let's head on down to the office and ask this Atwater some questions."

Grant stopped Brody as he asked, "Mind if I stay here with Jeff, Chief?"

Brody waved his hand as if he could have cared less, "Knock yourself out."

Grant joined Jeff at the side of the bed, asking, "All right, what can I do to help?"

Bookman, opening a fresh pack of facemasks, looked back out the door. "First, I need you to bring in a body bag from the back of my van."

Grant saw Brody and Lee Grimes disappear into the office. Cars were passing by on the Parkway but had slowed down considerably as the drivers viewed the activity at the Mountain Vista: caution tape encircling the entire area, three Townsend Police cruisers, the presence of the Blount County Sheriff and the county coroner's van. A small crowd of onlookers had gathered on the sidewalk watching all of the activity. It was a small community and they were curious. Soon the rumors would start to fly.

Opening the back of the van, Grant removed a body bag and returned to the room.

Jeff was busy searching for something in his medical bag.

Standing by the air conditioner, Grant tried to avoid the horrible odor that seemed to hang inside the room. "Jeff, I don't suppose you've got another one of those masks available?"

Removing a scalpel, Jeff answered, "Yeah, there in my bag. You can grab one."

After placing the mask over his nose and mouth, Grant joined Jeff next to the body as he asked, "By the time you get all that tape off, that body is going to be a mess, right?"

Jeff, peeling back the small section of tape covering the mouth area responded, "Yes, the adhesive backing on duct tape has a tendency to remove the top surface of what it is adhered to if left in place too long. When duct tape meets skin, after a period of time, skin loses." Removing the tape, he displayed the bloody, skin covered backside of the tape. "See there, rips the skin away from the body."

Replacing the tape, Jeff further explained, "Actually, some folks use duct tape to remove dead skin and I've heard it said that it has been used to reduce wrinkling, like beneath your eyes. The thing is, you have to be extremely careful when applying duct tape to skin. If you don't know what you're doing you can really damage your skin." Removing a section on the side of the head area, a bloody ear was exposed, skin hanging from the earlobe. "God, what a mess," Jeff said, as he replaced the tape and reached for the section covering where the eyes were more than likely located. Slowly peeling back the tape, he saw that the victim's eyes were wide open. Jeff shook his head as he placed the scalpel back in his bag. "From the look of the eyes I'd say the victim probably was alive when the last section was placed over the nose or mouth. The victim suffocated. Come on," Jeff ordered, "let's get him bagged up so I can get back to the morgue and get to work. This is going to take a couple of days. It's going to be a slow process removing all of the tape. About the only thing that will remove the adhesive on the back of the tape is kerosene or possibly rubbing alcohol. Still, it's going to be touch and go trying to salvage most of the skin."

Just as Grant and Jeff were carrying the body bag out to the van, Brody, Grimes and Atwater were walking out of the office and saw Zeb Gilling standing next to Ted's car. Brody, who didn't like Zeb to begin with, removed his hat and slapped the side of his leg. "What the hell, Gilling! What are you doin' here? Did you not see the bright yella caution tape surroundin' this place? That tape means keep out. It's not an invite for every Tom, Dick and Harry that wanders by!"

Zeb looked past Brody and gave Ted a dirty look. "I was passing by and saw Ted's Lincoln parked over here. That asshole owes me money. Two hundred dollars to be exact. He's been avoiding me for weeks. I'm here to collect before you haul his ass off to jail."

Brody stepped close to Zeb. "He ain't going to jail and I could care less what goes on between you two idiots. You've crossed a police barrier and you need to git...now! Understand?"

Looking toward the coroner's van, Zeb saw Grant and Bookman loading the body into the back. "Is that a body they're loading up?"

Ted stepped forward as he addressed Zeb, "I'm still the owner of this property, Gilling, and you're trespassing. I don't have the time to piss around with you right now. I've got enough problems. I mean hell! Somebody was murdered in one of my units."

Zeb looked back at Brody as he repeated, "Murdered?"

Great! thought Brody. That's just what they didn't need at the moment. Zeb knew everyone in town and the surrounding area. Within the next half hour the word would be out that another murder had been committed in Townsend. There would be calls from local citizens, the local radio and television stations, not to mention the newspaper. Brody was now just inches from Zeb. "Gilling, I'm only goin' to say this one more time...git!"

Giving Brody a quick, hard look, he turned and stared at Ted as he turned and walked toward the street. Halfway across the lot he turned back and yelled at Ted, "You still owe me money, Atwater!"

Ten minutes later, Grant found himself alone parked in front of The Mountain Vista. Bookman and Grimes had left to go back to Maryville, Brody to the Townsend Police Department, leaving Grant with orders to keep curiosity seekers away from the building until he was relieved later in the evening by Jacks. It was starting to rain as he rolled up the window. Staring at the rain running down over the windshield, Grant was confused to say the least. He was getting a sick feeling in the pit of his stomach. There had been another murder and from all indications the motive appeared to be animal related. Sitting back in the seat, he closed his eyes as he thought, *What's going on? I can't believe I have to go through this hell again.*

CHAPTER NINE

BALANCING THE LAST BITE of blueberry pie on his fork, Grant sipped on a mug of coffee. He stopped for a moment when he heard a tapping sound. Turning, he saw Dana Beth waving at him through the front window as she went about cleaning the house.

Smiling, he waved back, and then took his final taste of dessert. Dana Beth was due in two months and he could hardly wait until he held his little girl in his arms. Sitting on the front porch of Ruth and Conrad's home, which he and Dana Beth now owned, he reclined in the same cushioned wicker chair he had sat in last Thanksgiving when Conrad revealed to him that he was the serial killer. Now, months later, things hadn't returned to normal as he had expected. There had been another murder.

Just three days ago, a body had been discovered at The Mountain Vista Motel. During the autopsy conducted in Maryville, the county coroner reported that the body was indeed who they had suspected it to be; Daniel P. Bock. According to Bookman, Bock had more than likely been alive when wrapped in the duct tape. He probably held his breath for as long as he could, but eventually suffocated. Removing the duct tape had been extremely difficult. Most of Bock's top layer of skin tore from the body even though the tape was carefully removed. Bock's wallet had been discovered in his back pocket and despite the fact that he had defecated and urinated at some point, his driver's license was still readable.

Finishing his coffee, Grant got up from the chair and walked to the porch railing and looked out across the front yard as two squirrels chased one another around. His thoughts drifted to earlier in the day when he, Brody, Griner, Jacks, Sheriff Grimes, Jeff Bookman and the mayor had to face the media onslaught at the Townsend Police Station. It was a repeat performance of last year following Mildred Henks' murder.

In a meeting prior to the press conference, Brody decided to downplay the fact that they had two murders in the area already this year. The media, and especially many of the people who lived in Blount County, were saying the serial killer had struck again.

Grant wasn't buying into any of it since he knew the killer was no longer alive, but the Bock murder had knocked him for a loop. Duct tape had been used, the body had been placed where it could easily be found and there were animals involved. The only thing that was different from the murders of last year was there had been no drugs administered to Bock and all of his fingers and toes were still intact, but it was still puzzling. The most startling result that stemmed from the autopsy of Daniel Bock was that a number of fingerprints had been lifted from the duct tape and around the room where Bock had been found. The prints matched those found on the knife left at the Mackinaw murder scene and at the cabin Walt Lansing had rented out to the strange man that was suspected of stealing J.J. Pickler's bear. Possibly the same man Grant had seen at Conrad's funeral and at the nativity.

Grant sat on the porch steps as he reviewed what Conrad had told him about the murder of his family forty years ago. He had thought after talking with Conrad, the puzzle of the serial killer had been solved, but now it seemed as if there was a piece missing. One that didn't fit. The more he thought about it, the more he started to question Conrad's story. Maybe Conrad really wasn't the killer. Maybe he was covering for someone else. Maybe someone else had driven the van. He had no doubt that all of the clues he discovered in Conrad's garage were incriminating, but now he was thinking that Conrad might not be responsible for the murders of last year. He needed to verify the story Conrad shared with him; the story of a murder that happened forty years ago. There was only one way he was going to know the truth. He needed to talk with someone who knew what happened forty years ago on that farm. Getting up, he headed for the front door. He was going to call the County Sheriff over in Johnson County. He'd start there and see where it led.

Friday evening he called the County Sheriff and talked with Sheriff Tobias Reichenbaugh who said he would be glad to meet him at his office in Mountain City. On Saturday morning, he was up and out the door by six o'clock. Grant told Dana Beth that he had to drive over to Johnson County on police business. It was his weekend off and with any luck he'd be home later that night. If he was going to stay over he'd call.

Gassing up the Jeep at the Parkway Grocery, he grabbed a large coffee and two glazed donuts and headed north toward Knoxville. He had dressed casually in jeans and a light sweater.

He had placed his Townsend Police badge in his wallet and put his revolver in the console. Driving along, he thought about what they discovered about the latest victim. After Marge contacted the Des Moines Police Department, she received a fax back with the sparse information they had on Bock. He no longer lived at the address on the license, which was a unit in an apartment building. He had not left a forwarding address and as far as his record was concerned he had three parking tickets and a speeding violation. The Nebraska plates on the van turned out to be stolen. Bock was still somewhat of a mystery. The evidence they had found in the room definitely pointed in the direction that he or someone else had been poaching turtles. The van belonged to Bock and the smell inside the van indicated that someone, possibly Bock, had been transporting turtles back to The Mountain Vista Motel. If Bock was murdered because of turtle poaching then the crime fell right in line with last year's murders.

Arriving on the outskirts of Knoxville, Grant exited onto Route 81 North toward Bristol and settled in for the three hour drive to Mountain City located in the Northeastern corner of Tennessee. Normally the scenic drive up 81 was very relaxing, but at the moment his mind was occupied with thoughts about the strange man wearing dark clothes and a knit cap. Reaching up to the sun visor, he took down the article and the composite drawing of the man. It probably wasn't exact but it was close enough. It was based on the description that J.J. Pickler had given the Gatlinburg Police. That was the same description given to the police by Janis and a number of others who were at the Gatlinburg Grill the night Bobby Mackinaw had been murdered. The waitress from the Flapjack Cabin and Walt Lansing who had rented the man a cabin had also given the police the same description. The description given by those interviewed by the police matched the identity of the man that Grant noticed at Conrad's funeral and at the nativity. If it was the same man, why was he at Conrad's funeral? Maybe the man wasn't there because of the funeral. He hadn't actually gone down near the grave during the ceremony. Maybe he was simply passing by and stopped for a rest. What about the scent of peach brandy tobacco Grant had smelled as the man walked away following the funeral and at the nativity? Who was this man and why did he keep popping up at different locations in the area?

Looking down at the speedometer, Grant noticed he had slowed down to forty-seven miles per hour. It was just one of those quirky things he did while driving and concentrating on something other than the road ahead or what was going on around him. The more he daydreamed the slower he drove. Looking at a state highway speed limit sign that read 70 mph, he stepped on the accelerator as a semi passed him like he was standing still, the frustrated driver laying on his air horn. As the truck took its position in front of him, Grant read the backdoors of the semi: *BROTHERS TRUCKING.*

Suddenly, it was one of those "wake up moments" when his brain put two and two together. *Brothers,* he thought. Maybe that was the answer. *Brothers!* Maybe the missing part of the story Conrad had told him had to do with his brother. He had known Conrad since he started dating Dana Beth back in high school. The fact that Conrad had a brother was never mentioned. Why? Surely he would have come up in at least one conversation in all that time, but he hadn't. Conrad never mentioned he had a brother, nor had Dana Beth or Ruth said anything about him. It was like he didn't exist. Maybe he didn't exist and the story Conrad shared with him about his mother and father being murdered over in Mountain City forty years ago wasn't true. He jacked his speed up to seventy-five miles an hour anxious to get to Mountain City. If the story Conrad had told him was true, then he had to find out where his brother was and why he had never been mentioned by anyone in the Pearl family.

Before he knew it, the exit for Mountain City popped up. Getting off the exit, he made a right hand turn onto Route 421, which Dalton had told him would lead directly to Mountain City.

Ten miles down the two lane road, Grant thought that Dalton's directions where he used the word "directly" was misleading and a better way to describe the directions would be "haphazardly" as the road had more twists, turns and hairpin curves than any road he had ever been on.

Two miles later, after going around a number of sharp curves and a steep uphill climb he came to a small valley and finally a straight section of road. On the right, sitting back from the road, there was a long, one story log cabin with an attached garage on the left. A sign supported by two old telephone poles next to the road read:

DAVE'S 421
Mechanic on Duty
Gasoline
Flats Fixed
Maps, Coffee
"and a bunch of other stuff"

He needed to pull over for a couple of minutes and get something to drink. As he pulled into the lot, he noticed a number of old hubcaps nailed to one of the poles supporting the sign. An old greenish-brown pickup truck was parked at two old fashioned gas pumps in front of the garage. A long front porch with a number of old rocking chairs scattered about ran the distance of the log building. Two of the rockers were occupied by older men engaged in a game of checkers. An older woman sat behind a four-foot rickety table situated by the front door.

Parking in front of the building next to two motorcycles, Grant climbed out and stretched, the drive down 421 had taken its toll. Taking a deep knee bend, he looked back up the road and shook his head. So far, 421 wasn't one of those scenic mountain roads where you just sat back and relaxed as you cruised through the mountains. It was one of those roads that required constant attention.

Stepping up onto the porch, Grant passed the two checker playing men and nodded in their direction. "Morning." One of the men, too engrossed in the game, ignored him while the other nodded, but remained quiet. Passing the woman seated at the table, Grant saw a soda machine at the end of the porch. He inserted two quarters and made his selection, popped the top and took a long refreshing swig of the cold drink. Leaning up against the side of the building, he watched as two men exited the building, climbed on the motorcycles, backed out and left the lot in a cloud of dust. He placed his drink on top of an old whiskey barrel and reached into his jeans pocket and removed his handwritten directions to the Johnson County Sheriff's Office in Mountain City. According to the instructions Reichenbaugh had given him, he just had to keep following 421 into Mountain City until he came to Huckleberry Lane where he would then turn left. The office was up the street at number 999. Stuffing the directions back into his pocket, he took another drink and started back across the porch to his Jeep.

The old woman sitting at the table spoke to him as he passed by. "Mountain Jelly. Homemade. Four dollars a jar. Take home a gift fer yer family."

Looking at the assortment of jars stacked on the table, Grant asked, "Got any blueberry?"

Reaching for a jar, the woman held it up. "Spread some o' this on toast an' you'll think it's the best you ever et."

As he reached for his wallet, the woman continued speaking, "Buy a second jar, ya git a dollar off."

Grant smiled at the woman as he inquired, "Don't suppose you've got any peach? My wife loves peach."

Picking up another jar, the woman automatically began to bag both jars. "One blueberry and one peach. That'd be seven dollars."

He gave the woman a ten and refused the three one dollar bills she extracted from an old cigar box. "Keep it. Have a nice day."

"God bless," said the woman.

Climbing back in the Jeep, Grant figured he had at least a good half hour before he reached Mountain City. He pulled out of the exit, but had to stop as the old pickup made a slow right in the same direction he was going. The truck stalled and came to a stop.

The red hat driver stuck his arm out the open window and signaled Grant to go around. As Grant maneuvered around the pickup, he noticed five large white coolers with red lids bungeed on top of a tool box in the rear of the truck. Looking in the rearview mirror, he saw the driver get out, walk to the front of the truck and pop the hood. Before he realized it, he was going around the first of many curves on the way to his destination.

Twenty five minutes later, he passed the Mountain City town limits sign and within two minutes found himself in the midst of the tiny community swallowed on all four sides by what seemed to be an endless mountain range. The bulk of the town laid on the left with a few scattered buildings on the right backed up against the side of the mountain. Three streets down, he located Huckleberry Lane, made a left turn and halfway down the street spotted the Johnson County Sheriff's Office. The building appeared to be larger than Townsend's office, but looked much older. There were only two vehicles parked in front; a Johnson County Sheriff's cruiser and a yellow minivan.

Parking next to the van, Grant stepped out, drew in a deep breath of mountain air and walked to the front door.

Inside, standing at a file cabinet, was a woman with short red hair, dressed in a standard brown county sheriff's uniform. Noticing Grant as he entered, she smiled pleasantly then asked, "Good morning Sir, what can we do for you?"

Grant looked around the extremely organized office as he answered, "My name is Denlinger and I have an appointment with Sheriff Reichenbaugh."

The woman turned and reached to shake his hand. "That'd be Grant Denlinger from Townsend."

Surprised the officer knew who he was he laughed and remarked comically, "The one and only!"

"Sheriff told me this morning when we got here that he was expecting you. Follow me, he should be back in his office."

Following the female officer down a short hallway, Grant entered a back office that was just as organized as the front office; one of those "everything has its place" offices—neat as a pin.

Behind a centered desk toward the back of the office sat the county sheriff. He was a stocky man with grey hair, cut short, fashionable eye glasses, conservative mustache, and a pleasant smile.

The officer wasted little time in making the introductions, "Sheriff Reichenbaugh, this is Grant Denlinger." Motioning to a chair in front of the desk, she turned and left the room.

Just before Grant lowered himself into the chair, the sheriff stood and offered his hand, "Tobias Reichenbaugh, but please, call me Toby. How was the drive over this morning?"

Making himself comfortable in the chair, Grant responded, "Wasn't bad, well, I take that back. When I hit 421 it was kind of rough."

"Know what you mean," said Reichenbaugh. "You have to possess a NASCAR mentality to drive down 421 with any level of relaxation. I hate it every time I have to drive up that way and I grew up around these parts." Sitting back in his chair, Tobias placed his hands behind his head as he continued speaking, "So what can we do for the Townsend Police this morning?"

Grant corrected him as he answered, "First of all, I'm not here on official police business. I have the weekend off and thought I'd do a little snooping around on my own, but out of professional courtesy, I thought it best to get in touch with you first. You're probably already aware of the fact that we've had four murders in or around Townsend last year. This year hasn't gotten off to any better start. So far, this year we've already logged two more."

"Two," said Tobias. "I was only aware of one murder over in your neck of the woods this year. Some fella over in Gatlinburg up and got his head crushed in."

"The second murder just happened earlier this week on Monday. We found the victim at one of our local motels."

"And you think these two new murders are related to last year's?"

"The first one, no. Now the second one, maybe. A lot of the evidence has similar characteristics with the murders of last year."

"So, what's all this have to do with little ol' Mountain City?"

"Maybe nothing, I'm not sure. The reason I came over here to see you is I need some information on some murders you had here in the area about forty years ago. A farmer and his wife and most of the animals on their farm were killed by some drunken hunters. Sound familiar?"

Looking out a side window, Tobias seemed to be in deep thought as he estimated, "Well, let's see. That'd make it back around '69, '70...right?"

Snapping his fingers a number of times as if he were trying to revive his memory, he looked back at Grant. "If the murder was back in '69, well, hell I was just a senior in high school." Suddenly, as if he had a revelation he pointed his finger at Grant and snapped his fingers one more time. "You're right about the murders. I forgot all about that. It was up in the Iron Mountains. And, you're right; the entire family was killed except for the two boys." Shaking his head in wonder, he went on, "Those murders haven't been talked about by anybody around here in, I bet almost thirty-five years."

"Why do you suppose that is?" asked Grant.

"Forty years is a long time back," said Tobias. "People here, just like anywhere else, have a tendency to move on with their lives. A lot of folks that lived here back then are dead or might have moved away. Other families have moved into the area and have no idea those particular murders ever happened. This part of the state is a tad bit different than the rest of Tennessee. We're smack dab in the middle of the Appalachian Mountain Range; one of, if not the poorest section of the country. Here in Johnson County, we've got about 890 square miles, most of it dense forest. Our population in the county bounces around 18,000 folks. Twenty five hundred live in Mountain City, which leaves about 15,000 people scattered out through the rest of the county.

"The folks here in town and those who live in the other smaller communities are about as well off as most, but the people who live out in the mountains, they have their own laws and their own way of life. Most times, if a person from up in the mountains gets killed, well there's a reason for it. At times, it might never get reported. I know. I've gone up there to talk with those people about things that go on. They always treat me with respect, and I suppose that's because I represent the law around here, but still they're pretty close-mouthed about what goes on in their own backyard."

"So what you're saying is that it might be hard to find anybody we could talk to who would remember the murders," Grant asked.

"Exactly," said Tobias, "but I've got an idea. My sister-in-law works over at the public library. I know for a fact she's there every Saturday until two in the afternoon. Here in Mountain City we have the luxury of being the county seat. Anything that goes on around these parts would be filed away at the library. The local newspaper here in town is called the Tomahawk. It's been around since 1874. It comes out every Wednesday so two-thirds of the folks around the county are usually three steps behind on what the rest of the world is doing."

Standing, Sheriff Reichenbaugh suggested, "What say we take a run over there and see what Adele can dig up."

The journey across town from the county sheriff's office to the county library took all of three minutes. The library was a modern looking structure compared to most of the buildings they passed.

Pulling up in front of the library, Reichenbaugh pointed to a brand new truck, its sticker still pasted to the back window. "There's Adele's new truck. Come on, let's go on in and see what we can find out about the murders."

Following Tobias down a hallway with a polished slat wood floor, they entered the main room of the library, a circular room with two stories of wall-to-wall bookcases, a round service desk located in the center of the room. Two women stood behind the counter, a high school age girl and an older woman who Tobias spoke to. "Adele, I see you've still got this place running tight as a ship."

Adele, a woman in her mid-fifties with short brown hair and spectacles balanced on the end of her pug nose, looked out over top of the glasses. She smiled and commented sarcastically, "Well, well, if it isn't the local lawman. Surely you're not here to check a book out Toby. Probably the last time you read a book was back in high school and that's because the teachers made you."

Accepting his sister-in-law's comical slur on his apparent lack of reading, Tobias leaned on the counter as he introduced Grant to Adele and explained his reason for their visit. "Well, for a change you might just be wrong Adele. I might be tempted to read some newspaper articles, that is, if you can locate them for me. Grant is from Townsend and he's over here looking into some murders that happened about forty years ago. Ring a bell?"

Doing some quick math in her mind, Adele responded as she placed an ink pen behind her ear. "Forty years ago. I was a sophomore in high school...hmm." She thought for a moment. "Wait a minute...that was the year the Penders were murdered? I do recall that. They lived in that spooky place up in the Iron Mountains. I can't recall much of anything about those murders, but I do remember how everyone was saying it was dangerous to go up there. Of course that was after the murders and the place was abandoned. It was a falling down mess, but you know how that goes. Telling a bunch of kids they can't go somewhere is like sending them an engraved invitation. Back in those days I was a cheerleader. I hobnobbed with all the other cheerleaders and the football players, ya know, the cool crowd." Looking at Grant, she motioned toward Tobias as she went on, "Now, Toby here was always on the quiet side, actually quite lazy as I remember. He didn't play any sports, go to any of the dances, wasn't involved in any school activities. How on earth he became our county sheriff is beyond me." She gave Toby a gentle nudge as she continued, "Anyway, like I was saying, the old Pender farm was considered off limits especially after a bunch of kids went up there and returned with injuries. Like the time my best friend, Kathy went up there with her boyfriend. They got attacked by a swarm of bees and got the crap stung out of them. Turned out Kathy was allergic to bee stings. She was in the hospital for close to two weeks. I reckon the people around here finally learned that you don't go where you're not welcome, and no one was welcome up on Iron Mountain, especially on the Pender farm."

The young girl standing next to Adele politely interrupted, "Do you want me to get started on sorting those books today or should I wait?"

Turning to the girl, Adele gave her instructions, "That's a good idea. You need to get started. It's going to take us until next week. Besides that, looks like I'm going to be looking up some forty year old newspaper articles."

Picking up where she had left off, Adele remembered something else. "Remember the Diemler brothers, Toby?"

"Geez," Tobias remarked, "I haven't heard anyone mention their name, well, I guess for almost forty years." Looking at Grant, he explained, "Kevin and Lenny Diemler went to school with us. They were our resident hoodlums. They lived in a rundown house on the outskirts of town. Everyone, at least as far as the high school kids were concerned, were scared to death of those two hellions."

Interrupting Toby, Adele interjected, "Do you remember that hotrod they had. It was metallic blue, had big tires and was faster than any car in the county. I always wanted to take a ride in that car but was too scared of the Diemlers to ask. They were always in trouble. Their mother died sometime when they were in grade school so their old man raised them. He owned a gas station here in town and did some mechanic work. He was in and out of jail quite a bit, so the boys were on their own most of the time. We always figured they'd wind up in prison. The Diemler boys, well, they weren't afraid of anything or anybody. You give them a dare or make a bet with them and you were guaranteed to lose."

Grant, interested, asked, "What happened to them?"

"They never graduated from high school...they disappeared! That's another horror story all together about the old Pender farm and the reason why I never went up there," said Adele. "I guess it was a few months after the murders and everyone was saying no one in their right mind would go up there, let alone stay in the Pender house overnight since the place was considered haunted.

"One day at school, the Diemlers overheard some of us talking about how dangerous it was up there. Lenny said we were just a bunch of chickens and there wasn't anything to be afraid of at the Pender place. The long and short of the conversation was that they bet some of us twenty dollars they could spend the night in the farmhouse, saying that if there were any ghosts or demons up there they'd kick their butts. We just knew for sure we were going to lose the bet, but we wanted to make them spend a night up there anyway. The Diemler boys were tough as nails."

Grant's interest was piqued as he asked, "What happened... did they go up to the farm?"

"You bet they did," answered Adele. "They headed up there Friday afternoon when school let out. Said they'd be back Saturday morning to collect the money. Some of the football players followed them up there to make sure they went inside the old house. Sure enough the Diemlers parked their car as close to the house as they could get and went in. That's the last time they were ever seen. Saturday morning, they didn't show up back in town.

"When Monday came around and they weren't in school, we all laughed saying they had chickened out and were too embarrassed to show their faces. By Wednesday, when they were nowhere to be found, their old man contacted the police. They took a drive up there and found their car right where they had left it. The police went inside the house and found two sleeping bags, a half empty case of beer, a pack of cigarettes and some unopened sandwiches. There was evidence that they had indeed been there, but nowhere to be found. They searched the barn and the other assorted buildings on the property. They even searched the surrounding acreage...nothing. Those boys simply vanished."

"That's right," agreed Toby. "What happened to them still remains a mystery to this day, even after forty years. Some think the boys decided to go looking around and either fell into a pit or got lost in one of the caves in the area. Either way, they just disappeared." Reminding Adele of the reason for their visit, he asked, "So when do you think you might locate those articles about the Pender murders?"

"All depends," answered Adele. "That makes it around '69 or '70. What time of the year did the murders take place?"

Toby looked at Grant as he shrugged his shoulders, "Hell, I don't know. What do you think?"

Grant thought for a moment, trying to recall what Conrad had told him about the murders, then spoke up as if he knew what he was talking about. "Well, let's see, from what I've been told the Pender's were killed by hunters. Unless it was small game season, I'd say we're looking somewhere between late September to early December. That's deer season."

"There ya go," said Toby as he gestured at Adele. "We've pinpointed the approximate year and months. Should be a piece of cake to locate those articles."

Adele rolled her eyes as she gave Tobias a look that indicated he didn't know what he was talking about. "Apparently you haven't spent much time in a library, especially the Johnson County Library." Displaying the surrounding walls, she explained, "You just don't waltz in here, snap your fingers, and the information appears. Around here things start off slow and then taper off. What I'm saying is that when we open the doors each day there are no lines of people waiting to dig up old articles about the past history of this area. This might take five minutes or it might take five days, maybe longer."

Tobias seemed confused. "I can understand five minutes, even five hours, but *five days!* Why would it take that long?"

"Because it depends on where the information is. Forty years ago, the library always kept a copy of each edition of the Tomahawk. They were stored down in the basement in waterproof boxes. They were sorted by the day, month and year. Then about ten years ago, we decided to transfer all of the newspapers of the past to microfiche. Then, a few years after that all of the information was copied on to discs. So, to be honest, until I start looking, I'm not sure where they'll turn up."

Holding up his hands as if he understood, Tobias stated, "Okay, I see the problem. Look, I've got another idea. Adele, why don't you start your search for the articles. Give me a call later on my cell and let me know where we stand. Meanwhile, Grant and I are going to go have a talk with someone that might just be able to help us out." Turning, he started back down the hall. "Don't forget...call me later."

Grant, who was still standing at the counter, looked at Adele who simply shrugged. "Nice to meet you," said Grant as he half ran to catch up with Tobias.

Standing next to the cruiser, Grant asked Tobias, "Where are we going?"

Tobias answered, "Irma Green. She was my sixth grade teacher." With that he got in the car and turned the ignition.

Climbing in, Grant thought then asked, "I don't know who this Irma Green is but if my mathematical skills do me any justice if she was your six grade teacher and you were a senior when the Pender murders occurred what she could possibly know about the murders. I don't see the connection."

"The connection came later," pointed out Tobias. "The next year when I entered the seventh grade I found out Mrs. Green had retired from teaching. She was the best teacher I ever had. Anyways, she started to work over at Piney Meadows, an orphanage, no doubt, the state run home where the two Pender boys were sent following the murders. She was working there when the murders happened. She just might remember them."

Tapping his hands on the dash, Grant commented, "Okay, Piney Meadows, here we come."

"Can't go to Piney Meadows, it burned to the ground almost twenty years ago. I mean burned to the ground. It was a devastating fire. They lost everything, all of their equipment, records, everything. We're going to Shady Valley."

"Another state-run home?"

"No, Shady Valley is a nursing home where Irma has been for the last few years."

"She works there?" asked Grant.

"Hell no, she's a resident. She just turned eighty-seven. There was an article about her in the paper last month. She's lived in Mountain City all of her life. She just received some sort of a senior citizen award. Aside from being the best teacher we ever had here she sat on the city planners commission, was active with the girl scouts, was a contributor to our city park and a bunch of other civic activities. If anybody would know about the murders it would be her. She knows everyone in town, everyone who lives here today and everyone who lived here forty years ago."

It was only a ten minute drive to Shady Valley, the nursing home located a few miles north of town. Pulling into a circular drive, Tobias parked the cruiser in front of the main building.

Entering the main doors, they stopped at a service desk and Tobias asked what room Irma Green was in. A nurse at the front desk, answered, "Room thirty-seven."

Tobias removed his hat as he replied, "Thank you, is it all right if we drop by to pay her a visit today?"

"Sure," said the nurse, "but right now she's probably not in her room. She's in the dining hall having lunch."

Tobias, not familiar with the nursing home procedures asked, "Would it be all right if we visit her while she's eating?"

"Not a problem. Just let me buzz you in. After you get through those doors, make a right at the second hallway, about halfway down make a left and you'll see the dining hall. She normally sits at the second table in the third row."

Following the nurse's directions, they passed a number of older folks, some slowly making their way down the hall by use of a cane or a walker, others sitting outside of their rooms in wheelchairs.

Entering the dining hall, Tobias located the third row where he saw Irma seated by herself. She was picking at what appeared to be fried chicken, mixed vegetables, mashed potatoes and orange Jell-O. Irma was a heavyset woman, her body adorned in a loose fitting, yellow flowered dress. Her short, silver grey hair sat atop a rosy cheeked face that instantly lit up when Tobias and Grant approached. Peering over the top of her glasses, she looked Tobias up and down, noticing his uniform then asked jokingly, "Have you come to arrest me?"

Touching Irma lightly on her shoulder, Tobias explained, "No, we're not here to arrest you. I'm one of your former students. I was in your sixth grade class the last year you taught." Tobias went on, "Let's see that would be back in 1963. My name is Tobias Reichenbaugh. They called me Toby. Do you remember me?"

Fiddling with her mashed potatoes, Irma smiled at Grant then answered Tobias, "I had thousands of students during my teaching career and there was a time when I could remember all of their names. They were all special. Over the past few years my memory has started to leave me." Reaching out, she touched Tobias's sleeve and commented, "When you were in my class you must have listened to what I always told my students about working and studying hard when in school. You're a policeman. You've done well for yourself."

Pulling out a chair, Tobias asked, "Would it be all right if we sat with you for a while?"

Pushing her unfinished plate to the side, she responded, "Yes, you may. I'm done with this mess. Fried chicken, ha, how do they expect a person to eat that with dentures?"

Tobias gently objected to her not finishing her lunch. "Please, don't let us interfere with your lunch. That Jell-O looks good."

"It's all right. I'll just take what I can eat back to my room. I wasn't all that hungry anyway."

Now seated, Tobias smiled at Irma. "I remember when I used to tell you at lunch that I wasn't hungry, but you always explained to me how important it was for me to eat."

Ignoring his comment, Irma was now focused on Grant who had seated himself directly across from her. "Were you one of my students also?"

Grant smiled at the woman as he politely answered, "No ma'am, I'm just over here in Mountain City on business with the County Sheriff...Toby."

Seizing an opportunity to get the ball rolling, Toby spoke up, "This is Mr. Denlinger and he came over from Townsend this morning to ask me some questions about some murders that happened forty years ago. It was the Pender murders. You would have been retired from teaching by then, but I remembered that you went to work at Piney Meadows. Do you remember when the Penders were murdered?"

Staring at her plate of food she started to gently chew on one of her fingers as she looked up into the bright lighting above. "Can't remember that."

"Well, maybe you can remember their two sons who were not killed. They were sent to Piney Meadows and were there until they were adopted. I thought maybe you could tell us their first names."

Irma smiled and answered, "There were a lot of children who came to the home. They were all so sweet. All those poor darlings without any parents." Reaching out she grabbed a passing nurse by the arm as she pointed at her lunch. "I'm going to be finishing my lunch in my room. I feel tired." With that she pushed herself away from the table and guided her wheelchair toward the dining hall exit without saying another word.

The nurse standing by the door smiled as she passed and turned to Grant. "You've got to forgive Irma, her train of thought is very short these days. I'm sure by now she has forgotten you were even here to see her."

Tobias folded his hands together and looked across the table at Grant as he remarked, "Well, that certainly didn't work out, now did it?"

Grant was about to say something when an old man who had been sitting at the next table got up and approached them. He was a strange looking fellow: white mustache, a pair of sunglasses pushed back over his long white hair, an old, three-piece white suit, cowboy boots and a walking cane in his hand.

Tapping Tobias's arm, the man introduced himself, "Name's Hiram Tate. I was sitting over there at the next table trying my best to force down the terrible lunch when I overheard the conversation you had with Irma...Mrs. Green. You have to be very patient with Irma. She's a sweet ol' gal, but her memory is slipping like most of the old codgers in this place. Have a hell of a time carrying on any kind of conversation around here. Yeah, poor Irma, they say she's in the beginning stages of dementia." Taking a seat at the table, Hiram continued, "I heard you asking her about the Pender murders. Well I can tell you this. I know everything there is to know about those murders."

Tobias gave Grant a look indicating that the old man might be crazy.

Hiram picked up on Tobias's skepticism as he gently jammed Tobias in his left arm with his cane. "You think I'm nuts, don't you? I might be eighty-five years old and my hearing and eyesight are not what they used to be, but I can assure you my memory is sharp as a tack. I worked for Millard Pender for six years. I made his deliveries for him. Covered three states: East Tennessee, Western North Carolina and Southwestern Virginia. Ol' Pender was the best moonshiner in these parts. I had a sweet deal with him. I made quite a bit of money working for Pender." He cocked his head and let out a loud cackle. "I sure was surprised when I heard you mention the name Pender and that piqued my interest.

"Nobody has talked about those murders in years. Course, I never said anything to anyone. I didn't want the law down on me. Ya know, I was the first one on the scene after the Penders were killed. In all those forty past years I never mentioned anything about those murders until today. You're right about one thing though, they did have two young sons who witnessed everything and they did in fact wind up at Piney Meadows. I knew the boys, but not by name. I'd see them when I'd go up to the farm to pick up deliveries. I'd always say hello to them, but they were on the strange side. They'd just look at me and run off. After the murders, I followed the newspaper articles up until they were adopted by a family by the name of Pearl up in Knoxville. After that, I can't tell you much about those boys."

Grant suddenly interested at the mention of the Pearl family spoke up, "I'm surprised you remembered that they were adopted by the Pearls. What else can you tell us about the murders?"

Rubbing his hand across his mustache, Hiram thought for a moment then answered, "Here's the deal. I'll take you boys up to the Pender farm and give you a firsthand rundown on the murders, but there has to be something in this for me."

"We're listening," said Tobias.

Looking around, Hiram motioned at the surrounding room as he explained, "I'm here on the assisted living program which means I can come and go as I please. Problem is I can't drive a car any longer. The only time I get to leave this place is when they take the ol' biddies to Wal-Mart or to the movies. I'm in the mood for some action. So, here it is. I take you up to the Pender place and give you the lowdown, you take me out for a steak dinner with all the trimmings, maybe even a beer when we get back. Deal?"

Tobias looked at Grant then back to Hiram. "How do we know you're telling us the truth? This could just be a ploy to get a free meal away from this place."

"All right, tell you what. After we get back from the Penders if you're not satisfied then you can just return me here and we'll forget about the meal."

Tobias looked at Grant. "What do you think?"

"Well," said Grant. "Mr. Tate here has verified at least to me that he knows what he's talking about. He knew the last name of the family that adopted the two boys, and he remembered Pender's first name...Millard. Sounds interesting to me, but it's your county, it's your decision."

Pursing his lips, Tobias thought for moment, then spoke, "All right Mr. Tate, you've got yourself a deal. Now, how do we get you out of here?"

Standing, Hiram pointed toward the dining room exit. "We just go down to the front desk and check out. Actually, this could be fun. We don't need to tell them where we're going or what we plan on doing. They'll probably think you're arresting me. Five minutes after we're out of here, the word will be out: the county sheriff hauled ol' Hiram Tate out of here. Give them something to talk about. They'll probably think I was chasing after one of them old biddies and she called the cops."

CHAPTER TEN

HELPING HIRAM INTO THE BACKSEAT of the cruiser, Tobias told him to watch his head. Making himself comfortable, Hiram looked around the confines of the backseat. There was mesh security wire separating the front from the back, a twelve-gauge shotgun fastened to the mesh and no door handles. Strapping himself in, he joked as they pulled out of the lot. "Haven't been in a police cruiser since the last time, and the only time, they sent me off to prison."

Grant, turning in the seat gave Hiram a strange look. "You were in prison?"

"Sure was," said Hiram. "That was four years before I started working for Millard Pender, way back in '59. I was running stolen cars for a theft ring out of Cleveland, Tennessee. I was full of piss and vinegar back then and just trying to make a living. I knew every back road there was in these parts. No offense, Sheriff, but back then, the police couldn't have caught me if their life depended on it. Made good money stealing cars, but like most criminals, fate finally bit me in the ass. I stole me a brand new Chevy one night and the local police were right on my tail. Just before I got to the county line, wouldn't ya know it I blew a tire and spun off the road. I jumped out of the car and tried to run but it was no use. They nailed me and arrested me on the spot. The judge sentenced me to five years, but I got out in three for good behavior. I moved back here to town and to tell you the truth there wasn't a brass band waiting for me when I returned. I was an ex-con and to be honest with you not all that popular. When you live in a small town everybody knows your business and the gossip flew the day I got back home. My days of crime were at an end and I decided to straighten myself out, but most folks here in town weren't willing to forgive and forget.

"I got me a small rat hole apartment and set out to find employment. I couldn't get a decent paying job. With my record nobody wanted to hire me, so the only jobs I could get were dishwashing or working as a janitor. I was barely making ends meet. Then, I guess it was about 1963 I got a part time job over at the feed mill. That's when I met Millard Pender—"

Interrupting Hiram, Tobias asked, "Which way are we going?"

Leaning up toward the front seat, Hiram pointed south as he gave directions, "Get on 421 south and drive straight through town. After we get out of town a few miles there'll be a road on the left that leads up to Iron Mountain. I'll let you know when we come up on it."

Getting back to his life after prison story, Hiram continued, "Millard knew all about my past. Said he was looking to hire someone to work up at his place. Said the work paid good, but that it could be dangerous. He pulled out two hundred dollars right there on the spot and said it was mine if I started immediately. By the end of the week and with a little bit of training I was officially running Millard Pender's moonshine deliveries. He made the best hooch in a three state area. Had his still somewhere up in the woods on his property. I never saw it because he always had the deliveries ready and waiting for me under the barn. He had a root cellar hidden beneath a trapdoor under some bales of hay. Then, below that he had a sub root cellar. It was down there that he kept a safe and shelves of shine. I delivered three days a week. On Monday I'd pick up deliveries for the eastern part of Tennessee, then on Wednesday I'd deliver to Western North Carolina and finally on Friday I'd take deliveries up into Southwestern Virginia."

Leaving the town limits, Hiram motioned up the road. "About ten minutes or so we'll be coming to that road I told you about."

Looking in the rearview mirror, Tobias asked, "So what kind of a person was Millard Pender?"

"He was a tough, old bastard and as I recall, a mean looking son of a bitch to boot. He always had on the same clothes. He wore dirty coveralls over the top of his long johns and his sleeves were always rolled up. Never saw him without his straw hat. He had one of those long unkempt beards that kept you wondering if some small critter might be livin' in it. He was a shrewd businessman and a person you didn't want to cross or screw over. Sooner or later he'd get even with ya. The local police didn't mess with him much, but the state revenuers would come up to his farm two or three times a year waving their search warrants and what not. They'd search his house, the barn, his out buildings and the general area. They never found so much as a drop of moonshine." Laughing, Hiram went on to explain, "I remember one time when I was up there in the barn talking with Millard when them revenuers came barreling up the dirt road. They jumped out of their cars saying they were with the federal government and had a right to search the property. Millard never flinched. He was just as calm as I am right now.

"When they came in the barn they actually moved the hay bales and discovered the trapdoor to the root cellar. They opened the door and went down. What they discovered was some cured meat, some onions, radishes and potatoes and some canned goods. Little did the state boys realize it, but they were standing directly over the top of seventy some gallons of genuine Iron Mountain moonshine. The feds were really pissed. They knew there was hooch on the property, but they could never find it.

"After they left, me and Millard had a good laugh. Actually it's the only time over the six years I worked for him that I saw him laugh. Sometimes I wouldn't see him for two to three weeks, then other times I'd see him around the place quite a bit."

Tapping on the wire mesh with his cane, Hiram raised his voice as he ordered, "Okay, see that road coming up on the left. Shoot up there and in about two miles we'll be taking a right. I'll let you know when I see it."

Sitting back in the seat, he continued with his past moonshining delivery days. "It really wasn't necessary for me to see Millard every time I came by for deliveries. He had a full proof schedule that really didn't require any supervision on his part. He'd bring the hooch down from the still and place it down below the root cellar. Whenever I'd show up, I'd open the safe and put the money from the previous deliveries in a manila envelope. There was always an envelope in there for me, which contained my pay for the next deliveries and also a list of stops I had to make. I'd take the envelope and load up the hooch then I was on my way."

"So, would you say the Penders had a lot of money?" asked Grant.

"They got by, maybe a little better than most folks in the mountains, but it sure didn't seem like they had what I'd call a lot of money, leastwise, he never spent it if he did. There was talk amongst the mountain folks that Pender buried his money somewhere on the farm. Hell, it still might be buried up there."

Grant, quite interested in Hiram's story asked, "So, in all the time you said you went up there you never had much contact with Millard's sons or found out the two boys' names?"

"Nope, never did. Like I said they were a strange pair. Pretty much kept to themselves. Millard was hard on those boys. I always heard he beat the crap out of them if they didn't do what he said. Course, he was drunk most of the time. Pickled is more like it. I think he was drinking as much hooch as he was making. Why, I remember during the summer when it got hot out, you could smell the alcohol coming out of his pores, but that never stopped him from doing his work. But, as mean as he was, his wife Etta was even meaner. She was meaner than a snake. The part of the mountain where the Pender farm is located is a haven for snakes, mostly timber rattlers and copperheads. Etta Pender always reminded me of one of those old Greek characters, ya know Medusa, that creature with the snakes in her hair and if you looked at her you'd turn to stone. Etta was a snake handler and performed her snake handling at the Holiness Pentecostal Church. Many people in the hills thought she was a witch. She was always making potions and cures from snake venom.

"One time when I was up there picking up deliveries, Millard noticed a bad rash I had on my arm. He asked me about it and I said I couldn't get rid of it. He told me the next time I came by he'd have something for me. Sure enough, two days later when I went up, he gave me a small bottle of some kind of salve telling me it should do the trick. Well, I smeared it on my arm and two days later when I went back the rash was gone. Millard told me Etta had mixed it up and that it had rattlesnake venom in it. After that I figured she knew what she was doing. I figured that's how she got people to come to her church. Mountain medicine is powerful stuff. She cured a few people and that's all it took."

Looking out the front window, he stopped talking and pointed up ahead. "There, that road on the right. Turn up there."

Tobias, making the turn had to floor the accelerator as the road began a steep climb up the mountain, the road seemingly engulfed in tall pines on either side.

"Getting back to those two boys," said Hiram. "Millard told me Etta wanted the boys to go to church but he didn't want anything to do with church. He didn't have much faith in the Good Lord. He did demand the boys go to school, but he said they could make their own decision on church. The younger boy, who was on the slow side, tended to lean toward his mother and the older boy hung with Millard. The young one did go to church with Etta and would follow her into the woods to capture poisonous snakes. It was the strangest thing. Sometimes when I'd pull up in front of the barn, the young one would be sitting in the driveway playing with a rattler or a copperhead. That kid scared the hell out of me. He'd stare at me with those cold eyes and I'd get away from him real fast. Course, Etta scared the hell out of me too. To tell you the truth I think the only person alive she was afraid of was Millard. If he got drunk enough, he'd beat the hell out of her. Just like he would beat those boys. Sometimes when I went to pick up a delivery she'd be out in the yard hanging clothes and she'd be covered in bruises and cuts. Lots of times she'd have two black eyes. I could never figure it. It was like he held some sort of power over her for her to put up with those beatings. I mean hell; all she had to do was dump some of her venom into his coffee and that would have been the end of Pender. One time, he did tell me he had married her when she was just fourteen after her folks died. I guess she had nowhere else to go. If she would have poisoned Millard I don't think she would have been able to make it on her own."

Passing a long series of jagged cliffs on their right, Hiram leaned forward again as he explained, "All right, when we get to the end of these cliffs we need to take a right and go about a mile and a half. That'll put us smack dab in front of the dirt road that leads to the farm."

Grant, looking at the cliffs commented, "Doesn't seem to be any homes along the road that I can see."

"That's 'cause most mountain folks live further back in the woods. Don't want to be bothered much by people. Don't you worry. They're watching us."

For the next few minutes they drove along in silence, until Hiram ordered them, "Stop, pull over to that small clearing on the right."

Steering the car off the road and parking beneath an overhang of trees, Tobias looked across the dirt road at a six-foot high, rusted chain link fence that skirted the left side of the road. An old gate blocked the entrance to a weed infested side road. "That the entrance to the Pender farm?"

"Yep, that's it," said Hiram. "Most of the Pender property is fenced in because the state owns it now. That's another story I'll get to later."

Just then a pickup truck slowly passed them as it headed farther up the road. Grant, looking out the window, noticed the truck as it passed. The driver wore a red hat and there were coolers in the back. "That's strange," said Grant. "I saw that very same truck at a place I stopped at on my way down here this morning; what was it called, yeah, Dave's 421."

Tobias blew off Grant's comment as he remarked, "Probably just some country boy heading back home."

"We can't get in the front gate to the farm," said Hiram. "We'll have to drive up the road about a half mile where we'll come to a larger clearing that leads to the Southwestern corner of the Pender property."

Tobias pulled back out onto the road. "How much property did Pender own up here?"

"It was well over five hundred acres," answered Hiram. "Some of the roughest mountain country around: high cliffs, steep hills, caves and pits, all of which are infested with countless snakes not to mention poison ivy, poison oak and thorn bushes so thick you'd have to machete your way through if you didn't know your way around. Millard liked it that way. He said it kept folks away from his place."

Just as they were about to go around a long curve in the road, Hiram pointed at a small abandoned cinderblock building practically covered with vines. "That's the old Holiness Pentecostal Church where Etta and her youngest son used to do their snake handling. Snake handling is illegal here in Tennessee nowadays. Actually, the only state where it's still legal is West Virginia. There are still a handful of snake handlers in the state, but I think most of them are down in Del Rio, which is south of here."

As they passed the structure, Grant continued to stare at the strange looking building through the rear window. "There he is again," he said as he pointed.

Tobias, negotiating the curve, responded, "There who is again?"

"That man in the pickup truck that we just saw passing us. The same one I saw earlier today down on 421. He's parked behind the church."

Giving Grant an odd look, Tobias asked, "Is there something I should know about this man you claim you saw earlier?"

"No, guess not," answered Grant. "It's just strange that I keep running across that truck."

Hiram, who wasn't the least bit interested in the man in the pickup commented, "Like the Sheriff said, probably just some good ol' boy wondering what we're doing up here." Laying his cane on the seat he unfastened his seatbelt. "After we get around this curve we'll come to a straight section of road then just before the next curve there'll be a cleared power line section that cuts right through the forest. It's state maintained and the only feasible way to get into the Pender place, well, at least close to it. There it is...right there. Just pull into that dirt road and pull off to the side. We'll have to walk in from there."

Parking the car next to the rough looking side road, Tobias climbed out followed by Grant who opened the backdoor for Hiram. Hiram, once outside the car, stretched as he took a deep breath. "Ah, nothing like good ol' clean mountain air." Looking up the power line road, he explained, "We have to walk up the road for about a hundred yards, then we'll cut through the undergrowth which will lead us to the corner of the farm." Starting up the road he motioned with his cane. "Come on boys, let's go."

Following Hiram up the road, Tobias asked, "Was this road here when you were making deliveries for Pender?"

"The road was here, but it wasn't owned by the power company," said Hiram. "They didn't run the lines up here until a few years after the murders. Most of the hill folks used generators for power." Stopping and turning back to face Grant and Tobias, Hiram pointed his cane at both of them as he continued speaking, "What do you fellows know about snakes?"

Tobias was quick to answer, "I know which ones to stay away from. Long as they leave me be I'm fine with them. I'll stay in town and they can stay up here on the mountain and if we never cross paths, well, that's okay."

Grant agreed, "Know about as much as most folks I reckon. I know one thing for sure. I don't want to get bit."

Moving on up the road, Hiram held his hands out as he turned in a circle displaying the surrounding wilderness. "The Iron Mountains, especially around here seems to be a breeding ground for rattlers and copperheads. Always has been and since nobody lives up here anymore it's safe to say the snake population has increased dramatically on Pender's land. You get bit up here in the middle of nowhere, without immediate medical attention, you might not come out of here alive."

Grant, looking from side to side, now more aware than ever of the existence of local snakes asked, "When you say immediate medical attention what kind of timeframe are we talking when one gets bit?"

"Depends," said Hiram. "Depends on how healthy the bite victim is, where they have been bit, how old they are...stuff like that. You never know. A person could live five days or die in five minutes. A good rule of thumb to go by is about twenty to thirty minutes. You get to a hospital in that time more likely than not you'll live to see another day. The trick is not to get bit in the first place and I'm going to tell you how we can try our best to make sure that happens."

Walking to the side of the road, he bent down and picked up a section of branch that had fallen from a tree. Tossing it to Tobias, he explained, "When we get in the undergrowth we need to beat the weeds so any resident snakes can hear us coming. Snakes are terrified of humans and if we give them ample warning they'll skedaddle. They don't want to meet up with us anymore than we do them. Most folks think it's smart to remain quiet as they walk in the woods, however this can, and often does, lead to coming up on a snake, startling it and winding up getting bit. It's the only defense mechanism they have.

"Now, that being said we only have about fifty yards more to go until we enter the brush." Turning, Hiram started once again up the road. Tobias, looking at Grant shrugged and then followed.

"This oughta do, right about here," Hiram pointed out as he stopped. Bending down he picked up a softball sized rock and tossed it into the brush. Grant jumped when he heard a rustling sound as something moved in the tall weeds. "There that should make enough noise to get us started," said Hiram. Walking into the knee high weeds, he suggested, "Might want to pick up a few more of those rocks so we can toss them in front of us as we forge our way through."

Watching Hiram move forward, beating the weeds, while Tobias picked up two rocks and followed, Grant shouted ahead to Hiram. "Just in case, what do we do if one of us gets nabbed?"

Hiram, without looking back answered, "Hightail it back to town to the emergency room at the hospital. If by some chance both of you get bit we're in for a world of hurt. Just tell me what your last wishes are." He let out a loud howl of laughter. "I'll have to drive us back to town and seeing as how I no longer am in possession of a driver's license not to mention the fact that I haven't driven a car in seventeen years it could be touch and go."

Pointing to his left he went on, "Don't go getting in those bushes over there: poison ivy."

Duplicating Hiram's actions, Tobias beat at the brush to his right and left with the stick as he continued forward. Grant, looking to his right asked, "Hey, what about these low hanging branches in these trees. I know snakes can climb trees."

"I wouldn't worry about that much," said Hiram. "Rattlers and Copperheads are capable of climbing trees but normally stay on the ground in thick vegetation, around rocks or old logs. Their heavy body weight makes it difficult for them to climb trees. So, my advice to you is to look down, not up, as long as one ain't hanging on a branch and meets you eye to eye—"

A noise off to the left startled Tobias and he went into a defensive position and commented, "Was that a snake?"

"No, too loud," answered Hiram. "Probably a squirrel or some other critter."

Stopping for a breather, Hiram pointed forward with his cane. "We're about halfway through. Another fifty yards or so should put us in the clearing next to the Pender place."

Grant, looking out into the dense trees, asked, "During the years you worked for Pender, did you ever get bit?"

"Nope never did. Course, I was always careful. I knew they were around and just figured if I left them alone then they'd steer clear of me. I'd see one on occasion, but just went on about my business." Turning, he started through the brush once again, "We should be at the clearing in less than five minutes."

Minutes later they emerged into a clearing where the brush was only ankle high. Stopping in the middle of the clearing, Hiram pointed to an old rusted barbed wire fence just ten yards in front of them. "That, gentleman marks the edge of the Pender farm. Just about a hundred yards or so up over the hill is where the old house and barn are located."

Walking to the fence, he reached out with his cane and tapped the side of an old school bus sitting next to an equally rusted out dump truck. There were old bed springs and assorted rust covered appliances, surrounded by piles of trash. "This corner of the property is where Millard used to pitch all of his junk and this clearing is where the first incident took place the day the Penders were murdered."

Seating himself on a large rock, Hiram removed a handkerchief from his coat pocket, wiped his brow then began his story about the murders. "Like I said, my eyesight and hearing are not what they used to be, but my memory is quite good. According to the boys, at least what the paper said, they were up in a tree fort." He pointed at a tall maple tree located at the edge of the clearing. "That one right over there. If you look up you can still see some of the wooden boards the boys nailed up there.

"The paper reported that the boys said they heard voices. Remaining quiet, they saw four men dressed in hunting outfits walk into the clearing. They were laughing and joking and drunk. According to the boys, they were passing a bottle around and complaining about the sleet and the rain and how they hadn't seen a deer all day or even fired their guns. Then, one of the men took a shot at this school bus and before you know it all four men were taking target practice at the bus, knocking out the last few windows. Then they started shooting at cans and bottles laying around on the other side of the fence. They were having a good ol' time shooting, drinking, laughing. Then, all of a sudden, Millard appears out of nowhere and fires his shotgun over their heads. He had his three Rottweilers with him. I remember those dogs. They reminded me of the Hounds of the Baskervilles. When I first started to work for Millard, he told me that eventually they'd get used to me, but in the meanwhile I needed to bring some kind of a snack along for the dogs to keep them from attacking me. So from then on I'd always carry a box of milk bones with me in my car. Once in a while I'd bring hamburgers up here for the dogs. It didn't take long for those three monsters to figure out that ol' Hiram Tate was a human who always had a treat for them. It was a strange sight. I'd drive up in front of the barn and here they'd come. Three huge dogs from the pits of hell with their tails wagging ready to get their snacks."

Waving his cane in the air, he apologized, "Sorry, I'm getting away from the murders. The boys went on to report that Millard and the hunters argued. Millard said they needed to move on. The men argued right back at Millard claiming they had every right to hunt in the mountains as long as they were not on his property and it was none of his business. At that point, Millard aimed just above their heads and pulled off a second round from his shotgun and told them that if they didn't git, they could wind up dead and that would be the last they were heard of. There were some other things that were said, but eventually the men moved off down the fence line of Millard's property cursing him as they left.

"The boys by this time, had climbed down out of the tree and ran through the woods to yet another tree fort up the ways." Hiram stood and pointed with his cane. "Let's make our way up the fence and I'll show you where the murders took place."

Walking next to the rusted barbed wire, Hiram explained, "We've got about thirty yards or so of brush that we have to walk through so be on the lookout for our friends, the local snakes."

Looking up at the sun, he went on, "It's getting close to the hottest part of the day. They'll be out sunning themselves. So, keep a close eye." Thrashing the weeds with his cane, he walked on. As he passed the tree, Grant stared up at the remains of the tree fort.

As they made their way along the old wire fencing, Grant could just begin to see the roof of the Pender house coming into view up the hill on his left. Finding out Conrad's brother's name was turning out to be difficult. Hiram stated that he'd seen the boys plenty of times but never talked with them. Still, Adele back at the library was looking for the old articles on the Pender murders. Surely the two boys' names would be mentioned in the paper. All hope was not lost.

Bringing up the rear, Grant said, "The information I originally received about the Pender murders is pretty sparse, but I understand Pender was quite the mechanic and his wife baked pies and cakes and sold them in town."

Stopping, Hiram gave Grant a strange look. "You seem to know as much about the Penders as I do. How did you know Pender was a mechanic?"

"It just came up in a conversation over in Townsend, that's all," answered Grant.

Hiram, on the move again, verified Grant's statement, "You're right about Millard. He was a mechanic. Best one up here in the mountains. He could fix most anything. Etta was quite the baker. Once in a blue moon she'd go into town and sell baked goods; however, Millard's moonshine and her snake potions were their main source of income. They had to have some kind of legal income to keep the revenuers from getting suspicious about how they made a living."

Stepping into a larger clearing, Hiram walked to where there were rotted remnants of wood fencing. Placing his boot on an old fencepost that had fallen over, he pointed at the area that had been fenced in years ago. "The two boys had a makeshift pen right here where they were raising two young fawns whose mother had been killed by hunters. As soon as the fawns were old enough to fend for themselves they were going to turn them loose. Those boys were always taking care of animals. I saw them take care of young coons and squirrels who were orphaned or injured." Turning, he pointed at a large oak tree. "The two boys were up in that tree when the hunters entered this clearing. When the hunters saw the deer in the pen those bastards shot them for no reason. In the paper the boys said it seemed so senseless. Then, everything got nuts and the men started to fire across the field at Pender's horse. Before they knew it, Millard Pender comes running down from the house with his three hounds at his side. The boys reported that he never said a word, but just started shooting his shotgun at the

men. He hit one of the men in the arm, another in the leg. I guess
those hunters figured Pender was out to kill them so they shot him
before he could even reload. All three dogs were gunned down as
well. Etta, hearing all the shooting came running down from the
house and when she saw her husband laying there she picked up
the empty shotgun, but was cut down just like Millard. The boys
just sat silently up there in the tree, scared out of their minds,
afraid to move."

Walking to the right, Hiram stopped after traveling just a few
yards and pointed at the ground. "This is the spot where Millard
and Etta were shot. Their horse was found about twenty yards
past the fawns' pen." Looking back at the tree, Hiram shook his
head in wonder. "Those boys were so scared they stayed up in that
tree all through the night despite freezing rain. When morning
finally came around they climbed down and ran nearly four miles
to the nearest neighbor's place. The police were contacted and
drove up from Mountain City and hauled the boys back out here to
the crime scene where they reported everything I've told you."

Turning, he started up the slight hill. "Come on, let's get up to
the house because there's where the real interesting part starts.
Like I said earlier, I was the first one on the scene. I remember
that day. It was a Friday and I had to pick up deliveries for up in
Virginia. A nasty day; sleet, rain, colder than usual for November."

As Hiram continued to explain what happened that day long
ago, Grant stared at the old house and barn. The house was a two
story clapboard, covered in gray wood siding that was falling off in
a number of places. All of the windows were broken out and two-
thirds of the stone chimney had crumbled to the ground. The right
side of the front porch had collapsed long ago.

The barn was in an equally deplorable state of ruin. One of
the barn doors had fallen off and the left half of the building
covered with crawling vines. Three rusted cars sat to the left of
the barn.

"I must've shown up that day while the boys were already down
at the neighbors because there was no one around when I came up
the road, least I didn't think there was. I thought it was strange
that the dogs didn't run out to meet me. I parked right in front of
the barn like always. The fact that Millard and Etta were nowhere
in sight was not unusual. There were plenty of times when I came
by for the deliveries and wouldn't see a soul. I'd just go into the
barn pick up my deliveries and be on my way. But that day...was
different. When I got out of the car, I saw one of the dogs laying in

a pool of blood next to the barn doors. I followed the trail of blood the dog had left which led me back down to the pens. That's when I discovered Millard and Etta, the horse, two fawns and the other dogs all shot dead. I didn't hang around long. I knew I had to get the hell out of there. It was a sickening sight. Turned my stomach."

Grant, who was now standing in front of the barn asked, "And you didn't report any of what you saw to the police? And you didn't look for the boys?"

"Hell fire, no!" answered Hiram sharply. "Remember I was an ex-con. I was just one step ahead of the law back then running illegal moonshine in three states. I couldn't afford to get involved in something like that. I went into the barn and down into the root cellar, opened the safe, took my next pay envelope, kept the money from the previous deliveries and took all the shine I could load. Never said a word about what I had found that day in the last forty years. Figured it was just best if I stayed out of it. At that point I had no idea what happened to the boys."

Grant spoke up, "So you're telling me that you took the time to go down into the root cellar, but you couldn't even take five minutes to look for those boys?" How could you leave not knowing what happened to them?"

Hiram could sense that Grant was clearly irritated. "I guess that was one of the worst things I ever done, but I was scared."

Grant just shook his head and walked a few feet away.

Tobias spoke up, "So, you didn't go into the house or look around for them?"

"Nope...just hightailed it out of here. I reckon I was just thinking about my own hide at the time. Until I found out those boys were safe, I regretted what I did."

"Did you ever come back here?" Tobias asked.

"Yeah, I came back, but only after waiting for about a year. The police spent a couple of weeks up here running an investigation, but then things tapered off and folks went on about their lives."

"So, why did you come back?"

"More than anything else, I guess curiosity. The location of Pender's still was always a mystery and I wanted to see if I could locate it, plus there was the story about all the money he had buried somewhere on the property. I spent the better part of six months looking for the still whenever I had an opportunity to come up here. I walked every inch of his property...no still. Over the years a lot of folks came up here looking for that still and the buried money, but as far as I know they've never been found. Then, after a while folks stopped coming up here. The word was the place was haunted and besides that with all the snakes up here it got to the point where it was just too dangerous. Now, personally myself, I don't believe in all that spiritual mumbo jumbo crap; ghosts, demons and the like, but I've have to admit there's just something odd about this place."

Tobias, walking toward the house spoke up, "That's what my sister-in-law said when we went to visit her over at the library this morning. She said a lot of kids came up here and for the most part always returned with some sort of injury. Things like getting attacked by bees, or getting bit by a snake, severe poison ivy."

The sound of distant thunder rumbled across the sky. Looking to the east at the darkening clouds, Hiram suggested, "We better be heading back. Looks like a big storm coming our way. Don't want to get caught up here on the mountain in bad weather." Turning, he started back down the hill.

Grant objected to leaving so soon. "Wait, I wanted to go down in that root cellar, maybe inside the house and have a look around."

Without looking back, Hiram emphasized, "No time for that now. That storm will be on us in less than a half hour. Now that you know how to get up here you and the sheriff can come back tomorrow. As far as going in the barn and the house, well, I wouldn't advise that. Those buildings are no doubt loaded with snakes. Couldn't pay me to go in there."

Tobias agreed, "Hiram's right. I've been up here during storms. Gets pretty rough. We do need to get back to town."

As Tobias and Grant followed Hiram down the hill, they listened as he told them the story of Jake Diemler. "Jake was murdered up here, too. He was the Diemler twins' uncle. But that was a few years before the Penders were killed. I went to high school with Jake. He was a strange bird to say the least. Never knew what he wanted to do. He was always so unsettled. After we graduated I did a hitch in the army and I heard that Jake moved down south, think it was Alabama. When I got back from the service he had moved back to Mountain City. He hadn't changed a bit. Between getting evicted from the place where he was living, getting into bar fights and bumming around the area, he wasn't exactly the model citizen. As a matter of fact he joined the Ku Klux Klan who had a small branch down in Del Rio. But, as bad as the Klan is he couldn't get along with them either."

Looking back over his shoulder he commented, "That storm's moving quicker than I figured. We're gonna get wet before we get back to the car. We better pick up the pace."

Tobias, interested in the story of Jake Diemler asked, "You said that Diemler was murdered up here. How did that happen? I don't recall ever hearing about that."

Walking down the fence line, Hiram continued with his story. "I was just getting to that. You see, what happened was Jake was handling Pender's deliveries a couple of years before I was hired on. He was skimming Pender's hooch. After he'd pick up the deliveries he'd pour some out of each jug and then add water. He'd sell what he skimmed off and kept the money for himself. Well, after a while Millard starts to get complaints about the quality of his shine. Didn't take him long to figure out what was going on and he fired Jake. Later, that week Jake runs into Millard in town at the hardware store. One thing leads to another and before you know it they're goin' at one another. Pender nearly killed Jake and he surely would have if some people outside the store wouldn't have pulled Millard off him. Jake left that day saying that he'd get even.

"After that, Jake seemed to calm down. Folks started to say that the whipping he got from Pender straightened him out. He started to work with his brother Frank at the garage and eventually got a part time job with the school district driving a school bus. Back then, folks in town didn't get along that well with people up in the mountains and it was difficult to get a driver to pick up the mountain children and bring them into town to school.

"Jake volunteered for the job and since they had no other offer he got the assignment. Things went along okay for a few months but then Jake started to give the Pender boys a rough time. He'd never drop them off in front of the road where they lived. He'd always drop them a mile or so from their house and tell them to walk it. He was always calling the younger one, the slower one names, like inbred or retard or mountain trash.

"Jake had a habit of after dropping all the kids off he'd pull up into a clearing, which is located a little further down the road. He'd sit there and drink, maybe take a nap. He always told the Pender boys that if they ever said anything to their parents about him calling them names or dropping them off down the road, that they'd have to answer to him. The boys never said a word until one day when the younger boy came home late. He was wet and muddy from walking home in the rain. He told Etta what was going on.

The very next week, on a Wednesday, Jake didn't return the bus to the school. When he didn't report the following day, the police went looking for the bus. They found it parked in the clearing with all four tires flattened and an iron bar stuck in the door. Jake was inside in a position that looked like he had tried to get out of the bus. His face was pressed against the door, his eyes were wide open. The coroner said he had been drinking. They also found over two dozen rattlesnakes inside the bus. They said Jake was bitten a number of times and died from the bites."

Standing in the clearing where they first came out of the brush, Hiram pointed at the school bus. "That's the bus they found Jake in. After they hauled him out they left the doors open hoping the snakes would leave. Eventually they did, but for some reason somebody dropped the ball and the city never came up to take the bus back to town so Millard hauled it off to this spot where it has been for the past four plus decades."

Grant stood by the tree where the boys had witnessed the hunters when they first arrived and asked, "Did they ever find out who killed Jake?"

"Nope, never did," answered Hiram. "Everyone knew there was bad blood between Millard and Jake. We all knew that the Penders killed him but no one could prove anything. When things happen up here on the mountain folks just sort of clam up. I've got my own opinion of who I think killed Jake. I'd bet you a dime to a dollar that the young boy did him in. Maybe the older boy helped...not sure. All I know is that young one knew how to handle snakes and when the sheriff came up here and told the Penders what happened to Jake, none of them seemed surprised."

Grant was halfway up the tree before Tobias noticed him grabbing a branch and climbing higher. "Grant, what are you doing?"

Placing his foot on a protruding knot in the trunk he hoisted himself another two feet as he answered, "Just thought I'd like to see what those boys saw from up here."

Hiram, now at the base of the tree, looked up as he warned, "Don't take too long. Clouds are getting darker and the wind is picking up."

It had been over twenty years since Grant climbed a tree. As a youngster at Dalton's farm it had been one of his favorite things to do. It was like riding a bike; something you didn't forget. Finally, over thirty feet up, he hoisted himself into what was left of the tree fort: six old one by six boards nailed in between four large branches that provided a makeshift floor and a number of one by four boards that closed in three sides. The wood was old and discolored from years of rain and snow, many sections rotted away.

Grant, let his legs dangle over the side of the flooring and looked down at Tobias and Hiram then over at the bus and the fencing and finally up the hill where he could see most of the house and part of the barn. He tried to envision what the boys had witnessed that day forty years past from up in the tree. He tried to imagine the four hunters, drinking, laughing and eventually shooting at the bus, then the boys' father arriving on the scene, firing his shotgun, followed by an argument between him and the men. From up in the tree they had a front row seat.

Suddenly a clap of loud thunder followed by a band of lightning raced across the sky nearby. Hiram yelled to Grant, "Come on son, you better get down from there. It's gonna get nasty around here."

Grant, realizing that the old man was right, turned to climb back down when something caught his eye. Partially covered by some vines there were carved letters in one of the boards. Pushing back the vines the letters were completely revealed. There were two crude inscriptions, one on top of the other. They appeared to have been scratched into the wood with a nail or a pocket knife, part of the second name partially obscured from the rotting tree bark.

Conrad Pender
R   nder

Staring at the rough inscriptions he thought to himself, *This most definitely verifies that Conrad's story is true. Conrad had been in the tree, but who was R nder.* He had made an important discovery, but his concentration was being interrupted as Hiram yelled up the side of the tree just as the rain started to fall. "Come on...get down here. We need to leave."

By the time Grant stepped his foot back on the ground, the rain was pelting the area. Tobias stood at the edge of the clearing as he held fast to his hat, Hiram remarking, "Told you it was going to get nasty."

Twenty minutes later, they sat in the cruiser soaked to the skin. Tobias turned in the seat and apologized to Hiram. "Sorry you got soaked. Hope you don't get sick."

"Don't worry about me," said Hiram. "I'm just old...not sick. Hell, this is the most fun I've had in years and the day isn't even over yet. Don't forget, you fellas owe me a meal in town."

Tobias addressed Grant as he smiled. "Well, what do you think? Is Mr. Tate deserving of a meal?"

Keeping the information that he had discovered in the tree to himself, Grant replied, "Yeah, I learned quite a bit about the Pender murders today. Let's eat!"

Pulling his wet sweater away from his body, Grant looked out the window as they passed the old Holiness Pentecostal Church. "Think I might come back up here tomorrow. I'd like to take a look at that church, go back to the farm, go in the house and maybe the barn."

Tobias turned the windshield wipers on high as he spoke up, "Count me out. Me and the wife are taking our grandchildren over to Dollywood. You're on your own unless Hiram's up for another trip up here."

"No thanks," said Hiram. "I've had my fill of this Godforsaken place. Until we came up here today I almost forgot how spooky the place really is. It's almost like the devil himself has laid claim to the five hundred acres of the Pender farm. Nope, like the Sheriff said, 'You're on your own.' Besides that, Atlanta plays ball tomorrow afternoon on TV. Can't miss my Braves. If you're smart you'll wait until the Sheriff can come back up here with you. You'd be a fool to come back up here tomorrow by yourself. There's just something strange about this part of the Iron Mountains."

Just as they were passing the locked gate that led to the Pender farm, Hiram leaned up toward the front seat. "Remember what I told you when we first pulled over here? About how the state owned the Pender property. That's another story I'll pitch into the nightmare history of the farm. After the Penders were murdered, I kept track of what happened to the boys. Course, the newspaper could never mention their names since they were minors. First, they stayed with a widow lady in town, since they didn't have any relatives anyone knew of. She died two months later and the boys were sent over to Piney Meadows where they remained for two years until the Pearl family from up in Knoxville adopted them. From what I understand the Pearls were well off so from then on I just figured the boys would be fine. I guess I was still feeling guilty for going off that day and not looking to see if those two boys were all right.

"Then, a few years later a wealthy land developer from New York came down here looking for some property in the area. Ya see, what he wanted to do was the same thing they did over in your neck of the woods, Grant. He figured if they could make a lot of money from the tourist trade over in Pigeon Forge and Gatlinburg then why couldn't they do the same thing over here. The man's name was Chester L. Peabody and he was quite the promoter. He sold his idea to some investors from back east. The only problem he had was he needed someone who was local, someone who knew how things work in this part of the country. So, he hooked up with a young fella by the name of Franklin Barrett from over in Townsend."

Grant had been trying his best to concentrate on his discovery of the tree inscriptions, but it was difficult with Hiram going on and on. The name Barrett caused him to turn in his seat. "You're kidding me! I know Franklin Barrett. He owns a couple of riding stables, some motels and cabins and quite a few other businesses."

Hiram nodded and continued with his story, "Thirty five years ago when Peabody came to Mountain City Barrett wasn't a millionaire. He was just out of college two years, but already making his mark. He was known as a young, aggressive entrepreneur with a bright future ahead of him. Peabody hooks up with him and after explaining his plans, Barrett jumps in feet first seeing what a great moneymaking opportunity it is. The land that Peabody was interested in was a portion of the Pender property. There was and still is a seventy-two acre section about a quarter mile from the farm. It was the only part of the Pender property that was worth developing. It was flat and sat near the top of the mountain. Barrett, after some investigating, found out that after the Penders were murdered the property was deeded to their sons and would remain in a trust for them until it was sold. He and Peabody contacted the Pearls and offered the boys two million for the seventy-two acres. But, Mr. Pearl was smart and said that if they wanted the acreage they had to buy the entire five hundred plus acres. Finally, after some negotiating they settled for 3.6 million for the entire property. At that point I figured those two boys had it made. Never heard anything more about them after that."

Tobias turned onto 421 as Hiram continued, "The next thing you know the Pender farm is alive with construction and for the next three years they bulldozed, cleared trees, ran plumbing and electrical lines, constructed buildings. It was going to be called

Iron Mountain Lodge. Peabody supplied the money via the investors and Barrett was the idea man. Barrett said that since they had to purchase all five hundred acres why not utilize them.

"Besides building a huge lodge that resembled a log cabin they constructed a number of smaller cabins, a dining hall, game room, gift shop and swimming pool, then put in a riding stable with the idea of having hiking and riding trails in the area. And, if that worked out, they were going to put in amusement rides later on. It was a big deal. The news media was always up there reporting on how progress was going and how this new venture was going to create jobs in the area and would bring in a lot of tourists and money. But then, the bottom fell out. Apparently Peabody was a bit of a shyster. Turned out he had problems with the IRS and hadn't paid taxes for a number of years. The IRS stepped in and threw a padlock on the place and temporarily shut down the entire operation. Following an investigation, the project was shut down permanently since Barrett didn't have the funds to continue on his own. He had put every cent he had into the Iron Mountain project. He walked away broke from the whole mess, just glad that he wasn't found guilty of any wrongdoing. But, Peabody wasn't so lucky. The word was he was going to go to prison for income tax evasion."

Pulling into the lot of a local Mountain City restaurant, Grant asked, "So what happened?"

"Well, for starters, Peabody up and disappears. Everyone thought he took off to avoid going to prison. They found him about three weeks later up in the Iron Mountains. He hung himself in the main lodge just inside the front door. They said there wasn't much left of him. The local wildlife had their way with him. Settling back in his seat, Hiram remarked. "So you say this Barrett is a millionaire?"

"Yes, he's quite successful," said Grant.

"Well, then he must've bounced back from the failure of the Iron Mountain deal."

"According to you that was thirty-five years ago. A man with ambitions like Barrett can accomplish a lot in over three decades."

Pulling to a stop in front of the restaurant, Tobias had stepped out of the cruiser and opened the backdoor for their passenger. As Hiram stepped out, Grant asked, "You said something about the state owning the property now. How did that happen if the IRS seized it?"

Leaning up against the cruiser, Hiram explained, "The IRS has no use for property, especially five-hundred acres that are what they consider non-developmental land. A few companies looked at the property, but by the time the IRS decided to sell the land off, which was four years later, no one was interested. The seventy-two acres where the Iron Mountain Lodge was located was rotted out, rust covered and weed infested, not to mention our old friends the snakes who literally took over. So, for the past thirty years the place has turned into a ghost town. No one goes up there anymore. Why you can't even get into the place. When Peabody and Barrett were developing the property they bulldozed all of the trees and vegetation off to the sides of the seventy-two acres, figuring that they would clear it away later. That never happened so now there is an impassable blockade, the perfect area for snakes surrounding the Lodge. Come on, let's eat...I'm starved," said Tobias as he headed for the eatery.

Walking next to Grant he asked, "Hey, you weren't really serious about going back up there tomorrow by yourself, were you?"

"Yes, I am," answered Grant as he recalled the inscriptions in the tree. "I might be on to something here, but I'm not quite sure."

CHAPTER ELEVEN

FRANKLIN BARRETT PUSHED open the door to the Smoky Mountain Brewery and quickly surveyed the room. He stepped toward the reservation desk just as someone tapped him on the shoulder.

"Right on time, Franklin." Merle Pittman extended his hand.

Shaking Merle's hand, Franklin looked at his watch. "Let's get a table. I've only got an hour before I have to be back at my office. I've got a business meeting at one."

The young woman at the desk smiled and asked, "Table for two?"

Franklin, always the comic, looked behind him as he answered, "I don't see anyone else unless you'd like to join us."

"Thanks, but not today," she said jokingly as she picked up two menus and escorted them into the dining room.

Once seated, Franklin quickly scanned the menu, ordered a double-scotch, straight up and a club sandwich. Merle passed on the alcohol, but nodded okay on the club sandwich with an iced tea.

Sipping a glass of ice water, Franklin looked across the table at Merle. "Okay, what did you want to talk with me about that couldn't wait until next week?"

"This may sound a little bizarre to you and it did to me at first," said Merle, "but once I thought about it, I decided to get together and get your opinion. A couple of days ago, I was at Frank's Market and I ran into a couple of the old cronies that my brother, Asa used to hang with. One of them, Buddie Knapp asked me what I thought about the recent murders, as if I had some inside information. I told him his guess was as good as mine. Anyway, Knapp tells me he read an article in the Mountain View paper about a bounty hunter that tracked a fugitive from Idaho all the way to Cherokee. He said the fugitive had been on the run from the law for over seven months and this bounty hunter caught him four days after he got here. Knapp went on to say that if the local police here in Tennessee couldn't catch our murderer then maybe someone ought to think about hiring someone, like a bounty hunter, to come in and help us out. At first, I laughed, but then I really thought about it."

"Are you serious?" asked Franklin.

The waitress was returning with their lunch and Merle remained quiet until she left. "Think about it, Knapp and his friends may just be a bunch of good ol' boys, but they kind of set the tone around here. They know everything that goes on and if they're worried then a lot of other folks are too. Who knows, this new round of murders might just be the straw breaker in our tourist business. Besides that, both you and I are going to lose money this year if they don't catch this killer soon. I've got about two-thousand Pittman-Henks tee shirts stacked away in a storage space and I know you're considering closing one of your riding stables. How is that coming anyways?"

"I just made the decision yesterday. I spent a hell of a lot of money on those wagons for the Pittman-Henks tours and now no one wants to go to the sites. Last year, as you well know, we really raked in the money from the tours. The two stables I own couldn't handle all of the business so I opened a third. Here it is, not even a year later and my new stable is belly up!"

"Well, there you go," remarked Merle, as he took a bite out of his sandwich. "You and I are well aware of the fact there is always money to be made in almost any situation, even the worst situation. We didn't get to where we are in life by waiting for things to happen. You and I are cut from the same bolt of cloth. We make things happen. When we see an opportunity we don't waste a lot of time thinking about it. We have always been men who are willing to take a risk...a calculated risk. Men who venture out onto the edge of the branch where others won't go. Remember, that's where the fruit is...at the end of the branch. Look, maybe we could hire this guy to hunt down our killer. If he caught him it might just make us look pretty good. I can see some profitable business ventures for us as a result of a man that we hire catching the killer." Stabbing a bite of coleslaw, Merle continued, "So, it costs us a few bucks to hire this fellow. The way I see it is things could get a lot worse around here, especially if there are any more murders. What do you think?"

Franklin laid his sandwich down and wiped his mouth with a napkin. "You may be right, but what do we know about this... bounty hunter? I'm not up on the law like you, but I'm pretty sure you can't hire a bounty hunter to go after someone unless they have jumped bail or are wanted by the law. We don't know much at all, if anything about this nut that's killing people in our area. He may or may not be a fugitive."

"I don't know anymore about this bounty hunter than you do, but I do know that most bounty hunters carry a private investigator's license to cover themselves. At this point, we really don't know if our killer is a fugitive or not but we do know that the killer is definitely wanted by the law here in Tennessee. The paper said the bounty hunter was going to be in Cherokee for a few days. There are a couple of tourist traps over there that are going to use him to promote their business. Now look, this guy sounds to me like he's not only an ace at what he does but that he's all about being in the public eye. If he caught our killer and we are the ones who put up the money to hire him, then we could cash in on the publicity. What do you say? Maybe we could take a ride over there and at least talk with him."

Franklin downed the last swallow of his drink. "I guess I could get away for a few hours tomorrow if you can find out where he's staying. Give the man a call and see if he'd be willing to meet with us." Franklin stood. "I have to run. Call me when you find out something." He laid a twenty on the table and left.

Merle ran his finger around the rim of his iced tea glass, took the last gulp, then got up and followed Franklin. Walking to the parking lot he thought to himself, *Franklin's interested. I know him well. If he thinks he can make money he'll bite. Hell, he probably has more money than he knows what to do with, but if he thinks he can make a dollar more he'll at least take a look at investing in this bounty hunter.* Brushing a few specks of dust off the door of his black Mercedes, Merle climbed in and pulled out of the lot.

He had known Franklin and his family most of his life and he understood why Barrett was always successful at making money. He was a self-made millionaire who had amassed a fortune with a small landscaping company he started when he was in his early twenties, fresh out of college. He worked hard and established his company into one of the best-known lawn service companies in Blount County. He began to purchase rental properties and within the next five years turned his efforts into a multi-million dollar business.

Driving toward his office, Merle took his cell phone from his pocket and called his personal secretary. "Gerri, do me a favor. Look up the number for the police department in Cherokee. On second thought, get me the private number of Chief Blue. It should be in my rolodex on my desk."

With Chief Blue's number now in hand, Merle pulled over into a small shopping plaza and dialed the number. It rang twice before there was an answer.

"William Blue."

"Hello Bill, this is Merle Pittman. I need a favor from you. I'm looking for the cell number of that bounty hunter who is over in your neck of the woods. Can you give me his name? I understand he brought a fugitive into your jail two days ago."

There was silence on the other end, then Blue answered in a frustrating tone, "His name is Hawk Caine. I don't have his number and I don't know where he's staying. Anything else I can do for you?"

Merle looked at his cell, then spoke, "That's strange. I was sure you would have all the information on Mr. Caine."

"Well, I don't," Blue answered sharply. "The Feds picked up the prisoner yesterday and took the files with them. That case is closed as far as I'm concerned. Look, I'm really busy now. Try calling the paper. Maybe they can tell you how to find Caine."

Slamming down the phone, Chief Blue rolled his eyes, slung open his office door and walked down the hall to another office where two officers were seated at desks busy working. "Listen up!" ordered Blue in an irritated voice. "We are no longer the answering service for Hawk Caine. If you get a call asking where he can be located, just tell them you have no idea and then hang up."

He no sooner finished speaking when the front door opened and a voice rang out, "Have I got any calls today?"

Chief Blue turned, his fists clenched as he came face to face with Caine. "Listen Caine, you got your man. The FBI took him into custody, so therefore you and I have nothing further to discuss. Just go on and do whatever the hell you do and stay out of my way." *Look at him,* thought the Chief, *he's an idiot! Look at the way he's dressed. Camouflage pants tucked into army boots and that stupid sleeveless shirt and black leather vest. Look at that belt buckle. Must have been an award in one of his past fake wrestling matches. Who wears gloves with no fingers and fringe on them? I wonder how much that Green Beret hat cost him. Look at those stupid hawk feathers he's got sticking out of his hat.*

Hawk Caine approached the Chief as he spoke in his deep voice, "I'm talking to you Blue. Did you hear me?"

"It's Chief Blue to you," said William, "and *no,* I wasn't listening!"

"Well, then let me repeat myself. I said...I'm going to be around the area for a few more days, so if I *do* get any calls you can just forward them to my cell phone number." Turning, he removed one of his business cards from his vest pocket and stuck it up on the hallway bulletin board. Giving everyone in the office a cocky grin, he turned and walked toward the door then stopped, and said, "Have a nice day Chief. If you run across any more Indian fugitives in the area just give me a call." He let out a loud bellow and walked out the door to his truck.

Chief Blue followed him and looked out. The loud, duel five-foot chrome pipes that extended above the cab of the oversized Dodge Ram truck were getting quite a few people's attention. Blue watched as Caine backed the garish red truck out of a tight parking space, then turned and headed out of the lot, the picture of a red tail hawk painted boldly across the polished hood.

Blue returned to his office and sat down at his desk. He had to get hold of himself. He was a professional. Why in the world he let that piece of crap, Hawk Caine rattle him was beyond him. Leaning back in his chair, he closed his eyes as his thoughts returned to a time years ago when he had first heard of Purvis Baskum. The little known bully, Baskum from Great Falls, Montana who had been a scrawny, but tough minded blonde, had morphed himself into Hawk Caine, a muscular black-haired bulk of a man who wore his hair in a long braid down his back. He sported a thick horseshoe mustache and goatee, two earrings in each ear and a large tattoo of a hawk on his right arm. But, even with all of the changes, his new appearance didn't hide the fact that he was a liar and con man who hated Indians. Blue could accept the fact that Caine didn't like Indians, but he didn't have to like it. That was the feeling of a lot of people who lived around the reservation in Great Falls. It was Hawk Caine that made things worse for the Indians he brought to justice. They were his prime targets.

Blue remembered an article in a weekly news magazine ten years back that featured a story about bounty hunters. Of the three bounty hunters who were interviewed Caine was one of them. Caine had stated that the Indians from the reservation were creating most of the crime in Montana and that going after them was, in his vernacular, "Easy pickin's." Blue was furious that the magazine printed the article and even went so far as to write to the editor.

He wasn't surprised when the magazine didn't respond. If any other bounty hunter, other than Hawk Caine, had made the remark in the magazine, he would have just thought he was an idiot and let it go at that. Seeing Hawk's picture along with the article brought back a lot of bad memories.

It was a long time ago, but Blue remembered it like it was yesterday. He was eighteen years old when he opened the mailbox in front of the humble home where he was raised. The letter he had been expecting for weeks finally arrived. Nervously, he tore open the envelope and there inside was his ticket to success. Reading the document he had let out a loud whoop. He had been accepted to the University of Great Falls in Montana. He was going to college, the first one in his family to accomplish such an honor. Billy, even back then realized that very few American Indians were able to go to college. His parents had always been supportive of their son and told him that if he studied hard he could defy the odds and get a college education.

That fall he arrived at the university and found he was assigned to a dorm room with a roommate by the name of John Clearwater, a full-blooded Blackfoot. They had a good laugh about the fact that the dean of admissions had roomed two Indians, even though from different tribes, together.

He and John became the best of friends and after their first year they rented a house off campus along with two other students. John had a younger brother named Cole who would drive up from Cascade City to visit twice a month. Even though Cole was only a junior in high school, he liked to pretend he was one of the college boys.

One particular weekend, Cole arrived displaying a black eye and a deep cut on his right cheek. When John questioned him about what had happened, Cole went on to explain that he had gotten into a scuffle with another boy by the name of Purvis Baskum, a high school dropout, who hung around the school crowd selling pot. Cole said Baskum was always making crude remarks to him about his ethnic background and he finally got tired of it.

When Purvis referred to him as a hatchet carrying redskin and told him to go back to the reservation where his kind belonged, Cole lit into him. According to Cole, Purvis got the worst of it.

Then, two weeks later, John received a late-night call from his father saying Cole had been killed. He was coming home from band practice at school and a car ran him off the road into an embankment. The driver of the other car was none other than

Purvis Baskum. Needless to say, John was devastated at the loss of his younger brother. Billy went home with him for the funeral and they found out the mishap on the road was ruled an accident and Purvis walked away free as a bird.

John decided to take a few weeks off from school to be with his parents, especially his mother who was struggling with the death of her youngest son. John never returned to school. Billy found out that John couldn't get past the injustice of Purvis getting off Scott free and had gone after Baskum, but tragedy struck again. Purvis had John arrested for threatening his life and then the bottom just fell out. John lost his scholarship and his mother died of what most people claim was a broken heart. After that, John changed. He became a recluse, refused food most of the time, became a physical and mental wreck and a year later, despondent, he hung himself in his father's garage.

The name Purvis Baskum became a plague to Chief William Blue. He read about him in the Great Falls Tribune when he joined the marines and then a few years later when he was accepted into the World Wrestling Entertainment Organization where he had changed his name to Hawk Caine. The picture in the paper showed Caine with his booted foot on his opponent's chest. Baskum had changed his name and his appearance, but in Blue's eyes the man was the same underhanded bastard he had always been.

It wasn't until three years passed before Purvis Baskum, aka Hawk Caine, reared his ugly head in Blue's life once again when he came to Cherokee, North Carolina. William had been on the force for almost seven years and had just recently been elected to the position of sheriff in Cherokee. By this time Caine had given up the profession of wrestling and became a bounty hunter.

Blue recalled that day: he had only been at his newly elected position as sheriff for two weeks when a prisoner was ushered into the Cherokee Police Headquarters with a chain around his neck, a bloodied face and practically unable to walk. His captor was none other than Hawk Caine. The prisoner turned out to be a young Crow Indian whose crime was failing to pay an enormous amount of speeding tickets and then refusing to show up at his court date. A warrant was put out on the boy, Caine was called in and he tracked him all the way from Arizona. He claimed the young boy had given him a rough time, hence that's why he had most of his front teeth knocked out and a broken kneecap. Chief Blue asked the boy if what he was being told was the truth. The boy, scared out of his wits simply nodded yes, but Blue knew the beating had not been justified. Now, after all that time, Hawk Caine was back in his jurisdiction, once again testing his patience at the highest level.

Even though Caine made a mockery out of the justice system, he was considered very good at what he did and it seemed like he always had the press or television cameras around to tout his glory when he brought in a fugitive from justice. Chief Blue hoped that after today he'd never see or hear about Hawk Caine again.

Taking Chief Blue's advice, Merle called the editor of the local newspaper who was more than happy to give him Caine's number. He called the number three times over the next hour, each time getting Caine's voice mail at which point he left a message. It was almost five in the afternoon before Merle's secretary advised him that a man by the name of Hawk Caine was on the phone.

Merle picked up the phone and identified himself, "Merle Pittman."

There was a short pause then a gravelly, deep voice, "This is Hawk Caine. You called me three times. I'm busy, so start talking."

Merle hesitated for a moment surprised at how brash the man was. "Ah, yes, Mr. Caine. I understand that you're a bounty hunter. Is this correct?"

"Yeah, so what."

"I'm interested, well one of my business partners and I are interested in talking to you about a matter that is of great importance to this area. I don't suppose you're aware of it, but we have had a series of murders around here, beginning a year ago in the spring. So far, we've had six murders, four last year and two this year."

"Why are you calling me? I assume you hillbillies have police around here. They got any ideas on this killer?"

Realizing from the hillbilly remark Caine made that he was a crass individual, Merle sidestepped the slur on the local population as he answered the question. "Nothing concrete. One of the murders was on federal land so the Feds have been involved working side by side with our local police." Switching directions, Merle stated, "Look, Mr. Caine, I'm sure you're aware that the economy of this part of Tennessee depends on the tourist trade and that's what supports our local towns and communities."

"That a fact," said Caine snidely.

Merle, quite adept at handling people changed his mode from defensive to offensive as he stated strongly, "Perhaps I have been misled in regard to your qualifications, Mr. Caine. I was led to believe that you're the best in your business. Now, if you have reservations about your abilities to handle our killer...our *hillbilly killer,* then maybe I should call someone more qualified to deal with the situation we are faced with—"

Caine was quick to respond as he interrupted Merle, "I am *the best* in the business and I ain't afraid of nobody or nothing. When do you want to meet? I'm on a tight schedule. I gotta be back out west real soon."

"Suppose you come over to my office tomorrow afternoon, let's say one o'clock. I'm located in Gatlinburg."

"Suppose you tell me if it's gonna be worth my while."

"I do believe it will be, Mr. Caine."

"Okay then, give me the address and I'll be there."

Merle gave Caine the address and directions to his office and confirmed the time of their appointment. Hanging up the phone, Merle wondered if he was making a bad decision. Tomorrow Luke, Buddie and Zeb would be at the Parkway Grocery for coffee and local gossip. He'd drop by in the morning and discuss his plans with them. They were right on top of the pulse of what was being said out there in the surrounding area and their opinion and knowledge was important. He thought about calling Franklin and asking him to join them for coffee but decided against it. He would meet with the group alone and then depending on how things went, he'd give Barrett a call.

The next morning Merle Pittman circled the Parkway Grocery lot three times before locating a parking space. Friday was a heavy tourist day with people coming and going to and from the Smokies. The *Hot Coffee and Donuts* sign in the window of the grocery always brought in those who were in a hurry and didn't want to take the time to stop at one of the local restaurants. Today was no exception. Merle stood with the door open letting in four customers before it was his turn to enter. He looked out of place in his blue business suit, cream-colored shirt and grey tie among an array of women in shorts, flip flops and men in jeans, tee shirts and the ever present ball hats.

After purchasing a cup of coffee, Merle sidled down the crowded aisle of the store, until he was able to see the three small booths located in the corner by the front windows. As usual,

Buddie, Luke, and Zeb occupied the last booth. At one time, his brother, Asa had been part of the group along with Charley Droxler.

"Good morning, gentlemen," Merle said, as he raised his cup in a toasting fashion.

"Well, hot damn, if it ain't the fancy pants lawyer from Gatlinburg," said Zeb. "You old son of a gun, what happened? The coffee machine at your fancy office give out?"

Merle put on a smile as he responded, "Actually, if you don't mind, I'd like to join you fellows this morning." Setting his cup down on the table, he reached for the only other empty chair.

"No problem," said Zeb as he motioned toward the chair. Zeb and Asa, Merle's younger deceased brother, had been friends since they were kids. Merle, who had always been a bit of a nerd growing up, always wanted to tag along with them. Asa, despite being younger was a tough little kid and would always chase his older brother down the street throwing rocks at him and yelling at him to go back home. As the years passed, the two brothers took different paths, Asa dropping out of school at the age of sixteen, Merle graduating and going on to law school. Merle, later on became a lawyer and moved to Gatlinburg where he had set up what was to become a highly successful practice. Merle was well known in the surrounding area and his brother, Asa, a local lowlife, was an embarrassment to Merle, who constantly had to bail his brother out of one scrape after another. Zeb often bragged that one of his best friends growing up, Merle Pittman, was a high paid lawyer over in Gatlinburg.

Making himself comfortable at the table, Merle looked across the table at Buddie. "I've been thinking about that article you told me about the other day and I've decided to check into it."

Zeb squinted his eyes, looked at Buddie then back to Merle. "What article?"

Merle answered the question before Buddie could respond. "Buddie told me about an article that appeared in the paper about a bounty hunter named Hawk Caine who apprehended a fugitive from Idaho over in Cherokee. It was quite an impressive feat. The fugitive had been on the run for over seven months and this bounty hunter was able to not only locate him, but bring him to justice in less than a week."

Zeb looked totally confused as he addressed Buddie. "You know this guy...this bounty hunter? You didn't say anything to me about him."

"Look. I just ran into Merle here," said Buddie, "and we got to talking and I guess I was just thinking out loud and I mentioned that maybe we should consider hiring someone like this Caine fella to locate the nut that's been killing folks in the area."

Luke shook his head as he pointed out, "Yup, that's what we need. Some loony running around with a license to haul this guy in…dead or alive. Geez, Buddie, this is the twentieth century…not the old west. Where do you come up with these ideas?"

Merle folded his hands on the table. "I found myself thinking the same way when Buddie first mentioned it, but the more I thought about it, the more it began to make sense. Let me ask you this. How much faith do you boys have that the local police here in the county are going to catch this killer? Myself, well, I'm rapidly becoming less and less confident in Sheriff Grimes and even less confident in Axel Brody. The Feds have even been involved and still we can't find the killer. What next; the National Guard roaming around the Smokies and our towns? That would really do a number on our local tourist business."

"Aw, come on Merle," said Luke. "They ain't gonna bring in no National Guard."

"Not yet, but let's face it. Things are not getting any better. What if this killer becomes more aggressive than he already is and starts killing folks right here in town? There is already talk that the two murders we've had so far this year might be connected to the four from last year. What about this strange guy that's been reported seen in the area? He was hanging around J.J. Pickler's bear and now nobody knows where J.J. is. He was spotted in close proximity to the Mackinaw murder. He might be the killer. Hell, any one of us could have rubbed elbows with this nut and not even know it."

An uncomfortable silence settled in around the table, but then Merle started to talk again. "After I talked with you, Buddie, I contacted Franklin Barrett and he agreed that it might be a good idea. I did a background check on this Hawk Caine and I have to say he has a very impressive record of finding criminals no one else seems to be able to locate. After I finish talking with you fellows I'm going to give Barrett a call and we're going to meet with this Mr. Caine at one o'clock at my office. Depending on how the conversation goes, Barrett and I just might put up the cash to hire this Caine to catch our killer." Not waiting for their reaction, Merle emphasized, "I would think that after two of your friends were killed, one which just so happens to have been my brother, that you would be happy to see this maniac behind bars."

"Well damn!" said Luke. "When you put it that way it don't sound half bad. I've been sleeping with a gun under my pillow for over a year. First time in my life I haven't felt safe living here in Townsend. I even thought about moving, but I've lived here all my life and wouldn't know where else to go."

Twirling his cup of coffee in his hands, Zeb asked, "You asking us to put up money to hire this bounty hunter?"

"Not at all," said Merle. "All Barrett and I want is your support, especially when the news hits the paper. If we do hire Caine, and the news gets out that a bounty hunter is in town, the rumors will be flying. If people ask you anything about it, and they will, I need you boys to tell folks you support Caine being here, that you think it's a good idea. I need you to spread the word, but not until after I talk with Caine and it's a done deal. Right now, it's just on the table. A decision hasn't been made if we're going to hire Caine nor has he accepted. You three have a lot of friends not only here in town, but throughout the county. If people know you three are on board then a lot of people will be more willing to go along with the plan."

Luke seemed relieved, realizing that he didn't have to contribute. "Sounds good to me. I'm in. Just let me know what you and Barrett decide."

Merle slid away from the table and stood. "Thanks for your time gentlemen. Have a good day. I'm counting on your support."

Dropping a five-dollar bill on the table, he offered, "Next round of coffee is on me and thanks for being such a good friend to my brother."

As Merle walked away from the table, Zeb scooped up the five. "Do you guys buy any of that? Hell, you know damn well Pittman doesn't give a crap over who might get whacked next. And, as far as his brother, Asa goes, they didn't get along all that well. Something smells fishy. I bet ya this is just another one of his and Barrett's moneymaking schemes. But, kind of makes me feel important that Merle thinks we carry some weight in this town. Yep, I reckon we are sort of important."

That afternoon, Hawk Caine did not arrive at Merle Pittman's office until almost one thirty. Franklin Barrett had just given Merle a lesson on punctuality and was ready to leave, when Gerri, Pittman's secretary, opened the door and said that a Mr. Caine was in the outer office.

"Send him in," Merle said.

When Hawk walked into the office, the look on Franklin's face was priceless. His jaw dropped open and he looked as if he had seen his worst nightmare.

"Sorry, I'm late," said Caine. "This is a damn hard place to get to this time of the day. Damn cars everywhere. People gawking out their windows like they ain't never been out of the turnip patch." He plopped down in a chair opposite Franklin, the chains hanging from his pants rattling like Halloween fright night.

"Let me introduce myself," said Merle. "I'm Merle Pittman and this gentleman is Franklin Barrett."

Caine nodded. "The clock's ticking. What's on your mind?"

Right from the start, Merle could sense that Caine was not going to be easy to communicate with. "Well, first of all, let me say that I have done a background check on you and find you are quite astute at what you do. In the past fifteen years, you have helped to place twenty-seven criminals back where they belong. I also noticed that you were arrested three times yourself, but never convicted."

"That's right," said Caine as he leaned forward. "You seem to know more about me than most folks do. Those three arrests were piddly-assed things. In my business, at times you have to break the law...ya know, bend the rules a bit in order to catch those bastards." He tapped the end of his finger on top of Merle's desk. "Now, let me tell *you* a thing or two. I don't do drugs, I've got a keen eye and one hell of a temper. I'm a crack shot and have the nose of a bloodhound. You turn me loose on somebody's trail and I guarantee you, I'll catch the creep." He sat back in the chair. "Criminals get careless and sooner or later they mess up and that's when I'm on them. Now, let's get down to business. Who do you want me to nab?"

Merle cleared his throat. "Mr. Caine, we are faced with a serious state of affairs here in this part of the state, especially over in Townsend. We are quite anxious to locate someone who can bring it all to an end." For the next fifteen minutes Merle explained the situation starting with the murder of his own brother the previous April and ending up with the recent murder of Bock.

Caine didn't seem fazed by what he was being told and when Merle finished he commented confidently, "Yeah, I'd say it's about time someone got off the pot and caught this killer. Give me...two months. It'll cost you fifty thousand dollars, half up front, the remainder when I hand him over to the law. Plus, you pay all of my expenses; room, food and whatever else it takes to keep me happy while I'm searching for your killer."

Franklin had remained quiet, but finally spoke up, "Fifty thousand. That seems awfully steep."

Caine stood up. "Take it or leave it. Tracking a person down doesn't come cheap. In this case a killer. What you don't seem to understand is that I'm putting my life on the line. Don't try to con an old con. I know that you two *businessmen* are not doing this out of the kindness of your hearts. I know you have an ulterior motive. I don't care about that. Just pay me the cash. I'll get the job done."

Walking toward the door, Caine spoke back over his shoulder. "I'm going to drive back over to Cherokee. You have my number. When you make a decision…let me know."

Franklin began to regain his composure. "Hold on, Mr. Caine. I'd like to ask you some questions."

Caine turned as he reached for the doorknob. "I ain't up for no questions. When we have a signed contract then I'll answer any questions you have. You know my qualifications and the price tag."

Franklin stood. "At least let me ask you one question. Is it necessary for you to dress in such a garish manner?"

Hawk let out a laugh. "Ain't sure what that word means, but I happen to like the way I look and I don't think your killer will give a damn what I'm wearing or what I look like when I tie his ass to a tree." With that remark, he left the office.

After the door was closed, Franklin walked to the window. "So this is the man you want me to give twenty-five thousand dollars to? He's a joke, Merle. I think I'll pass and keep my money."

"That's your decision," said Merle, "but for my part I think he can get the job done. Sure, he's loud and dresses to make people notice him. He loves the limelight and what better praise could he get than that of catching a killer. I am prepared to make him a very lucrative offer and if he accepts it, then we'll both know he's our man."

Franklin leaned on the window sill. "I'm still listening."

Picking up the interoffice phone, Merle ordered his secretary, "Gerri, would you please run out to the lot and tell Mr. Caine that we are ready to make him an offer."

Two minutes later, Hawk Caine came back into the office, sat in the same chair and crossed his legs. "What's it gonna be, boys?"

"All right, Mr. Caine," said Merle, "here's the deal we're proposing. We'll give you two months to catch the killer. If you find him and bring him in we'll give you a cashier's check for fifty thousand, plus your expenses. But, if you don't produce this culprit, then we don't owe you a cent, not even your expenses. Also, during the time you're working for us you'll be referred to as Hawk Caine, Private Detective. I assume you have a current up to date P.I. license?"

Hawk ran his fingers over his mustache. "Fair enough, but with some minor changes. First off, I say when the two months start. I'll have to spend some time doing research on the killer and his victims. When I'm ready to start tracking the killer, I'll let you know. Second, you'll pay my expenses as I go. If I don't bring your man in you keep your fifty grand. Third, I do have a P.I. license and can act as a private detective. As far as how I'm referred to, you can't hide the fact that I'm a man who tracks criminals down, so you can call me anything you want, the fact still remains…I am a bounty hunter."

Merle looked at Franklin for his approval. "Do we have a deal, Franklin?"

Barrett nodded his head.

"Okay then, Mr. Caine. We have a deal," said Merle. "Tell you what. Why don't you go grab some lunch and I'll have my secretary draw up the contract." Looking at a clock on the wall, Merle confirmed. "Let's say you drop back by here at three. We'll seal the deal then you can get to work on your research and we'll wait for your call when you're ready to start the two months."

Caine smiled, stood and shook both of their hands. "I'll be back at three then."

As Caine left the office, Franklin sat on the edge of the desk. "How long do you think it'll take before the news is aware that we're hiring Hawk Caine, the bounty hunter?"

Merle smiled. "Probably about as long as it takes him to get to his cell phone. Get ready Franklin. The limelight is not only about to shine on Mr. Caine, but you and I as well."

CHAPTER TWELVE

THE PASTOR OF THE Mountain City United Methodist Church looked out over the early morning congregation, blessed everyone and then told them to go in peace. Out in the gathering area, Grant stood in line and eventually shook the pastor's hand. He commented that he had never seen Grant in church before. Grant explained that he was in town on business and was a regular member of the United Methodist Church over in Townsend, which the pastor responded to by telling him he was welcome anytime he was in town.

Walking to his Jeep, Grant glanced up at the sky. The weather channel had forecast a cloudy day with the possibility of scattered showers. The dreary sky indicated that the weathermen had hit it right on the mark. The endless grey clouds swallowed up the blue sky and a stiff wind was blowing across the church parking lot.

Climbing into the Jeep, he looked at his watch: 9:27 a.m. He double-checked to make sure he was prepared for his return trip to the Pender farm. He took out his revolver from the console and checked to make sure he had a full load. As he looked up, he noticed two older ladies who were getting ready to get in the car next to him. They both stood next to the door as they stared into the Jeep watching the new visitor to their church fiddling with a gun. Grant, seeing the look of concern and amazement on their faces, rolled down the window as he put the revolver back in the console. He reassured them, "It's all right. I'm a police officer from over in Townsend."

The women looked at each other in confusion and Grant decided it was best if he just pulled out. Any further explanation would only make things worse than they appeared. Turning the ignition key, he smiled at the ladies, rolled up the window and pulled out of the lot leaving them standing there no doubt wondering what they had just witnessed. *Oh well,* thought Grant, *It'll give them something to talk about next week in church; the man they had never seen before in church had a gun in his car.*

Just two blocks down the street, he pulled up next to the drive-thru of a restaurant and ordered a sausage biscuit and a small coffee. Parking in the corner of the lot, eating his breakfast, he laid his revolver on the seat and took out the two extra clips he brought. He also removed a flashlight and a Swiss army knife. Moving his jacket from the passenger seat, he checked to see if his camera, extra film and blue notepad were still there.

It was turning out to be a more expensive trip than he had anticipated. He estimated it would take at least a tank of gas, plus the cost of a motel room since he decided to stay overnight. There would also be the cost of a couple of meals. The previous night, after checking in at the Americourt Hotel in Mountain City, he spent $80.00 at a local sporting goods store. He decided at the last minute that the clothes he was wearing were not really suitable for tramping around in the woods. He purchased waterproof, heavy duty hiking boots, double stitched work jeans, a long sleeved flannel shirt, gloves and a baseball hat with the name of the local high school football team. On his way out of the store he spotted a snakebite kit as he grabbed batteries for his flashlight. He recalled an article he had read sometime in the past about snakebite kits and how they were somewhat difficult to use and not really all that effective, but at this point any added protection made him feel more secure.

The previous night he also stopped at a local Quick Stop and grabbed a six pack of bottled water, three candy bars, a large bag of chips and some beef jerky. Pulling out of the lot, he smiled to himself as he said aloud, "Iron Mountains, here I come!"

The previous night after checking into the hotel, he called Dana Beth to tell her he was staying overnight. He wanted to make sure she was feeling okay.

Making a right hand turn from 421, he started his journey into the mountains as he contemplated what he wanted to accomplish by returning to the scene of the forty-year-old crime. His primary reason for returning was to climb the tree again and examine the inscriptions since he had been interrupted on his first trip up the tree by Tate and Reichenbaugh. He decided he was also going to check out the Pentecostal Holiness Church, the old Pender house and the barn. He wasn't sure what he expected to discover—maybe nothing.

He still had hopes that Adele would come up with the old newspaper articles that would identify the two brothers, but he had his doubts. Hiram said his memory was sharp as a tack and he recalled what the articles said as he followed what happened to the boys after the murders up until they were adopted by the Pearl family. If their names were mentioned then why hadn't he remembered them? Adele and her efforts seemed to be his last hope unless he found something up at the farm. Maybe there would be some old documents or even a scrap of paper in the house that had been overlooked by the authorities, something that would identify Conrad's brother by name.

Following Hiram's previous directions up into the mountains, he opened a bottle of water and looked out at the passing forest and cliffs that occasionally lined the two-lane road at times. A doe ran across the road in front of him. Startled, he had to brake for an instant as the deer disappeared safely into the thick pines. Only one car had passed him since he entered the mountains. He thought about what could happen to someone if you got lost up in the mountains. He had charged his cell phone up over night. The phone might be his only contact with the outside world. Hell, he didn't even know if there was any reception in the Iron Mountains. Back in the Smokies he remembered times when he was in the mountains and the reception had been great while at other times it was non-existent.

Twenty minutes later, he pulled across the road from the main entrance leading to the Pender farm. Getting out of the Jeep, he walked across the road to the padlocked, rusted chain link gate. On the other side of the fencing, the dirt road was barely distinguishable. It was completely grown over with weeds and underbrush, the trees on either side hid the road from sight less than forty yards in the distance. He snapped a picture of the road and then stepped back and got a shot of the gate. Back in the Jeep he made a few quick notes in the notebook then headed for his next destination; the Holiness Pentecostal Church or what was left of it. It was only a couple of hundred yards up the road around the next curve.

In less than two minutes, he rounded the curve and the vine covered cinderblock structure came into view. Pulling off to the side of the road, he leaned out the window and snapped a picture of the old church, which didn't look anything like a church: no steeple, no stained glass windows, no cross of any sort or sign that indicated that it had been a functioning church at one time. It was a small building, maybe twenty by thirty feet with a slightly pitched rusted metal roof. Placing his revolver in his belt, he put a clip in his jeans pocket along with his Swiss army knife, grabbed the flashlight, hung the camera around his neck and started across a weed infested dirt lot.

Halfway across the lot, he stopped as he watched a large bird of prey glide over the top of the trees, circle around then disappear in the forest. He drew in a deep breath of mountain air as he listened to the different sounds of the birds and the wind as it blew through the pines. He always enjoyed the peacefulness of the mountains, but the air seemed heavy today and a bank of dark clouds was forming in the sky to the west. Just as he was about to take his next step, he heard a familiar sound, but not one he expected to hear in the middle of the forest: the sound of an engine; maybe a car being started.

Before he could even think about where the sound was coming from, a pickup nosed its way along the side of the church. Grant instantly identified the truck as the same one he had seen at Dave's 421 and at the abandoned church yesterday. The driver of the greenish-brown truck leaned toward the passenger window as he peered out at Grant. It was the same man he had seen before, the one with the red hat. The grey sky and the dark interior of the inside of the cab prevented Grant from clearly seeing the man's face, which appeared as an opaque shadow. The man continued to stare at Grant as the truck slowly headed for the road. Grant realized he was out in the open with no protection—protection from what he wasn't sure. It was just strange the way the driver stared at him as if Grant was trespassing or interrupting whatever the man had been doing.

Placing his hand on the revolver in his belt, with his free hand, he raised the camera and took a picture of the driver and the truck. The driver floored the gas pedal, the truck tires sending dirt and cinders back toward the church as he turned onto the road. With his eyes still fixed on Grant, he sped around the corner in the direction Grant had come from. Grant snapped off another shot hoping that he got the plate number.

For the next few moments, Grant looked up the road then back at the church undecided about if he should spend time looking around the old church or just leave. On one hand he was armed and could certainly defend himself if the man returned. What if the man was not alone and there were others hiding in the brush just waiting to get a clear shot at him? He was letting his imagination get the best of him. Checking the road once again, he moved toward the old church. As he approached the grey, weathered building he pulled the gun from his belt.

Walking around to the side of the church, which is where the entrance to the building was located, he saw a rotted wood door hanging by a single hinge. The open door did not seem very inviting. There were two windows where the glass had been broken out. Looking in one of the windows the interior was completely dark. The cloudy day was not allowing much light inside the building. Removing his flashlight from his pocket, he flipped it on and shined it inside the doorway. The church was a one-room structure, four old rotted pews; one with the legs completely missing occupied the center of the room. A small wooden podium was leaning up against the far wall and there were a number of old whiskey bottles and beer cans scattered around the floor.

Turning the light toward the ceiling, he saw a movement off to the left in the corner. Startled, he thought that it might have been a snake. The building was a perfect place to harbor all kind of critters from possums to bats. It was at that moment he decided not to enter the building. He took two pictures of the inside then stepped back and took a photograph of the front door and windows.

He walked completely around the building and at the back noticed tire marks in the mud along with boot prints from the recent rain. Thinking that they might be from the pickup truck and the man with the red hat, he took a picture of each then walked back to the Jeep and made a few more notes. Feeling hungry from the sparse breakfast he had eaten, his stomach growled. Unwrapping one of the candy bars, he pulled out and headed for the back entrance to the Pender farm.

Grant parked in the same spot where Reichenbaugh had parked the cruiser. Grant stepped out and made sure he had everything he needed for the final part of his venture. Placing fresh batteries in his flashlight, just for safe measure, he took a mental inventory: gun, extra clips, knife, flashlight, notebook and pen, camera and cell phone. He considered taking the snakebite kit along but it was going to be awkward to carry. If he was bitten it wasn't that far of a walk back to the Jeep.

He locked the Jeep and started up the road, but then stopped as he thought about the strange man in the pickup truck. What if he followed him and broke into the Jeep or slashed the tires while he was at the farm? Smiling to himself, he realized his imagination was running away with him again, causing him to think about what might happen. He recalled something one of his professors had taught him in school. Most of the things that come into our imagination are actually never going to happen. Deal with the situation at hand rather than what you think might happen. He imagined if the man in the truck lived in the area he could just simply have been concerned about what Grant was up to. He let out a long sigh and decided he needed to calm down and get on with his business.

Arriving at the approximate area where Hiram had led Reichenbaugh and him through the thick underbrush to the clearing, he searched the surrounding area for a stick he could use to beat the brush as he walked along. Locating a suitable stick, he also picked up three large rocks and tossed them into the weeds in front of him, following Hiram's instructions about warning any snakes that you were nearby. With his revolver in one hand and the stick in the other, he entered the thick bramble, still beating at the weeds. As he moved forward he remembered what Hiram had told him and Tobias. If anything, don't try to be quiet. Beating the weeds and stomping his feet, he yelled into the woods as if he were on a trail drive, "Yah, yah, go on snakes git!" He felt ridiculous at the moment but if ridiculous action prevented him from being bit then so be it.

Minutes later, he stepped into the clearing. Leaning his stick up against the fence that marked the edge of the old Pender property, he raised the camera and took a shot of the school bus where Jack Diemler had been murdered. Next, he took a photo of the tree where the boys had been when they first heard the hunters approaching the property.

Climbing the tree seemed easier than his first time. He sat with his back leaning up against two boards that were nailed to a large branch and surveyed the surrounding landscape. From up in the tree he could see the entire clearing, the Pender house and part of the barn, which was just up the hill.

His main reason for climbing the tree had been the inscriptions. He took a photo of the carved initials. He climbed back down the tree and started up the fence line. According to what Hiram had said, the boys must have climbed down and run up to the next clearing where they were waiting in another tree as the men approached. As he walked along, Hiram had said the boys reported the men as being drunk and they had overheard them complaining about how the day was going: rain and sleet, they hadn't even seen a single deer or fired their guns one time. Possibly, they had taken out their frustrations on the school bus. At the second clearing where the murders had actually taken place, Grant took photos of the second tree the boys climbed, the broken down pen where the fawns had been kept, the pen where the horse had been shot and the area where Pender and his wife and three dogs went down.

Laying the flashlight on the ground, he placed his foot on a knot as he reached for the lowest branch and started up the tree. Arriving at the spot where he thought the boys had been, he got an even better view of the house and the barn. Grant took a number of shots then leaned back and searched the tree and the old boards for any more inscriptions, but there were none. He sat for a moment surveying his surroundings. It started to rain, but from the looks of the rapidly moving clouds it was just a passing storm.

It wasn't quite as easy climbing the hill as it had been the previous day. The ground was still muddy from yesterday's rain and the wet weeds and branches grabbed at his clothing. Passing the area where the horse had been killed, he stopped and looked back down the hill and tried to envision what Pender saw as he ran from the house. The boys reported their father fired twice, wounding one of the hunters in the arm and another in the leg, but he had been cut down before he could reload. When their mother came running, she was also shot to death. Starting up the hill once again, he thought that all of the information he had learned was getting him no closer to discovering the identity of Conrad's younger brother.

Just as he got to the top of the hill and stepped onto the road that led to the house, the sun was starting to break through the clouds. Making his way to the front porch, he stopped and surveyed the old structure. A home at one time, it was now nothing more than a weathered shell that looked like it was about to keel over any second. Even though the front steps looked sound, on the third and top step the rotted wood gave way, his right foot and lower right leg broke through to the ground below. Taken completely by surprise, Grant just stood there for a moment, then quickly pulled his leg out from the tangle of vines that were growing through the boards. A sudden movement in a patch of tall grass let him know that snakes *or something* was indeed living under the porch.

Retreating to the front yard, he examined his right boot and pant leg. Grant took a deep breath. At the moment, he felt fine. He made the decision to continue on, but more carefully. If he started to feel sick, he'd head back to his Jeep.

As he started up the steps again, he carefully tested each step to make sure the wood beneath him would hold his weight.

Cautiously crossing the slatted porch, he looked in the opening where the front door to the house had been located. Taking two careful steps into the old house, he withdrew his revolver and placed the flashlight in his back pocket. There was plenty of light in the house. The back half of the roof had collapsed allowing the light to flood the interior. The room he was standing in was large with high walls that were practically covered with vines, mold and countless cobwebs. There was an old mirror frame hanging on the far wall with most of the glass broken out and scattered on the dirty floor. There was also a table with one of its legs missing and a single chair lay on its side. Just like back at the church, there were numerous whiskey bottles and cans strewn around on the floor.

Walking to his left, he peered into another room. There was an old rusted bed frame, a smashed nightstand and a broken table lamp. The walls were moldy and stained from the weather of the past forty years. An ugly looking spider moved quickly up a large web. Raising the camera he took a picture of the room, backed out and took two photos of what he thought was the living room.

Making his way ever so slowly across the room, he entered the kitchen. The cabinets had fallen to the floor and were in various stages of deterioration. The sink was still attached to the wall, but hanging at an angle. An ugly design of ripped and stained linoleum partially covered the floor.

Entering another room, he checked what remained of the walls to see if perhaps he could find some writing or carving. There was nothing. Just as he snapped a photo of the room an eerie feeling came over him. He could almost sense someone watching him. He turned quickly and walked carefully toward the open window. At the window, he looked out to the left then the right and out across the open field. There was no one in sight, but the strange feeling remained.

In the hallway there was a steep, narrow staircase leading to the second floor. The rumble of distant thunder sounded as he placed his foot on the first step. He removed the flashlight from his back pocket and shined it up the dark stairs. A bat fluttered past his head and out the back of the building. Startled, Grant regained his composure as he started up the stairs again. An empty picture frame hung sideways by a rusted nail, the shredded remains of a throw rug was scattered across the top step. He carefully ascended the stairs, holding onto the wall for support. Three steps from the top, he stopped when he heard a cracking sound. He could barely see the floor of the room above him. When the cracking noise stopped, he breathed a sigh of relief and placed his foot on the next step, but then as if the stairs had said "The hell with it," the rotted wood gave way to four decades of weather and termites. The entire stairwell fell to the ground. The steps along with Grant crashed down onto the flooring below in a cloud of old wood dust and splinters.

Stunned by the fall, he sat up and tried to regain his bearings. His gun was still in his right hand, but he had dropped the flashlight, which was still on, shining into the darkness of the moist ground beneath the house. He had fallen completely though the flooring. The natural light shined down through the hole he had made in the floor. Reaching for the flashlight, he scanned it around in front of where he was laying. Everywhere he looked, he could see nothing but damp dirt and rocks. Then he saw a movement. He wasn't going to lay there and try to figure out what it was that moved. He was beneath the house. *Snakes,* he thought as he quickly stood up and crawled back up into the kitchen.

Sitting safely on the floor, he examined himself for any signs of blood. He stood up, feeling a shot of pain race up his back and he noticed an abrasion on his right hand. Coughing, he waved away the lingering wood dust from his face while walking to the back of the house and looking out across an open field. The rain was just starting.

He walked across the back porch and held onto the back wall of the old house, stepping down off the rotted steps into the side yard. A sudden strong gust of wind whipped across a field behind the house causing a hanging, rusted gutter to clatter against the side of the old wood. Twenty yards away stood the barn, which was surprisingly in better shape than the house. The wind and rain beat at the barn, a loft door high up on the side of the structure banged back and forth. The wind picked up small dead branches and weeds blowing them across the side yard.

Approaching the open barn doors, he heard a crash. He turned and looked back at the house where the collapse of the stairway had weakened the back wall. A cloud of wood dust quickly disappeared from the wind and the rain.

Standing directly in front of the barn, Grant realized how lucky he had been when the stairs had fallen, since he had escaped without any broken bones. Aside from a few sporadic holes in the roof that allowed beams of daylight to filter down into the barn, the interior was dark and musty. Flipping on the flashlight, Grant withdrew his revolver and entered. A number of birds fluttered and flew through the roof openings. He could hear the buzz of insects flying around his face as he brushed away a mural of cobwebs. Just as in the house, green vines covered the barn walls and a number of local critters had taken up residence in the barn. Startled at his sudden appearance, three possums and a raccoon darted through holes in the walls. A rusty pitchfork and shovel lay next to an old tractor. There was still a faint smell of hay inside the structure, but not a single straw was evident. The dirt floor was covered in spots by shade loving weeds. A ladder that at one time had led up to the loft was broken and laid in a pile of rotted wood on the dirt. Three birds, obviously not concerned about his presence, perched high up in the loft as they stared down at the intruder.

Grant began to shine the light across the floor, as he searched for the trapdoor Hiram said led down to the root cellar and a sub root cellar. Recalling what Hiram had told Tobias and him, the trapdoor was beneath bales of hay. Walking the perimeter of the barn, he shined the light on the floor, but found no indication of a trapdoor. Circling the entire interior and finding nothing, he thought that maybe he had walked right over the door. He had been searching for a handle of some sort. The door might be concealed and had to be pried open. Common sense dictated that the root cellar was probably located near the center of the barn.

But then again, maybe Millard Pender did the opposite of what was considered common to avoid the cellar being found by the authorities. Kicking an old beer can to the side; Grant thought how stupid he had been for not asking Hiram where the door was located.

Walking to the center of the barn, he continued to look for the door. After a few minutes, he kicked at some low weeds. He stubbed his foot on something on the floor and nearly fell. Shining the light in the area where he had tripped, he saw it; a low, four inch section of thick wire rope. He bent down and placed the gun back in his belt. He hesitated before pulling on the handle. *Be careful—snakes!*

He tugged on the handle, the heavy wooden two by three foot door slowly began to open. When he had raised the door two feet, he dropped it back into place, a thud resounding through the barn, ample warning for the snakes. Raising the door a second time, he shined the light into the darkness below. A ladder constructed of metal rebar led down eight foot into the cellar. Laying the trapdoor over to its side, he examined the root cellar below before climbing down. The thin beam of light illuminated the five by five foot dirt chamber. The dirt walls were supported by timbers; thick four by fours every couple of feet that supported wooden headers.

Standing on the damp ground, he inspected one of the upright timbers. They looked like they were constructed of treated lumber and still, after all these years, appeared to have held up well. On the three walls surrounding the laddered wall there were wooden shelves that housed a number of dusty and mold covered glass jars. Taking one of the jars down from the shelf, he wiped away the dust only to discover that he was looking at a mason jar of peaches. Hiram had said the sub root cellar was beneath the regular root cellar and that's where Pender kept a safe and his moonshine. Shining the light back and forth across the dirt floor, Grant searched for another trapdoor, but once again, there was no handle. That made sense. Hiram said that the authorities had been down in the regular root cellar on one of their unannounced visits. They failed to locate the sub root cellar. All they found were canned goods, just like he had. Reviewing what Hiram told him, they had laughed as the Feds stood directly over the top of gallons of homemade brew and never knew it. The sub cellar was just beneath where he was standing; all he had to do was locate the hidden trapdoor. Pushing dirt back and forth with his foot, he discovered a small section of wood that had warped upward. Bending down he tried to open the door, but it was too heavy. He needed something to pry the door open. He remembered the pitchfork he had seen in the barn.

In less than a minute's time, he climbed back up to the barn, retrieved the old pitchfork and returned to the root cellar. The rain was beating on the rusted metal roofing as he inserted the edge of the pitchfork at the corner of the wooden door. He pushed down on the old handle, and it gave way and broke. Using the broken handle as a fulcrum, he forced the rusted metal prongs farther under the edge of the wood and stepped on the handle. When the edge opened a few inches, he stuck the broken end of the pitchfork in the wood, bent down and opened the door. The heavy door slipped from his hand and slammed into the dirt wall, three of the door slates broke loose and fell down into the small room below.

Circles of light moved across the dirt as he aimed the flashlight down into the sub room. Climbing down yet another metal ladder, he found the room was larger by about two feet and contained floor to ceiling wood shelves. There were three one-gallon jugs covered with dust on the top shelf of the back wall. He turned his attention to a wall safe that had been imbedded into the dirt wall and framed with lumber. He remembered what Hiram had told him about how he would, three times a week visit the Pender farm, go down into the sub cellar, place the collected money from the previous deliveries in the safe, take his pay for the next deliveries and customer list from the safe, load up and be on his way.

Shining the light around the small chamber, he thought it was amazing that he might just be the first one to climb down into the cellar in forty years.

Looking around the confines of the sub root cellar one last time to see if he had overlooked anything of interest, he started back up the ladder when suddenly, something heavy fell on his arm then dropped to the floor below. Before Grant could determine what hit his arm a second heavy object bounced off of his right shoulder. Shining the light back down into the black abyss, he saw two large dark colored snakes on the floor. He heard the dreaded sound of Timber Rattlers as they coiled into a defensive mode. One of the snakes lunged at him, but he was just out of reach on the ladder. He heard footsteps, "Hey," he yelled, but the trapdoor was slammed shut followed by the sounds of something heavy being placed over the door. Glancing back down the ladder, he saw one of the snakes winding itself around the third rung as it began its slow climb out of the cellar. The snakes were obviously pissed because they had been dropped nearly eight feet. He wasn't sure whether they were climbing the ladder to get to him or using it as a means of escape. Either way, it didn't make any difference. He was in their path and the one thing he was sure of was they were not just going to crawl past him completely ignoring his presence.

Reaching up, he began to pull himself up into the first root cellar, but felt a sharp pain in his wrist. Jerking his arm back, he fell back down the ladder, his flashlight falling down into the cellar. "Damn it," he cursed, just as a something moved by the opening. "I've been bit!"

The flashlight landed on the dirt below, its light shining on one of the snakes coiled in the corner, the other still hanging on the rung of the ladder. Grant took a deep breath as he tried to relax, despite the throbbing pain in his wrist. He tried to calm himself as he thought about his situation. He needed to climb back down and get his flashlight, but his two venomous friends below ruled that out. Hanging onto the ladder, he pulled his cell from his pocket and flipped it open. The dim light on the face would allow him to see at least a portion of the cellar above as he climbed up the ladder. Hoping to scare any snakes that might be above him, he banged the barrel of his revolver on the metal rungs. Looking up into the semi-darkness, he yelled, "Go on...git! Get out of here!"

He propped himself on the rim of the opening to the upper root cellar and carefully peered over the edge, moving the cell phone light from the right to the left. He saw a snake cowering in the corner and another was trying it's best to climb up the dirt wall.

He quickly looked down below. One of the snakes was now on the fourth rung, the other at the bottom of the ladder. What was it that Hiram had said? Fifteen to twenty minutes for the average size person to begin to feel the effects of a snake bite. He had to take control of the situation. He just couldn't hang on the ladder and wait to die. He didn't have a lot of time to think.

Shining the cell light on the coiled snake, he aimed his revolver and fired, the bullet ripping into the flesh of the snake's neck, its body slamming up against the dirt wall. Focused on the second snake, Grant quickly turned; concerned that it would react to the loud noise by striking out at him. The loud sound of the revolver being fired in such a small space had startled the snake as it crawled across the back of the wall. Grant fired quickly, but missed. Lining up a second shot at the snake's head he took a deep breath then fired again. The snake went into a curled position then died instantly.

Grant turned his attention to the two rattlers below him as he climbed down two rungs and shot the snake on the bottom of the ladder. The remaining snake cowered in the corner and Grant made quick work of it as he fired once again. Hesitating for a moment to make sure that both rattlers were indeed dead, he glanced back up at the closed trapdoor, small pebbles of dirt falling on his head.

Climbing down into the bottom cellar, he retrieved his flashlight then climbed back up, all the while realizing that he was not exactly remaining calm which was no doubt causing any venom in his wrist area to travel quicker through his system.

Sitting on the floor, he tried to relax for a few moments as he considered the predicament he was in and his options. Flipping open his cell phone again, he read the message displayed on the white screen: NO SERVICE. He closed his phone and he put it back inside his pocket. Shining the flashlight up at the bottom of the trapdoor he realized that whoever it was that threw the snakes down on him and closed the trap door intended for him to die. Why would that person try to kill him with snakes? The person could have simply just shot him or barricaded the door. Whoever it was, they might be waiting for him to open the door and then kill him. He opened the chamber of his revolver and removed the clip, which contained the single shell that was left. He placed it in his pocket and reloaded a new clip into the gun.

Spinning the chamber of his revolver, he leaned the flashlight in a position so it shined upwards on the bottom of the door. He aimed the revolver straight at the door and started up the ladder. He remembered how heavy the door was and the effort it would take to shove it open would give his unknown assailant time to club him over the head or shoot him. That was the chance he was going to have to take. His only other option was to stay down in the cellar and eventually die from the snakebite. If he did manage to escape from the cellar, he was going to have to get back to town immediately and go directly to the emergency room.

Placing his hand on the bottom of the wooden door, he thought about the fact that he had already wasted nearly five minutes since he had been bitten. His wrist was throbbing and a trickle of blood was beginning to seep through his shirtsleeve. He pushed on the door and it wouldn't budge. Taking a deep breath, he pushed again, but with more force. The door still didn't move. Whatever was placed over the door was holding it down. Looking back down below, he saw the rotted wood slats that had fallen from the sub cellar door. Maybe the wood on the door above was rotten as well. Placing his revolver in his belt, he removed his knife from his pocket, opened it to the screwdriver attachment and began poking at the bottom of the wood slats. The wood chipped away easily, dirt and small splinters of wood falling on his arms and shoulders. Giving up, he finally realized he really didn't have the time and could not exert the energy required due to the snakebite, to keep hacking away at the door. He needed to do something drastic *and quick!*

Climbing back down the ladder he shook his head at his own stupidity. Hiram and Reichenbaugh had both warned him about coming back up here alone. It was too dangerous. Leaning against one of the wood uprights, he looked around the small area and got an idea. If he could tear one of the uprights from the wall, providing the whole floor above didn't cave in and bury him, he might be able to use the timber as a battering ram. Sticking the knife in one of the timbers, he tugged at the wooden support, but it was deeply imbedded into the dirt wall. He stepped back and tripped over the metal ladder, which moved. It was then that he realized that the ladder was not secured. He stood the ladder up straight, estimating he had maybe a two-foot leeway he could utilize to gain momentum. He straddled the open door to the bottom cellar and positioned the ladder over the opening, lowered it, then with all the force he could muster rammed the end of the ladder up into the door above. The door itself didn't move, but a few chunks of the rotted wood along with a cloud of wood dust fell over his head, arms and shoulders. He repeated the process four more times as fragments of wood continued to fall at his feet. Frustrated that he was making little progress he rammed the ladder with all his might up into the bottom of the door as he swore, "Come on, dammit. Break!"

He no sooner stepped away from the opening below when the entire door above gave way. Wood, dirt, and much to his surprise a number of basketball-sized boulders crumbled down on top of him. He was knocked back against the wall as one of the rocks grazed the side of his head, another fell directly onto his right arm. Relieved that he had accomplished his goal of breaking through the door, he looked up at the light from above, then passed out.

The rainwater from the leaky barn roof dripped down on his face bringing him back to consciousness. Wiping the wetness from his face, he started to get up, but the pain in his arm and his side caused him to sit back down. The dim light from above didn't provide enough light for him to see much of anything in the cellar.

Remembering that he had been bitten by a poisonous snake, he got up on one knee. The pain in his side made it difficult for him to stand. Still in a daze, he tried to sort things out: *How long was I out? Where's the flashlight? Where's my gun? Where's my cell phone? Where's the ladder? I need to climb out of this hell hole and get to a hospital!*

Crawling on his hands and knees, he started to move the rocks around as he uncovered the ladder, at the same time being careful not to fall through the opening down to the lower cellar. Rolling four rocks down into the opening, he found his gun and cell phone.

A voice from somewhere above him called out, "Grant Denlinger, you in here? Denlinger, where in the hell are you? Denlinger!"

Grant yelled back up through the trapdoor opening, "Down here...I'm down here!"

Within seconds, a light was shined down through the opening and the familiar voice of Tobias Reichenbaugh followed, "You okay?"

Grant, located the ladder in the loose rocks and placed it up against the wall as he answered, "You've got to get me back to town. I was bitten by a snake."

Tobias offered his right hand to Grant. "I told you it was a bad idea to come back up here by yourself."

Grant, crawling out of the root cellar stood as he looked around the barn. "Did you see anybody around here?"

"No, why?" asked Tobias

"Someone tried to kill me...that's why!"

"What are you talking about? Who tried to kill you?"

Grant was covered with dirt and mud. His shirt was ripped where one of the small boulders had fallen on him, a small trail of blood was running down the side of his face from the falling rocks and the left knee of his pants was ripped open exposing an abrasion. "I can't worry about that right now. You've got to get me to the emergency room! I've been bitten by a rattler. I'll explain what happened on the way."

Outside in the pouring rain, Tobias asked, "Are you going to be able to walk down to where I'm parked?"

Grant, limped across the open area in front of the barn. "Yeah, I can make it. You'll have to drive. We'll come back and get my Jeep later."

"When I pulled into the clearing I saw a man looking in the window of your Jeep. When he saw me, he took off running into the woods," Tobias said.

"Must've been the same man that tried to kill me. I think it was the man I saw at the old church earlier today. The same guy we saw yesterday in that pickup truck. It was the man I saw at Dave's 421." Suddenly Grant got a strange look on his face. "What the hell are you doing up here anyway? I thought you were taking your grandchildren over to Dollywood today."

"The rain cancelled our trip and I got to thinking about you being up here alone. Didn't have anything else planned so I told the wife I was going to run up here and check on you. When I saw that man hanging around your Jeep, I started to get concerned. How long has it been since you were bit?"

"I don't know. It seems like about five minutes passed when that trapdoor caved in on me. The rocks from above that fell on me knocked me unconscious for...well, I really don't know how long. I've got a snakebite kit in the Jeep if you think it'll help."

Tobias objected, "I've heard those things only work if you apply them right way. If it's been a while they're not very effective. Where were you bitten?"

Standing in the clearing next to the old bus, Grant turned his hand over and displayed where the bite occurred. "Right here on my wrist."

Examining the bite area, Tobias commented as he ushered Grant into the nearby trees, "Unless the snake that bit you only had one fang, this might not be a bite mark. Are you sure this is where you were bitten?"

Looking at the single mark on his wrist, Grant confused, agreed, "You're right...only one fang mark. Maybe it's not a bite. Maybe I snagged myself on a nail or something."

"Well, we can't take that chance. We need to take you in anyway. So, tell me about this man who tried to kill you?"

Grant related the entire story from when he had arrived, including his confrontation with the strange man at the old church, to the stairs inside the house caving in, to being barricaded in the root cellar with poisonous snakes.

Walking the last few yards to Tobias's car, Tobias commented, "That's some story. Sounds to me like you must've run into some mountain man who's hiding something up here he didn't want you to see."

Grant looked at Tobias as if he weren't making sense. "But why would he want to kill me? I mean, why didn't he just tell me to get the hell out of here, away from the house and the barn?"

Tobias opened the passenger door as he answered, "Don't know Grant. People up here can be hard to figure out."

At the hospital, the doctor confirmed that Grant had not been bitten by a snake. The wound was simply a nasty puncture, probably from a rusty nail, that was cleaned and bandaged. The doctor gave him a tetanus shot and prescribed an antibiotic for him.

After leaving the hospital, Tobias took Grant back to his hotel where he changed his clothes and repacked his bag. Grant's Jeep was parked in front of his room. Tobias had two of his officers drive up to the Pender farm to retrieve it while he was in the emergency room.

Standing outside the hotel, Tobias looked back up toward the mountains. Motioning toward his Jeep, Tobias remarked, "I'm sorry your trip over here turned out so badly." He gave Grant a straight-faced look. "Some things are best left alone. I got a call from Adele earlier this morning and she told me she was unable to locate the names of the Pender boys. It's a closed case, Grant, and I really don't have enough to go on to reopen a forty-year-old murder. Tell you what, I'll keep the file on my desk and if you come up with any more information, just let me know. To tell you the truth, I don't see what any of this has to do with the murders over in Townsend. Now, stay out of trouble and keep yourself safe."

Later in the day, as he drove down Route 81 toward Townsend, Grant went over every detail of the day. Reichenbaugh hadn't been that concerned about the fact someone had tried to kill him up at the Pender farm. Grant wasn't wrong and he knew it. There was a killer up in the Iron Mountains and unless he could figure out who it was and make the connection between Conrad and his brother, there just might be more murders. He and he alone was the only person who even knew there might be a connection and that connection just might be one of the two carved names he had seen up in that tree. Who was R Pender?

CHAPTER THIRTEEN

GRANT UNLOCKED THE GARAGE DOOR and flipped on the switch lighting the interior of the garage. He hadn't planned or even considered how much yard work there was to do when he and Dana Beth had purchased the house from Ruth. When he lived on the farm with Dalton, the only lawn tool they ever used was a brush hog. Dalton would run it right up to the foundation of the front and backyards. There was no shrubbery or rose bushes to contend with. Now, he had a yard that was completely covered by a thick, plush carpet of grass, plus a row of holly bushes, a small flower garden and lots of trees. He had just mowed a little over a week ago and yet here he was, once again, getting ready to manicure the grass surrounding their new home. Aside from what seemed like weekly cutting of the grass, the hedges needed to be trimmed and some low hanging branches from the maple trees in the front yard needed to be cut back. Then there was the process of edging the lawn and then weed eating along the sidewalk and the small area in front of the house. These chores were all new to him, but had to be done to avoid being frowned upon by his new neighbors.

Walking to the corner of the garage, he pulled the power mower from beneath a workbench. Grabbing a five-gallon can he filled the mower with gas. Taking down the trimmers and pole pruner from where they hung on the garage wall, he stared at the hanging black tarp that concealed Conrad's old van and thought about that Thanksgiving day last year when he had not only discovered the van but the clues inside. There would be a time in the future when he would need to get rid of the van and all the rest of the things Conrad had used to kill his victims. A chilling thought, but one he needed to put out of his mind. He shook off his feeling of guilt and opened the overhead garage door then gathered up all the equipment and laid it on the driveway. Slipping on a pair of work gloves, he primed the gas on the mower and pulled the starter cord. The mower sputtered for a second then settled into a smooth rhythm. Grant entered the front yard and began the first swipe across the grass.

It was Wednesday, just three days since his return from Mountain City. He had lied to Dana Beth once again, not wanting to divulge the real reason why he had gone there in the first place. He explained his numerous bruises as the result of tripping over a boulder and then falling down the side of a rock covered hillside. She really hadn't asked him a lot of questions about the trip. She was preoccupied with her aching back and the upcoming birth of their new daughter. Eight months had passed and she was growing impatient. She was tired of feeling so sluggish and rundown, but the thought that soon there would be a new member of their family always brought a smile to her face. Turning at the hedges in the front of the yard, Grant started back across the grass in the opposite direction. He wondered how many times Conrad had cut the lawn over the years. He recalled times in high school when he had been dating Dana Beth and had been around her father. He had always been so precise about everything that nothing less than perfection would do, even when it came to cutting grass. Each swipe had to be exactly the same width as the last and always cut in the same direction. Grant thought about the gloves in the gym bag in the van and wondered if Conrad had used them to cut the lawn as well as murdering his victims.

Minutes later, he stopped on the other side of the sidewalk that separated the front yard and reached for the glass of iced tea he had left on the porch steps. Wiping his brow, he took three large gulps, placed the glass back on the steps and continued with the mowing. Looking though the front porch window, he could see Dana Beth sitting on the couch in the living room. He loved her so much. It was almost impossible to think about the pain she would have to bear if she learned the truth about her father. He knew Ruth would never believe him, no matter what proof he had. Poor Ruth, she had lived with Conrad all those years. She had been the dutiful wife who prepared her husband's breakfast every morning, kissed him when he left for work and slept in the same bed with him every night. Did he lie next to her and caress her back after coming home from killing Asa or Mildred? Grant remembered her sobbing at the funeral and how she still mourned for Conrad. He thought about his former father-in-law. The man who had lived in this house, the man who had owned the mower he was now pushing, the man who had planted the grass seed in the very yard he was presently mowing was responsible for the four murders last year.

Stopping at the corner of the yard, Grant turned off the mower. The front yard was finished. He walked by the front of the house and took another drink of tea. He went across the yard to the first tall maple. Adjusting the pruning shears, he placed the sharp blades around a branch and pulled the rope, the branch falling to the ground. The sound of the sharp blades snapping through the branch made him think about how Conrad had lopped the murder victims' fingers off. What kind of a person would do that to another human being, no matter how much they hated them? Conrad didn't really hate his victims. He hated what they had done to animals. He carefully chose his victims, just as if he were picking out a new shirt or tie. There was no sadness or remorse on his part, just a feeling of justification. Even though his victims mistreated animals, what gave Conrad the right to be their judge and jury? Things were really getting complicated and now his life was in jeopardy. There was someone back up at the Pender farm that wanted him dead.

After completing the edging and weed eating, he pushed the mower to the backyard. Just as he was about to start the mower, he heard a car pull in the driveway. Ruth was getting out of her car when she saw Grant walking around the side of the house.

Opening the rear door, she removed her suitcase and sat it on the driveway so she could hug her son-in-law. "Grant, why aren't you at work?"

Displaying his grass stained sneakers and sweat soaked tee-shirt, he pointed out, "Ah…I believe I am working."

"Now, you know what I meant. Why are you not out protecting the local citizens?"

Picking up her suitcase, he explained, "Went in early today. Got off at noon. Thought I'd knock out some yard work." Walking her to the side door of the house, he complimented her. "Looks like Chattanooga is treating you good. You look well rested. Listen, I want to thank you for agreeing to stay with us until Dana Beth has the baby. I know she's really looking forward to you being with her when the big moment comes. She could use your help and your support. I've tried to talk with her about some of the pain she's been going through. She just looks at me and tells me I couldn't possibly understand anything about the late months of pregnancy and I'm sure she's right. I'm starting to get a little frustrated. I'm not sure what to say or what I should do. I think sometimes she forgets I'm new at this sort of thing too."

Opening the screen door, Ruth kissed Grant on the cheek, "Don't you go worrying about Dana Beth. Everything is going to be all right. Now, give me that suitcase and go back to mowing the yard. I've got supper to get underway. I told Dana Beth I was making lasagna tonight."

After dinner, Grant pushed himself back from the table and complimented Ruth. "That was one great meal. Think I'll go watch the evening news."

"Not so fast," said Dana Beth. "We have some work to do tonight. I promised Mom we'd finish up going through those last two boxes of stuff we found up in the attic. Remember, I had you move them to the back bedroom last week. While mom and I clear the table, why don't you get the boxes and bring them into the living room. We'll load up the dishwasher and put away the leftovers. Shouldn't take us more than ten minutes, then we'll be in to help you sort through the stuff. We'll have our dessert in the living room while we go though the boxes."

Grant really wasn't up to going through someone else's belongings, but he realized it had to be done and Dana Beth expected him to help. He had to make two trips as the boxes were quite heavy. Setting them next to the coffee table in the living room, he sat down and opened the first box. It was filled with books and albums. Opening the first album on the top, he discovered that it was a photographic journey of Dana Beth's life from birth through high school. He even found a few pictures of himself and Dana Beth when they were dating. Pitching the album on the couch, he thought about his old high school days. Dana Beth Pearl was the prettiest girl in school. There were plenty of other boys she could have dated, but for some reason she picked him and now here it was almost seven years later and they were married, owned a home and were expecting their first child. If someone back then had told him where he was going to be today, he wouldn't have believed it. Here he was sitting in the home where his wife had been raised going through boxes of memories that for the most part had nothing to do with him.

Placing a number of books on the coffee table, he picked up another photo album, which in gold lettering stated: *Family Vacations*. There were pictures of Conrad and Ruth posing in front of various places of interest. Flipping through the pages it wasn't long until the pictures included Dana Beth as a baby. Ruth's voice interrupted his concentration on the album as she entered the room, with plates of strawberry shortcake and a bowl of whipped cream on a tray. Dana Beth followed her into the room, balancing a tray holding a pot of coffee, cups, utensils, and condiments. Ruth noticed Grant's interest in the album. "I see you've found our family photo albums. Conrad was always adamant about taking lots of pictures wherever we went. Which one are you looking at?"

Holding up the album for her to see, Grant answered, "Family vacations."

Setting the dessert tray down on the coffee table, Ruth commented, "There are a lot of good memories in that album. Lots of pictures of Conrad and I before Dana Beth came along. I remember one year when we went out to the Grand Canyon, then another time, up to Niagara Falls. After Dana Beth was born, we started to go up to Lake Itasca in Minnesota and after a few years as she got older we always went to the beach."

Dana Beth was in the process of pouring coffee, as she remarked, "I always loved the beach, but to be honest some of the best vacations I ever had were up on Itasca Lake." Handing a cup to Ruth, she went on, "I guess Grant and I will start building some vacation memories of our own." Handing a cup to Grant she reminded him, "Remember all the pictures we took up at Itasca on our honeymoon?"

Grant, setting down his coffee, answered, "Yep, that was a great week. I'd like to go back there sometime. It was so peaceful."

Ruth sat on a chair by the fireplace and poured creamer into her coffee. "Lake Itasca was always my favorite also. I loved the clean air and the sound of the loons skimming across the water just before sunset. I think we took Dana Beth there every year until she was ten. Then we started going to the beach each summer." Pointing to the album in Grant's hand, she suggested, "If you go back a few pages you'll find photos of the years we went to the lake. Conrad just loved it up there. He'd always take a week of vacation by himself in the fall and drive to Itasca and spend a week fishing on the lake."

Grant flipped through page after page until he came to a section that was marked *Itasca Lake*. Ruth walked around to the back of the couch looking over his shoulder. Reaching down, she tapped a photo with her index finger. "That's the first year we took Dana Beth. She was just one year old." Grant turned the pages as Ruth continued to point out various photos of Conrad, Dana Beth and her. Pointing to a photo as Grant turned another page she remarked, "There's one of my favorite pictures of Conrad with his friend, Rubin. Look at those goofy hats they're wearing." Grant hesitated before going on to the next page, looking at a number of photos of Conrad and Rubin: one where they were standing on a dock displaying fish they had caught, another sitting in a small boat and still another where they were holding drinks in front of a fireplace. Grant wasn't listening as Ruth rambled on, but was thinking, *What was the connection between Rubin and Conrad?* It was hard to tell from just looking at the black and white photos but then it hit him! For the past few days he had been racking his brain trying to figure out who R Pender was *and now* here it was right in front of him. Not wanting to appear too curious, he casually asked Dana Beth, "Rubin. Wasn't that the man we met the first morning we were up at Itasca? You remember, we talked with him while we were eating breakfast."

"Yeah, that's him. He was pretty close with our family."

Ruth jumped in on the conversation, "I think it was the third or fourth year we went to Itasca that we met Rubin. For some reason Conrad really took a liking to him. They both liked to fish and over the years, he treated Rubin like a brother. He came to a lot of our cookouts and outings and went fishing with Conrad all the time. You may have noticed when you first met him that he's on the slow side. I think Conrad felt sorry for him or just overlooked it. We never really talked about it. All I remember is that Conrad and Rubin got along quite well and it made it easier on me because I really don't like to fish. Every fall he'd go up to Itasca Lake on his own to fish and I guess spend some time with Rubin."

Grant had to be careful how he asked his next question. "Do you have any photographs of Conrad's parents?"

"No, we don't," answered Ruth. "We never talked about his parents. When we were dating he told me they died when he was young. He seemed rather uncomfortable talking about them and he made it perfectly clear that he did not want to discuss his parents or his childhood. He never even told me their names. He did tell me that he had been adopted, but really didn't want to talk about that either. He told me he didn't get along that well with his adoptive parents and that he left home when he was eighteen. I don't even know where he grew up as a young boy. I asked him a few questions over the years but he always became irritated. I could tell he felt uncomfortable, so I just let it be."

Grant asked another question, "So, you don't really know if he had any brothers or sisters?"

Ruth, now sitting in the chair picked up her coffee. "I don't know...I mean I doubt it. Like I said, he refused to discuss his family with Dana Beth or me. We never received any letters or phone calls. If he did have any siblings, they never contacted him. They didn't show up for his viewing or funeral, so I'd say, he probably didn't have any." Ruth seemed uncomfortable with continuing the conversation. "Any more questions, Officer Denlinger?"

"Nope," said Grant. "I'm going to go sit outside for a while."

It was just after ten o'clock when Grant sat down on the front porch. Holding a cup of coffee, he turned and gazed in the bay window. Ruth was still seated in the living room, sorting through the books and albums while Dana Beth busied herself in the kitchen, putting away the leftovers. No one thought anything about him retreating to the front porch. It had become an evening ritual for him to sit outside for an hour or so before turning in for the night. It was a quiet place; a place where he could relax and think. Looking out to the street, he noticed the streetlights casting their friendly glow throughout the neighborhood; he heard the barking of a dog up the street, the gentle whisper of a passing airliner high above. *What kind of man never tells his wife or daughter about his family or childhood? Even if it was awful, he surely would have told them something. Moreover, why would Ruth settle for not knowing about his parents. It seemed very odd to him.*

Based on what Ruth and Dana Beth had shared with him earlier in the living room, he couldn't turn away from what seemed obvious to him. Rubin, Conrad's friend from Itasca Lake had to be his brother. Ruth had said herself that Conrad treated Rubin like a brother. Maybe that's because Rubin was his brother. That's why Conrad took a yearly trip in the fall by himself up to Itasca. He could spend a week alone with his brother.

He thought back to when he and Dana Beth had breakfast the first day on their honeymoon at that restaurant on the lake. They met Rubin that morning and for some reason Grant couldn't put his finger on, he felt that Rubin had been attracted to Dana Beth. It all made sense now. It had been over ten years since Rubin last saw her. Hiram Tate said the younger brother was on the slow side. Rubin may have had vague memories of her, but just couldn't remember who she was.

His thoughts about Rubin were interrupted when Dana Beth stuck her head out the front door telling him she and Ruth were going to bed. Grant kissed her good night and said he would be up shortly. He was too keyed up to sleep. He had finally discovered who Conrad's brother was. If what he was thinking was true this could break the case wide open. But, who could he go to with this new information? He knew what he had to do and he would discuss it with both Dana Beth and Ruth at breakfast in the morning.

Thursday morning, Grant reached for his second slice of buttered toast as he looked across the table at Ruth. Dana Beth stood at the sink, her hands on her hips as she stretched her back muscles then commented, "I wish this baby would come on and get here so I can get a good night's rest."

Looking at Grant, Ruth smiled. "When the baby comes it's just the beginning of a series of sleepless nights. Get all the rest you can now, you're going to need it."

There was a moment of silence at which point Grant decided it was a good time to bring up Rubin. He had to be careful what he was about to share with his wife and mother-in-law. Up to this point he had lied to Dana Beth and Ruth, but now he was hoping he could confide in them and what he shared with them would not leave the kitchen. Clearing his throat, he took a drink of orange juice and spoke, "Listen, I want to share something with both of you, but you cannot tell this to anyone, especially Sheriff Brody or anyone else that's been involved with the past murders."

Ruth hesitated from taking a bite of her toast. Dana Beth turned and just stared at him. Realizing he needed to justify his previous statement, he touched Ruth on her arm and gestured for Dana Beth to have a seat at the table. "Look, I guess that sounded kind of out of place. I mean here we are having breakfast and I start talking about the past murders and how you can't say anything about what I'm about to say. It's just that Sheriff Brody and I don't see eye to eye on much of anything. It's just better if he doesn't know the direction I'm heading on this case, at least not yet." The puzzling looks on Ruth and Dana Beth's faces combined with their lack of a response made for another awkward moment.

Grant leaned forward as he set his empty glass down on the table. "Last night when we were going through that vacation album and we began discussing Rubin and what great friends he and Conrad were, it got me thinking. When Dana Beth and I were up there on vacation we met Rubin at the restaurant on the lake. He told us about all of the murders they had around the Itasca Lake area. At the time, I didn't think much about it. That is until last night. They have the same sort of thing going on up there that we have down here. I might be way out in left field here, but I think there might be a connection." Directing his next remark to Dana Beth he continued, "Last week I went over to Mountain City to follow up on a lead, which by the way Brody doesn't know about, so I'd appreciate it if you'd keep that tidbit a secret. It didn't pan out, but now I think I might be on to something here. I've got this coming weekend off and tomorrow I'd like to fly to Itasca Lake and talk with the County Sheriff. What do you guys think?"

Dana Beth smiled across the table at her husband. "Grant. When I married you I knew the line of work you were in and it really never bothered me. It's not like we're living in some big city where they have high incidents of homicides. The murders we've had here are not a normal way of life. I know it must be frustrating for you and everyone else that's involved in the case. I've never interfered with your work and I have no intention of starting now. If you feel you need to go up to Itasca Lake you'll get no objections from me. As far as Axel Brody is concerned I'd just as soon not talk to the man."

Ruth agreed with her daughter. "I'm with Dana Beth on this. Conrad and I never talked much about the murders, as a matter of fact the few times I brought them up, he always said he'd just as soon not discuss them. I'm hoping, along with everyone else in the area, that the police will soon bring the killer to justice. So, you go on up to Itasca and talk to whomever you need to. Don't worry about anything around here. I'm here and if anything happens I'll be right at your wife's side. As for Axel, I haven't spoken to him in years. There's no reason to start now."

Grant smiled. "All right then. I'll schedule a flight out of Knoxville for Friday. I should be back no later than Sunday."

Later that evening, following a routine day of patrolling the streets of Townsend, Grant sat down at the computer in their spare room. Within twenty minutes, he not only booked his flight, but also discovered that Itasca Lake was located in Clearwater County. The county seat was a town called Bagley where the county sheriff's office was located. He got the number of the courthouse and talked with Sheriff Chester Brickman, who said he would be more than glad to meet with him Friday afternoon when he arrived.

Grant settled into his window seat as the plane taxied down the runway prior to the direct flight from Knoxville to the

Minneapolis-St. Paul International Airport in Minnesota. He hadn't really thought too much about what he was going to say to the sheriff in Bagley. Their conversation had been brief. Grant said he needed to talk to him about some of the murders that happened at Itasca Lake and that they could possibly be connected to those that had occurred in Townsend. Brickman said that any information Grant had, would be welcomed.

He laid his head back and closed his eyes as he silently asked himself some questions: *Should he suggest to Brickman that they talk with Rubin? Would Rubin even be up at Itasca Lake? If it turned out that Rubin was the man in the red hat who had tried to kill him was he still over in Mountain City? If what he suspected was true, then who should he turn to next? Should he let the authorities in Minnesota take over or should he give the information to the Feds back in Townsend?*

Looking out at the passing clouds, he decided that any decisions he made prior to the meeting with Brickman was nothing more than guesswork. The results of his trip up to Bagley would hinge on what was said and what was discovered. The meeting might just be the beginning of a new investigation as far as the Minnesota authorities were concerned. He was going to try to get some rest.

He drifted in and out of a restless sleep as the wind turbulence caused the plane to dip on occasion. Finally, just as he was dosing off the landing gear hit the runway which jerked him back to reality. Bleary eyed, he looked out the window as the plane passed various hangers and airport buildings, eventually slowing down to taxi speed. When the plane came to a complete stop, he unbuckled himself, walked to the front of the plane where he said good-bye to the flight attendant. His next destination was a small municipal airline that would fly him up to Park Rapids where he would pick up a rental car and then drive to Bagley.

Looking at his watch, he noticed the time at 2:15 in the afternoon. He was right on schedule and had time for a quick lunch before his next flight which would only take about twenty minutes. Getting directions to the hanger near the end of the airport, he ate a hotdog and a bag of chips as he sat in the back of a four seated golf cart. An attendant drove him to the municipal hanger where he was told the flight to Park Rapids would be taking off in thirty minutes. He wasn't all that enthusiastic about flying in a puddle jumper, but it was the quickest way to get to Clearwater County. Renting a car in Minneapolis wasn't the problem. The problem was the three hour drive to get to Bagley.

He'd just have to put up with what he anticipated being a roller coaster twenty minute flight. Sitting in the tiny terminal, he thought that maybe he should have waited to eat until after he got to Park Rapids. His stomach didn't always agree with flying.

After fifteen minutes passed, he was approached by a young stewardess. "Good afternoon, sir. Are you Mr. Denlinger?"

Grant laid down the magazine he had been reading. "Yes, I am."

"If you'll follow me out to the runway we'll be boarding in five minutes."

Grant followed the young girl and once outside he found he was only one of two passengers on the short flight. Minutes later, they were instructed to board one of the smallest airplanes he had ever been in. Grant chose the very back of the plane, if for no other reason, than he didn't think he'd be able to handle staring out the front windshield of the plane as the cockpit was in full view from where the passengers were seated. Following some informal in-flight instructions from the stewardess, the pilot taxied out to the runway, waited for clearance from the main tower and within seconds they were airborne. Grant closed his eyes as the plane bounced and weaved with the wind. It was going to be a long twenty minutes.

He opened his eyes when the stewardess touched him on the shoulder. "Are you all right, Mr. Denlinger?"

Grant, trying his best to avoid getting airsick wiped his forehead with the back of his hand and took a deep breath as he answered, "I'll be fine if I could just get something to drink. I'm really not all that fond of flying, especially on these smaller planes."

The stewardess apologized, "I'm sorry, but we're making our approach now. We'll be on the ground in less than three minutes. I can get you a drink when we land if you'd like."

"Thank you, but if we're close to landing then I think I'll be fine."

The landing was surprisingly smooth and as Grant exited the plane the stewardess asked him once again, "Are you sure you're going to be okay?"

"Yes, I think I'm going to be all right," said Grant, "but I do need some information. Where do I pick up my rental car?"

Pointing to a large metal hanger she responded, "Everything here in Park Rapids is handled at the main counter." She laughed, "Actually the only counter. You can grab a drink, get a burger, check in, purchase a ticket, buy a magazine or in your case, rent a car. Have a nice day, Mr. Denlinger."

Grant walked across the small runway and entered the building where he immediately spotted the counter where an older man sat reading a newspaper. "Excuse me," said Grant, "I need to pick up my rental car? I ordered it on the net yesterday."

Putting down the paper the man answered, "Of course, and what is your name, Sir?"

"Denlinger...Grant Denlinger. I'm just driving up to Bagley. I may stay the night. I haven't decided yet."

"I see that you have prepaid so it's just a matter of signing one of our standard release forms and you'll be on your way."

Grant signed the form, scooped up the keys and asked, "Now where do I pick up the car and how do I get to Bagley?"

"Here, let me jot down some directions." Grabbing a pencil and a piece of paper, the man talked as he wrote, "Now, what you do is, take a right out of our parking lot then get on Route 71 North. Take that until you come to the town of Bemidji. I guess it's about a thirty minute drive. When you get on the other side of Bemidji, you'll come to Route 2. Take that for about another twenty minutes or so. That'll take you right into Bagley. Enjoy your trip."

Climbing into the Ford Focus, he pulled out of the lot and made the turn onto Route 71 North and within two minutes found himself entering the Itasca State Park. Even though he had been to Itasca Lake last September, he wasn't that familiar with the area. He and Dana Beth had hung around the lake for the most part.

He had read about the Itasca State Park. It covered nearly three thousand acres of old growth pines, an area that attracted over one half million visitors yearly, most of them going to the lake for vacation. Opening all the windows, he leaned back in the seat as he tried to relax and recuperate from his near sickness on the flight in from Minneapolis. The dark green trees shadowed the paved road on both sides creating a pleasant drive through the forest. He thought about what he had shared with Dana Beth and Ruth. He was glad that for once he had been truthful with them. He thought about Rubin and what the waitress at the restaurant where they had breakfast during their honeymoon said about him.

She said he was on the slow side, but highly functional. He tried to recall everything he could about that morning in the restaurant when Rubin walked in. That was a little over eight months ago. He had been on his honeymoon. The entire trip, he had been focused on his new wife, not some guy he had met at a restaurant. He tried to concentrate as he relived that morning.

They had been eating when Rubin had walked in. He was clean shaven but about the same height and weight as the man in the red hat who had a scruffy bearded appearance. Rubin had on a park ranger's uniform. Later, after he left, the waitress had told Dana Beth and him that he really wasn't a fish and game warden but that he had been given the unofficial honor since he spent everyday on the lake or walking in the woods. The local park police had bestowed it upon him. He was harmless, but liked to talk to anyone that would listen to him.

Grant remembered when he approached their table and asked to join them. When Grant told him they were from Townsend, it seemed like Rubin knew all about the Great Smoky Mountains. He said he loved that part of the country. *It made sense now.* If he was Conrad's brother then he had been raised over near Mountain City and then later on in Knoxville by his adopted parents. Then, on top of that, he mentioned how bad it was for them to be having those murders down in Tennessee. He went on to explain to Dana Beth and him about the murders they had over the past ten years. He also said he knew Dana Beth's father quite well. Dana Beth had some recollection of Rubin, but the last time she had seen him was over ten years ago. She was just a child at that time and was more interested in swimming and playing then spending time with Rubin.

Of course, he was Conrad's brother. Grant remembered that Rubin hadn't said much about Conrad. When Grant saw the pictures of Rubin and Conrad together and heard Ruth go on about how Rubin being almost one of the family, he wondered why Rubin hadn't said more about Conrad. Conrad had probably told him repeatedly not to talk too much about their relationship. It was obvious Conrad didn't want anyone to know Rubin was his brother.

Just on the other side of the town limits of Bemidji, he took a left turn onto Route 2 and saw a road sign that read: BAGLEY 18 MILES. He couldn't remember everything Rubin told him about the murders, but did remember he had been quite detailed. He remembered he had given one of his business cards to Rubin telling him he'd like to be updated later in the year if there was a new murder. *God,* he thought. He might have given the killer a business card. Maybe that's why the man in the red hat, who he now suspected to be Rubin, tried to kill him. While talking to them in the restaurant Rubin had commented that Grant was the first person in some time who was even interested in talking about the murders. He still needed to figure out what brought Rubin to Townsend. How did he know that Conrad had died? Realizing his mind was running away with him once again, he decided he would stop trying to figure everything out before he even talked with the County Sheriff.

It seemed like no time at all had passed when he found himself on the outskirts of Bagley. The town wasn't very large and he had little difficulty locating the courthouse on the square. Parking the rental car in a visitor's space, he got out, climbed the concrete steps and entered what appeared to be the oldest building in town. Stopping at an information desk directly on the right, he inquired as to where the County Sheriff's Office was located. He was directed down the hall. As he opened a door, he came face to face with a large man: crew cut hair, perfectly pressed uniform, spit shined shoes, holstered gun and a wide grin. The man had just turned from a copy machine that was just inside the doorway. He looked at his watch as he greeted Grant. "I'd guess that you'd be Grant Denlinger of the Townsend Police Department."

Grant, shocked that the man would know who he was, remarked, "Why, yes I am. I didn't realize I was that obvious."

Sticking out his hand, the man introduced himself, "Chester Brickman, Clearwater County Sheriff. Most folks call me Chet."

Grant shook the man's hand as he stated, "You already know who I am."

"I know most everyone in the county. Makes my job easier. Believe me, when a stranger rolls into Bagley, it just might be the most exciting thing that happens all day. Come on back to my office and let's have a chat."

Sitting behind a large oak desk, Brickman asked, "Care for a soda, maybe some water?"

"No, thank you," Grant said as he looked at a large map on the wall of the entire county.

Brickman noticed Grant's interest in the map. "There she is...Clearwater County. Sixty miles long and eighteen miles wide and most of that is water. We have over one hundred lakes here in the county. The county's population bounces somewhere around 8700, but between April and up until, I'd say, late October we get over a half million visitors most of which tend to go to Itasca Lake." Brickman seemed to be quite proud of his county.

Grant chimed in, "I'm a little familiar with Itasca Lake. My wife and I spent our honeymoon there last September. We rented a cabin next to Lake Itaska. Actually, it was her idea to come up here. Her family used to come here every year during the summer and her father always came back in the fall by himself to do some fishing. My wife and I really enjoyed the week we spent on the lake. We're planning on coming back, but probably not this year. My wife is expecting our first child, so it'll probably be next year before we get back."

Brickman, moving on to the reason why Grant was sitting in his office opened a file cabinet and removed two thick manila envelopes which he placed on the corner of the desk. "You said on the phone that you wanted to discuss the murders we've had in the past ten years. I have to admit you got my attention since there aren't many people who like or even want to talk about that subject."

Grant crossed his legs, settled back in his chair and began to reveal the reason for his trip to Bagley. "As I told you on the phone, down in Blount County, Tennessee where I'm from we've had a series of murders; six to be exact. Last year when I was here on my honeymoon, I heard about the murders up here and now, months later, I'm starting to think there may be some similarities. For instance, last year there was a murder in the spring, summer, fall and winter which suggest a pattern of sorts. This year it's a little different. We've had two in the spring. If I remember correctly your murders have occurred every fall, I think it was in early November each year."

Brickman seemed a little puzzled. "May I ask you, who told you about the murders that occurred in our area?"

"When we were eating at a place on the lake, we got to talking to a fellow named Rubin and..."

Brickman grinned. "So after Rubin told you all about the murders, did you do some investigating before coming up here?"

Grant shook his head. "No, that's why I'm here now."

"Well, Son, this may be a wasted trip for you. I only have two murders on my books that are unsolved. They were believed to have been committed by an estranged husband who caught his wife with another man. The man and woman were camping in the forest, and were found shot to death in a tent. They were up here on the pretense they were hunting. We were never able to locate the husband of the woman who was killed. We believe he left town the same day they were killed. I was under the impression that you had some information about the man we are still looking for. Every other death that has happened in the last ten years has been recorded as hunting accidents. We have had more than our share and for some reason, Rubin had it in his head that all of these hunters were being murdered. I'll admit that eleven deaths in ten years is a lot, but when hunting season starts, the woods up here are crawling with hunters. Some bring liquor along, others are just gun happy. They sit in their blinds and when anything moves, they start shooting. A few years back there was a hunter found dead at the bottom of a ravine. The coroner said the cause of death was a heart attack. Another hunter was attacked by a bear and died of a self-inflicted gunshot wound.

"The good news is that last year when November rolled around, no hunters or anyone was killed. You may not know this, but over a thousand people a year are injured or killed in hunting accidents."

Grant sat quietly as he tried to digest everything he was being told, when Brickman spoke again, "I took my family down to Gatlinburg last fall on vacation and I read an article in the local paper about three murders you had at that time. From what I read it's easy to see that you folks definitely have a serial killer on your hands. The deaths up here are simply about hunters being shot by other hunters. So...you said you got your information from Rubin."

"Yes. My wife hadn't been up here since she was ten, but she remembered a restaurant on the other side of the lake from where we were staying. We thought breakfast sounded good so we took a boat over there. I can't remember the name of the place but it was on the order of a log cabin."

"Know it well," said Brickman. "It's called The Country Store on the Lake. Whenever I'm down that way I always have breakfast there. Woman by the name of Hilda owns the place."

Grant smiled as if he knew exactly what the sheriff was talking about. "Hilda, that's right. She was the one who waited on us that day. While we were eating, another customer came in the place. He was dressed like a local park ranger. Hilda introduced us to this man and he came over to our table. Turned out that both he and Hilda knew my wife's father quite well from when he came up here fishing. This park ranger mentioned that it was too bad about all the murders we were having down in Townsend. Then, he went on to tell us all about the murders that you've had up here in the past ten years. However, he explained it much differently than you did. He said he felt the murders were all related and if something wasn't done, the killer would strike again. Later, after he left, Hilda told us he knew more about the killings than anyone did. She also told us he was slow and he really wasn't the fish and game warden but that was just an honorary title the park police had given him."

Sheriff Brickman shook his head as a look of sadness came across his face. "Yep, that was Rubin you met."

"That's right...his name was Rubin. And to tell you the truth he is the main reason why I made the trip up here. There was something odd about him I couldn't put my finger on, until just lately when we got a description of a suspect. Rubin somewhat fits the description of a man who has been seen for the past few weeks down in the Smokies. This man, who we haven' t been able to track down, might be responsible for one if not both murders we've had this year."

"I hate to be the bearer of bad news but if that's the main reason you made the trip up here to Bagley then you've wasted your time. If you would have asked me about Rubin when you called, I could have saved you a long trip."

Up to this point, Grant thought the meeting with Brickman had gone rather well, but now the bottom seemed to be falling out. "I don't understand," Grant said.

Picking up the last few papers in the second folder, Brickman laid them in front of him on the desk. Rubin died on January fifteenth, this year. There was no evidence of foul play. It appeared that his boat hit a log and turned over. Even though he had on a life jacket, he got caught underneath the boat and he drowned. There was a lot of ice in the water and he probably died of hypothermia. Rubin Carnes couldn't have killed either one of your victims this year. He was dead before those murders ever took place in Tennessee."

Grant didn't know what to say. Finally, after a few moments of silence, he asked, "Are you sure his last name was Carnes?"

"Sure as I'm sitting here," said Brickman. "I knew the man all his life. He lived in a small cabin near the restaurant. Everybody around these parts knew him. He was a likable sort of fella. Harmless, wouldn't hurt a flea. Always full of stories. He always managed to get by. Hilda and a few others around the lake always made sure he had what he needed. Problem is, he took his honorary post very seriously and every time someone was killed, he had it in his mind that they were murdered. Hilda sometimes played along with him just to get him to stop talking."

Brickman scooped up all the papers and placed them back in the folders as he asked, "So what are you going to do now?"

Grant rubbed his hand across his face, thought for a moment, then answered, "I guess it's back to the drawing board."

Grant walked slowly across the paved parking lot of the Knoxville Airport toward his Jeep. He was aggravated. His trip up to Clearwater County had been a bust. He had been almost positive that Rubin was the connection he had been looking for. He had expected, at some point after talking with Sheriff Brickman that they would go to where Rubin lived only to find him not at home. The reason being he was the man in the red hat, the man who still might be in the Mountain City area. He now found himself at another dead end. Rubin...Rubin Carnes was dead.

Climbing into his Jeep he sat back in the seat and let out a long breath as he stared at a directional sign that read: DOWNTOWN KNOXVILLE. *Dammit!* he thought. *Why hadn't he called Sheriff Brickman before making the trip to Minnesota?* He was wrong again. He had expected to return home with enough evidence to go after the man in the red hat. Slamming his fist down on the steering wheel, he shouted, "Conrad Pearl...I hate you!" Normally, he wasn't in the habit of talking to himself, but he repeated the name, "Conrad Pearl!" *Oh my God!* He thought. *I'm been looking for the wrong person. Not so much the wrong person—but the wrong name.* He had been searching for R Pender. What was it that Hiram Tate had said? The Pender boys had been adopted by a family in Knoxville.

Rather than looking for R Pender, he needed to be searching for R Pearl. He was sitting on the outskirts of Knoxville, the city where the two boys had been raised following their adoption. If anyone knew who Conrad's brother was it would have to be their adoptive parents. *Were the Pearls still alive? Were they still living in Knoxville?* Starting his Jeep, he pulled out of the lot. He had some research to do.

CHAPTER FOURTEEN

GRANT PULLED HIS JEEP into a gas station a few blocks from the airport. Picking up his cell phone, he dialed his home number. Following two rings, Dana Beth answered, "Hello."

"Hi, how's my little momma doing?" asked Grant.

"Just waddling around as usual. Where are you?"

"I'm in Knoxville."

"Did you find out what you needed at Itasca Lake?"

"No, I hit another dead end, but I'm still not giving up. There's something I need to follow up on here in Knoxville. As long as I'm here I might as well look into it. I'll have to spend the night, but I think I can wrap it up by tomorrow afternoon. I promise you when I get home I'm all yours. I'll stick to you like glue."

"Well, I don't know about that. It's hard to even get close to me. Sorry your trip up north didn't work out. Just go ahead and do what you have to, but I want to see your ugly mug tomorrow."

"Most definitely. Get some rest. Love you."

Grant threw his cell on the seat and headed for downtown Knoxville. He wanted to get in close proximity to the University of Tennessee. In the morning that would be his destination.

After a ten minute drive, he parked in the lot of the Best Western Motel on Strawberry Lane. He looked at his watch. It was 9:30 in the evening and too late to worry about dinner. He was tired. Checking in at the front desk, he signed his credit card slip and picked up the room keys and was reminded by the night clerk, "Don't forget...we have a continental breakfast starting at six in the morning."

"Believe me," said Grant, "I won't forget. I'll probably be the first in line."

His room was on the second floor at the end of the hall. Once inside, he laid his bag on the bed and turned on the television. He kicked off his shoes and lay down on the bed fully clothed. He watched the ten o'clock news, which had nothing major to report.

Thank goodness, he thought. *No more murders!* He yawned and stretched his hands over his head. He thought about getting up and taking a shower, but decided on a short nap first.

He was awakened by the sound of loud voices and car doors slamming. Sitting up, he looked at the alarm clock next to the bed. *Nine fifteen!* He sat on the side of the bed and shook his head. *Good grief, how did that happen?* He couldn't remember the last time he had slept until nine o'clock. Getting up from the bed, he shed his clothes and jumped in the shower, shaving while the warm water ran down his back. Fifteen minutes later he was dressed, packed and ready to leave.

"I thought you said you'd be the first in line this morning," said the desk clerk. "Looks like you're gonna be the last. Better hurry up before they put the food up."

Grant gave the girl a strange look. "What are you still doing here? Don't you ever go home."

"Just getting ready to get off. My shift runs from ten to ten. The ten o'clock girl just got here. Now, go eat!"

Filling a bowl with cornflakes from the small food bar, Grant tipped the coffeepot toward him to get the last cup out of the urn. Looking over the remnants of leftover food, he said to himself, "No orange juice or toast left. Looks like breakfast is going to be cereal." He took the bowl and a carton of milk and sat down at one of the four tables in the lobby.

An older woman who started to clean up the breakfast counter started to walk away with a tray of Danish. Stopping by his table, she offered, "You want a couple of these. If not, I'm just going to pitch them."

"Sure, thank you," said Grant as he lifted two of the pastries from the tray.

Minutes later, after eating his cereal and two Danish pastries, he walked to the counter to turn in his room keys. The ten o'clock lady asked him if he had a nice stay. He replied that he did.

Stepping out the front entrance he looked up at the bright sun. It felt like it was going to be a hot day. As he walked to his Jeep, he was ready to face the heat of the day and the only other lead he had in his search for the man named R Pearl.

Grant was familiar with the location of the university. He had been there on two different occasions with the Pearls when he dated Dana Beth in high school. Once he and Dana Beth had driven up to have lunch with Conrad and the other occasion had been when Professor Pearl gave a commencement speech to the graduating class. Grant recalled how proud Ruth and Dana Beth had been of Conrad that day. He remembered how they smiled when he had been introduced and then gave his speech. It was a speech about society's obligation to protect each other. Grant couldn't recall exactly what Conrad had said, but even the few parts he did recall, with what he knew about Conrad, was all a charade.

Arriving at the university grounds, Grant had no idea where the administration building was, so he stopped at the main gate at a school security station and asked for directions. Minutes later, he was winding his way through the maze of campus streets, ducking his head as he peered out the front windshield at the building addresses.

The administration building was an old brick structure, probably built when the university was founded back in the late seventeen hundreds. After locating a parking spot, Grant climbed the concrete steps leading up to the main hallway of the building.

He looked around, finally spotting a sign that read: INFORMATION. A woman sitting on a stool behind a marble counter smiled and asked, "May I help you, Sir?"

"Ah, yes," said Grant politely. "I'm trying to find some information on a professor who taught here."

"Are you a relative or are you working on a research paper?"

"Actually, I'm married to his daughter. Her father's name was Conrad Pearl, excuse me, Professor Pearl."

"Oh, my goodness! I knew your father-in-law quite well. I'm so sorry that he passed away. He was such a dear man. Every year on my birthday he would always bring me a dozen roses, saying that he really appreciated the job I did. It was so strange. The last year before he died was the only year he didn't bring me flowers. But the strangest part was he seemed so distant, like his mind was on other things. However, all that being said, as far as I'm concerned he was the nicest professor we've ever had here on campus."

"Listen," said Grant. "I'm trying to get some information on Conrad's parents. My wife is due to have our first child soon and she is working on her family tree, ya know, something to keep her busy until our new addition arrives..." Grant hesitated, thinking to himself, *Is this lady going to buy my lame story?* "...unfortunately, my father-in-law lost contact with his parents some years ago and we have no information on them whatsoever."

"I see. Well, Professor Pearl taught in the Humanities Department. I'll give you a pass to go to the offices in that department and I'm sure they'll be able to assist you." She pulled out a visitor's pass and a magic marker and handed them to him. "Write your name on that pass and it will let you go across campus without being questioned."

Grant printed his name on the pass, peeled off the back and stuck it on his shirt, thanked the lady and walked toward the front door as he thought, *Whew, one hurdle crossed.*

The Humanities Department was located just a block away. He walked across an expanse of lawn, exchanging nods and hellos with students and professors as they made their way to various classes. Inside the four story building, he ran his fingers down the list of names and departments posted inside the front doors. After he found the department he was looking for, he pushed the button for the elevator and following a short ride, got off on the third floor and entered the first door he came to. A young man wearing a name tag that read, Jason Wright, was sitting at a desk behind a computer. Grant found himself staring at yet another INFORMATION sign. The young man looked up from the screen and asked, "Yes sir, what can I do for you?"

Grant, not really sure if he was even in the correct department answered, "Could you tell me where I might get some information on Professor Conrad Pearl?"

Adjusting the glasses on his face, the young man inquired, "What type of information are you looking for? Class schedules, office hours or—"

Grant interrupted him, "Professor Pearl taught here for years, but he's deceased now. He died last year around Thanksgiving. I'm trying to get some information on his parents. I would like to get their names."

"Yes, I've heard of the professor, but I didn't know him. This is my first year. Let me look and see what I can find." Grant could hear the clicking of the young man's nimble fingers on the keyboard as he entered Conrad's name into the computer. Following a few seconds the man said, "Here it is. I pulled up his bio. His parents were, let me see, oh yeah, here it is, Dr. Marvin Pearl P.H.D and his wife's name is Irene."

Opening his blue notebook, Grant pulled a pen from inside as he responded, "Thanks, that's just what I need."

As he was writing down the names, he was about to ask his next question, but it was answered by the young man before he opened his mouth to speak. "Do you need their address?"

"Yes, that would be great. I didn't realize that information was available."

"None of this stuff is classified. Let's see, it says here, 2524 Cornell Drive. That's right here in Knoxville. It's about fifteen minutes from campus. Do you need directions?"

"Sure, that would be great."

After writing down the directions he was given, Grant closed the notebook and thanked the clerk. "You have been more than helpful. You saved me a lot of time."

"That's what I'm here for," said the young man.

Walking away from the desk, Grant smiled as he thought, *That was easy. I hope the rest of my day goes as well.*

Cornell Drive was located on a tree lined street in an older section of town next to a large expanse of grass called Adair Park. The towering mature trees that shaded Cornell Drive separated the row of brick homes fronted by manicured lawns and an occasional white fence. Grant slowed down as he read the passing house numbers. Pulling to the curb of 2524, he stopped the Jeep. *Okay,* he thought. *Take a minute. What are you going to say when and if you meet one or both of the Pearls? Maybe they don't live here anymore. They are going to be up in age. I don't want to alarm them.*

Lost in thought, he was startled by a knocking sound on the window. He turned, looking into the face of an elderly woman. He rolled down the window and the woman quickly asked in a stern tone, "Are you looking for somebody, Sonny? What are you selling?" In her hand she held a hoe.

Grant grinned, "I'm not selling anything. I'm looking for Marvin and Irene Pearl's house."

"Marvin and Irene!" the woman exclaimed. "Good Lord, they've both been dead for years. You a relative?"

Grant really didn't want to give the lady a long explanation so he answered, "Yes, I was hoping they might still be alive. I wanted to ask them some questions about their two sons."

The woman, still skeptical asked as she raised the hoe slightly. "You from around here?"

"No I'm not," said Grant. "I'm a police officer from down in Townsend. My name is Grant Denlinger."

The woman seemed more relaxed now that she knew who he was and where he was from. "Well, if you're not selling anything and seeing as how you're a policeman, I might be able to help you out. Turn off your engine and come sit on my front porch. Now mind you, I'm not inviting you in. Don't allow strangers inside my house. The porch is fine, but inside the house…not gonna happen."

As Grant stepped out of the Jeep, she stepped back still wielding the hoe in a defensive position. She gave Grant the impression that she was a feisty old bird who could do some severe damage with that garden tool if she wanted to. Moving to the sidewalk, Grant commented, "I don't want to intrude on your day or take up too much of your time."

Gesturing with the hoe toward her house she responded, "Hah, my day! This day is just like yesterday and it'll be the same crap tomorrow. All I have left is time." Leaning the hoe against the side of the house, she started up the steps to the porch.

Grant stopped and bent over to smell some roses that were planted on either side of the porch steps. "You really have some nice roses out front here. My wife loves flowers."

"So you're a married fella then?"

"Yes, for almost a year now."

"Guess that means you don't have any children yet."

"My wife is expecting our first in about a month or so. It's a little girl."

The fact that he was not only a policeman, but married and was a soon to be new father, she commented, "You seem all right young man. Listen, I've got some iced tea inside. Would you care for a glass?"

Grant, now on the porch, answered, "That sounds wonderful. Thank you."

She extended her hand. "My name is Martha Hellman. I've been living in this house for forty-five years. Raised two kids here. Been widowed for fifteen. Sometimes it seems like it was only yesterday that my husband Frank died." She shook her head. "Oh well, let me get that tea and then we'll talk."

Grant settled into a floral covered settee and looked out across the lawn at the house next door; 2524 Cornell. It seemed like a nice neighborhood. He tried to picture how it had looked back when Conrad and his brother had come to live there. *Were there kids riding bikes up and down the street? Were there basketball goals affixed to the front of garages? Were there moms sitting on the porches talking to neighbors and Sunday barbecues in backyards?* He looked again at the home where Conrad and his brother had lived after being adopted. *Who lived there now? What secrets did the house hold?* Soon he would know.

Martha pushed her foot against the screen door and backed out with a tray containing three large glasses of iced tea and six Oreo cookies on a small paper plate. Setting the tray down on a small wicker table she said, "Here we go. While I was in the house I called my dear friend, Bernice. She lives across the street and knew the Pearls better than I did. She'll be joining us in a few minutes."

Martha had barely gotten the last words out of her mouth, when a chubby, gray haired lady came across the street and up the walk. Once on the porch, she plopped down into a chair next to Grant and reached for a glass of the tea. After taking a long gulp, she wiped her forehead with a handkerchief.

"Well, Good Lord," remarked Martha, "you could at least say hello before you start swigging down that tea."

Bernice took another drink, then commented, "Couldn't, I was dying of thirst." Looking at Grant she offered her hand, "My name's Bernice Morris, and you're Grant, the police officer from Townsend. Martha told me all about you when she called. Anyway, it's good to meet a fellow officer."

"Oh poop!" said Martha. "Being a school crossing guard twenty years ago doesn't qualify you as an officer of the law."

Bernice objected to Martha's comment as she fired back, "Your comment doesn't surprise me. You never having worked a day in your life!"

For the next two minutes Grant sat quietly and listened as the two old ladies tried their best to better the other with friendly insults. He realized that the two women had a special relationship, but if he didn't get the ball rolling he could wind up sitting there all afternoon. "Excuse me ladies, but I was wondering if I could ask you some questions about the Pearl's. I believe they had two sons."

Martha folded her arms across her chest. "Those boys, they were something else, especially the younger one...Russell."

There it is, thought Grant. *The name he had been searching for...Russell! Russell was his name.* A significant piece of the puzzle fell into place. "Can you tell me about when they first came to live here?"

Martha flashed a suspicious look. "Why do you want to know this stuff?"

Grant knew that he owed them some sort of an explanation if he expected them to open up. Leaning forward in the chair, he went on to explain, "My wife's name is Dana Beth. Her maiden name was Pearl. Her father was Conrad Pearl, Russell's brother. Neither my wife or Ruth, Conrad's wife, know anything about his family. Conrad, for some reason never talked about his past. We can't help but wonder why he never would tell his family anything about his past life. He died last year and now my wife is expecting our first child, so you can see why my wife and I are interested to know more about the grandparents. Does that make any sense?"

"Of course it does," said Bernice. "Family is the most important thing and it's just wonderful about your baby. I know when I had my first he cried all the time. The grandparents were always around to help me out."

"Oh, for crying out loud Bernice," said Martha. "That was a long time ago, but I agree with you on the family part. I do remember reading about it in the paper when Conrad died. He had a very long obituary, since he was a professor at the university. He was a very well liked man, but here in the neighborhood we knew a different side of him and I can see why he never wanted to talk about his parents." Looking over at the house she said, "It was not what you would call a good situation in that house." She turned and looked across the porch, "Bernice, you tell him about the early years. You know more about what went on."

Bernice picked up an Oreo and split it in two. "My husband and I were living here about five years when Marvin and Irene moved in. They seemed nice, but kept to themselves most of the time. I thought for the longest time it was because they didn't have any children and they didn't think they had a lot in common with us young couples. They were a good ten years older than most of the people who lived around here, but it turned out that wasn't the reason at all. It was Marvin. He was downright anti-social. We invited the Pearls to everything that went on in the neighborhood but they never attended. At times, I thought it was because he was a psychiatrist and he thought he was better than anyone else. Irene was always making apologies for why they couldn't come to neighborhood festivities. I think she wanted to come but was too controlled by her husband. Every once in a while Irene would talk to me when I was out in the front yard piddling with my flowers. If Marvin pulled up into their driveway she'd hightail it back across the street as if she were afraid of the man. Then one day out of the blue she tells me she and her husband are going to adopt two boys, about the same age as mine. That was such a strange moment. She really seemed like she wanted to talk about it, so I invited her up onto the porch." Bernice stopped talking as she wiped her forehead again, took a drink of the tea, then stuffed another Oreo into her mouth.

"Was that your third Oreo?" snapped Martha. "I laid out two for each of us. I think that was your third! I've only eaten one and Mr. Denlinger hasn't had any!"

With her mouth half full, Bernice held up two fingers as she looked at the plate, then continued with her story about the Pearls. "Anyway, Irene proceeds to tell me about the boys' parents being murdered over in the Iron Mountains in the eastern part of the state. She said the boys had spent nearly two years at a state run facility and most recently they had been at a temporary foster home. Marvin worked with the state quite a bit and counseled a number of children. It was just something he did on the side to make a little extra cash. Irene said he told her that while counseling the Pender boys; that was their murdered parents' name, he got attached to them. Said he felt sorry for them and wanted them to have a better life and a good home. She told me Marvin took her to see the boys on three different occasions. They were living on a farm about five miles south of Knoxville. When the boys found out they were to be adopted they were upset. They were happy on the farm and didn't want to move to the city, but the powers to be dictated that they were to be adopted by the Pearls. Why not? They had a nice house, Marvin had a great job and the state agency realized that it was going to be hard to adopt out two boys their age.

"Later on, we found out what he didn't tell Irene was that both the boys had what is more commonly referred to as sociopath tendencies. Now, you tell me. What kind of a man would keep that from his wife?"

Bernice sipped at her tea as she went on, "I had no idea what the term sociopath meant, so I looked it up. The description fit those two boys like a glove. I don't think either one of them had a conscious except when it came to animals. They were manipulative and never felt remorse for anything they did wrong. Marvin knew all of this, but still went ahead and convinced Irene to adopt."

Martha jumped in on the conversation, "Well, I for one think it was a terrible thing for Mr. Pearl to keep a thing like that from his wife, who by the way, had never been a parent before and all of a sudden is expected to raise two half grown boys."

Bernice stood. "I have to go to the bathroom. Can I use yours Martha or do I have to go home?"

"Oh, go on and use mine," Martha said as she rolled her eyes at Grant.

After Bernice was inside, Martha turned to Grant and stated as if she knew what she was saying was a fact. "I know she's going to sneak in the kitchen and get some more Oreos. She's diabetic. She's not supposed to eat a lot of sweets."

Taking an Oreo from the plate, she offered the last one to Grant. Grant said, "No thanks," then asked a question, "What happened to the boys after they moved in?"

"Frank and I moved next door to the Pearls a year after the boys were adopted. The word is that after they arrived and for the first month or so no one in the neighborhood ever saw them. It was summertime and there was no school. The boys never came out of the house. Mr. Pearl...Marvin, had a cabin north of Knoxville near Jellico Mountain where he used to go fishing whenever he had a chance. I thought he always took the boys up there and that's why we never saw them. But then, one time I ran into Irene at the market up the street and we got to talking and I asked her how the boys were doing. She said they were doing okay but they were on the quiet side. Most of the time, except for their meals, they stayed in their rooms."

Suddenly, Martha stopped talking as she looked at the screen door. "Where is Bernice? It doesn't take this long to go to the bathroom. I know she's in my cookie jar! I know how many are in there. I counted them."

The door opened and Bernice came out, brushing crumbs from the front of her blouse. Martha shook her head in amazement and picked up where she had left off, "Finally the two boys began to venture outside and my two sons and all of the kids in the neighborhood were anxious to meet them. It didn't take long for my two boys to figure out that Russell, in particular wasn't all there. Now, I know that sounds cruel, but I don't know how else to put it. He could talk, if he wanted to, but he would stare at them like he was a mute. Conrad did all the talking. Russell was going into the eighth grade so I knew he couldn't be too stupid. He was strange and eventually none of the kids in the neighborhood wanted anything to do with him. Conrad seemed all right to a point, but he wasn't that interested in making friends so my boys just let it go. It seemed like the Pearl boys kept mostly to themselves."

Grant was like a sponge, soaking up everything he was being told. These two women were the key to everything he needed to know about Conrad and his brother Russell. Martha excused herself and went back inside to refill their glasses with tea and no doubt count the rest of the Oreos in her cookie jar. Grant made small talk with Bernice until Martha returned and set down three fresh glasses of tea. "Now, where were we? Oh yes, when school started that fall, Irene told me she was glad the boys were finally getting out of the house on a more regular basis. It was only a few days later that I noticed she seemed to be unhappy. When I asked her what was wrong she told me the boys were being bullied at school and they were coming home angry every day. The other kids were calling them hillbillies and hicks and constantly making fun of them. It got so bad Irene had to drive them to school, because they refused to walk the three blocks. I felt sorry for the boys and Irene as well. Marvin insisted that they stick it out. The boys hated him for making them go to school."

Bernice interjected, "I remember that time. You hadn't lived here all that long, Martha. Do you remember that morning when there was all that commotion going on up the street? Two fire trucks, three police cars and an ambulance sped up the street to the school. For a moment I thought it was one of those student shootings you hear about on television. It scared the dickens out of me. Remember how we hurried up to the school wondering what was going on. We just couldn't believe what we heard when we got there. My boys came running up to me saying that the school had to be evacuated. Someone had broken into the school overnight and had let over a hundred snakes loose in the hallways. Of course they were only garter snakes, but it didn't matter. They were snakes and they were everywhere."

Martha corrected Bernice, "It wasn't over a hundred. It was more like thirty."

"Well, I heard it was a hundred," said Bernice. "Anyway they had to close the school for two days to clear out all the snakes. They never found out who broke in, but I knew who it was. Remember, Martha, how we talked about it? We figured it was Russell. The night before the school was closed down, Martha and me were sitting on the porch and we saw Russell going up the street in the direction of the school on his bike. He had a number of sacks tied to the bike. I bet ya, he was the one who broke in and put those snakes in the school. I told my husband about it but he thought it best to just let it go. I really didn't have any proof that there were snakes in those bags and besides that, I could get Russell kicked out of school, which would piss Mr. Pearl off to no end. My husband felt they already had enough problems."

"It wasn't long after that," interjected Martha, "that Russell was removed from public school and placed in a special education program. Conrad didn't accept it very well. I recall one time, in the front yard, he was yelling and screaming at the Pearls for sending his younger brother to another school. Then things seemed to settle down for a while. The boys spent their weekends and most of the summer with Marvin up at the Jellico cabin. Every once in a while I'd see them. I'd always say hello, but they would just look at me and run off. When summer ended and it was time to return to school, Russell had grown two inches taller even though he was two years younger and taller than his older brother, but Conrad still looked out for Russell." Martha put her hands to her head as if she suddenly had a revelation. "What time is it? I have to put a roast on before four."

"Relax," said Bernice as she checked her watch. "It's only twelve thirty. You've got plenty of time."

"Maybe you two ladies would like to go to lunch," said Grant. "I'm buyin'."

Martha and Bernice looked at each other, then Martha spoke, "I can fix you a sandwich if you're hungry. I really don't like to eat at restaurants."

"Well, I do," stated Bernice. "I don't get out that much."

Grant could see that he was getting into the middle of an argument. "That's okay. Why don't we just go on with our conversation?"

Martha snapped her fingers. "I just remembered two other incidents that concerned those boys. I'm sure there were more, but I remember these two like they just happened yesterday. Since Russell attended a special school on the other side of town, he always took the school bus. One day when he got off, he came face to face with the Witlow twins. They were the same age as Conrad. They were mean little shits. They were always in trouble. They never said much to Conrad, but they were always giving Russell a rough time. Well, on that particular day, Russell comes across the twins who had found a small kitten. They were throwing the poor animal up in the air and laughing. Both of the Pearl boys, especially Russell, liked animals and seeing the Witlows mistreating that cat didn't sit well with him. He approached them and told them to stop. They gave him the finger and called him a couple of names and threw the cat into the air again. It was over in less than a minute. Russell attacked both of them. *I mean attacked!* He beat the living hell out of those boys. In fact, the parents sued Marvin and Irene for medical bills and damages.

"Anyway, Russell took the kitten home, but Marvin told him he had to keep that mangy critter out in the garage. Marvin could have cared less about that kitten. One morning when he left for work, he left the garage door open and the cat got out. Poor little thing got run over right over there on the other side of the street in front of Bernice's. Even though it was an accident, Conrad told Russell that Marvin might just as well have killed that kitten. When Russell asked Marvin if he had killed his cat, Marvin said that it was an accident but it really wasn't any big deal. It was just a worthless cat."

Holding up her finger to make a point, she kept right on talking, "Another time, and this was even worse, Russell and Conrad brought home two puppies that some people were giving away in front of the grocery store at the other end of the street. Irene didn't have a problem with the boys bringing home the dogs, but Marvin went into a rage and told them they had to return the puppies immediately. That night, Irene woke Marvin up and told him she was hearing noise on the roof. He listened and he heard it too. He went outside, grabbed a ladder from the garage and put it up against the side of the house above the window where the boys slept. Marvin was up on the top of the ladder looking around on the roof, when suddenly the ladder tipped sideways and he fell to the ground. He broke his right arm and left leg. He missed six months of work which resulted in the loss of some of his patients and cost him a great deal of money. After that, he always said that he had the ladder secured and he couldn't figure out how it tipped over. I know darn well what happened. Now, I never approached the Pearls and expressed my thoughts, but I know. I think one or both of those boys reached out the window and pushed that ladder over. Those boys had a mean streak about them that was hard to explain and it always seemed to revolve around animals. It wasn't until a few years later that we found out about how their parents were murdered and all their animals were killed. Irene said the boys were always saying that someday they were going to get even with people who mistreated animals. So, when you think about it, it's no wonder they went off on the Witlow twins and Marvin."

Everything Grant was hearing fell in line with what he already knew. Things like Russell liked to handle snakes, which meant that he very well could have taken all those snakes to school. Russell had attacked those two boys that were mistreating a kitten, a form of revenge for what he had witnessed as a young boy over in Mountain City. And then there was the fact that both Martha and Bernice knew about the Pender murders. It made sense that the boys would rebel against Marvin who didn't care for animals, but would they try to kill the man who had taken them into his home and offered them a better way of life?

Martha stood up. "I gotta walk off a cramp. It's hell getting old."

She limped across the porch, as Bernice elaborated on what Martha had said previously, "It seemed that after a while Conrad started to come around. He was doing well in high school and even started to date on occasion. Russell was doing bad in school and became almost impossible to deal with. Irene mentioned to me that her husband had a real problem with Russell, saying they should have only adopted Conrad and that Russell was nothing but trouble. Russell spent a lot of time in his room. Marvin was not happy with the way things turned out, but he had problems of his own to deal with. Besides, the stress of raising the two boys, his business was dropping off and he and Irene were not getting on that well. Marvin felt that he just couldn't deal with Russell, and Conrad told him to just let his brother be. He'd take care of him, just like he always had—"

Martha interrupted, "Then the letter came. I remember one day when Irene came over to pay me a visit. She was out of breath and so excited. Marvin got a letter from a lawyer from over in Mountain City stating that the five hundred acres that Millard Pender owned had been purchased for close to four million dollars and was to be placed in a trust for Conrad and Russell. Of course, Marvin was the executor of the trust fund. Can you imagine that? Two million dollars each! Irene was so excited, saying that Marvin could get his business back on track, maybe even retire and move out to the country. I was really excited for her. A couple of weeks later I asked her if they had received the money and she started to cry. Even though the boys were legally adopted, and still not of age to receive the money, it still belonged to them and Marvin and Irene were told by the court that they were not entitled to any of the money unless the boys agreed to it. She told me Conrad and Russell refused to sign over a single penny of the money. Conrad had been especially vicious, reminding them that they were not allowed to have a kitten in the house and how Marvin had killed their pet and how Marvin had refused to allow them to keep those two puppies. He said that he and Russell never wanted to be adopted by them and they should have let them stay on the farm where they were happy. Conrad looked at both Marvin and Irene and told them 'What goes around comes around!'"

Bernice chimed in, "Then later that year a bunch of stuff happened. Conrad turned eighteen and was a senior in high school. In May of that year just prior to Conrad graduating, Marvin died of a heart attack. Irene found him sitting in the kitchen with his head down on the table. She gave him a nice funeral and in some ways it almost seemed like she was glad he was gone. Now that Conrad was of age, and according to the trust entitled to get his money, he went to Irene and asked her for the paperwork. She turned it over to him without making a fuss. She even went along with him to the bank where his share of the money was transferred over to an account that was set up in his name. Russell's money had to remain in the fund until he turned eighteen. Now, Conrad Pearl, the orphan from Mountain City, was a millionaire.

"After Conrad graduated, he took Russell out of school. Conrad thought it was for the best since Russell was constantly getting into trouble and not learning much of anything. In July of that year Conrad and Russell left town."

Grant was confused. "That would have put Russell at about sixteen. How was it that he was allowed to go off and live on his own?"

Now, Martha was talking again, "Conrad offered Irene a substantial amount of money for Marvin's cabin up in Jellico. Irene really had only been up there a few times and had no reason to go back, so she sold it to Conrad. Conrad and Russell moved into the cabin. It was for the best, especially for Russell. I'm sure if the authorities knew about it they may have frowned on the situation. Irene just kept the whole thing to herself. The further Conrad kept Russell from people the better. Poor Irene was all alone in that big house so I started to visit her on occasion. She revealed to me that she had never been happy living with Marvin. After they adopted the two boys, things got worse. She told me that Marvin was abusive. He never hit her, but he was verbally abusive and kept her under his thumb. She never had a say so about anything. She was skeptical when they adopted the boys and was actually afraid of them. She went on to tell me that Russell was always bringing snakes home in jars and playing with them in his room. He would roam around the house in the middle of the night and sometimes she would wake up and find him staring at her. At times Russell and Conrad would get into fist fights, but even though, Conrad was very protective of his young brother."

"I think part of the problem," said Bernice, "was that Marvin never showed them any kindness or love. Irene tried, but those boys kept their distance. She told me one time that Russell would just glare at her with those steel cold eyes until she would turn away. I got my nerve up one day and asked her if Marvin knew about the money before they adopted the boys. She told me after Marvin died, one of his close golfing buddies confided in her telling her Marvin had learned about the upcoming sale of the Pender farm and that's the real reason why he adopted the boys. It was simply for the money. It had nothing to do with giving the two boys a better life."

Martha was back on the soapbox. "In the end, as they say I suppose everything worked out. Conrad got an apartment here in Knoxville and attended the university. With Conrad's help, Russell got his money and as far as I know continued to live in the Jellico Mountain cabin."

The phone from inside the house rang interrupting Martha. She stood as she announced, "There's the phone. Be right back."

After she went inside Bernice leaned over and whispered to Grant, "Martha won't admit it, but she was really afraid of the Pearl boys. It wasn't so bad when Frank was alive, but after he died she had an alarm system installed and had double locks put on all the doors and windows."

Martha opened the screen door. "I heard my name. What are you talking about?"

Bernice reached for the last Oreo as she answered, "Nothing about you, Martha. If no one is going to eat this cookie, then I will."

"Tell me, Ladies," said Grant, "Did Irene ever see Conrad or Russell again?"

"Only one time," answered Bernice, "and it was just Conrad, not Russell. What happened was, the house got to be too much for her and she couldn't see living there all alone so she sold the place and moved to a retirement village where eventually she could have assisted living if need be. Conrad, who of course was attending school here at the university found out and visited her at her new residence. Martha and I used to go visit her from time to time. She told us Conrad had come to see her. He informed her he had deposited a large amount of cash in an account so she would be taken care of the rest of her life. He also told her that along with the money came a stipulation that she would never see him or Russell ever again. It was for the best. She showed us articles in the paper when Conrad graduated from the university and then when he became a professor and when he got married. I guess it made her feel that he had turned out all right."

"Then one day," said Martha, "she showed us an article in the newspaper about some hunters finding some human remains up near the Jellico Mountain. The road they named was right in back of their old cabin. The paper said two hunters found a skeleton with its leg caught in a steel animal trap. At first Irene thought that it might have been Russell. It said in the paper that the man had a fractured skull and a number of old rusty traps were found nearby. The reporter wrote that it must have been a poacher who was setting traps. They surmised he fell and got caught in one of his own traps. Isn't that just horrible? Anyway, it couldn't have been Russell, because the man was only about five-foot-seven. Russell was well over six foot."

Placing her hands over her head, Martha yawned and said, "I'm getting tired. Time for a short nap before I start that roast. The end of this story is that Irene died at the age of eighty-six."

Grant realized his talk with the two ladies had come to an end. It was an abrupt ending but still, he had received more information than he had hoped for. "Well, I don't want to interfere with your nap or your roast. I really need to get on the road. I can't thank you enough for the help you have been."

As he stood, Martha said, "Now, when the baby comes I want a picture. Be sure and send me one."

Bernice chimed in, "Me, too!"

Opening his notebook to a blank page he unclipped his pen. "It will be my pleasure. Just let me write down your names and addresses and I'll make sure you each get one."

After he wrote down the information, he closed the notebook and turned to leave, but was stopped by Martha who gave him a big hug. "You're a nice young man. I know you will make a great father." She turned and went back into the house.

"She gets so emotional at times," said Bernice. "She really misses her two boys. Both live out of state and don't visit her very often."

Grant smiled as he walked down the porch steps. "Will you tell her I said goodbye?"

Once inside the Jeep, he waved at Bernice and pulled away from the curb as he thought to himself, *Martha said I was a nice young man. Am I? Are all the secrets I'm keeping and all the lies taking me farther away from that image?*

Grant arrived home at 3:30 in the afternoon. As he climbed out of the Jeep, Ruth came running out the front door of the house. "Don't get out! It's time! We need to go to the hospital!"

Dana Beth stepped out the front door and smiled. "We're going to have a baby."

CHAPTER FIFTEEN

THE SMALL THREE VEHICLE CARAVAN turned from Happy Valley Road onto a dirt road that crossed a field surrounded by tall pines. Buckwald Hiller, more commonly referred to as "Buck," the Townsend fire chief and scoutmaster, stopped the lead van in a clearing and stepped out. A second van and then a third parked next to the deep forest. Herman Black, a local insurance agent, who was the assistant scoutmaster, joined Buck as Dalton and Nelson Day, father of one of the scouts, climbed out of the church van. Dalton, a former scoutmaster, smiled while he watched thirteen, twelve to fifteen-year-old boy scouts clamor out of the first two vans as they gathered up knapsacks, bedrolls, tents and other assorted equipment for their three day hike into the mountains. Three church members, fathers of three of the young boys climbed out of the backseat of the last van, shook hands with Buck, Herman, Dalton and Nelson, said goodbye to the boys, then drove away, leaving the thirteen scouts and four adults standing at the edge of the forest. Buck, signaled everyone to gather near a posted sign that read: COOPER RUN TRAIL.

Getting everyone's attention, he tapped the top of the sign with a stick. "All right boys. In about ten minutes we'll get started. This will be a three-day hike, our final destination will be Abrams Falls over near Cades Cove. Today we'll knock out the two miles of Cooper Run Trail and about six miles of the Little Bottoms Trail where we'll make camp for the night. Tomorrow, we'll finish up the remaining six miles of Little Bottoms and two miles of the Abrams Creek Trail, then call it a day once again. On Sunday, we'll finish up the last six miles at Abrams Creek where the vans will be waiting for us." Walking in front of the group to get their undivided attention, Buck continued as he pointed the stick back at the forest. "Cooper Run is a relatively flat trail so the first two miles of our journey should be easy *but* the Little Bottoms Trail is not one of the more popular hiking trails in the area because the trail is not that well marked. A lot of folks who come out here alone have gotten lost, so stay together and don't wander off. If we should encounter any black bears or snakes remember the guidelines we laid out last week. If you follow the rules that we established no one should get injured. Any questions?"

The boys, who stood in a sloppy line, answered no or nodded their heads that they understood. Placing the stick over his shoulder, Buck motioned toward Dalton. "We have two additional adults along with us on our trip. Dalton, a former scoutmaster and Nelson, one of the parent volunteers, so if you have any questions or if any problems should arise you can go to them as well as Mr. Black and me." Hesitating, he instructed the boys to line up in a straight line, then count off starting at one and ending at number thirteen. "Here's the way we'll head out and we will resume this procedure throughout the three days. I'll take the point, then one through five will be next followed by Mr. Black, then comes six through nine, then Nelson, followed by numbers ten through thirteen, Dalton bringing up the rear. All right, let's move out!"

Buck led the way into the thick forest, everyone following according to their assigned positions. It was only a forty minute hike down to the Cooper Run Trail where the group turned right and started up the gradual path leading up into the mountains.

Dalton, the last in line thought about his new Great Granddaughter. Earlier in the year, when the scout troop from the Tuckaleechee Methodist Church in Townsend decided on a Memorial weekend three day hike both he and Grant had volunteered to go along as chaperones. Because of the birth of Crystal Ann, Grant was forced to cancel on his commitment. He felt it was far more important to remain at home with his wife, Ruth and the new baby. Walking along, Dalton smiled to himself as he thought about Crystal Ann. He would have liked it if Grant and Dana Beth were still living on the farm, but he understood that having a home of their own was important.

The last scout in line, turned and spoke to Dalton as he stepped over a large tree root. "Mr. Denlinger, I was talking with my father the other night about all the murders we had last year. When I told him you were going to be one of our chaperons he told me you were the former police chief in Townsend. He also told me a lot of folks in town are upset because the local police can't catch the killer. I asked my father if he was upset and he said he felt the police were doing the best they could."

Dalton knew the young boy as Jimmy Rollins, son of Nate Rollins, a local electrical contractor. Walking next to the boy, Dalton continued the conversation, "Your father is right. The police are doing everything they can, but at this point they still don't know who the killer is."

Jimmy kicked at a rock that was on the side of the trail. "All the kids at school think the killer is a hero. Everyone he killed was unkind to animals. Our teacher told us that even though the victims had been cruel to animals no one had the right to kill them. It's hard to understand."

Placing his hand on Jimmy's shoulder, Dalton tried to reassure the young boy. "They'll catch the killer eventually and the truth will come out." The conversation with Dalton quickly ended as the scout in front of Jimmy punched him on the shoulder while pointing out two grey squirrels that ran up the side of a nearby tree.

Dalton fell back a few feet as he thought about the brief discussion he had with the young boy. Jimmy had hit the nail right on the head. Most of the citizens in Townsend were upset with Brody and his inability to put an end to the killings. Just two weeks ago, he had attended a city council meeting where the topic of Brody's unpopularity had come up. Even though Axel Brody was the Police Chief, it was not entirely his fault that the killer was still out there somewhere. The Feds and Chief Blue from over in Cherokee, aside from coming up with a profile on the killer, hadn't so much as put a dent in the case.

Starting up the side of a steep incline of the trail, Dalton stopped, knelt down and retied his right boot as he looked at the surrounding forest. *The Great Smoky Mountains,* he thought. He had lived here in the Smokies all his life and even though he had never been in this section of the mountains before, he felt at home in the forest.

Climbing yet another steep grade, Dalton had to pay close attention to the boys walking in front of him due to the deep drop off on their left. The trail eventually went back down the side of the mountain into a valley next to a stream.

Over the next three miles, the group stopped on a number of occasions as Buck pointed out various trees: Honey Locust, Yellow Buckeye and Silver Maple all seemingly swallowed up by countless Fraser Firs. As the trail weaved its way through the thick green trees, there were numerous splashes of color from the mountain flowers.

Dalton recalled the days long ago when he had been a young scout and had memorized various trees and plants in order to acquire his forestry merit badge. Back then, there was hardly a tree that he could not identify. Now, years later he couldn't tell one from the next.

Stopping for a break, the group huddled together near the stream. They drank from their canteens and had healthy snacks from their backpacks. Buck's deep voice echoed down the path as he ordered the group, "Let's get moving, we'll be stopping for the night in about two hours."

The group once again formed up in their assigned hiking positions and started up the trail following the stream. Dalton, taking up his position, smiled as he remembered when Grant was that age. It seemed like the time had flown by and now Grant was not only married but a father. As of late, he seemed so distant. Maybe all of the new responsibilities of a wife, a new baby and owning a home in such a short time had become too much for him, but then again, Grant seemed to be handling that part of his life rather well.

Dalton thought about how his grandson had changed, especially since the beginning of the year. When Dalton brought up the subject of the recent murders, Grant said that he didn't have time to deal with it. It had become clear to Dalton, that for some reason, Grant didn't want to talk about it.

Buck raised his hand high in the air as he announced, "Hold up boys." Looking to his right, then left he commanded the group, "We'll camp right here. It's flat with the protection of the mountain on either side and we've got plenty of water from the stream."

Dalton glanced down at his watch: exactly five o'clock.

Signaling the boys to gather near the stream, Buck continued to give orders, "Listen up! We'll split up into three groups, the same way we hiked in. Group numbers one through five will remain here at the campsite and under the direction of Mr. Black and Mr. Day you'll begin to set up the tents in a circle surrounding the site. Group six through nine will be with me as we construct an area for the fire and prepare the evening meal. The third group, numbers ten though thirteen will accompany Mr. Denlinger over to the side of the mountain where you will gather enough firewood for the night. All right gentlemen...let's get to it."

Dalton smiled as he watched the boys scatter like ants, each one with an assigned duty. The boys in the wood gathering group stood at his side as they awaited his orders. Pointing at the side of the mountain twenty yards away, Dalton gave instructions. "You two need to gather smaller branches for kindling while myself and the other boys will collect larger branches. Be careful where you step. Don't reach down behind any logs or large rocks. With all of the noise we've made all of the snakes are more than likely gone, but just to be on the safe side, let's be extra careful."

As the boys made their way toward the base of the mountain, one of them asked, "Mr. Denlinger, have you ever been bitten by a snake?"

Dalton smiled as he answered, "No, never have been bit, but I've had a run in with a few snakes. I'd just as soon not run into any today so let's be careful."

At the base of the mountain, two of the boys began to pick up smaller twigs while Dalton and the others foraged for larger branches. The two gathering the kindling, their arms full of dried dead branches, returned to the campsite where they deposited the wood in a pile next to the stream. Dalton bent over and picked up a dead tree branch and snapped it over his upper right leg three times to create wood suitable for the fire. Spotting another branch, he was interrupted by the voice of Jimmy Rollins, "Mr. Denlinger...look at that weird green looking tree over there up the side of the mountain."

Dalton looked in the direction the boy pointed. A ray of sun that had filtered down through the tall trees glimmered off the side of what appeared to be the trunk of a metallic green tree encased in weeds and hanging tree vines. The bright green color seemed out of place as if it were not natural in the forest, like it was some sort of man-made color. Taking three steps toward the tree that was still a good ten yards off, Dalton squinted his eyes trying to make out what would cause such an unusual color on a tree. Three more steps and he stopped dead in his tracks. It wasn't a tree, but the left front side of a car fender jammed up against the side of the tree, a portion of the black tire now coming into view.

Three more steps and he saw what he thought was a human skull and part of a body that was nothing more than bones laying on the green hood just on the other side of where the windshield had been. Turning, he signaled for the boys to stop. "Jimmy! I want you to take the boys back to the campsite and tell Buck to get back over here."

Jimmy, curious as the others, asked, "Is there something wrong, Mr. Denlinger?"

"I'm not sure. Just take the boys back to the camp and tell Buck to come see me."

The small group of scouts followed Jimmy to the campsite where he told them that Dalton had ordered them back. After the boys left the area, Dalton stepped even closer to the car. He could now see that the tire was completely flat, the front windshield was broken out, glass was scattered across the metallic green hood and around the skeleton, which still had shreds of what had been a shirt clinging to the bones in a few spots. The left arm of the body was missing. Stepping as close as he could to the car, he pushed back some hanging vines and looked closely at the body. There wasn't a trace of skin left, no eyeballs and only a few small strands of dead hair left on the skull.

From behind him he heard the voice of Buck, "The boys told me something might be wrong over here."

Dalton pointed toward the car as he answered, "Yeah, there is something wrong, something that's out of place here in the middle of nowhere."

Buck's eyes grew large as he saw the car and then the skeleton. "My God! Did any of the boys see this?"

"No, I don't think so. What got their attention was the odd color of metallic green on the car. They thought that it was a strange colored tree. When I discovered what it was I sent them back for you. I don't think they know there's a car or a body over here."

Moving closer to the car, Buck commented, "Every time I go on one of these weekend trips with the scouts we always come across something interesting, but this tops them all." Looking up the side of the mountain, he remarked, "The car came from up there."

"Well, I'm not that familiar with this part of the mountains," pointed out Dalton. "I wasn't even aware there was a road up there."

Buck made his way around to the passenger side door as he pushed some low hanging tree branches to the side. "It's an old, one lane dirt road. Actually it's used by the county fire department. The electric company uses it to service the power lines in this area. I've been on the road a few times when we had to come up here for reported fires." He reached out and ran his hand down the side of the car.

Dalton immediately ordered him in a friendly fashion. "Don't touch anything unless you've got gloves on. We don't know what went on here. This just might turn out to be an automobile accident but until we know that for sure we have to be careful about how we handle things."

Buck removed a pair of brown work gloves from his back pocket as he apologized, "Sorry."

Looking back up the side of the mountain Dalton asked, "About how far up is that road?"

"I don't know," said Buck. "We're pretty far down. Hell, could be a couple of hundred yards or maybe a half mile. We won't know until we climb out if that's what you have in mind."

Dalton pointed at a number of smaller trees that had been sheared off and rocks scraped by the car when it descended down the mountain. "You can see the path the car took."

"We should call this in right away," said Buck. "Our cell phones are useless this far out in the mountains but I can use my two-way radio to call the fire station and they can contact the police."

"Sounds good," remarked Dalton, "but first maybe we can identify the driver. See if you can reach in and open the glove box. You'll be looking for a vehicle registration."

The car was setting at a downward angle and the passenger door was wedged shut by a tree. Buck, using a small rock cleared away the loose glass around the edges of the window and leaned in as he reached for the glove box. The latch was just out of his reach.

Looking through the broken front windshield at Dalton, Buck shook his head. "Can't get to it from this angle. Can you get in from the driver's side?"

"Not without disturbing the body," answered Dalton. "That's one thing we want to avoid if at all possible. Maybe you can crawl in the back window and then reach over the seat."

Buck pulled himself toward the rear door and once again made sure he knocked away all the jagged glass. "Here goes," he said as he slithered through the opening. Sitting awkwardly in the backseat he propped himself up by placing his feet on the front seat, took a deep breath, then leaned over the seat and reached for the glove box. After fumbling with the latch for a few moments it finally opened. Grabbing an old folder and a small box he returned to the backseat. Laying the folder on the floor, he opened the box and much to his surprise found that it was full of revolver shells. Holding up one of the shells he commented, "Maybe this guy is a cop or something. I mean, hell, regular folks don't normally drive around with ammunition in their car."

Dalton wasn't interested in the shells although it did seem odd. "Look in the folder and see if you can find the registration."

Opening the folder, Buck located an old owner's manual, a few old receipts for oil changes, a coupon for a free car wash and finally the vehicle registration. "Here it is...found it." Unfolding the official document he read the name at the bottom of the form, "Joshua James Pickler."

Dalton looked at Buck in amazement as he repeated the name, "Joshua James Pickler." He thought to himself, *Joshua James Pickler. Of course, J.J. Pickler!*

Buck picked up on Dalton's reaction to the name on the registration. "You know this guy?"

"I've heard of him. Look, put the box of shells and the folder back in the glove compartment, crawl out and throw me your gloves. I'm going to see if there's any ID on the driver."

Replacing the shells and the folder back where he found them, Buck crawled back out the window, made his way down to the front of the car and tossed his gloves to Dalton. Dalton, putting on the gloves pointed to the shredded pants on the skeleton where he thought he saw what appeared to be the edge of a wallet. Leaning in the driver's side window, he grabbed the wallet with little effort as the thin material ripped away. "Got it," he said. Sliding down the side of the embankment, he opened the wallet and located a license. Just like he thought. The driver was Joshua James Pickler. Holding up the license, he displayed it to Buck.

Buck thought for a moment then stated, "Wait a minute. Isn't that the guy from over in Gatlinburg that's been missing for what...almost two months?"

"Well, we can't be sure this Joshua James Pickler is the J.J. Pickler that's missing, but how many J.J. Picklers can there be?"

"What about the photo on the license. Is that the Pickler that's missing?"

"I don't know," answered Dalton. "I've never met the man. But, if it is him, then what we've discovered here is much more than an automobile accident."

Buck joined Dalton near the front of the car. "You're losing me now. I don't understand."

Dalton laid the wallet on the seat and looked in the back as he explained, "Do you remember the third murder we had last year?"

Buck, looking at the skeleton closely, answered, "Ah, let's see...that would have been Butch Miller. Yeah, I do remember that. It was horrible, I mean what they said in the paper about how he got ripped to bits by those dogs."

"Pickler disappeared after Miller's murder. Then a couple of weeks later he shows up back in town. He went to the police and was eventually cleared of any involvement in the murder. Then a couple of months back he reported some man stole a bear he had in front of his store and now he's disappeared again...well, up until now."

"So what you're saying is this might not be an accident."

"I don't know. Maybe it is, maybe it isn't. We won't actually know if this is the J.J. Pickler that's missing until somebody ID's his photo."

Buck walked past the car and climbed a few yards up the side of the mountain and looked up through the trees. "Well, this really screws the weekend up, now doesn't it. We can't very well just continue on like nothing happened. We'll have to call this in, especially, if this really is Pickler."

Dalton removed the gloves as he walked back down to the front of the car. "You need to call the fire station. Have them call Sheriff Grimes and the county coroner over in Maryville. I guess they better call Sheriff Brody as well. I'm not sure exactly where we are. We might be in the Townsend city limits. Anyways, have Grimes, the coroner and Brody meet at the firehouse. You can have one of your boys lead them up there to the road above. Someone will have to climb up and wait for them."

"Let's think about this first. What are they going to need to bring up here. I'm sure they'll want to haul the body up to the road...and maybe even the car," Buck said.

"You're right. When you call in, tell them to inform the coroner that we have a body up here. Now, as far as the car goes, that could be difficult. The way I see it the easiest way to get the car out would be by copter."

Looking up at the tall dense trees, Buck expelled that idea as he explained, "Naw, never work. Trees are too thick. First of all it'd be too difficult to navigate in between the mountains. Second, they wouldn't be able to get low enough and besides that, how would they know where to lower the tow line. What we need is a tow truck with an extra long heavy duty line. Here's what I think we should tell them. When Grimes, the coroner and Brody arrive at the fire station, I'll have four of my firefighters in two jeeps drive up here. They can drive the police in and bring along the equipment that's needed. If we try to pull this car back up it might be ripped to pieces. What we might have to do is cut it into more manageable sections. We'll also have to drain out any gas that might still be in the tank. After that, we can haul it up the mountainside in sections."

Dalton nodded in agreement, "Sounds like a plan. Make the call."

As Buck turned to get his two-way radio from the campsite, Dalton stopped him. "Wait a minute. How are you going to handle this...I mean as far as the boys are concerned?"

Buck thought for a moment, then answered, "I'll be honest with them just like I always have. I'll tell them we discovered a car with a body it in. That's all they have to know. The real decision is whether we continue the hike or cut it short."

Dalton stopped Buck again as he thought of something else. "Look, when you make the call have the fire station call the police over in Gatlinburg as well. They may want to be involved since Pickler lived over in that area."

The phone at the Townsend Police Station rang three times before Marge picked up. "Townsend Police Department." She listened while the voice on the other end explained the reason for the call. Axel Brody happened to walk into the front office as she was taking short notes and responding to what she was being told: "I see. The former Police Chief, Dalton Denlinger is already on the scene. Meet at the fire station within the hour. The victim might be J.J. Pickler. Thank you...I'll get the message to the Chief."

Brody didn't pay much attention to what Marge was saying until she mentioned the name of Pickler. Turning from the coffee machine, he set his cup down as Marge hung up the phone. "Did I hear you correctly? Did you say J.J. Pickler?"

"You did hear me correctly. That was the firehouse on the line. They said that Buck Hiller has the boy scouts out on a hike over in the mountains about eight miles past Happy Valley. Dalton is with them. They found a car, a green Cadillac at the bottom of a deep ravine. They also found a body behind the wheel, which is nothing more than a skeleton. The fire station said Hiller called in to get hold of the police. You're to get over to the fire station in the next hour where you'll meet up with Sheriff Grimes and the county coroner. Sheriff Blake from Gatlinburg has also been requested. They said they need a tow truck. I guess I'll call Nick's towing service and have them meet you guys at the station."

Brody couldn't get a word in as Marge was rattling off the instructions she had been given. "Wait a minute, just wait a minute!" snapped Brody. "What's all this have to do with Pickler?"

"They think the body found in the car might be J.J. Pickler."

Brody was about to say something else, but was interrupted by Marge, "Look Axel, you don't have time to hang around here and interrogate me. All I know is what I've been told. Now, you need to get moving. It's almost six o'clock. They're planning on leaving for the mountains by seven. They want to get up there before it gets dark."

Brody grabbed his hat and headed for the door as he ordered Marge, "Call Griner and Jacks and let them know what's going on. Tell them to mind the store. If anything else develops on this, call me and let me know. I'm outta here!"

Climbing into his red pickup, Brody as usual squeezed every possible dramatic moment that he could out of a situation, flipping on the flashing red and blue lights and hitting the siren as he sped out of the parking lot. Exceeding the speed limit by a good twenty miles per hour, he raced up the Parkway thinking about the ramifications of discovering J.J. Pickler's body. He recalled that night nearly eight months ago when he had received the call that one of his officers had been found murdered over at J.J.'s Junk Emporium in Sevierville. One of the strangest clues found at the junkyard had been a note duct taped to the fence along with two of Miller's severed fingers attached to it. The note simply read. Pickler...you're next! Pickler was the first to discover Miller's body and fled town when he saw the note. Now, months later, it appears that he is discovered at the bottom of a ravine in his car.

Grant, exhausted, was sitting on the couch as Dana Beth had just put Crystal Ann to sleep. Ruth was busy in the kitchen washing up the last of the dinner dishes when the phone rang. Dana Beth walked across the living room and answered the phone, "Denlinger residence." After listening for a few seconds, she turned and offered the phone to Grant, "It's Marge over at the station. She needs to talk with you."

Taking the receiver from Dana Beth, Grant spoke, "Hey Marge, what's up?"

Marge's voice was filled with a sense of urgency as she explained, "Grant, I apologize for interrupting you at home. We just got a call from the fire station. A boy scout troop discovered a car with a body in it at the bottom of a ravine near Little Bottoms Trail. Dalton thinks it might be J.J. Pickler. Anyway, Axel is meeting Sheriff Grimes, the county coroner and Chief Blake from Gatlinburg at the firehouse. They plan on leaving for the mountains by seven. The reason I'm calling is I thought you might want to tag along since no one else on the investigating team has been notified. Agents Gephart and Green took the week off and Chief Blue lives too far away. I know you're at home this week with the new baby, but I thought you'd like to know what's going on."

The thought that J.J. Pickler had been found caused a moment of silence from Grant as he stared out the front window, then finally responded, "Listen Marge...thanks for calling."

Dana Beth noticed the look on his face. "You look like you've seen a ghost. Is there something wrong?"

Grant walked to the chair next to the fireplace and sat down as he answered, "Yeah, there is something wrong. They think they found J.J. Pickler's body up in the mountains."

Ruth walked into the living room as she overheard the conversation. "Oh no...not another murder!"

Grant stood as he walked back to the front window. He desperately wanted to be involved, but at the moment his place was at his wife and new baby's side.

Dana Beth joined him as she asked, "Did they say how it happened?"

"I really don't know," said Grant. "Marge said they found a body in a wrecked car at the bottom of a ravine in the mountains. They said it might be Pickler. Everyone is meeting at the firehouse at seven to head up there."

Placing her hand on his shoulder, she looked him squarely in the eyes. "Well, what are you waiting for? You better get a move on if you want to get to the firehouse before they leave."

Grant looked at Dana Beth and Ruth as he apologized. "I didn't mean that I had to go. Look, I took the week off to help you out with the baby. Right now, my place is here at home with you."

Ruth joined them at the window. "Everything here is going to be fine. Crystal Ann is sleeping. There isn't anything that could possibly happen that Dana Beth and I can't handle. Now, go on, get out of here and do your job."

"Are you sure it'll be all right if I go?" asked Grant.

Dana Beth walked to the front door and grabbed Grant's keys from a wooden bowl and tossed them to her husband. "If you don't leave now you're not going to get there on time." She opened the door and ordered, "Go on, now get out of here."

Grant kissed her on the cheek and as he backed out the front door hollered, "I might not be back until tomorrow morning."

It wasn't five minutes before Brody pulled into the fire station. He parked his truck off to the side of the parking lot and walked up to four firemen who were in the process of loading the needed equipment for the trip up the mountains. Gesturing towards the Jeeps he asked, "What's all this?"

One of the firemen, loading a heavy duty reciprocating saw into the back of one of the Jeeps answered the question, "Fire chief said we might need to cut the car apart in order to drag it up."

Another fireman who was placing a coil of rope in the back of the Jeep looked Brody up and down. "You're going to have a tough go of it going down the side of the mountain in those duds."

Brody, placing his left cowboy booted foot on the rear bumper of the Jeep answered sarcastically, "Who said anythin' about goin' down the side of a mountain?"

Rolling his eyes at the others, the fireman remarked, "Well, if you're just going along for the ride I guess you'll be okay. I thought with you being the Chief of Police and all you might want to get down to the scene, that's all."

Brody, offended at the young man's attitude, snapped back instantly, "Look son, this is a police matter. If anybody's goin' along for the ride, it's the fire company. When we get up there I'll be givin' the orders."

A young, tall muscular fireman who was arranging two tool boxes in the back of a Jeep stepped close to Brody. Towering over Axel, the young man not intimidated by Brody's brashness responded, "Here's the way it is, Chief Brody. We checked the county map and the car that we're going to be pulling up is about three miles past the Townsend City limits. That makes it a county issue...out of your jurisdiction. When we get up there I have no doubt the County Sheriff will be running the show, giving the orders about what will or will not be done, how things are handled. The County Coroner will be in control of bringing the body up and the Fire Chief will be in charge of pulling the car out, so I guess that puts you pretty far down the pecking order." The young man didn't wait for a response from Brody but turned and walked back toward the firehouse.

"Well, ain't you just some kind of smart ass," growled Brody. "Do you think I don't know the laws in this county. Don't tell me how to do my job."

The other three firemen tried their best not to laugh as they went about getting ready for the trip to the mountains.

Brody was at a loss for words when he noticed Sheriff Grimes' cruiser and the Blount County Coroner van pull into the lot. Grimes was no sooner out of the car when a tow truck came rambling up the road.

Grimes, approaching Brody, asked, "What we got, Axel?"

Brody, disgusted, gestured at the firemen, "Ask them, they seem to be the experts around here."

One of the firemen approached and addressed the coroner and Grimes. "Fire Chief has a group of scouts out on a three day hike when they discovered a car at the bottom of a steep ravine. There's a body in the car. They said it looked like it had been there for a while. We're to run you boys up there. They'll have someone waiting on the fire road for us."

Looking at Jeff Bookman, the coroner, he continued, "You're to pull the body up and we'll take care of the vehicle when you're finished up. As soon as Sheriff Blake from Gatlinburg gets here we'll take off. We need to get up there before it gets too dark. Hell, we'll probably be up there all night. We're taking a generator and some spotlights along just in case."

The tow truck pulled up next to Axel's truck, the driver leaned out the open window, "Where to, Axel?"

Brody, wondering why he was even asked to come along waved his hand in frustration, "Your guess is as good as mine."

Grant's Jeep pulled in right behind the tow truck and before he was even out of the vehicle Brody approached him. "Denlinger… what in the hell are you doin' here? You're supposed to be on leave. Get the hell out of here and go back home. I can handle this by myself."

Grant objected, "Can't do that, Chief. Somebody from the investigating team has to go up there. Gephart and Green are out of town and Chief Blue wouldn't be able to get here before we leave…so, I'm going. What's the plan?"

Buck leaned up against the side of a moss covered tree as he looked back down the mountain. Taking a deep breath he spoke to Nelson, who was out of breath, sitting on a log. "We've been climbing for nearly twenty minutes. When I told my wife I was going to be hiking this weekend this wasn't what I had in mind."

Looking at Nelson, Buck suggested, "Maybe this wasn't such a hot idea. You look tired. Do you think you'll be able to make it to the top?"

"Just give me a couple of seconds," said Nelson. "I'll be fine. I went in for my yearly physical about a month back. The doctor said I needed to start exercising."

Buck looked at his watch, then joked, "Yeah, well I don't think he had climbing up the side of a mountain in mind when he gave you that bit of medical advice."

Nelson stood as he stepped over a boulder. "Come on, we've got to keep moving. They left the firehouse ten minutes ago. We've got to get up to the road before they arrive so they know where to stop. They'll be here in less than thirty minutes."

Pushing himself away from the tree, Buck groaned, "Straight up we go!"

Dalton threw two large logs on the hot coals of the fire as Horace addressed the group of scouts gathered around the fire. "All right, here it is boys. We discovered a car and a dead body over there at the base of the mountainside. Buck and Nelson, are as we speak, climbing up the mountain to meet the police and the fire company on a road that's up above us somewhere. Now, I know that being boys you're probably interested in going over to have a look at the car and the body, but that is not going to happen. Before Buck left he gave me instructions. We can't touch or disturb anything or go near the car and body. Later on this evening the police, the coroner and the fire company will be arriving to pull the body and the car back up the mountainside. As far as the remainder of our trip is concerned, Buck will decide tonight, depending on what the police say about whether we continue or turn back. Now, if you have any questions go ahead and ask."

Buck stopped as he placed his hands on his knees and then pointed up through the trees. "Looks like the road is about twenty yards ahead."

Nelson put his hands on his hips as he tried to catch his breath. "I don't know about you, but I'm bushed!"

"Come on," said Buck. "We can rest when we get on the road."

Following Buck the last few yards, Nelson comically commented, "Yeah at least for a few minutes. We're gonna be cutting it close. They'll be here in about ten minutes, then it's back down the side we go."

Pulling himself up onto the road by means of a low hanging branch, Buck stretched and then removed a pack of cigarettes from his shirt pocket. Placing a smoke in between his lips he offered the pack to Nelson. "Care for a smoke?"

"No thanks," said Nelson. "Don't smoke."

Their conversation was interrupted as Nelson looked up the dirt road as he heard the sound of approaching vehicles. "I think they're here."

The lead Jeep appeared, followed by the second Jeep, Brody's truck and then the tow truck bringing up the rear, a trail of road dust engulfing Nelson and Buck as the convoy came to a halt. Two firemen along with Sheriff Grimes and Sheriff Blake hopped out of the first Jeep, the two remaining firefighters and the county coroner climbed out of the second.

Grant, who had elected to go along in the tow truck, walked past Brody who was standing next to his truck. "You coming, Chief?"

Brody, feeling like a fifth wheel, realizing that no one was going to listen to anything he had to say, answered, "I'll be along shortly."

Carrying a black body bag and his medical kit, Bookman smiled when he saw Buck standing on the side of the road. Looking at the surrounding forest Bookman asked, "Where's the body?"

Buck pointed down the ravine. "About three to four hundred feet down yonder."

"Did you get a chance to look things over? Find anything interesting I should know?"

"Didn't have that much time. The body, which isn't much more than bones, is still inside the car, except for the left arm that must've got ripped off. Found the car registration in the glove compartment along with a box of revolver cartridges." Reaching into his back pocket he pulled out the wallet he had taken from the corpse. "Found this wallet on the victim." He handed it over to Sheriff Grimes.

Nelson looked at his watch. "It's almost seven thirty. We've only got about two hours of light left."

Opening the wallet, Grimes removed the driver's license which he handed to Sheriff Blake. "Joshua James Pickler. That the J.J. Pickler that's missing?"

Blake looked at the plastic covered photo. "The one and only... that's him." Handing the license back to Grimes he asked, "What's the plan, Sheriff?"

Looking back down the ravine, he shook his head. "First of all we've got to get down in there. That'll probably put us at around eight thirty. I'm sure Jeff wants to get the body up out of there first. As far as bringing up the car is concerned, we'll have to wait until we get down there and have a look." Looking at Buck, Grimes asked, "What do you think, Buck? How and when we bring the car up is your decision."

Buck looked at Bookman, hesitated then asked one of the firemen, "Did you bring the generator and some lights?"

"Yes sir," came the immediate answer.

A long roll of thunder sounded in the distant mountains. Jeff started down over the side of the road as he strongly suggested, "Let's get down there. That body isn't going to get back up here on its own."

Charley, the tow truck driver, standing next to Grimes asked, "What do you need me to do Sheriff?"

"For now, just stay put. We won't know how to handle this until we see the condition of the car."

One of the firemen asked Buck, "Are we going to take the saws down now or wait?"

Buck, who was starting back down over the side answered, "Let's take everything down now." One of you men needs to stay up here in case we need you to start the generator."

Grant looked at Brody. "You coming along, Chief?"

"No, I'll just stay here," said Axel. "Sounds like it's gonna rain, besides that, I don't think they'll be pullin' that car up until tomorrow. But, what the hell do I know?"

Grant, realizing that Axel was in one of his moods gave the Chief a half-assed salute as he turned and walked back down the road.

Buck led the way down the mountainside, followed by the rest of his team, along with three firemen carrying the needed equipment. Grant, who had volunteered to carry a coil of rope over his shoulder. was last in line.

Ten yards down, Grant lost his footing as a small log broke loose beneath his right foot causing him to fall backwards. He slid forward bumping into the fireman in front of him who grabbed at a tree to prevent him from falling also. The downhill journey was a constant challenge. Small avalanches of rocks, boulders and logs became dislodged and rolled down creating havoc for those down the line.

Halfway down the side, Grant stopped and watched as the men in front of him proceeded slowly while struggling with the tool boxes and saws.

On his way once again, he stepped on yet another log that caused him to go down, a small cascade of rocks and loose branches bouncing and rolling down toward the others below.

Finally at the bottom of the ravine, everyone gathered around the car, some staring at the corpse, others bending over trying to regain a normal pattern of breathing. Grimes, whose face and arms were streaked with dirt and mud, looked at his watch as he spoke to Bookman. "Jeff, if you want to get the body up out of here you better get cracking. It's eight fifteen."

Jeff gestured to Grant for assistance. "Lay the body bag down on the ground where it's relatively flat. We want to try to keep the body in some sort of natural order." Putting on a pair of plastic gloves, he gently moved the skull to the side as he closely examined it. "This is interesting. Looks like there is a 22 caliber shell imbedded in the back of the skull. This could very well mean the cause of death had nothing to do with the descent of the car down the side of the ravine. Our friend Pickler here was shot. From the looks of the deterioration of the body and the clothing I'd say he's been down here for some time. I'd say well over a month."

Reaching in the driver's window, he ordered Grant, "See if you can secure the head while I try to remove the torso." Grant snapped on a pair of plastic gloves and leaned across the hood as he gently picked up the head and shoulders as if he were handling a priceless, irreplaceable object. As Jeff raised the legs and upper body toward the window the hip bone broke loose causing the body to break in two pieces. "I was afraid that was going to happen. Just do the best you can. I can reconstruct the body back at the lab."

Turning to Grimes, Bookmen remarked, "I'd really like to get the body out of here tonight, but we might not have enough light left. We can't drag the bag over the rough terrain and if we carry it it'll take two people to keep it level and steady. Going uphill and trying to keep your balance at the same time to avoid tipping or bending the body bag is almost an impossibility."

"What other choice do we have?" said Grimes.

Addressing Buck, Jeff asked, "If you started right now could we get the car back up to the road before it gets dark?"

Buck, shaking his head walked toward Jeff as he held out his hands. "No way...that's impossible." Another rumble of thunder sounded. "Hear that...the weather is going to turn on us soon. If we started right now we might get the gas tank drained and the car cut into a number of more movable sections. By the time we get the tow line dropped down here and get the generator and lighting rigged up, it'll be pitch black out here."

"So, what are you suggesting?"

"I think we should get as much as possible done while we still have some light. When it gets dark, we can call it a night and finish up tomorrow."

"All right, but what about the body?"

Jeff crossed his arms as he looked down at the black bag. "The body isn't going anywhere. It can wait until tomorrow. What we need to do is rig up some sort of flat surface that we can secure the bag to and then we can drag it up to the road. I agree with Buck. Let's get what we can done for now and finish up in the morning."

Buck held up his right hand, "Hold on a sec. There's something else we need to discuss. If you're all going to go home for the night and return tomorrow you need to get started back up. If you spend any time at all working on the car you'll be cutting down on the amount of daylight you'll have left to climb out. Now, if you want, everyone can stay the night down here with the scouts. We've got plenty of tents. Some of the boys can double up. We've got plenty of food and water. Looks like it might be a wet night. We can use the two-way to contact the fire station who in turn can notify your families that you're staying up here for the night."

Sheriff Grimes looked at Alan Blake. "Whaddya say, Alan? Is it up the mountain and then down again tomorrow or do you just want to stay put?"

"If you're gonna stay Sheriff, then count me in."

"Me too," said Jeff. "But we'll have to keep the body bag near the campsite so that it won't be disturbed by any local critters."

"It's settled then," said Buck. Turning to one of the fireman he ordered the young man. "John, I need you to climb back up and tell Darren that you guys are heading back to town in the fire Jeeps and will return at first light. Tell Brody and the tow truck driver the same thing." Turning to the other two firemen he ordered them, "All right fellas, let's see if we can get that tank drained. If we have enough time then we'll start cutting."

Grant glanced at the glowing face of his watch: eleven fifteen. All of the boys were tucked away in their tents. With all the excitement he doubted quite seriously if they were asleep. What a story they would have to share with their parents and friends when they returned from their weekend hike.

CHAPTER SIXTEEN

AXEL BRODY PULLED UP THE SHADE on his kitchen window. He smiled. It was going to be a nice day, sunny, but not too hot. It was his first Sunday off in over a month and he intended to enjoy every minute of it. It was the perfect day for going out to the lake and getting in some serious fishing: ice up a twelve pack, make some thick bologna sandwiches and take off. But first, he needed breakfast, something cold. Taking a beer out of the refrigerator, he grabbed the Sunday paper from the kitchen table and stuck it under his arm.

Out on the front porch he settled into his favorite chair and leaned back. After a long swig of cold brew, he opened the paper and suddenly his Sunday was ruined. "Son of a bitch!" he said out loud. There it was on the front page: the ugly face of Hawk Caine staring back at him. Pulling his cell phone from his pocket, he hit speed dial and waited.

"Townsend Police Department, Officer Griner."

"Lee, this is the Chief. Who all's in the office?"

"Right now, all of us, but Kenny is getting ready to go home. He just finished up the night shift."

"You tell him to stay put. All of you stay in the office. Don't leave unless it's a case of life or death. I'll be there in fifteen minutes."

Lee hung up the phone and stopped Kenny who was about to leave the office. "Hold on Kenny. Looks like the Chief got another bug up his ass. You have to stick around...we all do. He's on his way into the office. Sounds really pissed!"

Kenny yawned. "Well, he better make it quick. I need some sleep." Plopping down in a nearby chair, he propped his feet up and placed his hands behind his head as he leaned back and yawned again.

Fourteen minutes later, Axel entered the office, slapping the newspaper against his right leg. Throwing the paper down on the desk, he snarled, "You guys see this?"

Kenny leaned forward and looked at the paper. "If you mean this ugly looking character on the front page...yeah. Saw it down at the Parkway Grocery this morning. Some of the customers were reading it when I went in. They asked me about it and I told them I really didn't know anything about it. As a matter of fact, one of the customers really pissed me off when he laughed and said, 'What's new, imagine that. One of our officers not knowing what's going on. It's about time we get someone on these murders that can get the job done.'"

"I knew it!" said Brody. "I knew Pittman and Barrett couldn't keep their damn noses out of our business long."

Kenny stared down at the paper. "Well, if this guy, Hawk Caine, can find the murderer in two months like he says in the paper then I say more power to him."

Brody glared at Kenny. "Look, this guy's a bounty hunter. He might carry a private investigator's license, but he's still a damn bounty hunter. We sure as hell don't need his kind in our town."

Pointing at all three of his officers he emphasized, "We're gonna stick to this guy like a fly on flypaper. He makes one false move and we're gonna nail him!"

Lee Griner spoke up, "So in other words, with everything else that's going on, we're going to take time out to baby sit a bounty hunter? Who are you mad at, Chief? Hawk Caine or Merle Pittman and Franklin Barrett?"

"The whole lot of them, damn it! You got any other suggestions. I'm tired of my town being turned into a three ring circus!"

"Yeah, I do have a better idea," answered Lee. "Leave it alone. If Caine catches our killer, good for him. If he doesn't, it'll play itself out."

Brody walked to the office window and looked out then turned and addressed Grant, "What about you Denlinger? You haven't said a word."

Grant shrugged, "What is there *to say?* If the man's a legal bounty hunter and a licensed private investigator there's nothing we can do about it. I ran into Agent Gephart last night when I first heard about this Caine character being in the area. He just laughed, saying that a lot of folks are grasping at straws. That's the reason why most folks support this bounty hunter. This guy doesn't have near the information we have on the killer. The FBI doesn't seem concerned about him and we shouldn't be either."

Brody waved off the comments Gephart made as he remarked, "Hell no! The Feds don't have to worry. When they're finished they can just pick up and leave. This is our town. We need to be damned concerned about this guy."

Grant walked to the coffee maker. As usual, Brody was difficult to deal with. Pouring himself a cup of coffee, he realized that this bounty hunter thing was just something else in his life he really didn't need at the moment. He was still trying to figure out what to do about the latest turn of events that had occurred in his life.

A loud rumble was heard coming from the parking lot. Brody, clearly upset about Hawk Caine, was on a short fuse as he turned and looked in the direction of the loud noise, "See, that's what I mean about people! They just don't understand the law. That sum bitch should get a ticket for noise disturbance." Brody sat down in a chair next to the window as his voice softened, "I'm sittin' here lookin' at three good lawmen in front of me. You all know the law is serious business. You took an oath when you took this position. It's our job to protect the people in this town and right now we're losin' by seven murders."

Grant could feel the muscles in his neck tightening. He wished he could just tell Axel and the others what he knew and be done with it, but he couldn't. It was his secret to keep. Hoping to change the subject, he asked, "Do you know this Hawk Caine, Chief?"

Brody perked up as he answered, "Let me tell you about Hawk Caine. I used to be a big wrestlin' fan. Watched it every Friday night like clockwork. Hell, I knew it was fake, but I still liked it. Caine was a pretty big star back in the late eighties. Then, one night he came up against a wrestler by the name of Wolf Big Bear. He was a full-blooded Apache and he was a mean bastard. Story has it that Caine was scheduled to lose to Big Bear on this particular night, but his pride got the best of him and after he was knocked down twice he began to pummel Big Bear. Big Bear got confused since Caine wasn't followin' the script they had practiced. Hawk punched him in the mouth a couple of times and all hell broke loose. Big Bear started to fight back, if nothin' else for his own protection. Man, it was a free for all. The audience was screamin' and then there were three referees tryin' to separate the two wrestlers. Finally, Big Bear hit Caine so hard that he flew out of the ring. Caine wound up losin' the match just like the promoters had planned, but was disqualified and kicked out of the wrestlin' federation. That's the reason he hates Indians so much. It's a stupid reason, but I guess it's good enough for him. I followed him for a while after that. He was doin' some non-sanctioned matches and eventually wound up wrestlin' alligators down in

Florida and competed in some of those Iron Men competitions. I have no idea how he got into the bounty huntin' business, but I do know this. He's good at what he does, but he's a showman first. A few days back I read about the interviews he's been givin' over in Cherokee. Now, with Merle Pittman and Franklin Barrett behind him, I can imagine what he'll do if he shows up here in Townsend."

The revving up of an engine followed by more loud rumbling seemed to shake the building. "Got dammit!" yelled Brody. "Who in the hell's makin' all that racket? I'm gonna give that sum bitch a ticket right now!" He stomped over to the door and shoved it open. Hawk Caine's bright red, enormous Dodge Ram truck sat high up on the largest Goodyear tires made for the street, the five-foot chrome exhaust pipes situated on either side of the elevated cab spewing out black diesel fumes.

Caine laid on the air horn as he gunned the powerful engine, more black fumes filling the air above the parking lot. He was leaning out the driver's side window as he waved his feathered hat at the gathering crowd. Two young boys climbed up the passenger side and peered in the window. Two local reporters, each carrying a microphone, and the third, a cameraman, pushed their way through the growing crowd. One of the reporters, a young woman, pushed the microphone toward Brody's face as she asked, "Chief Brody...what do you think about the fact that Hawk Caine has joined your team to track down the killer who has caused havoc in the area?"

Brody was fuming. He grabbed the mic from the reporter, got close to her face and answered, "Look, let's get one thing straight. The man in that truck is workin' on his own. He is not a member of the police force here in Townsend or for that matter even welcome here."

The woman took back the mic and continued the interview, "Doesn't it impress you that Mr. Caine claims he can locate the killer within two months when you consider it's been well over a year and your department and the FBI have not been able to come up with a single lead?"

Brody leaned toward the mic. "Now, that statement is not entirely correct. We've discovered quite a few clues about the killer. It's only a matter of time before we apprehend him." Pointing to the large truck, he emphasized, "We don't need the likes of Hawk Caine gettin' in our way."

Brody was finished talking, but the reporter kept pressing, "It seems to me from what I've heard the locals are not satisfied with the job the police here in Townsend are doing. I would think you'd appreciate any help you can get." She turned and looked directly into the camera for effect as she continued talking, "Could it be the police here in town are at odds with Mr. Caine?"

Pushing the cameraman to the side Brody came within inches of the female reporter's face. "The only people I'm at odds with right now is the media, which you sadly enough, are a part of."

The reporter signaled for the cameraman to move in for a close up as she moved close to Brody. "Chief Brody, are you aware of the first amendment to the Constitution of the United States that clearly protects the freedom of the press and the right to assemble."

Brody had enough of the pushy reporter. "Look lady, you people think you can go anywhere you please and say anythin' you want. We happen to be investigatin' seven different murders *and* as the police chief here in Townsend I have the right to arrest anyone that interferes with police business. Now, here's the way it's gonna go. You've got fifteen minutes to clear out of the parkin' lot or you'll be filmin' from the opposite side of one of our holdin' cells." Brody stared directly into the camera as he stated boldly, "And that is the news for the day. Thank you." Turning to the reporter he spoke calmly, "Now, get that damn microphone out of my face and get your ass off police property."

Brody wheeled around and retreated to the office, the reporter still not willing to vacate the premises as the cameraman suggested that they should leave. They had what he called enough *interesting film* for the evening news.

Inside, Brody yelled, "Denlinger! You go back out there and tell that damn Hawk Caine I want to see him in my office right now!"

Grant slowly walked toward the door. "Are you sure, Chief?"

"Damn straight I am! Tell him to get his ass in here."

Minutes later, Hawk Caine strode into the office. "Howdy, boys! How in the hell are ya?"

Grant pointed down the hallway. "Straight back."

Brody was ready for him as he entered the office. Axel looked Caine up and down. He was much shorter than he appeared in his old wrestling days. He didn't resemble anything remotely close to a lawman, but more like a performer in a wild west show: leather vest, snakeskin boots, fringed gloves, fancy hat.

Brody stood against his desk, his arms folded across his chest. Caine, not the least bit intimidated spoke first. "Mind if I sit? My feet are killing me." Before Brody could even answer, Caine sat down in a chair positioned in front of the desk, spreading his legs out in front of him. "Damn, that's better." Looking at Axel, he said, "You must be Chief Brody. Just in case you've been hiding under a rock, my name's Hawk Caine." He let out an irritating chuckle as he gestured at Brody. "Why don't you have a seat?"

"This is my office and if I want to sit, I will," commanded Brody. He lowered himself slowly down into his familiar chair.

Caine blew off Brody's attempt to control the meeting. "Now, the way I see things, Chief Brody, we got two choices on this case I'm investigating. We can work together or against each other. What's your druthers?"

Brody was temporarily dumbfounded. What Caine had just said to him was the exact same speech he was going to give Caine. Composing himself, he spoke, "Let's get one thing straight, Mr. Caine. I know why you're here and I ain't one bit against gettin' this killer apprehended, but the way we go about it is a different matter."

Hawk shook his head, his long braids of hair moving from side to side. "You say you know why I'm here. Well, you might be wrong. First off, the way you and the Feds are going about it hasn't exactly worked so far." Pointing his thumbs at his chest he went on, "Me, I'm about getting the job done right. I'm the real deal and I'm going to make a bundle of cash when I catch this bastard and get a lot of publicity to go along with it. Let me tell you something. I ain't no amateur at this sordid business. I've been shot at, stabbed, thrown off of a building out in Omaha and almost run over by a car in Arizona. I've had more stitches in my body than in the jeans I'm wearing. I've got to think about my future. I've been damn lucky up to this point, but who's to say that one of these days one of these creeps I'm chasing won't get the best of me and do me in. That being said, my new business partners: Mr. Pittman and Mr. Barrett, who by the way are not exactly my type, are willing to pay the ticket and I'm taking the bus ride. With their help, I just might wind up doing what I really want to do. Mr. Pittman, I believe his name is Merle, said I might just be ripe for a reality show on television. He knows some entertainment lawyers out west and after I catch your killer he said he's gonna hook me up."

"Merle Pittman, my ass!" said Brody. "If I were you I wouldn't count on anythin' from him other than him makin' money and leavin' you in the dirt. Pittman and his pal, Barrett, will slice a dime if they think they can make three nickels out of it. You might be lucky enough to end up with your picture on the front of a tee-shirt, but that's about it."

"Look, I'm damn good at what I do. From what I've been told a damn site better than what you do. So, don't think because you're wearing a badge that represents some hick town in the middle of Tennessee that you're qualified to give me advice."

"Yeah," said Brody, "well here's some advice for ya. Get the hell out of my office!"

Hawk stood. "So be it. Now I know where you stand, but you can bet your sweet ass when I bring in your killer, you and I won't be taking any pictures together. It'll be all about me in all my glory." He turned and without another word walked down the hall and out to the parking lot.

Brody, who had followed Caine down the hallway, watched the man walk out the door. Turning, his fists clenched, with a stupid look on his face, Axel exclaimed, "Guess what boys? Our bounty hunter wants to be a TV star. He ain't satisfied with catchin' criminals, he wants to be on television."

Kenny began laughing. "So he's gonna be another, Walker, Texas Ranger. Chuck Norris ain't no pretty boy, but he's done rather well for himself."

The look on Brody's face clued Kenny into the fact that he'd better shut up. Kenny reached for the door. "I'm outta here. Have a nice day."

Grant, following Kenny out the door offered a half-assed salute. "Guess I better hit the streets. Looks like there's going to be a lot of tourists in town today." Leaving Lee behind to deal with Brody, Grant walked to his cruiser as he noticed the crowd that had gathered out in the parking lot starting to break up. Hawk Caine's large truck pulled out of the lot, a trail of diesel fumes clouding the air.

Grant drove three blocks on the Parkway before he was called to an accident scene on Hilltop Drive. Veering left, he turned on his lights, but refrained from flipping on the siren. Minutes later he pulled up at the scene. It was just a minor fender bender, but unfortunately a vacationing young couple from Georgia had run into the back of Ambrose Stroud's truck. Ambrose had the young man pinned up against the side of their car as he yelled a series of profanities at the boy, his young wife standing off to the side screaming.

Getting out of his cruiser, Grant yelled, "Ambrose...back off!"

Ambrose wasn't about to let up as he shoved the young man again. "This asshole ran into the back of me!"

Grant knew he had to be careful with Ambrose who had a reputation of having a short fuse. Stepping closer, Grant ordered him a second time, "Ambrose...leave him be!"

Ambrose shot Grant a hard look, then commented sarcastically. "Who's gonna stop me...you?"

"Yes," Grant said, placing his hand on his gun. "I'm asking you one more time to back off."

Ambrose spat on the ground and shoved his way past the boy. He turned and faced Grant. "Why are you yellin' at me? They hit my truck!"

Grant inspected where the two vehicles had collided. The damage was minimal.

"Ambrose, your truck is so beat up, why you can't even tell where he hit you. Come on, let's just call it a day. It's not even worth swapping insurance information."

The young man now at his wife's side spoke up, "Officer, if it's alright we don't want this man's insurance info. We don't want to press charges either. We just want to get the hell out of here!"

Ambrose climbed in his truck as he cursed, "Damn tourists!"

Climbing back into his cruiser, Grant waited until the two vehicles pulled away. His mind wasn't on work today. He was concerned about Dana Beth. She was having some post-pregnancy difficulties. After two trips to the doctor, Grant was glad that Ruth had come to stay with them so Dana Beth wouldn't be so nervous and frustrated.

All morning long, the Smoky Mountain airwaves were bombarded with the news that two businessmen, Merle Pittman from Gatlinburg and Franklin Barrett from Townsend, were putting up $50,000 dollars to find the killer of the rash of murders in Blount and Sevier Counties. A news conference was announced to be held at noon on WBXX television's regularly scheduled program: NEWS AT NOON.

Brody had Marge call Lee and Grant back into the office so they could all view what Axel was calling nothing more than another moneymaking scheme on Pittman and Barrett's part.

Grant walked into the station at 11:55, five minutes before the interview was to begin. Marge told Grant to go back to Brody's office as she handed him two large pizza boxes. "Can you believe it? Axel bought lunch." Grabbing a two liter soda, she followed Grant down the hall.

Placing the pizzas on Brody's desk, Grant thanked Axel, "Thanks for lunch, Chief. What's the occasion?"

Lee was pouring himself a cup of soda and grabbing a slice of pizza as Brody answered, "I want you all to see a news conference that's on television at noon." Looking at the clock on the wall he ordered Marge, "Turn on the set."

Within seconds the small, fifteen inch television that sat on top of a file cabinet came to life as Brody bit into a slice of pizza. "Merle Pittman and our own Franklin Barrett are at it again, but this time it's more than just tours and tee-shirts. The word is they're puttin' up $50,000 to catch our killer. Myself, I think it's nothin' more than nonsense."

Marge, standing in the opposite corner, commented, "My father always said you can't make any sense out of nonsense."

Brody nodded in agreement and added, "News conference, my ass. If I know Merle and Franklin they're just blowin' smoke. There's got to be an angle to all of this and I bet ya there's a lot more to it than just catchin' the killer."

The office conversation was interrupted as a familiar face appeared on the screen. *"Good afternoon. I'm Becky Lyons of WBXX Channel News. Today on the news at noon we are televising a special edition."* Across from Becky sat Pittman, Barrett and Caine. After a brief rundown of the murders, Becky followed up with a statement saying the police departments in Townsend, Maryville and Sevierville and the FBI as well, were stymied and seemingly at a roadblock because the murders still remained unsolved. Introducing Pittman and Barrett, she explained that the two local businessmen were putting up $50,000 to apprehend the killer.

After introducing Hawk Caine, she asked Merle, *"Mr. Pittman, I suppose you are aware that our listeners are wondering why it is you think Mr. Caine will be able to locate the killer when the local authorities have come up with nothing that can be considered concrete?"*

Merle scooted toward the edge of his chair and sat up straight. *"I will be more than glad to answer your question, Becky. Mr. Barrett and I are deeply concerned about the murders we've experienced here in the area. This sort of thing just doesn't happen here in the Smokies. I'm sure I don't have to tell your viewers that the economy of the general area depends on the tourist trade to a great extent. If we do not apprehend this killer, at some point people are going to shy away from coming to this area for their vacation. Franklin and I are not only business owners but citizens of this area as well. We conducted extensive research before hiring Mr. Caine...*"

"That's a crock of bullshit!" Brody yelled at the screen.

Merle continued, *"...Sometimes it requires a new perspective to figure out the clues and then act on them. We think Mr. Caine will be able to do just that."*

"What the hell does that mean?" growled Brody. "Talk about double-talk."

Becky turned to Caine. *"I understand that your appearance over in Townsend caused quite a stir."*

"Exactly," said Hawk. *"It's all part of the plan. This killer needs to know that he's being hunted...by me! I'm the best in the business. After today, he'll know I'm in the area and that I'm after him. He'll slip up and then he's mine!"*

The interview lasted for another few seconds then Becky wrapped things up by stating that if anyone in the viewing area had any information they should contact the station and the information would get to Mr. Caine.

Brody sat on the edge of his desk. "Just like I thought. They got nothin'. What in the hell are Pittman and Barrett up to? Their last idea about tee-shirts and tours faded and went belly-up. All those tee-shirts are good for now is washin' your car. This Hawk Caine is a clown. How could anyone take him serious?"

"It would appear," said Grant, "that Merle and Franklin have taken him very seriously. Fifty grand is nothing to sneeze at."

"There's more to this than what meets the eye," said Brody. Walking toward the door he grabbed his hat. "I'm headin' home for the rest of the day. See you in the mornin.'"

The man sat in the Mountain Café watching an elevated television above a door leading to the kitchen. Sitting alone by the front window in a corner booth, his lunch in front of him, he dipped his French fries into a glob of catsup on his plate and stuffed three at a time into his mouth. Watching the television intently, he stared at the face of Hawk Caine. Clearly disturbed, he pushed his unfinished lunch to the side and wiped his bearded face with a napkin, laid a ten dollar bill on the table, picked up his red hat and quickly walked out of the restaurant.

It was 12:45 by the time Grant was back out on patrol. He had skipped breakfast and his stomach was grumbling. Pulling into the

Timbers Restaurant just off the Parkway, he nodded at some tourists who were getting off a bus. Brody, for the past few months, had been adamant about all of his officers being friendly and making sure that the tourists were made to feel welcome *and safe.*

As he walked toward the entrance of the restaurant, he noticed Caine's oversized red truck with a hawk emblazoned on the hood taking up two parking spaces. *Oh no!* thought Grant. Of all the restaurants up and down the Parkway, why did Caine have to go and pick this particular one to eat lunch at?

It was cool inside, a nice respite from the warm day. Taking off his sunglasses his eyes adjusted to the light in the giant dining room. He spotted Caine seated at a corner booth near the back wall. *What the hey!* thought Grant. *Maybe I should talk with him. It can't hurt. It can't do any harm to introduce myself.*

The introduction wasn't necessary. Caine noticed Grant as he approached his table. Laying down his fork, Hawk smiled and said, "Well, well, if it isn't one of Townsend's finest, Officer Grant Denlinger."

Grant, taken off-guard, hesitated then answered, "I'm surprised you know who I am. I mean, I saw you back in the office but we were never really introduced."

Caine seemed more genuine than he had when he was talking to Axel. He invited Grant to sit. "Please, join me. Are you here on official police business or just some lunch?"

Grant pulled out a chair and sat as the waitress approached, handed him a menu, and placed a glass of water in front of him. "Good afternoon, Grant. Will you be having lunch today?"

"Yes, yes I am," said Grant. "I'll just have a burger and fries and let's see, a Coke."

Grant, still amazed that Hawk Caine knew who he was pushed the menu to the side, then sipped at his water. "I'm still surprised you would know who I am."

"Just part of the job," responded Hawk. "I've been doing this sort of thing for years now. It's more than just a job. It's a game. A game I play for money. A game that can get dangerous at times. It's important that I know all of the players, not just the man I'm after. Pittman filled me in on everyone on the Townsend Police Department. According to what I've been told, your boss, Chief Axel Brody, is a bit of an ass and after meeting and talking with him, I'd say Merle was correct. He and Barrett think you're a fine officer and could possibly in the future be the chief of police here in Townsend. I know that your grandfather, Dalton, was the former police chief. Let's see, this coming fall you'll be married for a year and your wife, Dana Beth just had your first child. Little girl... wasn't it?"

Grant, stunned, just sat quietly, not sure what to say.

Caine, seeing the look on Grant's face spoke up, "Relax son, it's not a big deal. I just like to do my homework. I like to know the players in the game. You know, who's got my back and who I have to watch out for." Pouring dressing on his salad, he continued to talk, "Speaking of meetings, I guess I went and pissed off your boss, didn't I?"

"Yeah, I guess you could say that," answered Grant. "Tell me something. Do you really think you can find the man we've been looking for?"

Caine stabbed a forkful of salad and took it to his mouth. "Sure, why not? It's not rocket science. Unless he's left the area, which I doubt, I have a good description of him. Besides being a killer, he's got to do things that normal people do: eat, get gas for his vehicle. He's bound to turn up sooner or later. He'll slip up. Besides that, up until this point he really hasn't had anyone of my talent and caliber tracking him. My arrival here in the area signals the beginning of this killer coming to the end of his rope."

The waitress delivered a fourteen ounce t-bone steak to the table and sat it in front of Caine. Smiling at Grant she gestured back toward the kitchen. "It'll just be a few minutes on your burger."

"Hope you don't mind if I eat in front of you," said Caine as he cut into the steak, the blood running out onto the plate.

"No, go right ahead," said Grant as he thought to himself, *Maybe this strange man can help me. This might be my one shot to get some help. Maybe I can tell him just enough about what I know to get him over to Iron Mountain. If he's as good as he claims he is, then he can do the rest.* Probing, he asked, "What do you know about this killer?"

Putting a large bite of salad in his mouth, Caine pointed his fork at Grant. "You mean *killers!* The first four murders, the ones last year were committed by someone else, not the man we're currently looking for. I still haven't figured out the connection, but I know for a fact there are two killers. Last year's killer was very organized. He made sure he didn't leave one single clue that you could connect to him. Now, this year's killer, possibly this guy that wears the knit cap, is sloppy. He left fingerprints on the knife found at the scene of the Mackinaw murder, which happen to match up with prints found at the cabin he rented and again at the Mountain Vista Motel where they found Bock's body. The way I see it our killer didn't plan to kill Mackinaw. So that would account for him not being too careful about leaving clues behind. From what I've been told by those who witnessed what went on at the Gatlinburg Grill, the man was provoked. He might have just been defending himself. At this point we can't be sure, but that's the way it looks so far to me.

"Now, Bock's murder is a totally different story. Bock was more than likely killed because of his mistreatment of turtles and that's where I can't seem to connect the dots. Bock was killed for the very same reasons as the first four murders; animal cruelty. Could be, the killer was planning on leaving the area and didn't worry too much about leaving fingerprints behind. One more thing; this J.J. Pickler who they found in that ravine up in the mountains. From what I've been told I think he butted heads with the killer, which was a mistake. That bear he had stolen from him is the reason why he disappeared and was found murdered. I talked with the clerk at the grocery store here in Townsend who saw Pickler run out of the store after another customer. I'd lay odds on it that was our killer." He continued to cut away at his steak. "And that's a clue no one else knows about." Touching the knife to the side of his head he remarked proudly, "Smart move on my part...right?"

"If you don't mind me asking, what's your next move?"

"I've got to try and pinpoint the last location of this guy. From that point I can pick up his scent. I figure Gatlinburg might be my best bet."

Grant's order arrived and he busied himself with putting catsup on his fries. Taking a drink of his soda, he stuffed a fry in his mouth then spoke, "Look, Mr. Caine, I'm not going to beat around the bush. I consider myself on the smart side also. Like you, I have discovered not just one clue but a number of clues that no one else knows. I think this information might just help you find the killer."

Caine didn't miss a beat as he sat back in his chair and looked at Grant suspiciously, "That a fact? Why are you interested in sharing this *information* no one else seems to know with me rather than with your own boss, Brody?"

"Simple, Brody and I don't get along all that well. You see, I'm one year away from getting my degree in crime scene investigation. Brody is just a good ol' boy who, by some twist of fate, has done well for himself here in Townsend by becoming the

Chief of Police. He calls me Wonder Boy, which pisses me off to no end. He won't listen to anything I have to say. He's impossible to work with. If I were to share the information that I have with him, he'd just botch it up or shove it under the rug. You said earlier that Barrett and Pittman thought I was a fine officer and a candidate to be the future chief of police. Well, Merle and Franklin hate Brody and the way he handles things. If I'm going to hand out information I want it to be in the hands of someone I can trust. Let this be understood, you and I never had this conversation. If Brody found out I had confided in you, he'd fire me immediately."

Caine took another large bite of steak. "I'm listening. Tell me more and why in the hell do you think you can trust me."

Grant looked around the restaurant to make sure no one nearby could hear what they were talking about. Caine's calm attitude unnerved him. He stammered as he continued, " You're in it for the money. Any information you get to help you find the killer will just make it easier for you to collect the $50,000. I think that's reason enough to trust you. I have reason to believe that the killer is still in Tennessee, not far from here, but out of Brody's jurisdiction. I've seen a man that fits the description you have been given. He's no longer in Gatlinburg, so if you start there you'll wind up going nowhere. Presently, I believe he's in Mountain City, which is about three hours east of here, near the North Carolina border. He was seen in a pickup truck in the Iron Mountains. I made a trip over there and sure enough spotted his truck parked at a deserted church. There is an old abandoned farm nearby the church. I snooped around the old house and the barn. The whole time I was there I got the strangest feeling I was being watched. Turned out I was. While I was in the barn I crawled down into an old root cellar. The next thing I know, four rattlesnakes are tossed down on top of me and then I'm locked in. To make a long story short, I killed the rattlers and got out of the cellar."

Tearing a piece of bread off of a roll, Caine stuffed it inside his mouth and spoke at the same time, "So, who tipped you off about this Iron Mountain business. How do I know this isn't just some cock and bull story engineered by Brody to get me out of town? Your story doesn't add up."

"I can't give you that information. You're just going to have to trust me." Grant continued to evade the complete truth as he lied, "The person who gave me this information doesn't want to be involved. There are other reasons, too. My wife just had our first child. I need to take care of my family and to be honest with you, this case is consuming almost all of my time. Besides that, I don't know how much longer I can go on working with Sheriff Brody. He hasn't liked me since the day I started. I want to continue to be an officer, but not here in Townsend under Brody's supervision. I want to leave on my own terms, but if Brody doesn't get off my back, one of these days I might pop him square in the mouth. That wouldn't look very good on my resume."

Grant scooted forward on his chair leaning toward Caine. "Look, all I'm saying is you might want to take a drive over to Mountain City and have a look around. And, one other thing, If you decide to go down in the root cellar, mixed in with some rocks that fell down on me, you'll find a flashlight, a Swiss army knife and a camera I dropped. Something else, I have a contact you can talk with over there. Sheriff Tobias Reichenbaugh. He can verify every word I've told you."

Caine pushed his unfinished steak to the side and stuck a toothpick in his teeth. "What makes you think I won't hightail it over to Brody's office and spill the beans...tell him everything you just told me?"

"I know Brody," said Grant. "He wouldn't believe you and besides that I'd deny we ever talked."

Caine took a long swig of water. "You seem like a smart fella, Denlinger. I like you. But, remember, even smart men can make mistakes. Now, how do I get to this Mountain City, if and when I decide to go?"

Grant gave Caine quick directions, which Hawk wrote down on a small notepad. Putting the pad back into his shirt pocket, he asked, "You ain't expecting part of the fifty grand when I bring this killer in, right?"

"Absolutely not. I want this killer caught before he kills again."

Caine removed two more toothpicks from a jar on the table and stuck them in his pocket. "I got a few other things to tend to before I head on over to this Mountain City. I'll give you a holler when I get back, that is, unless you read an article in the paper saying that I caught the killer."

"Be careful," warned Grant. "This man seems to know the woods. He can sneak up on you before you know it. He's extremely dangerous."

"Don't go worrying about me. I've run across about every kind of varmint there is. I'm used to danger."

Caine stood and lumbered down the aisle, tipping his hat to three ladies that were seated at a table by the door. As he passed the waitress he stopped, said something to her then left.

A few seconds passed when the waitress came over to Grant's table. "Excuse me, Grant, but the man that was with you said you'd take care of lunch." She laid the bill for twenty-seven dollars on the table.

CHAPTER SEVENTEEN

A BUSINESSMAN AND HIS SECRETARY stopped in front of the Trader's Gap Restaurant on N. Shady Street and stared in disbelief as the gigantic, red, Dodge Ram pickup truck rumbled up the street, plumes of black diesel smoke spewing from the chrome exhaust pipes. Further down Shady Street at Millers Flower Shop, a husband picking up some flowers for his wife's birthday couldn't believe his eyes as the monstrous truck rolled by, the driver waving as he sounded the air horn, the loud noise echoing up the street. Minutes later, a man getting his battery changed at Napa Auto Parts on W. Main Street pointed at the massive tires of the truck as it slowly passed by. A woman, coming out of the Farmers State Bank further down Main hugged her daughter as the loud air horn startled the young child. Hawk Caine knew how to make an entrance.

On Church Street, Caine passed a dental office and an antique shop then guided the huge truck into an empty lot of a business that was for sale. Turning, so the large black hawk on the red hood of the truck was facing the street, Caine gunned the diesel engine again, the powerful sound of the motor reverberated up and down the normally quiet street. A woman, passing by pushing a stroller, picked up her pace as Caine removed his feathered hat and waved at her. *One more trip though town*, thought Caine as he pulled back onto the street.

Twenty minutes later, satisfied that everyone in town knew he had arrived, he turned onto Honeysuckle Lane, drove one block then wheeled the truck into the parking lot of the Johnson County Sheriff's office. Taking up two parking spots in front of the building, he opened the door, pulled out the chrome, built-in step ladder and stepped down to the ground. The hood of the monstrous truck was at least a foot and a half above his head. Cleaning off his snakeskin boots on the back of his custom-fit studded jeans, he placed his hat squarely on his head and walked to the main door.

Once inside, he strode up to a desk where a female officer was talking on the phone. Just as the officer hung up, Hawk leaned on the desk, his fingerless gloved hands supporting his short, muscular frame. Removing his hat, he asked, "Might there be a Tobias Reichenbaugh here today? I believe he's the County Sheriff. I've got business with him."

The officer looked him up and down, his flamboyant dress attire causing her to hesitate before answering. "Is he expecting you, sir?"

Caine gave a cocky smile as he stated smartly, "No one ever expects me! I'm kind of like a surprise. Now, if you would be so kind, go tell your boss that Hawk Caine is here to see him."

Getting up, the officer smiled then rolled her eyes as she turned to walk to the back office. "Have a seat, Mr. Caine. I'll let him know you're here."

Caine, who wasn't that fond of female police officers made a chauvinistic comment as she left the room. "You do that, Babe!"

Tobias was just hanging up the phone when the officer entered his office. Looking up he remarked, "That's the third call I've gotten in the last five minutes about some maniac in a feathered hat driving around town in a giant pickup truck blowing diesel fumes all over the place and scaring folks half to death with an air horn."

Pointing over her shoulder with her thumb, she confirmed, "His name is Hawk Caine and he's out in the lobby waiting to see you. Just so you know: he's a short, little shit with a big mouth."

As he ran his hands through his hair, Tobias looked toward the ceiling as he commented sadly, "I had a feeling when I got up this morning this was going to be a bad day. Send him back here."

Hawk was staring at a number of police photographs on the wall as the officer returned. "Mr. Caine, Sheriff Reichenbaugh will see you now. End of the hall, last door."

Giving the officer a disdainful look he started down the hall without a word of thanks, but hesitated when the officer asked him, "Where is everyone else?"

Hawk turned and responded, "Everyone else who?"

The officer looked him up and down, then answered, "The rest of the circus."

Caine really didn't have the time to get into an argument with the officer, so he just blew her comment off with a wave of his hand and continued down the hall. Entering the office, he saw Tobias sitting behind his desk. "You Reichenbaugh?" he asked curtly.

Tobias stared at the man standing across the room: five-foot eight at best, extremely well-toned muscles, black leather fringed vest, hairy chest and arms, jet black goatee and mustache, earrings in both ears, tight jeans complete with a large silver belt buckle, the feathered hat in his right hand. "Yes, I am Reichenbaugh. Tobias Reichenbaugh, Johnson County Sheriff."

Before Tobias could utter another word, Caine spoke up, "I'm Hawk Caine. You've no doubt heard of me."

"To be completely honest with you, in all of my fifty-eight years I've never heard the name."

Sitting in a chair, Caine propped his boots on the edge of the desk. "I guess you must not be much of a sports fan, Tobias."

"And what, pray tell, does that have to do with anything?"

"Years back I was a professional wrestler. I was on television all the time."

Tobias corrected Caine as he answered, "I am a sports fan. Baseball, football, basketball and the like. I've never really considered wrestling, at least the type that you were involved in a sport. I've always thought of it as fake; entertaining, but still fake."

Caine sidestepped Tobias's attempt at humiliating him as he pointed across the desk while laughing. "You look like you're a good fifty pounds or so overweight. You wouldn't last five minutes in the ring."

Tobias pointed at Caine's boots as he responded, "Unless you move those boots from my desk you're not gonna make it five minutes in my office."

"Fair enough," said Caine, removing his feet from the desk. "Occasionally, I run across someone who hasn't heard of me. You just happen to be one of them. It's not that big of a deal."

Tobias leaned forward as he gestured toward the phone. "Well, perhaps I should take that back. I do know of you, not your name, but that you're in town. Five minutes before you arrived, I got three calls from citizens complaining about some nitwit driving a big noisy truck through town, scaring the hell out of folks with his air horn."

Caine was not easily insulted. "Just wanted to let everyone know I was in town."

"So, why are you in town, Mr. Caine?"

"Aside from my past wrestling days," said Caine, "I've got a lot of other talents, one being that I'm a bounty hunter...the best in the U S of A, by the way. I specialize in running down criminal Indians, but I'll track most anybody if the price is right. I'm in the beginning process of tracking down a killer I understand is currently in this area."

Tobias, not sure what Caine was talking about pointed to a map of the county on the wall. "That's Johnson County, my jurisdiction. I know of no criminal Indians in the area. So, who are you after *and* who hired you?"

Caine gave Tobias a snide grin as he answered, "Actually, I'm not obligated to tell you who I'm working for, but I don't think they would object to me mentioning their names: Merle Pittman and Franklin Barrett from over in Gatlinburg. They're paying me big bucks, plus expenses to track the killer from over in Blount County."

Tobias held up his hand. "Just hold on a minute. Let's back up the truck here. I don't know all that much about this bounty hunter business, but I do know that you have to have a warrant in Tennessee if you're as you say, running this man down."

"You got me there, Sheriff. I don't have a warrant on this killer because they haven't identified him as of yet. So, at the moment I'm sort of walking into a blind date."

"Well, I hate to be the bearer of bad news, Mr. Caine. But until you have a warrant, at least in my county, you're not going to be running anybody down."

"Remember, I said I had many talents." Reaching into his pants pocket, Caine removed a leather bound wallet, took out a plastic coated card and tossed it on the desk. "I'm also a licensed private investigator. The back of that government issued identification card clearly states that I can practice my profession anywhere in the country, which by the way happens to include little ol' Johnson County, Tennessee. As a private investigator, I don't need a warrant. I can come and go as I please. I can ask folks in these parts any questions I want *and* believe it or not, I can track down and apprehend a suspect." Nodding at the card, Caine spoke with an air of confidence, "Try that on for size, Sheriff."

Reluctantly picking up the card, Tobias read the front and back then tossed it back on the desk. "All right, so you're a private investigator. What makes you think the killer from Blount County is now here...in Mountain City?"

Placing the card back in his wallet, Caine answered as if he had some inside information, "Let's just say a very reliable source approached me when I was in Townsend and gave me the lowdown."

Tobias smiled. "Don't tell me your reliable source is Pittman or Barrett."

Caine grinned. "No, it's not. They're just fronting the money. My source happens to be Grant Denlinger, who is an officer with the Townsend Police. Apparently he doesn't get along all that well with the chief over there and has been trying to solve the mystery of who this killer is on his own. He told me he had been over here recently and had seen a man he thinks might be the killer. Said he went to some old church, house and barn. Went down in a root cellar, had some rattlers tossed down on top of him, then he got locked in. Said his knife and flashlight are still in the cellar. Any of this sound familiar?"

Tobias nodded his head as he answered, "Quite familiar. Officer Denlinger was here a while back. He asked me some questions about a forty-year-old murder that happened up in the Iron Mountains. We went over to our library and couldn't get the information he was looking for. Talked with a couple of folks in town who were around when the murders happened. Eventually, we took a drive up there. When we drove past an old abandoned church we saw a fella in an old pickup truck parked behind the church. Denlinger mentioned that it seemed strange he had seen the same man in the same truck earlier in the day at a place called Dave's 421. It's a gas station, general store sort of place on the outskirts of town. I told him it was probably just one of the locals."

Removing a pack of toothpicks from his vest pocket Caine began to clean his front teeth. "So, what did you find out about this *local?*"

"Didn't even look into it," said Tobias. "No reason to."

Caine, with a look of confusion, exclaimed, "No reason! An officer from another part of the state comes over here to investigate a forty-year-old murder, almost gets killed in the process and you say there's no reason to look into it. Ya know, that's the problem with these small town, backwoods police departments. When something happens there's no sense of urgency." Scooting forward on the chair, Caine further explained, "There have been seven murders over in Blount and Sevier Counties which happens to be about three hours from here. Denlinger comes over here to look into a forty-year-old murder he thinks might be tied in with the murders somehow and almost winds up losing his life. Can you explain to me Sheriff Reichenbaugh, how that constitutes not looking into?"

Now it was Tobias who leaned forward as he tried to avoid Caine's attempt at controlling the conversation. "Look Caine, it was Denlinger's decision to go back up to the Pender farm the day after we were there. We suggested very strongly that he not go back up there by himself. It's a dangerous place."

"Apparently so," remarked Caine. "Denlinger gets rattlesnakes thrown down on top of him and then gets locked in. Sounds like attempted murder to me. Why would you, *the local law,* not look into something like that?"

"Because I don't have enough to go on. Denlinger said someone tried to kill him. I wasn't there at the time so I don't know what happened beyond what I was told. For all I know, the man who threw the rattlers down into that cellar might have been a local moonshiner or maybe some local who is raising pot up there somewhere. We have no proof that this man in the pickup truck is even the same man as the one who locked Denlinger in the cellar. If I went up into the mountains every time somebody gets their neck out of joint I'd be up there every day."

Caine eased back in the chair. "I wasn't aware that making hooch and growing pot was legal here in this part of Tennessee. Out west, where I'm from we don't put up with that sort of nonsense."

"Making bootleg liquor and growing pot is just as illegal in Tennessee as it is anywhere else," confirmed Tobias. "That being said, we here at the Johnson County Sheriff's Office are well aware that this sort of thing goes on up in the Iron Mountains." Picking up a ruler, Tobias tapped a county map on the wall behind where he was seated, "Part of the Iron Mountains are in my jurisdiction. There are folks who live way back up in there that for the most part want to be left alone. There are children up there that don't go to school and people up there who don't pay taxes. Hell, there are people living in that area that have never been seen by the folks here in town. Mountain people are not concerned with what goes on down here in town, nor are most of the folks in town concerned about what happens up in the mountains. Some of the folks in the mountains make moonshine or grow pot because that's the only way they can survive. As long as we don't get any complaints on their activities, we leave well enough alone."

Caine waved off Tobias's statement as he gestured toward the map. "You make it sound like these mountain people are dangerous. I've dealt with worse."

"And I assume by worse that you're referring to the Indians, who you called criminals earlier."

Pointing at Tobias, Caine answered loudly, "Listen, some of those Indians when they're on the run can be some of the meanest bastards you'd ever want to meet. They don't scare me none. That's why the authorities always call me to bring them in. These mountain folks you talk about sound on the tame side compared to a lot of the people I've dealt with." Standing, Caine made his point as he pointed to the map. "I'm gonna be going up into those mountains, to that old church and that farm. I'm gonna be knocking on some doors up there and asking a lot of questions. If anybody gives me any grief they'll wish they hadn't run across ol' Hawk Caine."

Tobias stood, but refrained from offering his hand. "Two things before you leave my office, Caine. First, I appreciate you dropping by and letting me know you're in the area. If and when you discover that the killer from over in Blount County is here in Johnson County, let me know and I'll help you in any way I can. Second, if you plan on going up into the Iron Mountains and knocking on doors and asking a lot of questions, just a word of advice. Don't get too pushy and start sticking your nose in where it doesn't belong. People have been known to go up there and for some reason not return. So, just be careful. You're going to be in their territory."

Caine turned to leave as he stated confidently, "Thanks for the warning, Sheriff, but when the day comes I can't handle a bunch of uneducated hillbillies, I guess that'll be the day I hang up my spurs and get out of this business."

"Like I said, I'll help you any way I can. Just make sure you operate within the law and we won't have any problems."

Walking down the hall, Caine spoke back over his shoulder, "The only way we're going to have a problem is if you *get in my way*. By the way, where's the nicest place to stay around these parts?"

Tobias thought for a moment, then answered, "The nicest place or the nicest place that will let you stay there?"

"I want the nicest place there is. I don't care how expensive it is. Long as I'm on Pittman's and Barrett's dime, I might as well live it up."

"Well, since you put it that way then I'd suggest Prospect Hill. It's a high end bed and breakfast south of town on the way to Boone."

Placing his hat back on his head, Caine nodded and remarked, "I'll tell them you recommended the place. See ya around, Reichenbaugh."

Hawk Caine pulled his huge truck into the circular paved entrance of the Prospect Hill Bed and Breakfast. Two couples seated on the massive front porch that fronted the elegant three story turn of the century home stared in awe as Caine stepped down from the cab. He removed his plumed hat, ran his gloved fingers through his long hair, spit on the ground and walked toward the front steps of the old mansion. Climbing the curved steps, he stopped and addressed two couples who had stopped rocking in their chairs. "Afternoon, folks. I understand this place has the nicest accommodations in the area. How about the vittles? They any good?"

One of the men, seeing that his wife was appalled at the sight of what appeared to be someone from another galaxy, spoke up, "If you're referring to the food, they have a wonderful breakfast here."

Winking at the women, Hawk smiled as he gazed out across the manicured lawn, professionally cut trees and hedges, flower gardens and a four-tier water fountain. "Well, I might see about getting me a room here." Gesturing at an empty rocker, he informed the woman. "Save me a seat. Might join ya later."

The inside of the mansion was just as elegant as the grounds that surrounded the building, with polished hardwood floors, oriental throw rugs, antique couch and chairs, expensive wall coverings, elegant paintings on the walls and a large chandelier centered in the middle of the arched ceiling. Walking up to a marble topped oak desk, Caine hit an antique ringer on the desk next to a sign that said: RING FOR SERVICE.

A woman in a long, satin green dress, a string of pearls hanging from her neck, entered the room from behind a floor to ceiling green flocked curtain. The woman held her head high as if she were royalty. Adjusting her shoulder length hair, she raised her eyeglasses to her eyes and stared at Hawk, giving him the head to toe once over. Clearing her throat she commented, "I didn't realize we had any deliveries today."

Out of respect, Hawk removed his hat, bowed at the waist, grinned and answered, "I couldn't tell you if you have any deliveries today or not. I'm just here to get a room for a couple of weeks."

The woman, completely taken by surprise, sat down instantly, as if she were going to faint. "Oh my, I see." Trying to dissuade Hawk Caine, who must have appeared to her as an odd sort of character, she replied, "It's quite expensive to stay here at Prospect Hill. Most people prefer to stay in town where it's not *as expensive!*"

Hawk made himself comfortable in a red velvet chair next to the desk and looked directly at the woman, "Define *quite expensive.*"

The woman touched her glasses again as she answered with pride. "The rooms are $179.00 per night, not per week, but per night."

Removing his wallet from his pocket, he took out a credit card and laid it on the desk. "Let's start off with two weeks. That'll be around $2500.00. Let's put about a two hundred dollar tip on there and make it $2700.00."

She stared at the card, not sure what to say. Caine, feeling that he now had the upper hand, added, "I assume you know the County Sheriff, Tobias Reichenbaugh. Well, he recommended this as the best place to stay in the area. You see, I'm a bit of a celebrity. Name's Hawk Caine. Used to be on television quite a bit. Presently, I'm a bounty hunter, slash private investigator." He placed his investigator license next to the credit card. "Currently, I'm being employed by two of the wealthiest businessmen from over in Blount County. I need a quiet out of the way place where I can relax while I'm conducting my investigation. It is believed that the killer from Blount County, responsible for seven murders thus far, is now operating here in Johnson County. When, not if, I catch this killer there's going to be a lot of publicity in the area. Might just be good for your business for folks to know that the man who finally nailed the killer actually stayed right here at Prospect Hill. Might be good advertising."

The woman needed no further prodding as to whether she was going to allow this strange looking man to stay at the prestigious Prospect Hill Bed and Breakfast. She was no match for Hawk Caine. Reaching for the credit card she smiled and said, "Just let me run your card, sir."

An hour later, Hawk relaxed in an oversized Jacuzzi situated next to a large picture window overlooking the elaborate grounds of Prospect Hill. Taking a drink of expensive wine directly from the bottle, he looked at the silver platter of assorted cheeses and grapes that had been delivered to his luxurious room. Resting his head on a soft Jacuzzi pillow, he puffed away on a cigar and smiled to himself. Between his bullshit and Pittman and Barrett's money he had talked and bought his way into a room fit for a king. As long as Pittman and Barrett were footing his expenses he was going to enjoy himself. Setting the wine bottle down, he grabbed the Mountain City yellow pages, turned to the restaurant section and tore out the page. He repeated the same process with the lodging and gas station pages. Tomorrow he would begin his search for the killer.

CHAPTER EIGHTEEN

MONDAY MORNING, AT PRECISELY SIX O'CLOCK, Nadine Farnsworth, proprietor of Prospect Hill, peered out a second story window as she ran her finger across an antique bookshelf at the end of the hall. Her early morning cleaning inspection was interrupted by the loud noise of the diesel engine, as Hawk Caine allowed the motor to warm up. The normally tranquil setting of the surrounding forest suddenly took on the sights and sounds of a truck stop, the constant deep rumbling of the engine, the black diesel fumes filling the air and drifting out into the trees.

Sitting back in the seat, Caine reviewed his plan for the day. He held up the ripped yellow page of gas stations in Mountain City and the surrounding area and counted the number of stops he would have to make. Seventeen businesses offered gas: five service stations, ten convenient marts, one grocery store and Dave's 421, which is where he was headed first. It was at this location Reichenbaugh said Denlinger had first seen the man who wore the red hat and drove an old pickup.

Pulling out of the paved parking lot, Hawk thought since the man he was after had been seen there, it only made sense to make that his first stop for the day.

As he left the city limits of Mountain City, he headed up 421 North. He looked at the endless mountain range in his rearview mirror. *The Iron Mountains,* he thought. *Depending on how things pan out over the next few days I might have to drive up into the mountains and start asking folks who live up there if they've ever seen the man I'm looking for.* He glanced down at the console where he had laid the composite picture of the suspect. The face that stared back at him looked sinister, foreboding. The knit cap pulled down over the ears combined with the piercing eyes would no doubt bother most folks, but not Hawk Caine. He was used to dealing with criminals, lowlifes, those who broke the law. If the man was in the area, eventually they would cross paths, and when they did, this killer will have met his match.

Twenty minutes later, he saw the sign for Dave's 421. Pulling into the dirt lot, he checked his fuel gauge and noticed he was down to a little less than a half tank. He parked his truck next to the diesel pumps and climbed down, surveying the surrounding mountains in every direction. Sliding his credit card into the slot, he knew it was going to be far easier to catch his prey in Mountain City rather than in the mountains. Out of all the men he had tracked down and brought to justice, all but three had been apprehended in a town or city. No matter how careful they were they always made a mistake. He had apprehended one man in a grocery store, another getting a haircut, and ironically, one while getting gas. He always did his homework, asked a lot of questions and listened to what people said. He counted on the men he tracked to slip up and let their guard down. The tank full, he replaced the nozzle back into the pump, closed the gas cap and headed for what appeared to be a general store.

The store was crammed with roadmaps, snacks, magazines, novelties and just about anything else one could imagine. Approaching the sales counter, he inquired of a young girl who was fiddling with the cash register, "Excuse me, young lady, is the manager or the owner in this morning?"

The girl looked at Caine and from his attire assumed he was just another trucker. "Yes, he's back in the office doing some paperwork," she answered.

After answering Caine's question, she just stood there staring at him. Caine spoke up as if she were stupid, "I can't very well speak with him unless you go back there and tell him I'm out here. The name's Hawk Caine."

Another girl who had been stocking cigarettes spoke from across the store. "I'll get him. Be right back."

It was less than a minute when the girl followed by a tall, thin man came out from behind a wall of soda machines. The man walked right up to Caine and offered his hand. "Dave Simes, owner. What can I do for you, Mr. Caine? Hope you don't have a complaint, but if you do I'll do my best to solve it."

Hawk opened his wallet and displayed his ID as he explained, "Don't have anything to complain about, but I do have a problem you might be able to help me solve."

Dave looked closely at the card. "Private investigator. Who did I piss off now?" he said, laughing nervously.

"I have no idea," said Hawk. "I could care less who you piss off. I'm in the area looking for a man who might be responsible for all of the killings they've had over in Blount County. I have reason to believe he's in this area."

"God!" said one of the girls. "My father was just talking about those murders the other night. Said he was glad they were over in Blount County and not over here where we live."

The other girl lit up a cigarette, as she commented, "And you say the killer is in our area now?"

"I have it from a rather good source that he is," said Caine as he produced the drawing of the suspect. "Here, take a look at this composite drawing. It's not exactly what the suspect looks like, but it's close enough."

The girl who was smoking, placed her hand over her mouth as she mumbled, "Oh, my God! That man was just in here, not more than ten minutes ago. He paid for a fill up, a carton of chocolate milk and a package of cupcakes."

The other girl chimed in, "Yeah, I remember him. Course, he wasn't wearing that knit cap. He had a bright red ball cap on. He's been coming in here every week for about the last month I guess. I noticed him right off. Most everybody that comes in here are regulars. He always comes in on Monday or Tuesday, gases up, buys a carton of chocolate milk and a snack and then leaves."

"Strange sort of a guy," added the other girl. "Real quiet... never says a word."

Caine placed his hands on his hips, "Well, I'll be damned! What kind of vehicle was this man driving?"

"Old greenish-brown pickup truck."

"How did the man pay for his purchase?"

"He always pays with cash."

"Did you happen to notice which way he went when he left this morning?"

"No, we had other customers."

"Look, I gotta git," stated Caine. "Think I'll head back into Mountain City and snoop around." Opening his wallet, he removed one of his business cards and handed it to one of the girls. "Do me a favor. If he happens to drop by again, see if you can get him to say something, maybe his name. Oh, and one other thing. If you can I'd appreciate it if you'd slip out and write down his license plate number. My cell phone number is on the back of that card. If I don't catch this guy before next Monday I'll be back to stake out your place. And I wouldn't worry so much about him being in the area. Hawk Caine is on the case!"

The two girls and Dave stood outside beneath the overhang of the store as they watched Caine's diesel truck pull out and speed down the highway toward Mountain City. One of the girls handed the business card to Dave as she said, "Never a dull moment. Is that guy nuts or what? If that killer comes back again I'm not gonna talk to him. I'm gonna call 911. This has got me scared to death."

Around noon, Hawk Caine pulled his truck to the curb and checked his watch. It was time for lunch. Grabbing the ripped yellow page that contained the list of eating establishments in and around Mountain City he climbed down and walked up the street to the Mountain Café.

After leaving Dave's 421 earlier that morning, he immediately drove back to town and cruised up and down every street in Mountain City looking for his suspect that he had just missed by ten minutes at Dave's. There wasn't any sense in visiting the rest of the places selling gas since the girls had told him the man he was looking for had been in once a week for the past month, usually on a Monday or Tuesday. Unless the man was filling up more than once a week then Dave's 421 was his favorite gas station. Most people were creatures of habit and Hawk figured the man he was looking for was no different than most folks. He had spent the entire morning visiting various restaurants in town hoping someone had seen the man he was searching for. Out of the twelve places where one could grab a bite, he had already visited eight with no luck. No one had seen the man in the knit cap. Since he had missed out on breakfast he decided to eat lunch, relax and review what he had accomplished so far.

Entering the small café, he took a table next to the front window so he could keep an eye on the street in case the pickup drove by. He spread out the ripped yellow pages he had taken from the phone book at Prospect Hill. There were only four places to eat that he hadn't visited yet. Taking out his pen he drew a line through the Mountain Cafe which left only three. Later in the afternoon he'd check out the remaining restaurants, which were all fast food joints. The chances of someone remembering a particular customer there would be far less than at a regular sit down restaurant. He put the page of restaurants on the bottom and started to look at the page of hotels, motels and bed and breakfast places in the area when an older waitress approached, "Good afternoon, sir. I'll be taking your order. Let me get your drink order first."

Hawk was short and to the point. He held up his hand so that she would not interrupt him. "I'll have the meatloaf special, only with fries, no mashed potatoes. Give me gravy on the fries and I'll have spiced apples. Bring me a pitcher of iced tea with lemon."

Glancing out the front window again, he noticed a pickup pass slowly by. It was black, a newer model. The girls at Dave's said the man he was looking for drove an old greenish-brown pickup. He shook his head in amazement as he thought about how he had missed his suspect by a mere ten minutes. Hell, he had probably passed him on his way to Dave's driving in the opposite lane. He had probably been no more than ten feet from the man.

It seemed like no time at all before the waitress returned with his lunch. Placing the meatloaf and a pitcher of iced tea on the table, she looked out the window noticing Caine's truck. "You must be that bounty hunter everyone in town is talking about. My name is Alma. You look so familiar to me, like I've seen you somewhere before. I've lived here in Mountain City all my life and I know you're not from these parts." Placing her hands on her hips she stared up at the ceiling in deep thought as she continued to speak, "I know I've seen you somewhere."

Caine unwrapped his silverware and answered, "Probably on TV. I used to be a professional wrestler. Wrestled for the WWE for a number of years."

Snapping her fingers, Alma pointed at Caine. "That's exactly where I've seen you. My husband is a big wrestling fan. Watches it every Friday night. Never watched it much myself but I'd catch an occasional glimpse as I was walking around the house. You were one of the bad guys...right?"

"Yep, I sure was," answered Caine as he poured himself a glass of tea. "That was years ago. Now, I'm the good guy. As a bounty hunter, I track down real bad guys. Listen, maybe you could help me out." Pulling the composite drawing from his vest, he laid it on the table and smoothed the edges. "This is the guy I'm currently looking for. He's been reported in this area. They think he might be responsible for the murders they've had over in Blount County."

Alma stared at the picture in disbelief then sat down at the table as she picked up the drawing and signaled to another waitress who was walking by, "Sally, look at this drawing. Isn't that Bubba?"

Sally placed a tray of dirty dishes on an adjacent table and joined Alma and Caine. Looking at the drawing, Sally commented without the slightest hesitation. "Damn straight, that's Bubba.

Matter of fact, he had breakfast in here this morning. Got the same thing he always orders: double pancakes with extra syrup and hash browns on the side."

Caine was just about to cut into his meatloaf, but suddenly stopped, pointing his fork at Sally. "You mean to tell me this man was here this morning...for breakfast?"

Sally picked up the drawing and confirmed, "Yep, that's Bubba. He comes in quite often to eat. Sometimes for breakfast, sometimes for lunch, even dinner, but mostly breakfast."

Caine laid his fork down. He was too excited to eat. "What time was this man here this morning?"

"Hmm...let me think. I guess it was around 7:30, maybe 8:00."

Alma jumped in on the conversation. "I really couldn't say. I didn't come in until ten." Taking the drawing from Sally, Alma explained, "This is Hawk Caine, the bounty hunter everyone has been talking about. This is the man he's looking for. He thinks he's in the area—"

Caine interrupted her as he asked, "Are you sure a man matching that description was in here earlier today?"

Sally looked directly at Caine. "Of course it's him."

Alma agreed, "Yep, that's Bubba. I've waited on him quite a few times myself. Nice fella, doesn't say much. Always has a smile for me. He doesn't look mean, like in this picture."

"Something else," said Sally. "When he first started to come in here he wore that knit cap, but then he started to show up wearing a red ball cap."

"How long has he been coming here?" asked Caine.

Alma looked at Sally then answered, "I guess maybe a month or so."

"And you say his name is Bubba?"

"We have no idea what his name is. He's such a great tipper that we decided to give him a name...so we started to call him Bubba, not to his face, but just amongst ourselves. He just looks like a Bubba."

Sally motioned for Alma to move over to a chair next to the window as she took a seat herself. Tapping the drawing with one of her long fingernails she stated. "Actually, his real name is Russell."

Alma shot Sally a strange look. "How would you know that?"

"I didn't, until this morning when he came in for breakfast. As usual he was having a second cup of coffee after he finished eating. When I laid his bill on the table and started to clean up the dishes, he laid his wallet on the table so he could pay me. His wallet happened to flip open and for a brief moment I saw a driver's license with his photo on it. The license was from Tennessee and his first name happens to be Russell. I didn't have time to catch the last name."

Caine was beside himself. "Did this Russell say anything?"

Sally shrugged. "Just that he'd see me tomorrow."

Alma added, "Bubba...or Russell or whoever he is, never really has all that much to say. The longest conversation I ever had with him was the first time he came in. When I asked him if he was on vacation he told me he was just visiting for a while. I asked him where he was from and he said up north. He was always nice to me and he's a great tipper."

Caine pushed his unfinished meal to the side. He was on to something here. Eating at the moment was not a priority. Opening his wallet he pulled out two fifty dollar bills. Handing one to each waitress he explained, "This is hush money. What I'm about to share with you can't be discussed with anybody; not the other waitresses, the manager or owner, not even your family."

Sally fingered one of the fifties, "I don't understand."

"It's simple," said Caine. "This man...this Russell told you he'd see you tomorrow which means he's coming here to eat sometime during the day. Since he didn't indicate whether it was breakfast, lunch or dinner, I may have to stake this place out all day. If you mention that I'm going to try and apprehend this killer here in this restaurant, the word will get out and our killer might flee town. So, you just take that money and keep quiet about what I'm going to say."

Looking around the restaurant to make sure no one nearby was listening, he explained, "Here's what we'll do. I'll park my truck across the street out of sight early tomorrow morning before you even open up. I'll station myself behind those bushes on the other side of the street. When he arrives, whenever that may be, I'll wait until he gets inside and orders his meal. That way he'll be relaxed...off guard, so to speak. As soon as you deliver his meal one of you needs to walk out the front door and give me a signal. Let's say, you run your right hand through your hair. That'll be the signal for me to take action. Now, let me ask you. Is there a back door I can get access to?"

Alma pointed toward the kitchen door. "Sure, but it's only to be used by the employees. We always park out back. The backdoor leads right into the kitchen area."

"Perfect," said Caine. "After you give me the signal I'll go around to the back and you can let me in. Where does this Russell usually sit?"

"Normally, in one of the four booths by the front window," Sally said. "Actually, he's sat in the very seat where you're sitting."

Looking back at the kitchen door, Caine spoke with confidence. "Good, then his back will be to me. He'll never see me coming until it's too late. It'll be over in a matter of seconds. It might get rough, but I doubt it. I might have to club him over the head or wrestle him to the floor depending on how he reacts. If that happens you guys need to keep the customers out of the way and tell them I'm with the law."

Alma looked at the kitchen door then back to Caine. "This sounds dangerous."

"It can be...but only for me. You and the customers will have nothing to be worried about. This could be good for business. The press and the people who have hired me have been told by me that I can catch this killer in two months. Today is my first day of actually being on the job. It'll be a big deal when Hawk Caine captures this killer in less than twenty-four hours. The news media will be in town and right here at the Mountain Café to get the lowdown. When they interview me I'll mention both your names and explain about how I couldn't have done it without you. This place will be packed for weeks with curious customers. This could be the biggest thing to hit this town in years and you'll be right in the middle of it. Now, are there any questions?"

Sally looked at Alma. "Seems simple enough, but I don't know. Do you think he'll have a gun? We could get shot."

Alma hit Sally on her arm. "Come on girl, where's your sense of adventure. Besides that, Hawk said it'd be over in seconds. After Bubba has a seat and his order is brought to the table one of us goes out and gives Hawk the signal then we let him in the back and he takes over." Picking up the fifty she waved it in the air. "Easiest fifty bucks I ever made." Sally picked up her money and finally nodded in agreement.

Caine reached for his meatloaf. "Remember, not a word to anyone. Now, let me finish my lunch and I'll see you girls tomorrow." Returning to his meal Caine lost himself in thought. *I hope those waitresses can keep their mouths shut. Dammit, I can't believe that I missed him twice today. I'll get him tomorrow. He won't know what hit him.*

After eating lunch, Caine returned to Prospect Hill. He walked around the back of the luxurious property and surveyed the tennis courts and the Olympic size pool. He couldn't remember the last time he had been swimming. More than likely it had been over thirty some years ago when he was a kid. He didn't even own a swim suit, but nonetheless he decided to sit out by the pool. There were three other couples at the pool; two in the water, basking in the sun on floating devices, the other couple engaged in a conversation as they sipped at drinks beneath a bright red umbrella. Caine wasn't the typical person that would normally frequent a swimming pool and he had no doubt his presence at the edge of the water caused people to stare in wonder. Lying back in a plastic covered lounge chair in his jeans, he had removed his shirt and vest and kicked off his boots and socks. His hairy, tattooed body didn't exactly fit in with the regular guests that stayed at Prospect Hill.

Looking at his watch, he noticed it was two o'clock in the afternoon. He smiled. It was time to call Merle Pittman and give him an update. Punching in Pittman's number on his cell phone he waited as he looked up into the bright afternoon sun. A pleasant voice answered the call, "Pittman Law Office, may I help you?"

Caine got right to the point, "This is Hawk Caine. Put Pittman on. I need to speak with him."

The secretary hesitated, but then responded, "Let me see if he's available."

"He'll be available to speak with me," said Caine. "Just get him."

There was silence on the other end, then following a few seconds the voice of Merle Pittman spoke, "Caine, I've been waiting for a call from you. When are you going to get started on running down this killer? Like we agreed, you've only got two months if you want to collect that fifty grand."

Caine laughed. "You can start the meter ticking. Looks like I might nail your killer tomorrow."

"Really!" exclaimed Merle. "Where are you?"

"Can't share that information with you. The less you know the better. If I go telling everyone where I'm at it might screw things up. I don't want the news media here just yet. I will tell you this: I'm going to nab him while he's eating at a restaurant in the town where I'm presently staying. That's all you need to know for now. There are a few things you need to prepare yourself for. When the news breaks that I've got the killer it's gonna be big news. You'll have to schedule a massive news conference with all of the local media present. I'll hand the killer over and you'll present me with a check for fifty grand. When the news gets out that Hawk Caine caught the killer in just one day instead of two months it'll be front page news. I want this to go national. This is the break I've been waiting for. I'll keep my end of the deal, you just make sure you keep yours. Now, I've got to get a good night's rest. Tomorrow is going to be quite interesting." Hawk hung up the phone. Merle just stared at the phone in his hand, but then smiled. This was going to be bigger than he and Franklin had planned on. The apprehension of the killer was going to be quite profitable for both Barrett and him.

Hawk Caine sat on an empty five-gallon bucket he found behind the building where he parked his truck. He peered through the bushes across the street from the café. Glancing at the glowing face of his watch, he noted the time at four-thirty in the morning, an hour and a half before the café would be open for business.

Sipping on the coffee he had purchased at an all night gas station north of town, he reached into a bag of day old donuts and took a large bite out of a chocolate donut. He looked toward the dark sky, the drizzling rain falling on his face. It had been raining all night and the forecast for the day was for more of the same. Pulling the collar of his jean jacket up around his neck, he frowned and thought to himself, *Just my luck...rain!* Conducting a stakeout in bad weather was nothing new to Caine. It came with the territory. At times, it was just part of the job.

Removing the lens cap from the binoculars hanging from his neck, he adjusted the focus bringing the interior of the café to life. A light came on and someone walked across the café by the front windows. *Probably the owner or the morning cook,* he thought.

That made sense as the café would be open for business in a little over an hour. The waitresses would be arriving soon, the cook would be organizing strips of bacon and laying out dozens of eggs. Someone had to get the coffee going. Breakfast sounded good, but for the moment he would have to be satisfied with his gas station coffee and stale donuts.

Later on in the week, if everything went according to plan, he'd be fifty thousand dollars richer and would be dining in the finest restaurant the Smoky Mountains offered. He hoped that when Russell said he'd see Sally tomorrow it meant he was coming in for breakfast. Since Russell hadn't been specific, Caine resigned himself to the fact he might have to remain behind the bushes until lunch or possibly supper. It could wind up being a long day. Caine always had a "what if" plan in place and today was no exception. He had prepared himself for the long haul if need be. The cooler at his side was filled with sodas, three sandwiches, beef jerky and chips.

The street was dark and lonely looking, the only sound, the gently falling rain on the brim of his hat. It was too early for most of the residents of Mountain City to be up and around. In the last half hour only two cars had passed by on the wet street. Caine looked at his watch again: ten after five. The café would be open for business in fifty minutes. If he remembered correctly, Sally had said that Russell had come in for breakfast yesterday between seven thirty and eight o'clock. If the man followed the same routine as he did yesterday then that meant in less than three hours he'd have Russell in handcuffs.

Between five-thirty and six o'clock there was a lot of activity at the café. Alma and Sally entered from the kitchen door and sat at a table by the window as they enjoyed breakfast before the morning rush. A car stopped out front and a man delivered a small bundle of newspapers. Next, a truck pulled up to the curb for the café's regular bread delivery.

The rain was coming down harder as the first customer of the day entered the café. He was obviously a regular as he waved at Alma and Sally then took a seat at the counter. He no sooner had his coffee in front of him than he was joined by two other older men who sat on either side of him.

For the next hour and a half, Caine kept a close watch on the café. His coffee was gone and he had finished the donuts. The rain had slowed down, but remained steady. His clothes were soaked and his butt was sore from sitting on the bucket. A number of customers had come and gone, but there had been no sign of Russell. Letting the binoculars fall to his chest, he looked at his watch; exactly seven-thirty. The next half hour was crucial.

According to the waitresses, it was during this time that Russell normally showed up for breakfast. He stood up and stretched. He checked his revolver again and then made sure he had his cuffs attached to his belt. He pounded both of his fists into his palms and rotated his neck then did a deep knee bend. Even though he had somewhat of a pot belly, Caine still prided himself in his physical abilities. Despite the fact that he was out of shape, many a man had underestimated his strength and quickness. Popping a stick of gum in his mouth, he sat back down on the bucket and looked through the binoculars.

A Mountain City police cruiser pulled up to the curb just down from the café. Caine stared in disbelief as Sheriff Reichenbaugh climbed out of the car, walked up the street and entered the café.

"Damn it!" he swore. "What the hell is Reichenbaugh doing there." Then, it hit him. *What if Sally and Alma screwed me over and called the County Sheriff about my plans to apprehend Russell at the café. If Russell drives by and sees the County Sheriff's vehicle parked near the café, he won't go in. Damn it all to hell! Those two daffy waitresses are going to screw me out of my fifty grand!*

He continued to watch Reichenbaugh's every move as he entered the café, waved at Sally then moved to the counter where he started to talk with Alma. *What are they talking about? Is Alma spilling the beans about my plans?* Caine stood and tried to move closer in the bushes to get a better view of Reichenbaugh and Alma. Speaking in a low whisper, he clenched his teeth, "If those two dumb broads screw up my plans there's gonna be hell to pay!"

The situation suddenly changed as Sally handed Reichenbaugh a cup of coffee. He said something to her, tipped his hat and turned to walk out the door, but was stopped by the old men at the counter. Caine, all of a sudden realized that Reichenbaugh's appearance at the café was nothing more than his stopping by for morning coffee, but still, the County Sheriff had to get his ass out of there before Russell showed up. "Move your ass...move your ass!" said Caine. Following a few seconds of conversation Sheriff Reichenbaugh exited the café, walked to his cruiser, climbed in and drove off. Lowering the binoculars, Caine let out a long sigh of relief.

He looked at his watch again. It was seven-forty-six. If Russell was going to show for breakfast, it would be in the next few minutes. He was just about to sit down on the bucket when an older, greenish-brown pickup slowly passed by and pulled into a parking spot about twenty yards past the café. Bringing the binoculars to his eyes, Caine focused on the truck and the driver.

The man stepped out of the truck, looked both ways up and down the street, stretched, yawned then started to walk toward the café.

Caine smiled approvingly as he identified the man. He fit the description that he had been given: big man, old work clothes, heavy work boots, bearded face and red ball hat. It was most definitely Russell, the man he was being paid to bring in. Within the next fifteen minutes, he would experience his most successful and profitable capture.

Caine watched as Russell seated himself at a window table. Alma approached, and after taking Russell's breakfast order, she looked out the window in the direction of the bushes, knowing that Hawk Caine was out there somewhere watching.

Minutes passed and Alma brought Russell's meal to his table. After refilling his coffee she put the pot on the counter, walked across the café and stepped out the front door as she ran her right hand through her hair. "Showtime," Caine said as he jogged up the street staying close to the bushes that lined the sidewalk. Hawk cut across the street and ran down a small alley, took a right past two buildings and ended up behind the café. Sally was waiting for him in the rain by the back door. Before she could say a word, Caine asked, "What the hell was the County Sheriff doing here? Did you or Alma say something to him about what we talked about?"

Sally, puffing on a cigarette, held an umbrella over her head and answered as if she were being accused of something she hadn't done. "No way! We didn't say a word to anyone, just like we agreed. Reichenbaugh occasionally stops by for a cup of coffee and this morning just happened to be one of those days. He doesn't have a clue Russell is in there or that you plan on nabbing him."

"Good," said Caine as he breathed a sigh of relief. "Now, do you guys remember the plan we discussed?"

"Yeah, I think so. Alma and I talked about it last night before we left work. You said it could be dangerous, but only for you. I'm nervous as a cat. I hope your plan works."

"Quit worrying" said Caine as he wiped the rain from his face. "My ass is on the line, not yours. Now, is this the door that leads inside?"

Stubbing out the cigarette on the side of a trashcan, Sally nodded, took a deep breath and reached for the handle on the screen door. "Let's get this over with. Follow me." As they entered the kitchen, the cook looked up in surprise. Before he could say a word Sally patted him on the shoulder, "It's all right Carl, this is Hawk Caine and he's a friend of mine. Don't pay us no mind. You just keep cooking."

Stopping at a metal door, Sally pointed to the window in the kitchen door. "Take a look in there and tell me what you think."

Caine looked through the glass and saw Russell sitting ten yards away at the window table with his back turned to him. "Perfect" Caine said. "He'll never know what hit him. This is going to be easier than I thought." Turning back to Sally, he gave final instructions, "In a few seconds I'm going out there. It'll be over before you know it. He'll probably struggle but it won't do him any good. Once I get him on the floor, I'll slap the cuffs on him. Remember what I said. You and Alma have to keep the customers calm. Once I have him cuffed you need to call Reichenbaugh to get over here immediately so we can get this guy locked up."

Sally folded her hands in front of her as she began to get nervous. Caine, noticing her uneasiness, remarked calmly, "Don't worry. This is going to be a piece of cake. In less than an hour from now Russell will be in jail and I'll be back over here having breakfast. Now, you need to go out there, grab that coffeepot and go over in front of his table and ask him if he wants a refill. While he's distracted, I'll come up from behind him and put him in a neck hold, taking him to the floor. Ready?"

Sally reached up and opened a cabinet door and removed a bottle of brown liquid. Holding the bottle up, she unscrewed the top and took a long drink, then let out a long breath. "Owner's whiskey stash. Keeps it up there for special occasions." Taking another drink, she smiled. "I'm ready. Let's do this!" After she walked through the door, Caine watched through the window as she went to the counter, picked up the coffeepot and approached Russell. Russell no sooner looked up at Sally when Caine was through the door and across the room.

The look of panic on Sally's face caused Russell to turn just as Caine clamped his muscular left forearm around Russell's neck, at the same time locking his left hand into his right. Caine pulled Russell backward trying to take him to the floor, but Russell was able to keep his balance. The chair fell back over and Russell straightened up as he flung both of his elbows simultaneously into Caine's rib cage and then stomped his huge feet down on Caine's boots. Caine, from his old wrestling days was used to having his body pummeled. He tightened his grip on Russell's neck as he yelled, "You're going down, you son of a bitch!" Russell grunted loudly as he struggled to free himself, but Caine's death lock hold was winning the battle.

The customers, taken by surprise, jumped up from their tables and backed against the far wall. Some of the women were screaming, while other customers ran out the front door.

Over the loud commotion Alma yelled, "It's okay; he's with the law!" Sally was doing her best to calm the patrons seated at the counter who had nowhere to go.

Hearing the disturbance in the dining area, the cook came out the kitchen. When he saw Caine and Russell fighting, he yelled, "What the hell's going on out here!"

Some of the customers were screaming, "Someone call the police!"

"Stay back...don't get involved!" Sally yelled.

"I'm getting out of here!" a man said as he managed to get off his stool by the counter.

The cook grabbed a nearby mop and clubbed Caine on the back as he yelled, "Leave Bubba alone, you bastard!"

Sally ran across the room and shoved the cook against the wall as she ordered, "You're hitting the wrong man. Bubba's the murderer!"

Hearing Sally's outburst, another man bolted for the door as he yelled, "Everybody better clear out! That guy's a murderer!"

Russell, using the table for leverage raised his right foot and shoved backward driving both he and Caine into a coat rack which tumbled to the floor, metal coat hangers flying in every direction.

Caine, realizing his opponent was not going to give in easily rammed Russell face first into the wall. Russell let out a loud yell and bit down on Caine's left arm. At first Caine had been relaxed feeling he had the upper hand, but when Russell began to loosen Caine's grip he let go and shoved Russell into the wall again. Russell's right arm swung back and caught Caine in the chest sending him stumbling backward. Russell turned, blood running down his face from a broken nose he got when his face was being slammed into the wall. He gritted his teeth as he took a step toward Caine, but was once again driven back against the wall from a flying drop kick from Hawk. Caine, out of practice from his old wrestling days fell to the floor. Before he could react Russell picked him up like he was a rag doll and hoisted him above his head. Taking three long strides toward the counter Russell tossed Caine into the air, his body crashing down on the counter and then falling onto the floor on the other side, cups and dishes falling on his head and body.

Russell, now free of his assailant, looked at the front door that was blocked by a number of customers who were frozen, not sure what to do. Turning, Russell picked up one of the metal tables and hurled it through the plate glass front window. Just as Caine was getting up from behind the counter, he saw Russell jump through the opening and run up the street. Caine, hopping over the counter was livid. "Got dammit all to hell. I'm gonna kill that son of a bitch!" Pushing Alma roughly to the side he yelled, "Get the hell out of my way!"

Jumping through the opening, he withdrew his revolver from the back of his belt and ran up the street in the direction he had seen Russell run. A man standing next to his car pointed up the street as he yelled, "He went up there to that old truck!"

Caine slipped on the edge of the wet curb and went down hard. Cursing, he got to his feet and realized he had injured his right ankle. Not able to run, he limped as quickly as he could toward the truck. He had to get to it and stop Russell before he pulled out onto the street. If he got away he might not get another chance to capture him. As he approached the truck, he slowed down.

Ducking down, he approached the driver's side of the truck. Bringing his revolver up into a defensive position he yelled, "Put your hands over your head and get out of the truck. Caine backed up against the side of the truck and quickly turned, pointing the gun into the open window. *Where in the hell did that bastard go?* He said to himself as he looked into the empty cab. Walking around to the front of the truck, a look of surprise came over his face as Russell stood up in the truck bed and pulled off a quick shot. The bullet hit Caine in his right shoulder. Holding onto his injured arm, his hand trembled as he squeezed off a reactive shot. The bullet ricocheted off a stop sign and shattered a nearby gift shop window. Russell jumped down from the back of the truck and took aim at Caine.

Realizing that Russell had the drop on him, Caine threw down his revolver, and yelled, "Don't shoot! I'm not armed!" Russell hesitated for a split second, then slowly pulled the trigger. The second shot hit Caine right between the eyes. Caine's knees wobbled and he fell backward in a sitting position on the sidewalk, blood running down his face. He felt dizzy, his eyes were glazing over. He watched through bleary eyes as Russell walked back to his truck and got in. Pulling forward, he peered down at Caine, then sped away.

"I'll be damned," mumbled Caine as he touched his bloody forehead and looked up into the falling rain. His head slumped forward and he drew his last breath.

In the distance, the sounds of sirens broke the silence from the crowd of people who were in disbelief at what they had just witnessed.

CHAPTER NINETEEN

THE MURDER OF HAWK CAINE echoed through the Smoky Mountains. The ex-professional wrestler turned bounty hunter got his wish. The account of his death was splashed across television and radio stations and newspapers from coast to coast.

The media was calling it the Mountain City Shootout. The county seat of Johnson County was transformed from a sleepy-eyed town into a Mecca for reporters, television and radio station vans and those who just wanted to see the spot were Hawk Caine was shot and where the Smoky Mountain killer had escaped. Most of the residents retreated into their homes to avoid having a camera shoved into their face while others took to the streets to talk to anyone and everyone who was interested in their story. Every business in Mountain City was prospering; restaurants, motels and gas stations overwhelmed with customers. A ripple effect from the murder touched every person who knew about it and those who held a special interest in the Smoky Mountain killer.

Alma and Sally, the waitresses at the Mountain City Café were enjoying their fifteen minutes of fame relating and embellishing their story. They told everyone who was willing to listen to them about their favorite customer, A.K.A. Bubba. The Feds from Townsend, Harold Green and Ralph Gephart, arrived in Mountain City later on the day of the shooting. They notified the local authorities that they were requesting twenty agents to the surrounding area to block off every main road in the county.

Along with the state police a massive manhunt was underway. As soon as the story broke, Merle Pittman and Franklin Barrett were on the phone lamenting that they hadn't secured the rights to Caine's story. They had both expected to cash in when Caine brought the killer in and now all they had to show for all their planning and negotiating was Caine's expense account that needed to be paid.

When Merle suggested they head over to Mountain City and remind everyone that they had hired Caine in the first place, Franklin objected, saying he was not going to return to the place where he had years ago lost his first fortune. "I have no desire to make money off of a dead man," said Barrett. "We went down that road before following the death of your brother, and then Mildred Henks. It started out to be profitable, but wound up being a financial mistake. The story of Hawk Caine being shot down on the street will be old news in the weeks to come and eventually will fade into the background. Unless someone finds this killer soon, the tourist trade in the area will take a serious plunge. This killer is becoming more visible and most folks are really getting nervous. I think I'm going to take some time off and go on vacation somewhere far away from the Smokies."

Chief Axel Brody stood in the corner of his small office as he addressed his three officers: "By now you all have no doubt heard about what went on this mornin' over in Mountain City, so I'm gonna skip the details. Chief Grimes phoned earlier and informed me that he is dispatchin' six deputies from Maryville to assist us. We'll be workin' overlappin' twelve hour shifts until we either catch this bastard or things cool down. We'll have three men on patrol at all times. If the killer comes back here he's gonna see police everywhere he looks. It doesn't appear to me this guy has any intention of leavin' the area soon so we've got to stay on top of things. He's a bold sum bitch and he's gonna surface again."

Taking a seat in his chair, Brody further explained, "I wasn't all that fond of Hawk Caine, but in the back of my mind I was half hopin' he'd catch this killer and that would be the end of it. Well, that didn't happen so it looks like the ball is back in our court once again." Looking around the room he held up his hands. "Is everyone on board with this?"

All three officers nodded, but remained quiet. Brody stood, finished his coffee then ordered, "Good. Let's hit the streets and keep your eyes open for anythin' out of the ordinary."

Grant was no sooner in his patrol car when his cell phone rang. Removing his sunglasses from the visor, he sat back in the seat and answered, "Hello."

A familiar voice on the other end responded, "Grant, it's Tobias Reichenbaugh. Man, what a day! Mountain City has been turned upside down. A lot of folks over this way are still in shock. I mean, this sort of thing just doesn't happen in Johnson County. We've never experienced anything like this over here. A man shot down in broad daylight on the main street of town. It's a nightmare."

Grant tried to speak, but Tobias kept right on talking, "The Feds called me when they caught wind of the shooting. They kept me on the hot seat for nearly an hour grilling me with one question after another. They wanted to know if I knew the killer was in the area and if I was aware that quite a few people in the area had witnessed his comings and goings. They also wanted to know if I had ever met with Hawk Caine. I started to get nervous when they asked me if I knew where the killer might be. I decided to tell them everything I knew except for the fact that you had been over here snooping around. I just told them that I received an anonymous call from someone who informed me they saw a man fitting the suspect's description up by the old Pender farm on Iron Mountain.

"They kept asking me if I knew the identity of the caller, but I simply told them it was probably someone who lived up in the mountains and that most of those folks like to stick to themselves." Hesitating, Tobias then continued, "Ya know, Grant, I should have taken you more serious when you told me someone tried to kill you at the Pender place. Now, someone *has been killed* and I feel partly to blame for not checking further into what you told me. Hold on, I've got another call coming in."

Seconds later Tobias was back on the phone. "Just another reporter wanting information on the shooting. Look, Grant, I didn't bring up your name because I didn't want to see you get into any trouble. I don't know your boss, Brody, all that well, but I did run into him at a golf outing years ago. It didn't take me long to figure out that he's pretty much an ass. I can't imagine working for the man. If he found out you were over here he'd probably fire you for withholding evidence."

Grant let out a sigh of relief. "Thanks for not mentioning my little trip over to see you. If anyone found out I was over there it would be an issue, especially for Chief Brody. To tell you the truth, Tobias, I'm just about at the end of my rope on this investigation. This whole case has got me stymied." Suddenly, Grant had a horrible thought, "What about Hiram Tate and Adele over at the library? What if the Feds get around to talking with them. I'm sure they'll mention that we talked with them about the Pender case. Hiram will no doubt tell them we went up to the farm and that I decided to return the next day. If that happens the Feds could have a lot of questions for not only you, but me as well."

"I've thought about that," said Tobias. "I'll cross that bridge when I come to it. Listen, I've got another call coming in. Keep in touch."

Throwing his cell phone onto the passenger seat Grant pulled out onto the Parkway. He felt drained. He had no idea what to do at this point. He had allowed himself to become mired so deeply in the case that there didn't seem to be any way of keeping the secret of Conrad Pearl much longer. Now, Conrad's brother, Russell had come to the area for some reason. What was it? The sound of a car horn sounded behind him, snapping him out of his daydreaming.

Turning, he noticed the Ohio plates, a man and a woman, two children in the backseat. *Tourists,* he thought. They were always in a rush to get to their next moment of vacation, having little regard for local citizens who were not in a hurry and just going about their everyday lives.

Turning into the parking lot of the Parkway Grocery, Grant decided to get a cup of coffee. Fatigue weighed on his body like a suit of armor. He was faced with twelve hours of patrolling the streets and a good cup of coffee might help him stay awake. As usual, the place was bustling with a mixture of tourists and locals. Walking up to the coffee dispenser, he overheard a couple discussing the shooting of Hawk Caine. There were only two newspapers left from the stack that was normally on the edge of the counter. Pouring himself a cupful of steaming coffee, it seemed strange to him how easily the bold headline on the front page could be so easily ignored: **BOUNTY HUNTER SHOT DOWN IN MOUNTAIN CITY.** He gazed around the busy store as people were grabbing beer, cigarettes and ice, others paying for gas. It seemed odd how conditioned people became to tragedy—how they could just go on with their lives in the midst of turmoil.

Someone called out his name. "Hey Grant!" Looking toward the front of the store he saw Zeb and Buddie seated at their usual table by the front window. He really wasn't in the mood to talk with them—not today. He knew they would want to talk about the shooting. Giving them a wave he walked out the door.

Zeb looked out the window at Grant crossing the lot. "Wonder what's up with him? Couldn't even stop by and say hello." Taking a swig of coffee Zeb answered his own question, "Guess he's got a lot on his mind what with Hawk Caine taking a bullet. Ol' Brody is probably cracking the whip on his officers. Damn, I wish they'd catch this killer."

Buddie nodded. "Yeah, Brody would sure like to be the one who cracks this case, but I think the chance of that happening is remote to say the least. Hell, the killer was right here in Townsend and they couldn't nail him and now he's over in Mountain City."

Buddie stared off out the window across the street. "Imagine that...another shooting over in Johnson County."

Zeb gave Buddie a strange look then dumped three packets of sugar into his coffee.

"Why'd you do that?" asked Buddie.

"What?" shrugged Zeb.

"You just put three sugars in your coffee which is half gone and cold to boot. You've really been acting weird this morning, sitting there drumming your fingers on the table and now dumping sugar in coffee you're probably not going to drink. You nervous or something?"

"No, not nervous...just concerned. You seen Luke lately? He hasn't been here in three days. It's not like him to not show up for coffee. I went by his house yesterday. His car was in the driveway, but he didn't answer the door. I called him later and he told me he was taking a nap. Now, when's the last time you remember Luke taking a nap in the middle of the day? When I called him he said he'd just been tired lately."

"Tired, my ass!" said Buddie. "He's just plain ignoring us and you know why. We have to keep an eye on him just like we always have." Pushing his coffee to the side, Buddie stood. "The hell with all this shit. Speaking of taking a nap, I think I'm gonna go home and lay down."

Three miles above the Watauga River, Russell guided his truck around the bends and turns of an old abandoned road that led to an outcropping of rocks. He had found a small cave that was now to be his temporary home. His truck bounced from side to side, at one point almost turning over as he crossed a creek littered with large rocks. On the other side of the creek he drove up a steep incline then followed an old weed-covered logging road that ran along the rim of a ravine. Parking the truck beneath a rock ledge, he jumped out and began to gather up handfuls of branches and pine boughs which he threw over the truck until it was concealed from sight. Satisfied that the truck was camouflaged, he walked briskly as he backtracked his way down the logging road gathering leaves and small branches as he went, throwing them over the tire tracks the truck had left behind.

Finally, back at the creek he placed two logs across the road at the bottom of the incline, then waded in the shallow water of the creek as he picked up two large rocks and placed them in the ruts the truck had made in the mud just below the water. Satisfied that no one could detect his trail he returned to the cave.

Out of breath and thirsty he sat down on his cot and grabbed a jug of water. He opened one of the bags and removed a package of crackers. The box had gotten wet on one side and the crackers were moldy. He threw the crackers on the ground. Placing his head in his hands, he rocked back and forth, thoughts running threw his mind: *I really liked living in the barn back at the farm even if it was only for a short time. Why did that man come to the barn and why did he go down in the root cellar? I'm glad I found this cave further back in the forest. I'm safe now, but how much longer will it be before they come looking for me? Why won't they leave me alone? I didn't even know that man who was in the barn. Was he looking for me? All these bad things have happened to me. All I wanted to do was tell my brother good-bye and then I was going to go home.*

Taking another long swig from the jug, he wiped his mouth with the back of his hand. Thoughts continued to race through his brain. *Why are things so messed up? Yesterday I was going to have a nice breakfast and then leave the Iron Mountains and go back home. Now, it's all bad again. It's always been bad for me. When I was just a little kid living at the farm Conrad always tried to protect me from Pa. When Pa was drinking, Conrad would always warn me to run off into the woods. I remember all those times when I wasn't fast enough and Pa would catch me, drag me by my feet into the barn, and beat me. He called me stupid and dumb and I hated him. When he was killed by those hunters I never shed a tear. I cried for my mother and the animals that were killed that day.*

He recalled the bus driver that was mean to him. *I can't remember his name, but he was always making fun of me. He called me names and made me stand up in the bus and the other kids laughed at me. He got what he deserved. My friends...the snakes paid him a visit.*

Wiping tears from his face, Russell smiled as he thought about some of the good times he had as a boy growing up on Iron Mountain. He recalled all the time he had spent with his mother and how she had taken him into the woods many a time to collect Rattlers and Copperheads. She was the one who taught him how to handle snakes. The snakes were his friends. They had always protected him.

Russell sadly looked around the interior of the cave and in his heart he yearned to be back home. *Why did they take us to live with the Pearls?* he thought. *Mr. Pearl was mean and would always grab me by my arm, squeeze it and push me into a chair. He killed my cat and took my dog away. I'm glad he had a heart attack. At least, that's what they thought it was...a heart attack.*

A crackling sound startled him and interrupted his thoughts. Getting up quickly he went to the entrance of the cave, his rifle at the ready in his hands. He watched as a doe disappeared into a thicket of tall grass on the left. Lowering the rifle he went back inside. He rummaged through one of the containers of food, opened a package of Pop-tarts and unwrapped them. Stuffing half a Pop-tart into his mouth, he washed it down with a slug of water.

Sitting back down, he leaned against the cave wall. He thought about how good his life had been after Conrad had taken him out of school. *Conrad took me to the cabin up in the Jellico Mountains. I love it there. I love the cabin, the woods, the streams, the fields. I love everything about it. I had running water, electricity and heat. Conrad bought me a television set and a radio. Conrad taught me how to drive and bought me the truck. I had my freedom. I could come and go as I please. I could drive into Jellico or Newcomb for supplies and to eat meals sometimes. The towns up there are friendly and small. I felt safe up in the mountains away from people. Conrad told me that I would never feel comfortable living in Knoxville. It was big and noisy and had way too many people living there for me to feel at home. No, I like my cabin...except for the hunters. There are always hunters coming and trying to hurt the animals. There are poachers I have to watch for. I have to destroy their traps. There are deer stands that have to be knocked down. If they come into my forest I have to shoot at them sometimes to scare them off and sometimes I have to kill them.*

Stuffing the remainder of the Pop-tart in the side of his mouth, he thought about his older brother. *Conrad always came to see me on Tuesday and Friday. He always brought me money and chocolate candy. Then we would take a walk in the woods and talk about things. Sometimes Conrad would go away for a week or two but he would always tell me when he would be gone. But now it's different. I remember the first Tuesday he didn't come. Then Friday came and the same thing. Conrad did not come to my cabin. I looked in the notebook he gave me with a telephone number written in it and some instructions about what to do if anything ever happened to him. He told me to never call the number unless I was ill or injured. It had to be an emergency before I could call. The next Tuesday he didn't come and I worried. I called the number from a payphone at a gas station. A lady at the University of Tennessee where Conrad worked answered. She told me that Conrad had died recently and was being buried in Townsend. I didn't know what to do. I was so confused. He always took care of me. He always took care of my money. He is dead and he is never coming to see me again. Why did they bury my brother in Townsend? I shouldn't have come here, but I couldn't let my brother be buried alone. There were all those people at the funeral. Maybe I should have talked to them, but Conrad always told me to stay away from strangers. They would never understand me.*

Shadows were beginning to creep up the side of the cave as the sun began its slow descent into the mountains. He took out one of the three pipes that Conrad had bought him over the years. Filling the bowl with the leafy tobacco he sat back against the wall as he lit the pipe. The pleasant aroma of Peach Brandy always had a calming effect for Russell. He remembered how he and Conrad would take long walks in the forest as they smoked their pipes.

Russell was still wrapped in his thoughts. *After the funeral I should have gone back to my cabin up in Jellico. I should have gone back home and read Conrad's instructions that he wrote in my notebook. But then everything bad started happening. Those men at the restaurant, they wanted to hurt me. Conrad was right. People would not understand me and they would make fun of me. I should have killed them both instead of letting one of them go. I had no choice but to kill the man called Danny. He was hurting those turtles and that wasn't right. I had to save the bear from that mean man who owned that store. He followed me and wanted to kill me. I couldn't let that happen. What if he found the bear and put her back in that horrible cage? Everyone I killed while I've been here were bad men. Conrad would have wanted me to kill them just like he told me to kill the bus driver and Mr. Pearl. Why did that man try to kill me this morning? I saw him on television and I thought he was after me. I didn't even know him. He gave me no choice. He wanted to hurt me.*

Reaching under the blanket that was spread on the cot, he pulled out a soiled newspaper called the Mountain News. Turning the pages, he put his dirty finger on a picture of a young couple, the woman holding a baby. He traced his finger over the words as he slowly read them out loud:

Birth Announcement
Congratulations to Grant and
Dana Beth Denlinger
of Townsend Tennessee, are the
proud parents of a baby girl,
Crystal Ann, born on June 25, 2011
Crystal Ann weighed six
pounds, seven ounces at the time
of her birth. Grant Denlinger is
the son of Greta Denlinger and
the grandson of Dalton Denlinger
the former Police Chief and long
time resident of Townsend. Dana
Beth is the daughter of Ruth Pearl
and the late Professor Conrad Pearl
who passed away last year.

He stumbled over the words as he read the article several times. He was finally beginning to understand. He was Dana Beth Denlinger's uncle and the baby was his great niece. Ruth was his sister-in-law. He had relatives. He really wasn't alone. A smile crossed his lips, but then he frowned. *Why had Conrad kept his family a secret all these years? He never told me that he got married or that he had a daughter. It would have been nice having Thanksgiving dinner with them or to spend Christmas at their house. Were they mean people? Is that why Conrad never told me about them or let me come visit? Maybe Conrad was ashamed of them. It doesn't matter now. Conrad is gone and they are still my family. I want to meet them. Maybe they could help me figure out why all those bad people wanted to kill me.* He looked at the man in the picture next to Dana Beth. He looked familiar. *Where had he seen him before?*

Afraid to light a fire to cook food or to keep warm, he ate three raw hotdogs and a can of peaches. Lighting his lantern, he spread out the Tennessee map he had bought days before at Dave's 421. Tracing his finger across the map, he would walk down the mountain as soon as the sun was up tomorrow. He figured it would take nearly thirteen hours to hike up to Bristol. After he arrived, he'd find a Wal-Mart or some sort of store in town, buy himself a new set of clothes and change in the restroom. He would then get a shave and a haircut before finding a used car dealer where he would buy a used truck for cash. It had taken him hours to figure out his next move. Conrad had always been there for him when it came to making decisions. It was hard without his older brother to depend on, but soon, if everything worked out, he would have relatives who would look out for him. *Yes, soon everything will be alright,* he thought. Smiling, he laid down on his cot and fell asleep.

In the morning, he was awakened by the sound of a low flying aircraft. He quickly dressed and began packing a few of his possessions in a canvas knapsack. He took two bottles of water, a roll of toilet paper, an overripe banana and the other pack of Pop-tarts.

He rummaged through the other bags, before he decided to take a box of Band-Aids, his hunting knife, a pouch of Peach Brandy tobacco and his pipe. He checked to make sure his rifle was loaded and slung his second rifle over his shoulder. He realized he was going to have to abandon both guns before he reached Bristol. This was upsetting to him, but he couldn't be seen walking around town with two rifles. He didn't want to draw any attention to himself. When he arrived at Bristol he was going to have to hide his guns on the outskirts of town, then retrieve them when his business there was finished. Putting on his red hat, he stepped out of the cave. It looked like it was going to be a nice day for a long walk in the woods.

The trickle down effect from Hawk Caine's death had filtered into the Denlinger household. Grant, after working twelve hours a day would drag himself home and head straight to bed. In the morning he would usually try to spend a few quality hours with Dana Beth and the baby before he left the house for another long day on the streets of Townsend. Dana Beth realized the last year and a half had been stressful on Grant, due to the ongoing investigation that seemed to be going nowhere. Grant always displayed a pleasant demeanor when he was around her.

Everything seemed to change since he had returned from Knoxville. He barely spoke to her unless she initiated a conversation. He seemed lost in his thoughts. She could tell he was losing weight. Most of the time he left the dinner table after eating just a few bites. When she asked him what was wrong, he always blamed his attitude on his work and the fact that they were no closer to solving the murders. She knew he was under a lot of pressure and she was extra careful making sure she did nothing to upset her husband.

On the fourth day of his twelve hour shifts, Dana Beth waited up for him. He was working noon to midnight. She curled up on the couch at eleven thirty and set the baby monitor on the coffee table. She was comfortable in this house. Everything looked much the same as when she had been a little girl. Since buying her parents' home, she really hadn't changed anything. The grandfather clock in the corner chimed the time at eleven forty-five as she closed her eyes. The pleasant "four times on the hour chiming" had been putting her to sleep since she was a baby.

She awoke at two o'clock in the morning, the chiming reverberating through the house. Checking the baby monitor everything seemed at peace. Grant must have come home and gone to bed without waking her. She needed to check on Crystal Ann then go to bed herself. She found Grant in the baby's room, sitting in the rocking chair as he fed Crystal Ann her bottle. He smiled pleasantly when she entered the room. "Good morning, Sleepy Head. Did you have a good rest?"

"I've never done that before...I mean fall asleep downstairs while Crystal is up here. I wanted to wait up for you. I guess I'm not much of a night owl anymore. Was Crystal crying? I didn't even hear her."

"Everything is just fine," said Grant. "When I got home you were asleep on the couch so I came up here to check on her. She was just laying in her crib staring at her mobile."

Dana Beth sat down on a window bench as tears welled up in her eyes. Grant, concerned, asked, "What's wrong...are you sick?"

"No Grant, I'm not sick. It's just that lately I feel like I'm not being a good wife and mother. Maybe you don't love me as much as you used to. I feel when I talk to you you're somewhere else and not even listening to me."

Grant laid the baby down in the crib and sat beside Dana Beth. "What in the world would make you say something like that? You're the best mother there could ever be." He put his arms around her as she laid her head on his shoulder. "Dana Beth, I love you as much now if not more than the day I married you. You and Crystal Ann are my whole life. I'm so sorry you would even think there's something wrong between us. I wish I could explain everything that's going on with these murders, but even if I did, the bottom line is that the killer is still out there and who knows when this will end. I guess I'm just plain stupid. I never stopped to think how all of this was affecting you. You're so patient and kind and you've never complained."

Dana Beth looked into Grant's eyes. "I knew when we got married, even before that, the type of work you do. I accepted that as a part of our life together." Touching his hair she placed her hand on his cheek. "I love you, Grant."

Grant held her out at arms' length. "Never doubt my love for you and our daughter. No matter what the outcome of all this is, I'll always be here for you."

Dana Beth dropped her head and spoke softly, "I have something to tell you. I wasn't going to bring it up, but I've decided I should."

Grant gave her a puzzled look. "What is it?"

"Well, on Tuesday when I backed out of the driveway to go to the grocery store, I noticed a red truck parked halfway down the block. There was a man standing next to the truck. I know everyone on the block, so when I got to the IGA and the same truck pulled in behind me I thought it was someone I knew. It took me a couple of minutes to get Crystal Ann out of the car seat and when I turned around the truck was gone."

Grant, still puzzled, spoke, "I still don't understand what you're trying to tell me. What truck? What man?"

"Grant, please, just let me finish before you start asking me a lot of questions. Anyway, I passed the same man a number of times in the grocery store and he smiled at me and nodded as if he knew me. The strange part is, he didn't have a cart with him or any groceries in his hands. He looked at Crystal Ann and commented about what a pretty baby she was."

Grant held up his hand as he stopped her from talking. "I have to ask you one question before you go any further. What did this man look like?"

"Oh, he was tall. A big guy, you know, not fat, just big. He had short, dark hair and was clean shaven. He had on tan pants and a tan shirt. Kind of looked like a work uniform."

"Was he wearing a hat?"

"Yes, he had on a black baseball hat. Let me finish what I was saying before. When I came out of the store I saw him pulling away in the truck. Later on, when I was at the post office, I saw him again. He was standing next to the truck at the edge of the parking lot by the exit. When he saw that I noticed him, he started to walk toward me. He looked like he wanted to talk to me. Something just didn't feel right so I hurried up and got back in the car and drove off."

"What made you feel uncomfortable about this man?"

"It was just something about his eyes. They looked like they could stare right through you."

Crystal began to cry and Dana Beth picked her up and began to rock her gently in her arms. "I felt stupid thinking that the man was dangerous. He didn't do anything that was threatening to me. I thought maybe he was someone visiting one of our neighbors or even a tourist...until last night." Dana Beth hesitated for a moment, but then continued, "Last night, after I put Crystal to bed I went to the window to close the blinds and there he was standing at the end of the driveway just leaning against a tree. I immediately turned out the light and when I looked back out the window he was gone."

Grant could feel the color draining from his face. "And this man, you say he was here at the house? Are you sure it was the same man that approached you?"

"Yes, I had a clear view of him and I know it was the same man from the grocery and the post office. I thought I was being foolish. Maybe the man lives around here somewhere and was just out taking a walk."

Grant was more concerned than he wanted to let on. "I'll check around the neighborhood tomorrow and see if anybody has noticed the man and knows who he is." Standing, Grant kissed Crystal on her head, then spoke, "I'll be right back." Walking down the hall to the upstairs bathroom, he closed the door and leaned over the commode. He felt sick to his stomach. He tried to throw up, but he simply had the dry heaves since he had nothing in his stomach. He stood and looked in the mirror above the vanity. Beads of perspiration had formed on his forehead and he looked pale. Leaning on the vanity he thought to himself, *This is more serious than Dana Beth realizes. It sounds like this man, whoever he is, is stalking my family.* Then he had an even more frightening thought. *What if he's the killer, but that didn't make any sense.*

Dana Beth had said the truck was red. The killer's truck was greenish-brown. Besides that the description she had given him didn't match the killer's. The killer wore dark clothes and had a beard. He also wore a knit cap, or at times a red hat. The man described by Dana Beth was clean shaven and wore tan clothes and a black hat. It didn't add up. Grant placed his hands over his head as he tried to sort things out. Even if the man Dana Beth saw standing at the end of their driveway wasn't the killer, it still warranted looking into. If the man was the killer he was turning out to be more intelligent than Grant had given him credit for. Maybe after he fled Mountain City he got a different truck, a haircut, shaved and bought a new set of clothes. Either way, a strange man was paying unwelcome attention to his wife and child.

Splashing cold water on his face, he walked back down the hall to the bedroom. "Listen, Dana Beth, things are really getting nutty around here. I think it would be wise if you take the baby and go down to Chattanooga and stay with your mother for a while. Trust me on this."

"No Grant, I don't want to—"

Interrupting her, he explained. "I'm working practically around the clock. I worry about you being alone with this killer still on the loose and now it looks like we have a strange man showing up here right in our own driveway. That's too close for comfort as far as I'm concerned. I would feel much better if you and Crystal Ann were away from here. I'm going to call Sheriff Brody and let him know about this man who's following you. In the morning you can call your mother, pack whatever you and the baby need, and then I'll drive you down to Chattanooga."

Dana Beth wanted to object, but there was just something in the tone of her husband's voice that prevented her from questioning his decision. "All right, if that's what you think is best then Crystal Ann and I will go. I know mom will be more than glad to have us stay for a while. But tell me this, are you going to be in any danger after I leave?"

He put his arms around her. "Nothing I can't handle. You and the baby's safety are my main concern. Now, you need to get some rest." He kissed her on the forehead and turned to go back downstairs. "I'm just going to get a glass of cold milk then I'll be up."

Standing in the kitchen, he decided on coffee rather than milk. He was too keyed up to try to sleep. He walked around the house checking all of the locks on the windows and doors. Turning on the back porch light, he stepped out the backdoor. Taking his gun from his shoulder holster, he stood for a moment, letting his eyes adjust to the dim light. Slowly, he walked around the yard, stepping away from the shrubbery that hugged the foundation of the house. At the front of the house, he walked down the driveway and looked both ways up and down the dark street. It was quiet, except for the sound of the crickets singing their night song.

Where is he? He thought. *Is he staying in a motel right here in Townsend or is he sitting in his truck somewhere waiting to make his next move.* A set of car lights shined on the pavement as a car passed slowly by. Grant waved to the driver as the car moved on down the street and turned the corner.

Back inside, Grant poured water into the coffeemaker and added three scoops of coffee. He went upstairs to check on Dana Beth and the baby. He found them both fast asleep. There would be no sleep for him this night. He had to keep watch and protect his family. It was ten after three in the morning. *The hell with it,* he thought. *I'll give Brody a call.*

Grant could hear Axel fumbling for the phone just before his scratchy voice answered with a sleepy, "Hello."

"Axel, it's me Grant! Sorry to wake you up this time of night, but I'm calling to let you know that I'll be out of the office for a few days. I just wanted to let you know so you can send someone by to pick up the cruiser. I know you'll need it."

"What the hell are you talkin' about?" snapped Axel as the late night call brought him to an instant state of awareness. "There's no way you can take time off now! Are you crazy? Unless this is a matter of life and death you get your ass into work tomorrow just like always."

"Look, Axel, I have something I have to take care of and it just might be a matter of life and death. If you want to fire me...then go right ahead. My family comes first."

There was silence on the other end then Axel's disgruntled voice, "Aw hell! Take care of your business and be quick about it."

The last thing Grant heard was Brody slamming down the phone. Grant stayed downstairs all night. He emptied the coffeepot and tried to remain awake but sleep overtook his mind and body around four in the morning. He awoke with a jolt when Crystal began crying. It was already light outside. He heard footsteps above him and then Dana Beth's soft voice as she took the baby out of the crib. Grant rubbed his eyes and tried to sit up. His back ached from sleeping in the chair. A few minutes later he heard Dana Beth talking with her mother on the phone.

Going into the kitchen, he made a fresh pot of coffee and was preparing his first cup of the day when Dana Beth and Crystal came down the stairs. "Morning, Grant. I just called mom and told her you were driving me down for a few days. She was really excited and said she and her sister would be more than glad to have us. I'm just about packed. I've got a couple more things to pack for Crystal then I'll be ready to go if you are."

Grant was surprised at how smoothly his suggestion of going down to Ruth's was going over. Holding up his cup he asked. "What about breakfast."

Handing the baby to him, she answered, "Why don't we just grab something on the way."

Half an hour later, Dana Beth was ready to go. Grant put her three suitcases in the trunk and backed out of the driveway. Driving slowly down the street, he looked left and right constantly looking for the red truck and the man he was sure was Russell. Finally turning onto Route 321 he felt a little more relaxed.

They talked about the baby and their vacation plans. Of course, the weather was always a good topic and so was the amount of traffic on the road so early in the day. When there was a lull in the conversation, he fiddled with the radio. At one point, Dana Beth laid her head back and closed her eyes. He tried to clear his mind and keep his eye on the road; the lingering thought that Russell had been stalking his wife was a constant distraction.

Two and a half hours later they arrived at Ruth's sister's place. Ruth and her sister, Grace, welcomed them warmly. Following some verbal pleasantries, Grant explained that he had to get on the road and head back home. He kissed Crystal on her head and gave Dana Beth a hug as he spoke to Ruth, "I'll be back in a few days. Don't worry about anything." Getting into his Jeep he addressed his last remark to Ruth. "When I get back I'll be expecting a big pot of chicken and dumplings."

As he drove away he looked in the rearview mirror, seeing them standing in the driveway, Dana Beth probably in tears as she explained what was going on back in Townsend.

Stopping just outside the city limits of Chattanooga, Grant stopped at a McDonalds and ordered lunch at the drive-thru. His life seemed to be running at full speed and there was no time to slow down. He knew exactly what he was going to do when he got back to Townsend. At least, he thought he knew what he was going to do.

He no sooner pulled into their driveway when his neighbor, Bob Hampton, came walking across the yard. "Grant! Listen, I know you're probably busy, but I wanted to tell you about a man that came by this morning looking for Dana Beth. I noticed a red truck parked in your driveway and while I was picking up my newspaper, I saw a man come around from the back of your house. At first I thought that maybe it was someone you had hired to work on the house, ya know, gutters or siding or something, but then he walked up onto your porch. He just stood there for quite a while and when he didn't ring your bell or knock on the door I thought it was strange. I guess I was just being nosy so I walked over to find out who he was. He said he was waiting for Dana Beth. He mumbled something about being Dana Beth's uncle. I never saw him around here before. Do you know who I'm talking about?"

Grant tried to remain calm. "What did this man look like?"

Bob looked toward the porch as he answered, "Big fellow, kind of on the clumsy side. He seemed slow and very nervous, as if he wasn't sure of where he was. He was wearing a brown, no it was a tan work outfit and a black baseball hat. He had the strangest eyes. I really couldn't look at him too long. I was going to call the police, but then he smiled at me and sat down in one of your porch chairs saying he was just going to wait. Then he said something else but he was sort of hard to understand. About an hour later, when I was getting my mower out of my shed, he comes walking over to my place. He told me that he had to leave and he was going home because he couldn't stay here anymore. I really didn't have a clue as to what he was talking about. Then he got in his truck and left. Maybe it's just my imagination. Maybe he is one of your relatives. It just seemed strange the way he acted and all."

"Thanks, Bob," said Grant. "You did the right thing in coming over here and saying something. Dana Beth doesn't have an uncle, at least that I know of. I appreciate you looking out for us. Don't worry I'll take care of this. Thanks again."

Bob turned and walked back across the lawn. "Hey, that's what neighbors are for."

Watching his neighbor walk back to his house, Grant walked up onto the porch. He could feel the anger building inside of him. *The man that was on my porch said he was going home. What home? If the man on his porch was Russell and he was confident that it was, then where was home? Somewhere in Townsend, Mountain City, the Pender farm, or Knoxville. Russell is either not afraid or just doesn't understand. He sat right on my front porch waiting for us. He sat in the chair that Conrad used to sit in, the same chair that I sit in. But why? This just doesn't make any sense!*

Frustrated, Grant picked up the chair and tossed it out onto the front sidewalk. One of the legs broke loose and landed in the grass. Grant, composing himself, sat on the porch steps as he tried to reason things out. *Everyone in the state, including the state police and the Feds are looking for Russell and he winds up sitting on my front porch. I can't handle this by myself anymore. I need help.*

Reaching into his pocket he pulled out his cell phone and hit number 11 on his speed dial. The call went to the voicemail of Chief William Blue. "Chief Blue. This is Grant Denlinger. I need to see you as soon as possible. I'm heading over your way right now."

CHAPTER TWENTY

GRANT TOOK HIS 22 CALIBER RIFLE and a box of ammunition out of the gun cabinet and placed them in the backseat of the Jeep. He locked the door to the house and concealed a section of string beneath the latch on the front gate. If anyone opened the gate, the string would fall to the ground; a warning that someone had been to the house. Getting back in the Jeep he hit the message button on his cell phone. There was a message from William Blue: *Good to hear from you. I'll be home all evening.* William followed up with directions to his house.

Pulling out into the street, he made a left and headed for the Parkway. He wondered if he was doing the right thing. He could no longer keep the secret about Conrad Pearl being last year's killer to himself. Now that he knew Conrad's brother, Russell, had killed four more people he realized he was not capable of bringing Russell in by himself. He needed help. Was turning to Chief William Blue the right move? He certainly couldn't go to Brody with the information he had withheld. Brody would go through the roof, he'd lose his job; it would be a nightmare. The Feds would be more understanding but they still had a job to do and probably would not be happy he had not stepped forward with the information he had discovered. He would be arrested for withholding crucial evidence. He wasn't close to Sheriff Grimes and really didn't know Sheriff Reichenbaugh that well. No, Chief Blue was his best and only option at this point. Would Blue understand his predicament and work with him to track down Russell? Would he sidestep Grant's reasons for not divulging what he knew and contact the authorities, leaving Grant hanging out to dry? What would Blue say about all the clues Grant had discovered? Would he be supportive or go in the other direction? In the next hour or so, he would know.

William Blue lived three miles outside of Cherokee on Route 144. His house was a one story log cabin nestled back in a wooded area. There was a large redwood barn with an attached corral that housed three pinto ponies. When Grant arrived, he saw Blue leaning on the corral fence as he watched his horses. He turned when he heard the crunching of Grant's Jeep tires on the gravel driveway. As Grant stepped out of the Jeep, Blue waved and called out, "Come here, I want to show you something."

Grant walked over to the fence and William extended his hand. "Good to see you, Grant." He pointed to one of the horses. "That's my newest baby. I found her tied to an abandoned house. When I got her a few months ago she looked as bad as those horses we found on Charley Droxler's farm. But, look at her now. She's a beauty." Before Grant had an opportunity to say anything, Blue placed his arm around his shoulder. "We better head up to the house. Just before you pulled in, my wife told me supper would be on in ten minutes. You're in for a real treat. She's quite the little cook."

Grant hadn't planned on a social visit as he humbly objected, "I wouldn't want to interfere with your meal. I can just wait out here until you finish up."

Blue began to usher Grant toward the house. "Are you kidding? Unless you want to insult her, you better just tag along with me."

The interior of the cabin was rustic, the log walls were lined with native Indian pictures and artifacts, the furniture appeared to be handmade from cut logs and the hardwood floors were partially covered with western throw rugs. Entering the dining room, Grant saw a long wooden table that was set for three, a wagon wheel with buffalo carved lights centered above the table.

William's wife entered from the kitchen as they approached the table. Setting down a bowl of mashed potatoes, she smiled pleasantly at Grant. "Good evening, Mr. Denlinger. Welcome to our home."

William offered a seat to Grant as he explained, "This is my wife, Lilly. Her Cherokee name is White Flower. She's a full-blooded Cherokee and was raised on the reservation. We met in college."

Walking around to the opposite side of the table, Blue held his wife's hand. "She's the love of my life. I've been married to this wonderful woman now for eleven years."

Lilly shook her head as she corrected her husband. "Have a seat, William, *and* it's been twelve years."

Minutes later the meal was on the table. Blue bowed his head and said grace. Even though, as of late, Grant hadn't been eating that much, the food smelled delicious and just after his first bite he was hooked: pot roast, mashed potatoes, corn on the cob, applesauce and an awesome Caesar salad.

For the next half hour Grant put the reason for his visit to the back of his mind as they indulged in light conversation about the log cabin and about Dana Beth and the new baby. William had yet to ask him why he had stopped by and for the moment Grant was simply enjoying their company and hospitality.

A Grandfather clock in the front of the house announced the time at six o'clock. Grant took his final bite of apple cobbler. "That was great Mrs. Blue. I'm going to have to get your roast recipe for my wife." Pushing himself away from the table he placed his napkin on his plate and offered, "I'll be more than happy to help you clean up. At my house I'm pretty good at kitchen patrol."

Lilly stood as she started to gather up the plates and utensils. "Sorry, but I don't allow men in my kitchen. You two just go on and entertain each other for a while." Grant figured William probably had said something to Lilly before he arrived about them having something to talk about.

"Let's take a walk," said William. Heading for the front door Blue motioned with his hands as if he were displaying the entire house. "We have a custom; actually it's an old Cherokee custom, of not discussing any negative thoughts inside. We, as Indians don't want to inhabit our home with any bad spirits. When you called I got the strangest feeling that what you have on your mind might be, let's say…heavy duty."

Walking around the side of the house, William led Grant down a stone walkway to some tall trees where they stopped at a bench next to a small pond. "This is my Koi pond," said William. "I like to come out here in the evening just before it gets dark and just enjoy the sounds of nature. It gives me time to clear my head. Problem is, the local critters keep eating my fish." Gesturing for Grant to sit, he went on, "Now, let's get down to business. What's on your mind?"

Grant, now seated, stared at the pond for a moment, then spoke, "I'd like to ask you a couple of questions before I get started."

William sat on a nearby large boulder. "Sure, go ahead."

"When you heard about the murders we've had this year, did you in any way connect them with the murders from last year? I mean, do you think it's the same killer?"

Blue didn't even hesitate in his answer. "Not at all. But I will say this. Last year's killings were all animal related. This year's killings are somewhat baffling. I think there are two killers and that they're connected in some fashion."

Grant nodded his head. "So did you talk with anybody about your theory?"

"Yes, as a matter of fact I did. I spoke with Chief Grimes over in Maryville and I've met with the Feds on three different occasions this year. We're all on the same page on this. We're almost one-hundred percent positive that there are two killers. Last year the killer was illusive and left very few clues for us. This year, the killer seems to be sloppy and not afraid to be seen in public. Do you agree with that theory?"

Grant lowered his head as he ran his fingers through his hair and over his face. Looking directly at Blue, Grant took a long, deep breath then spoke, "You're right. There are two killers. The killer from last year *has* vanished because he's dead and buried right in Townsend. I talked with him the day before he died. The second killer tried to kill me when I went over to Mountain City on a hunch. I know who both killers are."

Blue stared back at Grant as if he were trying to analyze what he had just been told. His silence caused Grant to ask, "Did you hear what I said?"

"Yes, I heard what you said," answered Blue, "and now it makes sense. Remember last year after Thanksgiving when we had those meetings at the FBI Headquarters in Townsend? I don't know if you'll recall this, but after our first day I asked you if you were all right and also commented that you didn't seem to be yourself. Now, I realize I'm putting the cart before the horse here but if you knew who the first killer was back then, I can now see how going to those meetings must have been difficult. I mean hell...there we all were trying to catch a killer that may have already been dead." Squinting at Grant, Blue asked, "Does any of this have to do with that?"

"It has everything to do with that," said Grant, "but for you to understand why I didn't say anything, I need to tell you the entire story from the beginning." Moving forward on the bench, Grant continued, "What I'm about to tell you I haven't spoken about with anyone else; not my wife, Chief Brody or the Feds." Grant thought to himself, *Here goes!* "Initially, I thought things would just sort of go by the wayside and everything would return to normal. Then when last April rolled around and there were no more animal related killings, I thought it was over. But, now, despite the fact that the first killer is dead, the murders have continued. I've tried to solve this case by myself and all I wind up doing is getting deeper and deeper in the case with seemingly no way out. Like I said, the second killer tried to kill me when I went to Mountain City and I believe that now he is stalking my wife. I have come to the conclusion that I can't handle this by myself. I need some help, William, and you're the only one I can trust."

"Look, you know I'll do whatever I can to stop these murders and bring down the killer, but I can't commit to something until I have all the facts. You can understand that?"

Folding his hands in front of him, Grant spoke as he looked down at the ground. "I'll try to make this as short as possible, but there's a lot to explain. Last year when the four murders happened, I was just as concerned as anyone else in the area, maybe more so. It seemed like I was right in the middle of things. I, like everyone else, wanted to see the killer brought to justice, but what I discovered stopped me in my tracks. I know this is going to sound corny, but I guess you could say that I owe my discovery to a can of pumpkin pie filling. We were at my in-laws house for Thanksgiving. It was obvious that Dana Beth and Ruth, Conrad's wife, were concerned about Conrad's health. I even noticed it myself. He seemed to be deteriorating. He was losing weight, had very little energy and coughed quite a bit. I found out later, after he died, that he refused to discuss his health problems with his family and actually got upset and told them to stop asking him how he felt. On that day, everyone was trying to avoid the subject of his poor health, but it was obvious to me and probably everyone else that he was in pain.

"After we had dinner, I was helping Ruth and Dana Beth in the kitchen when I was handed some cans to be put up in the pantry out in the garage..." Grant continued with the story as he revealed how he had discovered the hidden van and its incriminating contents: the Peach Brandy tobacco, the pipe, the gym bag, lopping shears, vial of chloroform and rubber gloves. Minutes later, he finished up by saying, "And the business card I found in the bag not only belonged to Mildred Henks, but it was blood stained."

Blue had heard enough. "Whoa, whoa, whoa, wait a sec. You found all of these things in your father-in-law's garage?"

Grant nodded his head as he confirmed, "Yes, I did. My mind was racing when it finally hit me that these things were all connected to the murders. At first, I really didn't think they had anything to do with Conrad and I never had a chance to do anything about what I had discovered, because Conrad, unknown to me, had been sitting on the porch and saw me when I went into the garage. To make a long story short, we had quite a conversation on the porch that afternoon. He confessed to me that he was the killer." For the next fifteen minutes, Grant explained what Conrad had revealed to him that day ending the story by telling Blue about Conrad's cancer and the choice he had been given about telling the authorities. Grant stopped talking as he noticed that William seemed to have no facial reaction to what he was being told. "William, you don't seem all that surprised at what I'm telling you."

"No, I guess not," answered William. "I didn't know your father-in-law. I never had an opportunity to meet the man, but I can tell you this: most serial killers live seemingly normal lives in between their bouts of lunacy. I'm sorry, but that's the only word I can think of to describe their actions." Holding up his right hand he remarked, "Before we go any farther we need to back up for a moment. I need to understand exactly what you're telling me. From what you have told me so far, your father-in-law really dropped a bomb on you. He gave you the choice of either turning him in as the killer, at which point the murders would be solved or, you could just let things slide and remain quiet about what you had discovered. I'm not sure what I would have done if I were in your shoes."

"That's exactly the way I felt. I remember going home that night without any idea of what I was going to do. I guess I was still in a state of shock. I mean I had just married this man's daughter two months prior and I had just had Thanksgiving dinner with him and his family. That night there was no sleep for me. I laid in bed next to my wife. She was so happy. At dinner, she had announced to her parents that she was pregnant and so looking forward to spending Christmas together as a family. I knew the following day, depending on what decision I made, our lives were going to get turned upside down. All I could think about was what her reaction was going to be when she found out her father was the man who had committed the four murders.

"Early the next morning, driving to work, I was still undecided as to what I was going to do. Just before I arrived in Townsend I made my decision. I had taken an oath as an officer of the law and I was determined to abide by that oath. I was ready to tell the Federal agents about Conrad. Then, I got a call on my cell phone. It was my wife telling me that her father had died in his sleep and that I needed to come home." Grant stopped talking for a moment to calm himself. He had kept this secret for a year and a half and now he was telling it to someone, the words flowing from his mouth faster than he could think.

Composed again, he continued, "Ya know, it's amazing how your life can change in a matter of two or three seconds. On my way home, I realized that with Conrad being dead there just didn't seem to be a reason to tell the FBI what I knew. The murders were not going to continue. I could just let things go and hope that in time life would return to normal. Dana Beth and Ruth's opinion of their wonderful father and husband would be salvaged. I knew it was going to be difficult for me until April and when there was not another murder, everything would be all right."

"Now things are really coming together," said William. "That first day at the meeting, after we found Charley Droxler, my thoughts about you were right. Looking back now I can see that you were distant and disinterested when we were trying to profile our killer. You already knew he was dead."

Grant stood and began to pace back and forth. "I swear, William, I just wanted it to be over. I hoped and prayed it would soon come to an end, but then the murders started up again."

Shaking his head in agreement, Blue asked, "What did you think about the Bock and Pickler murders?"

"I was completely confused. But when it was discovered that fingerprints found on his car matched up with prints taken from the knife at the Mackinaw killing and at the motel where they found Bock, I put two and two together. Pickler had said that a man had been pestering him about the bear he had at his store and reported to the police the bear had been stolen. I figure Pickler and the killer had a run in and Pickler came out on the losing end.

"I didn't find out about Pickler's murder until after I went over to Mountain City to conduct an investigation of my own. Ya see, there was just something about Conrad's story about how his parents got killed that didn't seem to add up. I went over there to see if the story about the forty year old murders were true and to find out his brother's name. I saw who I now believe is the killer at two different locations. Like I said earlier, someone tried to kill me up at the farm where Conrad's parents had been murdered. I found out the story Conrad had told me was true and I learned that he did have a brother. His name at that time was still unknown to me, except I knew his name began with the letter R."

"And you didn't tell anyone someone had tried to kill you?"

"Yeah, I did. I told the Johnson County Sheriff, but he really didn't take me all that serious and said he didn't have enough proof to open a forty year old case. I came back from Mountain City with little more information than I went over there with. Then, I remembered that Conrad had a friend up in Minnesota he used to go up there and spend a week with every fall. I met him when Dana Beth and I went up there on our honeymoon. He was on the slow side which struck a chord with me because when I was in Mountain City one of the things I learned was that Conrad's brother was slow. I remembered that Conrad's friend's name was Rubin. Off I went to Minnesota positive I was on the right track. Conrad's brother's name started with the letter R and I was so sure that Rubin was in fact his brother. But when I got up to Minnesota and talked with the sheriff in the county where Rubin lived I was informed he had drowned in the lake. So, once again I came to a dead end.

"On my way home from Minnesota, I got another bright idea. Since Conrad and his brother were adopted by a family from Knoxville I decided to see if I could track down their folks. I wound up talking with two older ladies who were neighbors with the Pearls, that's the name of the folks who adopted the two boys. After talking with them for a while, I found out that Conrad's brother was named Russell. That's not all I found out. Both the boys had psychological problems and Russell was slow witted. Turns out Conrad never said anything to anyone about the fact that he had a younger brother. He didn't even tell his wife. Over the years Conrad kept his brother a secret. I think it was because Russell had killed several people over the years and Conrad was trying to protect him."

Grant continued as he told William about the deaths of the bus driver and then Mr. Pearl, whom he suspected were both killed by Russell. He went on to explain that there could even be more victims that were unsolved murders or thought to be hunting accidents.

William couldn't get a word in as Grant rambled on, "When Hawk Caine was hired by Pittman and Barrett, I thought that maybe this bounty hunter would catch him and it would finally be over. But, as you know, Caine was shot down in Mountain City. The description given by the people who witnessed the shooting matches the description of the man I saw up in the Iron Mountains. The same man that I think tried to kill me at the Pender farm."

Looking directly at William, Grant emphasized, "You're right about this killer coming and going as he pleases. I saw a man who I believe is Russell at Conrad's funeral last year and then later in Townsend around Christmas. I believe this same man was in the

Gatlinburg and Sevierville area for a time, and then went over to Mountain City to the farm where he was raised in the Iron Mountains. He tried to kill me when I went over there, but failed. He did succeed in killing Hawk Caine and now I believe he's in Townsend." Grant was beginning to get upset as he went on, "It's amazing that this man seems to travel about the area and no one can catch him. There are a ton of people searching for Russell and yet I believe the man who was seen by Dana Beth standing in our driveway and also reported by a neighbor as sitting on my front porch is in fact, Russell Pearl, Conrad's brother."

Grant sat back down on the bench and wiped tears from his eyes, the emotion of explaining his dilemma caused him to lose control.

William stood and placed his hand on Grant's shoulder. "Take it easy, Son. I can imagine how hard this has been on you, but you've got to tell me everything you know about Russell."

Grant, composing himself, spoke softly, "I'll be all right. Just let me catch my breath." Taking a deep breath he continued, "I think Russell Pearl has changed his appearance. I think that now he is clean shaven and has changed his style of clothing. I also think he got rid of his old truck which was a greenish-brown and is now driving a red pickup." Wiping his eyes again, he stated very firmly, "Thank God, he left my home before Dana Beth showed up. I have no idea what he would have done. It scares the hell out of me to think that Dana Beth or the baby could have been harmed or kidnapped. I sent the baby and her down to Chattanooga to her mother's until we get this thing cleared up. We have to catch this Russell, William. We have to bring him down before he kills someone else."

Sitting down on the boulder, William agreed, "You're right, but I'm not sure this is something we can handle by ourselves. We may have to call in the authorities at some point...possibly the Feds. For now, I think we need to gather as much information as possible. You said that Russell was in Townsend yesterday, right?"

Grant nodded as William remarked, "Well, that doesn't mean he's still there. Here's what I think we should do. First thing tomorrow morning, we take a trip over to Mountain City. We'll talk with the folks at the restaurant where Caine tangled with Russell then we'll head on up to this farm you mentioned. We might be able to pick up some clues that were overlooked. You can stay here tonight. The drive from here to Mountain City is shorter than from Townsend. Let's go on in the house. I'll have Lilly make you a cup of herbal tea. It'll help to calm your nerves and you can get a good night's sleep. We'll leave at first light in the morning."

An hour later Grant called Dana Beth and told her he was spending the night at Blue's house. The last thing he remembered after he took his last swallow of tea and lay down on the eider filled bed, was the distant rumbling of thunder across the mountains and the occasional flash of lighting that lit up the room. Whether it was from pure exhaustion or the hot tea, he fell to sleep quickly.

"Good Morning," William said as Grant entered the kitchen. The aroma of fresh coffee and bacon sizzling on the stove filled his nostrils. William gestured toward a small table centered in the kitchen as he put a plate of bacon and eggs in front of Grant then filled his coffee cup. William sat opposite Grant with his own plate of food. Sipping his coffee, Blue started the early morning conversation, "On the way to Mountain City I'm going to pick your brain. There are still some blanks that need to be filled in based upon what you told me last night. I want you to try and remember even the smallest detail, even if you think it may not seem important."

Twenty minutes later, on the road, William made Grant start over with his story, constantly interrupting him, asking him to repeat things and asking him a ton of questions. He wanted to know more about Grant's trip up to Bagley. Blue went over Grant's visit with the two neighbor ladies in Knoxville making sure he remembered everything about that day. They talked a lot about what happened when Grant went to the Holiness Pentecostal Church and the Pender farm.

Mountain City seemed to be back to normal since the murder of Hawk Caine. A few people were out and about walking around town, the traffic was light. Passing the Mountain Café, Grant pointed out the spot where Caine had been gunned down. Blue commented that they could come back to the restaurant later in the day for a bite and to interview anyone who knew anything about what went on the day that Caine and Russell had tangled. On the outskirts of town, Grant gave directions to the Pender farm to Blue as they headed for the Iron Mountains. Grant could feel the tension returning to his body, the thought of returning to the farm held bad memories.

Minutes later they stopped in front of the gate to the Pender farm, which now stood wide open. Large patches of overgrowth and brambles had been cut away to make way for the FBI vehicles that had been there in hopes of capturing the killer. Parking the Jeep in the front yard, Grant noticed that the house had now completely fallen down. Walking toward the barn, Blue followed as Grant explained, "When I was here before some of the house was still standing. The place is a falling down mess, a haven for rattlers and copperheads. I felt someone watching me when I was in the house."

The barn doors stood wide open as they entered. The dust covered floor was marred with countless footprints of the agents who had scanned every inch of the barn. Looking around, Blue commented, "We'll be lucky to find any clues in here. With the FBI and whoever else was up here it looks like a herd of cattle went through this barn." Walking over to the opening that led down to the cellar, Blue asked, "Down there, is that where he tried to kill you?"

"That's the place," said Grant. "If you want to go on down go ahead. I'd just as soon stay up here."

"I am going down. You need to stay up here and keep an eye out for any unwelcome visitors, namely Russell Pearl. He could be up here somewhere. He could be watching us right now. We don't want to wind up in the same fix you got into when you were here before."

Shining his flashlight down the ladder, Blue descended into the cellar. Grant withdrew his revolver and turned in a complete circle as he looked around the barn, at the same time listening to what Blue was yelling back up from below, "Nothing much down here. You're right; the entire place caved in. The snakes you said you killed are still down here. Well, look here!" There was a few seconds of silence followed by Blue's voice, "Ah, genuine Tennessee moonshine. Haven't had a taste of this in years."

Climbing back up the ladder, he handed one of the plastic jugs to Grant. "Care For a nip?"

Grant refused, "No thanks. I got sick as a dog when I was a youngster drinking that stuff."

Setting the jug on the floor, Blue looked around. "Didn't find anything that will be of any help down there. Russell may have returned here, but he didn't stay long. Since this is where he was raised until he was eight years old it makes sense that he would come here. Might have been living up here when you showed up.

Why he tried to kill you, I'm not too clear on that. Maybe he felt threatened. If he's killed before, it wouldn't be any big deal to him. He probably thought he was just protecting himself." Walking back out of the barn, Blue explained, "From what you've told me I believe Russell is responsible for the four murders we've had this year. But here's the thing. I think he came here for his brother's funeral with no intentions of killing anyone and wound up being forced to kill three out of the four men he killed."

Grant was confused, "How do you figure that?"

Leaning up against the side of the barn, Blue answered, "You said Conrad never told anybody he had a brother. He kept him away from people, more than likely because he had killed before. Russell strikes me as the type of person who is not only slow, but is unstable; an individual who doesn't like to be around a lot of people. I figure it this way. First of all, the Mackinaw murder, Russell may just have simply defended himself and wound up killing Mackinaw. He didn't plan on killing him; it just turned out that way. Next, we have Daniel Bock, a worthless drifter who was poaching turtles. Russell vowed to get even with people who mistreat animals. It makes sense that if Russell's meeting with Bock was purely accidental, and he found out what Bock was doing, he killed him. Once again, in his own mind he wasn't doing anything wrong.

"As far as Pickler is concerned, Russell, stole his bear. Pickler made a mistake and went after Russell on his own. Pickler might have located Russell and once again, feeling threatened, he killed Pickler. It's easy to figure out what happened with Hawk Caine. Russell again, with his back against the wall, did the only thing he could to defend himself, he killed Caine."

"Do you think he would have killed my wife and baby?"

"I don't think so. That doesn't make any sense. Your wife and baby were not a threat to him. Unless we take him alive and talk with him we may never know the reason why he wanted to be near your wife. One thing for sure, Russell will not hesitate to kill anyone who he feels threatened by. That's what makes him so dangerous. He's the worst type of killer to figure out. He won't do what a normal person would do. He's very unpredictable."

Walking a few feet, he looked down over the side of a large field. "Is that the old bus down there in that clearing you were talking about earlier; the one the bus driver was killed in?"

"That's the one," said Grant. "That's where this whole mess started forty years ago."

"Life is strange, isn't it?" remarked William. "We weren't even born yet and here we are trying to track down a killer who back then was an innocent young boy, a victim of circumstances. If his parents hadn't been killed that day, his life might have turned out much differently."

Staring at the tree line fifty feet away, William turned back to Grant. "See those dead tree branches laying on the ground between those two large pines. They were placed there by someone. See how all the other branches that have fallen are in their natural state? The branches between those pines were stacked there to cover something up. Let's go have a look." William didn't wait for Grant to respond but started across the field, Grant followed.

At the edge of the field William bent down and started to remove the branches carefully as Grant warned him, "Careful, this part of the mountain is loaded with snakes."

William continued picking up the branches and tossing them to the side. "I know a thing or two about snakes. These branches were recently stacked here, which means that snakes are going to avoid this area for a few days." The branches finally cleared away, William stepped into the tree line and pointed into the thick forest. "I think there's an old road back in there." Motioning for Grant to come close, he reached up and pointed to a number of cut branches. "See there, someone recently cleared a path through here." Bending down he pointed to tire tracks that had been left in the forest floor and other areas where the grass was bent downward where the tires passed over. "A vehicle recently passed through here and those branches were placed across the road so that no one would find it. Somebody doesn't want anyone to know they went down this way. Get the Jeep. Let's see where this leads."

Grant was back with the Jeep in less than two minutes.

Climbing in the passenger side William pointed down the rugged road.

"Hold on," said Grant as he started down the narrow corridor. Grant rolled up his window as the branches from the trees were forced inside the Jeep making it hard to see the road ahead.

Moving slowly forward Grant thought to himself, *If anyone could track down Russell it was William Blue.*

A mile into the forest the road made a long sweeping curve to the left then went downhill for another half mile where the road was blocked by a fallen tree trunk. Getting out of the truck

William moved the small tree to the side of the road and climbed back in as he explained, "That tree was still green. It was just recently cut and placed across the road to prevent anyone from going any further."

At the bottom of the hill, Grant stopped the Jeep when they approached a small stream. Getting out once again, William told Grant to come with him. Crossing the shallow, cold, stream, William pointed out a number of large rocks that had been placed in the mud on the opposite side to cover up the tire tracks. "You see all those rocks, Grant? They are green and muddy. Look at the other rocks around the area. They are brown or white on top. Somebody placed those rocks in the tire tracks. Whoever drove down here was very careless in the manner in which they tried to conceal they had been here. Appears to me they were in a hurry."

Driving across the stream, they followed the road at the base of the mountain for a mile. The road took a sharp left up a steep grade into the trees. It was a gradual climb and William pointed out a number of occasions where the truck tires had spun from the difficult road. When they got to the top of a long rise, William told Grant to stop as he climbed out and inspected the road ahead for the next few yards. "No more tire tracks, only footprints. He ditched the truck around here someplace. The truck has to be close. Lock the Jeep and start looking on the left side of the road, I'll take the right. Be careful, he might be close by."

It was only a few minutes before William's voice echoed through the woods, "Grant, over here, I found the truck!" As Grant approached, William was brushing leaves from the hood and removing tree branches from the roof of the cab.

Grant, looking carefully in the passenger side window reached for the glove box. "This is the truck I saw at Dave's 421 and then at the old church. I'm gonna see if there's any ID in here."

William inspected the bed after removing more branches.

"Nothing back here except an old tire, a rusted tire jack and some coolers. Find anything up front?"

Grant walked to the front of the truck as he held up the items he had found. "Flashlight that doesn't work, a receipt for a trailer rental from Home Depot, couple of old magazines and some out dated coupons. No ID." Reaching for the bungeed coolers, Grant opened one, the acrid smell coming from inside the container, made him wrinkle his nose. "Same smell that we were faced with at the motel where we found Bock murdered. These coolers are identical to the ones we found in the motel room. Come to think of it, when I first saw this truck pulling out of Dave's 421, I saw these coolers in the back of the truck. It all adds up now."

Looking under the seat, William came up with an old pair of gloves and an ice scraper. Throwing the items on the seat, he looked out into the surrounding trees and then up the road. "You said the man, you think might be Russell, was seen by your wife and your neighbor two days ago in Townsend. You also said that you thought he had gotten a haircut and tried to change his appearance by purchasing new clothes not to mention that he now has another truck, a red one. He couldn't have made it on foot all the way back to Townsend hiking through the mountains. He had to go to a nearby town that could offer the things he needed to survive. Somewhere like Bristol which is to the north. Townsend is more to the west. We have two choices. We can leave the Jeep here and track him, but that doesn't make much sense since we know he showed up in Townsend. The other thing we can do is return to Townsend and start from there, but first we have to see if he spent any time around here; maybe a campsite or a place to hide out. I'll take the left, you take the right. If we don't find anything else in about an hour or so then we'll head back."

Once again, it was William who found what they were looking for. Walking back down the road he signaled for Grant to remain quiet as he placed his finger over his lips and whispered, "I found a cave up the road about two hundred feet from here. The same footprints we found back by the truck are all around the cave area. He might be in there, maybe not." Pulling out his revolver he ordered, "Follow me, but be careful."

Pulling his own gun out, Grant followed William into the surrounding trees. When they got close to the cave entrance William picked up a sizeable rock and tossed it inside. There was the sound of fluttering wings followed by three bats that flew out of the entrance, circled then returned to the cave. Pointing his gun at the cave, William explained, "Come on, let's have a look."

Shining the flashlight into the cave, William saw an empty peanut butter jar on the dirt floor. There were insects feeding on open food packages and a few empty bottles. A cot near the back of the cave was covered with bedding that had been shredded by local critters.

Kicking an empty two-liter bottle to the side, William shined the light on a spot where a campfire had been built. "Looks like our boy moved on. He left here on foot, probably carrying only what he needed." Walking out of the cave, he walked back to the road where the footprints continued on. "The way I figure it, the longer we stay here the more time we're wasting. We know that he went to Townsend. We need to head back. If we leave now we can be back before it gets dark."

It was only after they stopped for a bite at a Cracker Barrel that William began to clarify all his questions. After they ordered, William fiddled with his glass of water as he addressed Grant, "I've given everything you've told me a lot of thought. I've come to the conclusion that I probably would have done the same thing when it comes to your father-in-law. I would have turned him in just like you had intended. I can understand why you changed your mind after you found out that he died. But, I'm not so sure I still wouldn't have gone to the authorities. The only thing I can say is until someone walks in your shoes they are in no position to judge others. I am very much a family man, just like you. I love my wife dearly. We were never blessed with children, but that doesn't mean I can't sympathize with you. You thought the murders would come to an end *and* they did. At least, as far as Conrad was concerned. At the time you had no way of knowing that Russell, his brother, would whether he realized it or not, take over where Conrad left off. All of this is in the past now and we can't change any of it. All we can do now is try to change the future. When and if we catch this Russell, depending on the outcome, the authorities just might pin all eight murders on him, leaving Conrad in the clear."

"When you say, 'depending on the outcome,' what do you mean?"

"If we manage to take Russell alive and they question him, he'll more than likely fess up to the four people that he and he alone killed. The previous murders, those committed by Conrad will still be unsolved. Now, whether Russell knows that Conrad killed those people or not, well, we don't know. By bringing Russell in, only four of the murders get solved. If, on the other hand Russell winds up getting killed, the authorities might put an end to this whole thing and like I said...pin all eight murders on him. If both brothers are dead does it really make any difference who killed who?"

Grant nodded as he answered, "I see what you mean. Kind of like letting sleeping dogs lie."

"While we're on the subject of not exactly lying, but just leaving some of the facts out, what are we going to do about all those clues in your garage?"

"I thought I'd just hide them up in the overhead storage area of the garage just in case the truth somehow ever came out about Conrad. At that point, I could say that I started to look around and found the items."

"Look," said William, "Since I'm in this boat with you now, we need to destroy anything that could connect Conrad to any of the murders, that is if you still want to keep his secret from your wife and your mother-in-law."

"I don't want them to ever know the truth about Conrad," said Grant.

"That settles it then. Tonight when we get back to Townsend we need to put the items in the garage up in the storage area you talked about and then later on we can dispose of them."

It was dark when they arrived at Grant's house. When they pulled in the driveway, Grant still had an apprehensive feeling that Russell might be lurking around his home. Everything looked in place and when he unlocked the front door and turned on the light in the hallway, he felt sure the house was empty. Walking toward the kitchen he turned and spoke to William, "Make yourself comfortable. I'm not sure if there is anything in the house to eat. I think Dana Beth cleaned out the fridge before she left. I'll find us something."

William removed his moccasins and sat down in front of the coffee table. He opened his notebook and began to jot down some things he wanted to discuss with Grant.

Minutes later, Grant entered the living room with a plate of cheese, summer sausage, crackers and pickles. "Sorry, this is all I could find. I do have some cold beer in the fridge. Like one?"

William stretched as he answered, "Sounds good."

While they munched on the snacks, William quizzed Grant on what actually happened when Russell approached Dana Beth. Grant went over everything Dana Beth told him and finished up saying, "She said he really didn't scare her until she saw him standing at the end of the driveway." Grant looked around the living room, "Ya know William, I'm starting to hate this house. Everywhere I look I see things that remind me of Conrad. Hell, that's why Ruth moved out. She just couldn't deal with it. I'll never convince Dana Beth to move. She's really happy living here. She still has a picture of Ruth and Conrad on the nightstand next to our bed. It was taken right after Conrad started teaching up in Knoxville."

William looked confused. "So, if Conrad was working in Knoxville where was Russell living?"

Grant was just about to take a bite of cheese as he answered, "He was living in a cabin up in the Jellico Mountains. Conrad bought the cabin from Mrs. Pearl and then moved Russell in. Conrad would visit Russell on occasion to make sure he was getting by…" Grant stopped talking and quickly stood up. "That's it! That's where he is or at least where he's going. Russell told my neighbor that he was going home. He went home to his cabin in Jellico."

CHAPTER TWENTY-ONE

GRANT PUSHED OPEN THE DOOR of the Hearth and Kettle in Townsend. It was six-thirty in the morning, a little too early for most of the tourists to be out looking for a restaurant that serves breakfast. Chief William Blue was already seated at a window table as he nursed a cup of coffee. Grant, not quite awake, yawned as he crossed the restaurant's polished wooden floor. Signaling to the waitress, he pulled out one of the chairs. "Coffee, please." Looking across the table at Chief Blue, Grant continued to speak, "You look well rested this morning."

"I did get a good night's rest," said William. "It was good to be home with the wife. The Cherokee People believe that a married man and woman should not be separated at night. Besides that, I had to go home and tell Lilly that unfortunately, we might be up in Northern Tennessee for a few days."

Gulping down a glass of water, Grant splashed the last few drops on his hands and ran them across his face. "I feel like crap myself, after all the running around we did over in Mountain City, but the prospect of bringing Russell in and finally putting this nightmare to an end is encouraging."

Blue smiled as he commented, "Of course that's only true if your hunch about Russell returning to his cabin up in the Jellico Mountains turns out to be right. The problem is that before we can grab Russell we need to locate the cabin. I did some research last night after I got back home. The Jellico Mountain region itself is not nearly the size of the Smokies, but it's still a large area that's made up of a number of mountain ranges and smaller towns. So, unless we have some sort of an idea as to where this cabin is located it could take us some time to locate Russell."

Grant seemed to perk up as he informed Blue, "I also did some research on the Jellico Mountain area myself last night. I called one of the two ladies that I told you I talked with from Knoxville. I promised them I'd send them pictures of Crystal after she was born. I used that as an excuse to call them. Anyway, while I was talking to the one who lived next door to the Pearls I just happened to ask her if she knew where the cabin Russell lived was located. She told me she thought it was near a town by the name of Newcomb, which according to my research is just under five miles down the road on Route 297 from the town of Jellico."

Downing the last of his coffee, Blue stood as he gestured toward the exit. "Well, then I say we hit the road."

Grant remained seated as he looked for a waitress. "But, what about breakfast?"

"I already had breakfast an hour ago; ate it on the way over here from Cherokee. Why don't you just order something to go. The sooner we get to Jellico the sooner we can begin tracking down our killer."

The waitress was just returning with Grant's coffee when he suggested, "Better put a lid on that coffee. It's gonna be to go. I'll take a bacon, egg and cheese on toast also."

Twenty minutes later, Grant turned from 115N onto US 129N and headed for Knoxville. Looking in the rearview mirror, he asked, "So what's the plan when we get to Newcomb? Do we contact the local police or just start asking some questions around town?"

"Neither," said Blue. "First, we're going to Jellico, which is in Campbell County. I took the liberty last night and called the County Sheriff who works out of a town by the name of Jacksboro, which is fifteen miles southwest of Jellico. I told him we were coming up to apprehend a suspect we've been looking for. I didn't mention Russell's name but I did tell him he's, for lack of a better phrase, armed and dangerous."

"How many men will we have?" asked Grant.

"There should be a total of nine of us: the Campbell County Sheriff and two of his deputies, the Chief of Police from Jellico and one of his men, you, me, and I also called Gephart and Green who are back in Knoxville right now ready to join us. I figure with the Feds along things might go easier when it comes to jurisdiction and who has the right to go where and do what. It'll just make things a lot smoother. We are all to meet at nine o'clock this morning at the sheriff's office on Fifth Street in Jellico." Looking at his watch, Blue commented, "It's just after seven o'clock now. It'll take us about an hour and a half to get to Jellico. That'll put us in town at eight thirty."

Passing a sixteen wheeler, Grant asked, "How big is Jellico?"

"About twenty-five hundred people. Just a typical Tennessee mountain town. Not much goes on there. There is hardly any tourism to speak of. It used to be a big mining town back in its day. Kind of reminds me of Mountain City. Peaceful place where folks just go on about their lives."

Grant shook his head in wonder. "Mountain City, *used to* be peaceful. I almost got killed over there. Right about now I bet the folks in Mountain City would beg to differ with you on how peaceful it is there since Hawk Caine got shot down right in the middle of town." Grant nodded at a passing sign that read: KNOXVILLE CITY LIMITS. "We should be pulling into Jellico in about an hour."

At eight-thirty-five Grant passed a gas station on Main Street in Jellico. Chief Blue surveyed the surrounding structures. "Yep, typical mountain town."

Grant stopped at an intersection and made a right hand turn onto Fifth Street. "Do you think anyone around these parts knows Russell?"

"That depends," answered Blue. "Remember, he doesn't live here in Jellico. He lives down near Newcomb, which according to you is five miles down the road. I'm sure he had to come to town on occasion for supplies. Now, whether he went into Newcomb or drove up here to Jellico remains to be seen. Hell, his cabin could be miles out in the mountains."

Pulling into the parking lot of the Jellico City Hall, Grant commented, "We should know more after we talk with the local authorities."

Blue was the first to enter the two-story stone building, Grant trailing behind. Off to the left there was a large room where two long tables had been pushed together. Ralph Gephart stood and motioned for them. As they approached, Harold Green also stood and greeted them. Five uniformed officers all stood and shook Grant and Blue's hands as Ralph made the introductions, "This is Office Grant Denlinger from Townsend and Chief William Blue from over in Cherokee." Pointing across the table he introduced Sheriff Frank Turnbull from Campbell County, two of his officers, Steve Kerr and Lamont Devers from Jacksboro. Grant also shook hands with Drake Houseman, the Jellico Police Chief and one of his officers, Jerry Flynn.

When all of the introductions were complete, Grant and Blue took seats as Gephart motioned to the middle of the tables. "We have juice, donuts and coffee."

"Thank you," said Blue. "Just coffee for me."

"Ditto," added Grant.

After Grant and Blue seated themselves, Gephart took control of the meeting. "Okay, before we get started I think it's important we establish who is actually going to be calling the shots. Agent Green and myself represent the federal government and in a case like this where one of the murders was committed on federal land, we always take the lead. However, we're not convinced the killer we're after actually committed that particular murder, so at this point I think I'm going to turn things over to Chief Blue."

Blue responded quickly as he suggested, "I think Officer Denlinger is more familiar with this killer than I, so I think he should have the floor first."

Grant, realizing that he was on the bubble hadn't expected to ramrod the meeting. After all, out of the nine men seated around the table he was outranked by five of them: two federal agents, a county sheriff and two police chiefs. As far as the other three officers were concerned he had no idea how long they had served as lawmen.

All eyes were on Grant as he looked around the table at the collection of law officers who awaited his words. *Knights of the roundtable,* thought Grant. Then again, he thought, *No, this is more like the old west when a posse is formed to track down an outlaw.* Clearing his throat, he took a drink of the coffee, then began, "Most of you are probably aware that we've had eight murders in or near Blount County during the past two years. We have reason to believe that the man we are after lives here in Campbell County or at least close to it. We have found out that our suspect lives in a cabin down near a town called Newcomb. We think he has lived there for more than twenty years. He is somewhat of a loner, doesn't like to be around a lot of people and is quick to kill if he feels threatened."

Frank Turnbull spoke up, "Why, hell, that sounds like a lot of folks who live up here in the mountains. Well, not the killing part, but the rest of it. There are quite a few folks around these parts that are loners and want to be left alone."

Drake Houseman asked, "Do we have a photo of this suspect. Do you know his name?"

William reached inside his coat pocket and produced the composite newspaper drawing of the killer. Handing it across the table to Houseman, he answered the question, "This is an artist's concept of the killer based on people who have seen him. His name is Russell Pearl."

Picking up the drawing, Sheriff Houseman shook his head in disbelief as he slid the drawing across the table to Turnbull. "You gotta be shittin' me. I know Russell Pearl. He's lived here most of his life. He comes into town about once a week for supplies. As far as I know, he's never bothered anybody. He's different, not retarded, just sort of on the slow side. Never causes any trouble."

Jerry Flynn spoke up, "Yeah, I know Russell. I always knew there was something strange about him. If you tried to talk to him, he would just stare at you and never say a word." Looking at Grant, he continued, "You're right on the money about him being a loner and not wanting to be around folks that much. The most he's ever said to me, and I've known him for years, is hello and that's because I spoke to him first."

Sheriff Houseman pointed his finger at Flynn, "Come to think of it I haven't seen Russell in town for the past couple of months. I haven't seen him driving through town in that old pickup truck, either."

"Greenish-brown truck, right?" interjected Grant.

Houseman sat back in his chair as he answered, "That's exactly right...greenish-brown."

William added, "We found the truck abandoned over in the Iron Mountains in the eastern part of the state. We think he is now driving a red pickup. We don't, at this time, have a plate number or even the year or model of the truck. All we know is that it's red."

Grant poured himself a cup of coffee," We also believe that Russell has changed his appearance: haircut and shave, newer clothing." Gesturing at the composite drawing, he explained, "Probably doesn't look anything like that drawing now."

"Do any of you know where his cabin is located?" asked William.

Turnbull jumped in the conversation once again, "I know where it is. I've only been up there one time to investigate a body that was discovered near his cabin. The remains of a man were found in an animal trap. He'd been there for some time. A couple of hunters found him. Russell owns about ten acres that surround his cabin. We've had a number of complaints over the years from hunters reporting that a man who lives up in that vicinity has threatened them at gunpoint, telling them he doesn't allow any hunting near his cabin or for that matter anywhere up there. There have been other reports of shots being fired at them. In the past twenty years or so we've lost three hunters up on Lamb Mountain; that's where Russell's cabin is located. They were recorded as hunting accidents."

"I hate to tell you this," Grant said, "but those hunters may have been murdered by none other than Russell Pearl."

"Wait a minute," said Houseman. "Before we go jumping to any conclusions, what type of proof do we have that Russell Pearl is the man you're looking for, or for that matter, the man who killed all those people down in your neck of the woods?"

Gephart, realizing he needed to verify what Grant and Blue said, spoke up boldly, "Gentlemen. At this time, Russell Pearl is our prime suspect, a person of interest, someone that we'd like to question. His fingerprints were found at three of the four murder scenes and a person fitting his description was seen by a number of people in Mountain City when he gunned down Hawk Caine. We need to cut to the chase and discuss how we're going to go about locating this man."

Turnbull, realizing the power the FBI wielded, answered, "Like I said, I've only been up to the cabin one time. It's about eight miles from Newcomb on Lamb Mountain. It's pretty far in the backcountry. You can get turned around up there in no time at all. There are no hiking trails or tourist attractions. It's nothing more than mile after mile of wilderness. If we're going up there we need to be organized and prepared. Russell Pearl knows that mountain like the back of his hand. Before he moved into the cabin, his father, Marvin Pearl, used to bring Russell and his brother, what was his name, I think it was Conrad, up here from Knoxville on the weekends and during the summer. We heard that Marvin had died and the next thing you know Russell moves into the cabin. Conrad would show up from time to time. I believe he was a professor down in Knoxville. Anyway, he seemed like a nice sort of fella. He had changed from when he was a boy. He would bring Russell into town and help him shop for stuff."

Lamont Devers stood up as he slammed his fist on the table. "I say we quit pussy-footin' around and go nab this bastard! All this talkin' ain't gonna get the job done."

Turnbull, surprised at the outburst from one of his deputies ordered him, "Sit down Lamont. What the hell got your dander up?"

Lamont sat down as he addressed everyone at the table. "My brother Pete was over near Pearl's place fishin' three years ago. He said some big clumsy lookin' fella comes out of the woods tellin' him that there ain't no huntin' or fishin' allowed in the area. Pete said the guy didn't look like a game warden so he tells this clown to just mind his own business. The guy gives him a funny look and walks off into the trees. Ten minutes later, my brother gets shot in the arm. He swore up and down that it was Russell Pearl."

Steve Kerr, the other deputy from Jacksboro spoke up, "I remember that. You were on vacation when all that happened, Frank. I went up there to talk with Russell about what had happened and he told me he didn't know anything about it. I told you about it when you got back."

"I do recall that," said Frank. "There wasn't much we could do. We didn't have any proof that it was Russell. But after hearing all I've been told this morning, well, maybe he did shoot your brother, but we can't go off half-cocked with a lynch mob attitude." Looking at Lamont he suggested strongly, "Take it easy, Lamont. You need to chill some or you won't be going with us. I'll slap your ass on desk duty. Got it?" Lamont, embarrassed and having been put in his place lowered his head, but Grant could tell from the look on his face that he was still upset.

A moment of awkwardness followed when finally Turnbull broke the silence as he gestured to Gephart and spoke, "What's next? How do we get the ball rolling?"

"First of all," said Gephart, "we're not even sure that Pearl has returned to his cabin. He might still be in the Smokies somewhere. One of Grant's neighbors was confronted by Pearl who told him that he was going home. We're assuming he meant the place where he has lived for the past twenty or so years. That's why we're here today. We might get up there and find the place empty. We could run into yet another dead end which we seem to be doing a lot of lately." Looking at his watch, he kept right on talking, "It's now nine-thirty." He directed his next comment to Houseman. "Is there a place where we can all meet up at, let's say eleven?"

Drake thought for a moment then answered, "Yeah, there's an old fruit market about a half mile outside of town of Route 297 South. Can't miss it. There's an old dilapidated billboard by the roadside that reads Clyde's Market. We have to go that way to get to Newcomb. We can meet there."

"Good idea," remarked Turnbull. "Remember, everything we have discussed in this meeting is confidential. If the word gets out and Russell Pearl gets wind of our unexpected visit, he might take off and we could miss a golden opportunity to grab him."

Gephart stood, "Well I guess this meeting is adjourned. Where's the closest store where I can get clothes more suitable for tramping around in the woods?"

Houseman stood as he answered, "There's a Wal-Mart just north of town. They should have everything you need."

Grant and William stood next to the Jeep, watching the various police vehicles pull out of the lot and head in different directions. Looking up at the sky and then at Grant, Blue asked, "You got everything you need for this little adventure or do we have to go to the store. Myself, I came dressed for the occasion," as he displayed his dress attire of flannel shirt, jeans and full length moccasins.

Grant, pointing his thumb toward the backseat answered, "Brought everything I'll need with me. Just need to find a place to change."

Ten minutes later, driving down Route 297, Grant pulled the Jeep into a dirt parking lot just after the billboard they had been told to watch for. Parking directly in front of the old one story building that was nothing more than a gigantic, weather beaten shed topped with a rusted metal roof, Grant got out and kicked an old fruit crate to the side as he stated, "Home, sweet home."

Getting out of the Jeep, Blue looked at the old structure with its faded, rotting wood walls that were crisscrossed with vines, the roof covered in areas by old tree limbs that had been blown from trees from years past. "I wonder how long this place has been out of business."

Grant, collecting a canvas bag from the back of the Jeep commented, "Think I'll just mosey over behind that old trailer and change my clothes."

While Grant was busy changing, Blue leaned up against the Jeep and looked at the surrounding landscape. He imagined that the mountains here in Jellico were similar to those over near Mountain City. Mountains that did not benefit from a great and often overwhelming tourist trade like in the Smokies. He had no doubt that some of the mountains in this area were what a lot of folks would refer to as uncivilized; places where a lot of people never ventured. Just the type of environment Russell Pearl thrived in. A place where he could live his private life without being bothered by the outside world. He hoped they weren't going to have to track Russell out into these mountains. This was his backyard, his territory. It if came down to that, Russell would hold the advantage.

A red pickup sped by going south as Grant approached from the trailer. From behind him, Blue heard his excited and concerned voice, "You see that red truck? Maybe that was Russell!"

William turned and smiled, "Now don't go getting all paranoid on me. Do you have any idea how many red pickup trucks there must be here in Campbell County or for that matter, the state."

Grant, realizing how ridiculous he must have sounded, opened the back of the Jeep and placed the sack in the back. "Yeah, I guess you're right. The chances of that being Russell are probably pretty slim." Placing his gear on the hood of the Jeep, he took a vocal inventory. "All right, I've got my revolver, three extra clips, my camera, notebook, pen and rifle."

William looked at the articles Grant laid on the hood as he remarked, "If Russell is our killer, once we step on his property, I don't think he's going to be all that neighborly. He'll probably react just like he has in the past when he is threatened. He'll try to protect himself and one of us may be his next victim." Pointing to the collection of things on the hood, he explained, "I don't really think you're going to have much time for taking pictures and writing things down. If I were you I'd keep that revolver and rifle close at hand."

Placing his revolver in his shoulder holster, Grant checked his rifle to make sure it was loaded. "So, what did you think about the meeting back there at the sheriff's office?"

"I think it went well," said William. "We're off to a good start. I thought we were going to have to spend a few days locating the cabin, but they seem to know exactly where it is. I didn't expect them to know who Russell was either."

Grant looked down the road as he placed the camera and notebook back inside the Jeep. "What did you think of that Devers fella?"

"I've seen his kind before. He's a real hothead. He's the type of officer who wants to shoot someone or club then over the head first before thinking things out logically. He's the worst kind of officer you can have on this kind of a case. But, I wouldn't worry too much about him. Seems to me, Sheriff Turnbull has him in check."

Grant leaned his rifle up against the Jeep and placed his foot on the front bumper. "I'll be glad when this is finally over, when things get back to normal."

Popping a stick of gum in his mouth, William answered, "What is normal? I don't recall a time in my whole life as a police officer when life was normal. There are always those that will challenge the law. I suppose when all of this is over, things will settle down, but don't expect normal."

"That sounds good enough for me, William, except for the fact I'm not so sure I want to continue to work for Axel Brody. He has never liked me, and he dislikes you even more."

"On the drive up here you said something about how folks in Townsend are upset with ol' Brody...that he might lose his job if he doesn't come on and get this killer."

"I don't think they'll fire him. His term as sheriff is up this coming November. They just won't reelect him."

William smiled. "Why don't you run for sheriff? You were born and raised in Townsend. You've served on the Townsend Police now for what, going on three years. Everyone knows you. Your grandfather, Dalton, served as sheriff for years. He'd back you. He swings a lot of weight in Townsend. I think you'd have a great shot."

"No, I don't think I'm ready to be a sheriff yet. Maybe after a couple of years on another force somewhere, but not yet, and not here."

Opening the passenger side door, Blue spoke as he climbed into the seat. "It's not quite ten-thirty. It'll be a good half hour before the others show up. I'm gonna grab a short nap."

Placing his rifle in the backseat, Grant looked at his own watch as he commented, "Think I'll go for a short walk. I'm too keyed up to relax."

He crossed the dirt path and walked past the trailer to the rear of the old building. A few yards away, a tree line separated a small grass and weed covered area from the base of a mountain. Grant stopped at the trees and looked up the side of the mountain. The woods were dense, filled with fallen trees and boulders. He thought about how strange life could be at times. The area where he was standing was clear of obstacles and he could move about without any difficulty, but no more than two feet away the earth presented an uphill area strewn with countless obstacles; fallen trees, large rocks, vines. Life was all about making choices. If he remained where he was he could move about with ease, but on the other hand if he decided to start up the side of the mountain things would suddenly become a challenge.

Russell was up in that area somewhere and he wouldn't be coming down on his own accord. He wasn't too sure how Russell was going to react to him and the others stepping onto his property and invading his small world. Chief Blue was right on one thing. If they took Russell alive he would only confess to the last four murders, the first four would remain unsolved. If Russell was killed, then more than likely he might take the fall for all eight murders, leaving Conrad in the clear and the plan of keeping the truth about Conrad from Ruth and Dana Beth would still be intact. Within the next couple of hours, if Russell was at his cabin, everything he had experienced over the past year and a half might finally end. What the end of the story could wind up being, he was not sure.

Grant's thoughts were interrupted by the sound of a vehicle pulling into the lot on the other side of the building. He walked around the side of the trailer just as Sheriff Turnbull and his two deputies were getting out of their cruiser. Blue got out of the Jeep as Turnbull waved at him. As Grant approached, Devers and Kerr were checking their revolvers and talking. Kerr nodded to Grant as he walked past, while Devers just gave him a cold stare as if Grant were treading on his territory. Chief Blue had been right. Devers did appear to be a hothead, an officer who, at the moment, Grant was not too sure he trusted.

Grant was a few feet past where Devers and Kerr were standing when he heard his name mentioned, "Denlinger, isn't it?" Devers asked.

Grant stopped and turned. "You can just call me Grant."

Devers took a step forward as he looked at the surrounding mountains. "Ya know something? The mountains up here haven't been tampered with like down where you're from, The Great Smoky Mountains." He laughed, and then went on in a sarcastic tone, "Up here there are no well-marked hiking trails, no benches for tourists to sit on if they get too tired to go on, no directional signs. This is the real thing up here, Denlinger. I grew up in these mountains and I can tell you from firsthand experience that it's no place for some small time tourist town deputy like you. If you're smart you'll stay close to me. Who knows, you just might make it through this day."

Grant was going to say something, but thought better of it as he turned and started to walk away, then turning around he said, "Devers, isn't it? I believe your first name is Lamont. Well, Lamont, it really doesn't make any difference to me whether it's the Smokies or here in Jellico. We're tracking a killer. Let me ask you. How many murders have you had up here in these mountains in the past two years?"

Devers hesitated, but Kerr answered, "None, we haven't had any."

"Well, there ya go," Grant said, as he stepped toward Devers. "I guess maybe you just better stay close to me and *maybe you'll* just make it through this day."

Walking away, Grant heard Devers remark, "Smart ass."

The conversation ended as two more vehicles pulled into the lot, Gephart and Green stepping out of the first then Sheriff Houseman and his deputy out of the second. Gephart wasted little time in getting everyone to gather at the front of the building.

"All right gentlemen, there are a few things we need to discuss before we head out to the cabin. Sheriff Turnbull will lead the way since he knows the location. We'll take three vehicles: Sheriff Turnbull and his two deputies in the lead car, then Agent Green, Sheriff Houseman and his deputy in the second and I'll be with Grant and Chief Blue in the last car. When we get up to the vicinity of the cabin, Agent Green and myself will be in charge of apprehending the suspect. Everyone here is important and there are a few things to keep in mind. We intend to bring Russell Pearl in alive, but, unfortunately things don't always work out the way they are planned. We've already discussed the fact that he's slow, but that doesn't mean he's stupid. He will be very familiar with not only the cabin grounds but the surrounding area. So remember, we will try to take him alive, but if he retaliates by shooting at us we have the authority to take him out. No one and I mean no one is to discharge their weapon, until I give the go ahead. Are there any questions? Does everyone understand our objective?" Everyone nodded in response to Gephart's short speech except Devers who wore a look of disapproval.

Satisfied that everyone was on the same page, Gephart made a circular motion with his index finger signaling that they should get moving. Pointing to Turnbull, he stated, "We'll follow you. When we get up there we'll have a short meeting then we'll go in."

Climbing in the Jeep, Grant spoke to Gephart who was seated in the back, "You need to keep an eye on Devers. I don't trust him. He's got his own agenda. He could blow this whole thing for us."

"I picked up on his attitude," said Gephart. "He doesn't seem to be much of a team player, but I've got a plan for keeping him at bay."

Pulling out of the lot following the second car, Grant put his sunglasses on as the sun was shining directly in the front windshield. Minutes later, they passed the town limits sign for Newcomb. They drove through town, which took all of forty-five seconds then exited on the other side. Grant, looking in the rearview mirror, asked, "Wonder why the Newcomb Police were not invited?"

Gephart answered the question, "Because there aren't any. Newcomb is a small unincorporated town. They fall under the jurisdiction of Sheriff Turnbull, but the Jellico Police Department and the State Police patrol Newcomb on a regular basis."

Starting up a steep curve that led up into the mountains, Grant asked a second question, "How far out is the cabin?"

Gephart, rolling down the window answered again, "Turnbull said it was about eight miles up in the mountains from Newcomb. He said hardly anybody lives in the area where Russell's cabin is located. We've got to nail him at the cabin. If he gets loose in the mountains, we'll play hell trying to capture him."

The two-lane road twisted and turned up the mountain and reminded Grant of Route 421 on the way to Mountain City. The only difference was that Route 297 was a constant uphill battle. Finally, at the top of the mountain, Gephart pointed out as he looked at a Tennessee roadmap. "According to this map we've just reached the top of Negro Mountain. When we get down the other side then we'll be climbing Lamb Mountain, the area where Russell's cabin is located."

Twenty minutes later, Turnbull made a left hand turn onto a narrow paved road that was quickly swallowed up by the surrounding forest. Houseman and Grant followed for another five minutes when Turnbull turned left again, but this time onto a dirt road. Fifty yards down the road he pulled onto the shoulder, he, Kerr and Devers stepping out. The other two vehicles followed suit and soon all nine men were standing in a tight group. Grant looked at the small band of men who, rather than looking like members of the law enforcement community, they resembled a hunting party: heavy-duty hiking boots, camouflage pants and shirts, hunting caps, rifles slung over their shoulders.

Opening a large equipment bag, Turnbull removed five two-way radios, a first aid kit and a bullhorn. "I thought these radios would come in handy in case we get separated."

Gephart addressed Turnbull as he checked his revolver. "Okay, Sheriff, this is your county, so how do you want to handle this?"

"That's all up to you Agent Gephart. Since this is considered a federal case, we'll go with whatever you feel is best."

Gephart stepped to the front of the group as he asked, "Where is the cabin situated from here?"

Turnbull pointed up the road. "About fifty yards up the road curves to the left, then another forty yards or so down the road sits the cabin. It's in a clearing of sorts. The road leads right up to the front door. There is a steep drop off on the left side of the cabin and the rear of the cabin and the right side is bordered by the mountain. I'd suggest we walk in from here."

"Sounds good," said Gephart. "When we get to the cabin, we need to surround it with four groups of two." Handing out the two-way radios he assigned each group their position. "Grant and Chief Blue, I want you at the back of the cabin. Sheriff Houseman and Deputy Flynn will take the right side, while Agent Green and Deputy Kerr will be on the left. Sheriff Turnbull and I will be at the front. After everyone is in position, call me and then we'll give Pearl an opportunity to surrender. If we discover that he's not at home we'll break in and see what we can find."

Devers spoke up as if he were the last child chosen on the playground, "What about me? Where do I go?"

Gephart looked at Grant as he answered the question. "Devers, your job is to remain here at the vehicles and make sure they are not tampered with." Tossing Devers a radio, he went on, "You'll be our command post."

Devers objected, "That's bullshit. I'm not going to be left behind."

Turnbull pointed at Devers. "You'll do exactly what Agent Gephart tells you to…understand?"

Devers, realizing he had no choice answered sharply, "Yes, Sir!"

Turnbull started up the road. "Let's get this show underway."

Grant, the last in line looked back at Devers who was physically upset as he kicked at some rocks in the road and cursed. When he noticed Grant looking at him, Devers gave him the finger.

Grant smiled and continued up the dirt road.

Two minutes later, Turnbull signaled for the group to stop as he pointed to the cabin that was nestled back in a group of tall pines. Kneeling behind a fallen tree, Turnbull motioned for the group to join him. Peering through a set of binoculars he spoke. "He's probably home. I can just see the rear end of what looks like a red pickup parked in that overhang attached to the left side of the cabin."

Gephart, also looking through a set of binoculars, commented, "I don't see any movement. Looks quiet." Looking to his right and left he ordered the men, "Head out to your assigned positions.

When you get there call me and then we'll get started. And remember, no matter what happens, no one fires a shot unless I give the order."

Each group had to circle out wide into the woods to get to their positions without being seen from the cabin. Grant and Chief Blue were the last to get into position as they crouched behind a fallen tree on the side of the mountain. From where they were situated they could see the front of the pickup. "Gephart was right. Looks like he's home," said Grant.

"Just because his truck is parked on the side of the cabin doesn't mean he's inside," remarked Blue. "He could be anywhere on the property or out in the woods."

Grant picked up the two-way and spoke into it softly, "This is Grant. Chief Blue and I are in position."

Gephart, after receiving the last call, nodded at Turnbull and spoke, "Everyone is in position."

Turnbull picked up the bullhorn and suddenly the solitude of the forest was invaded by his deep magnified voice, "Russell Pearl! This is the county sheriff. We have your cabin surrounded. Come out with your hands raised high in the air."

CHAPTER TWENTY-TWO

RUSSELL STOPPED FOR A MOMENT and took a long swig of lemonade from his old canteen. The sweet tasting liquid ran down his throat as he screwed the top of the canteen back in place. He looked out across the deep, tree-filled valley separating Negro and Lamb Mountains and smiled. He was glad he was finally home where he was safe. Today was his first full day back and he arose early, had a good breakfast of bacon, eggs and sausage and an entire carton of orange juice. He had been walking for over three hours; first inspecting his ten acres and then the surrounding forest. He had been away for quite a while and now that he was back he wanted to make sure that *his land, his home* was just the way he had left it; a place far away from mean people, a place where no one could hurt him. The Smoky Mountains had been a disappointment to him. Conrad had been right all along when he said most folks would not understand him and he should stay away from them. He had made a mistake going to his brother's funeral. Most of the people he met were mean and wanted to hurt him. Well, not everyone. He remembered Irene at The Flapjack Cabin and Walt who rented him that cabin and then there was the waitresses at the Mountain Café in Mountain City. They were nice to him. There was no reason to kill them. Why couldn't everyone just be nice?

He was tired and hungry from his long walk in the surrounding mountains. He was satisfied that all of the animals on his land were okay. They would be safe as long as he was around. Turning, he started back down the side of the mountain to his cabin. Maybe he'd have a big bowl of soup and a couple of hotdogs. After lunch, he'd sit out on the front porch and whittle and smoke his pipe.

On a ridge, fifty yards above the cabin, Russell was stopped in his tracks when he heard a booming voice echo through the deep woods: *Russell Pearl! This is the county sheriff. We have your cabin surrounded. Come out with your hands raised above your head!* He cocked his head at the mention of his name. He looked up into the towering trees. It sounded like the voice of God: loud, powerful, filling up every corner of the forest. Then, there was silence. The voice had startled the birds and caused them to fly out of the trees.

Where had the voice come from? Who was calling his name? Thinking that someone meant him harm, he raised his rifle and turned carefully in a complete circle as he peered out into the surrounding woods. Not a movement—not a sound. Just when he had convinced himself it was his imagination, the voice echoed through the woods again: *Russell Pearl, this is County Sheriff, Frank Turnbull. Your cabin is surrounded. Come out with your hands raised in the air.*

Russell crouched in a defensive position as he looked to the right and then the left. Turning around, he glanced back in the direction he had come from. He looked up into the trees as he aimed the rifle everywhere he looked. Nothing – not a sound.

Suddenly, he was afraid. He needed to get back to the safety of his cabin. He started quickly down the ridge when he heard the loud voice once again, *Russell Pearl! This is your last warning. Come out with your hands in the air or we are coming in.*

Stopping on the ridge, Russell looked down at the cabin where he saw a man holding a bullhorn to his mouth. Another man knelt next to him, a rifle in his hands aimed at the cabin. Quickly concealing himself behind a tree, he noticed two more men to the right of the cabin behind some boulders, their rifles trained on the cabin. A movement at the bottom of the ridge near the back of the cabin caught his attention. Two more men were hiding behind a fallen tree trunk, one staring through a set of binoculars.

Lying on the ground, Russell leveled his rifle and took careful aim at the man holding the bullhorn. The crosshairs on the sight fell on the man's head as he spoke into the horn, *Russell Pearl, this is your last chance!*

Russell didn't like the man calling out his name. He and the others had no right to come to his cabin and scare all the birds with their loud horn. These men were probably mean and wanted to harm him. He couldn't allow that to happen—not on his land. Just as he was about to squeeze the trigger, he felt the cold metal rifle barrel tap the side of his face, followed by a voice, "You so much as flinch and I'll blow your head right off."

Russell froze as he released his finger from the trigger. The voice ordered, "Now pitch that rifle off to the side, you son of a bitch!"

Russell didn't react quickly enough. A heavy work boot kicked him in the side then the voice sounded again, "I said pitch the rifle...now!"

Throwing the rifle into some leaves two feet away, Russell tried to turn his head so he could see who had stopped him from killing the man with the horn. The rifle barrel was pressed against the back of his head as the voice ordered sternly, "Not so fast, you freak! Don't move a muscle until I say otherwise." Russell received another painful kick to his side as he let out a gasp of pain. The voice ordered him again, "Get your face in the dirt...now! They thought they were so smart, didn't they. Sheriff Turnbull and that stupid ass federal agent, Gephart, tellin' me to stay down by the cars. Well, they've got a thing or two comin'." Russell was kicked again as the voice ordered, "I want you to roll over on your back so you can see the man who's gonna put your ass in prison for the rest of your life."

Russell slowly rolled onto his back as he looked up into the face of a man he had seen before in Jellico. He didn't know the man's name, but was quickly introduced as the man spoke, "My name is Lamont Devers and three years back you shot my brother Pete. I could shoot you right now and get away with it, but I've got too much to gain by keepin' you alive. Word is you killed a bunch of people in the Smokies. They've been tryin' to catch you for nearly two years. From here on out whenever ol' Lamont Devers walks down the street folks will talk about me; the man who captured the Smoky Mountain Killer. Why, I'll be a local hero...maybe the next county sheriff. Now, you need to get back on your stomach so I can cuff your ass."

Russell began to roll over, but before Lamont could react, Russell with his right leg swept Lamont's left leg from beneath him. Lamont lost his balance and fell forward.

Lamont realizing that he was in trouble discharged the rifle, the shot hitting Russell in his left lower leg. Falling on top of Russell, Lamont tried to regain his position, but Russell was too quick. He rolled to the side, picked up his rifle and shot Lamont just below his left shoulder.

Lamont fell backwards, his rifle flying off into the nearby weeds. Russell was on his feet in seconds as he chanced a look back down toward the cabin. All of the men were staring up toward the ridge. Realizing he couldn't shoot them all before they climbed the ridge, he painfully limped slowly up the side of the mountain into the trees. He wasn't sure if Lamont was dead or not. He didn't have time to finish him off. He needed to get farther back in the forest where he would be safe.

Gephart was instantly on the two-way as he yelled, "Who in the hell fired without my order?"

Blue answered, "No one down here fired. Those shots came from behind us up on that ridge. Is anybody hit?"

Sheriff Houseman yelled out, "We're okay over here!"

"Same here," hollered Agent Green.

Gephart was about to speak again when another call came in. "Frank...this is...Lamont. I'm...up on...the ridge. That bastard Pearl...shot me. He took...off up the...side of the...mountain."

Gephart stepped over the tree he had been hiding behind and ran around the side of the cabin as he announced loudly to the other three groups, "Pearl shot Devers up on the ridge. He fled up the side of the mountain. We've got to get up there. We've got a man down."

Frank started up the side of the ridge, Deputy Kerr following. Sheriff Houseman was next as Flynn reluctantly followed.

"What the hell." said Gephart as he signaled to Agent Green. "Let's go!"

All six men ran past Chief Blue and Grant, "Do you think it's wise to just go running up the side of that ridge?" Grant asked. "Russell could pick off two or three of us before we get to Lamont."

"We don't have a choice," said Blue. "There's an officer up there who's been shot. Come on."

Devers, realizing the dilemma of climbing the ridge with Russell still nearby called down to Turnbull. "Frank...Pearl took...off running. I think...it's clear."

In just over a minute all eight men gathered around Lamont who was holding his left shoulder and grimacing in pain. Frank knelt as he touched Lamont on his good shoulder. Blue gently removed Lamont's hand from the wound as he inspected the blood soaked area. "Looks like he took a shell just below his shoulder."

Concerned, Frank asked, "How are you feeling, Lamont?"

Lamont tried to move as he winced in pain, "I think...I'll be alright. You need...to get up the mountain...and get that son of a bitch!"

Frank looked at Blue. "How bad is the wound?"

"Looks like the shell missed his heart, not by much. It was close. He's losing a lot of blood. We need to get him to a hospital. He could bleed to death if we don't get him some medical attention soon."

Gephart took over as he ordered, "Kerr, Flynn. You two need to get Devers back down to the vehicles now. We'll call in an ambulance to meet up with you in Newcomb. They'll never find their way up here. Now, get moving."

As Lamont was helped to his feet, he mumbled, "I think...I can walk. Just keep...me steady."

Frank patted Lamont on his back as the three men started back down the ridge. "Don't worry Lamont, you'll be fine."

Gephart looked up the mountain as he asked Houseman, "What's up there?"

Drake shook his head as he answered, "Goes up for almost a mile or so I guess. We're going into some pretty rugged country."

"This is just what we didn't want to happen," barked Gephart. "Devers stupidity gave Russell more time to get away from us. He knows this country. He's probably been up there hundreds of times."

Houseman looked up the mountain. "It's your call, Agent Gephart. What's the plan?"

Turning back to the group, he thought for a moment then ordered, "Sheriff Houseman, I need you and Green to go back down and keep an eye on the cabin in case Pearl circles around. Frank, Grant, Chief Blue and myself, are going up the mountain and try to pick up his trail. I thought we could bring him in alive, but that might not be possible now. It's gonna be tough trailing him up through those trees and rocks."

"Not really," said Blue. "There's a blood trail. There were two shots. Devers must have wounded Russell." Pointing at the ground, he indicated a spot where there was blood. "This area is too far from where Lamont was shot. This has to be Russell's blood. He's hit." Walking a little further on, Blue pointed out, "Look here on the ground. The right footprint is deep in the dirt indicating were Russell applied more pressure on his right foot because he was shot in the left foot or leg. You can also see where he is slightly dragging his left foot. Depending on how bad the wound is and the amount of blood loss, Russell is going to get weaker especially traveling uphill. Now, if we're going to track him we just can't go charging up the mountain. We need to spread out, let's say, ten yards apart. It's hard to say what he's thinking. He might go a ways and then lay up and wait for us. Pick us off one at a time. Or, he might be scared and just keep running until he tires out."

Gephart suggested, "Sounds good, but I think now that we've got him on the run we should call in additional help." Addressing Turnbull, he asked, "Are there any copters in the area that we could get up here?"

"Sure," said Turnbull. "The State Police have a helicopter they can bring in."

"Go ahead and call them in and let them know about our situation. I'm also going to call my office in Knoxville and have them bring two additional copters up here, plus I'll have the State Police send us more officers to assist us in the search."

Speaking to Turnbull again, Gephart inquired, "How far can Russell get if he has the time?"

Turnbull shrugged, "The mountains up here are not like the Smokies. There are no well defined trails...it's hard to get around up here. A lot of the country is dense wilderness where people in general never go." Looking north, he explained, "The Kentucky border is just a few miles to the north. If we don't nail him within the next few hours he might make it across the state line. Southern Kentucky has its own share of mountains."

Blue looked through the binoculars as he started up the side of the mountain, "Let's get moving. The longer we stand around here the farther away he's getting."

Ten yards up the mountainside William pointed to a splattering of blood on some leaves. "Looks like he's headed straight up. He'll be easy to follow. Try to stay behind the trees and boulders as much as possible."

Forty minutes later, they arrived at a clearing where the mountain leveled off for a few hundred feet and then rose higher toward the summit. William knelt down as he inspected a blotch of blood. "He's still bleeding and as long as he keeps moving the blood won't coagulate. He's simply aggravating his wound. He's probably scared and confused, which makes him all the more dangerous."

Sitting with his back against a large boulder, Blue opened his canteen and took a short swig of water. Looking at the rest of the group he asked, "Did anyone else think to bring a canteen along?"

Everyone shook their head no. William passed the canteen to Grant. "Here, everyone needs to take one swallow. We don't know how long we'll be up here. We might not run into any streams, so we need to conserve."

"Good idea," said Gephart. "Do you think we can rest for a couple of minutes or should we continue to push on?"

"A few minutes won't hurt. Actually it's the smart thing to do. We need to pace ourselves. A wounded human being will react much the same way as a wounded animal when they're on the run from a hunter. They'll push themselves farther than they should and when they finally do stop for a rest they're exhausted. Many times, a wounded deer, for instance will run until they can go no farther. When they finally lay down to rest it never gets back up. They simply bleed to death. This is what Russell is no doubt faced with. As long as he's running, we have nothing to worry about. It's when he stops, when he can go no further, when he feels he is cornered. That's when he'll be the most dangerous. He'll get to the point where he has nothing to lose. When he gets his back to the wall and decides to fight back, we'll have our hands full."

Grant handed the canteen to Turnbull as he looked off into the distant sky. "Do you hear that? Sounds like a copter."

Turnbull cocked his head and answered, "That'll be the State Police copter."

Seconds later, the copter flew over the clearing, circled around and hovered over top of where they were seated. An officer leaned out of the cockpit and waved at them then circled around and put the copter down in the weed covered clearing no more than thirty yards away. Ducking his head from the rotating blades, the pilot ran across the field and knelt behind the boulder and asked, "Who's Gephart?"

Gephart reached out, shaking the officer's hand. "I'm Agent Gephart."

The officer introduced himself then asked, "What've we got?"

Gephart quickly ran down the series of events they had encountered since arriving at the cabin, and finished up by stating that the suspect had fled up into the mountains after shooting one of their group."

Before the officer could respond, he was signaled back to the copter where he spoke with the pilot then returned. "Bad news, gentlemen. Officer Devers didn't make it. They got him to Newcomb where the paramedics were waiting. They got him stabilized, but on the way to the hospital he expired. I'm sorry."

Turnbull picked up a rock and tossed it with all his might across the open field. "Damn it all to hell! If Lamont would have just followed the orders he was given he'd still be alive." This Russell Pearl...well, it won't break my heart if we kill this bastard."

Everyone remained silent for a few seconds until Gephart gave the officer his orders. "You boys need to circle above us in about a quarter mile sweep. Your presence will probably distract Pearl. He'll have to be more careful about being out in the open. With you boys being in the air, it'll slow his progress down. Don't get too low because he'll probably take a potshot at you. This guy's nuts!"

The officer stood, and running back across the field, yelled back, "If we see him we'll give you a shout out!"

William stood. "The cards just got stacked a little more in our favor. That copter gives us a leg up. Russell will have to concentrate on it as it circles overhead. It'll give him less time to focus on us." Peering around the edge of the boulder he suggested, "The tree line is about thirty yards across that clearing. We need to spread out and get to the trees quickly. We'll be easy targets out in the open. Hopefully he moved further up into the mountain."

Grant was relieved that one of the copters had shown up. Taking a deep breath, he thought about the extra state troopers and federal agents they summoned to come and assist in the manhunt. It could be hours before they caught up with them. For now, it was up to Blue, Turnbull, Gephart and him to keep the pressure on Russell Pearl. He wondered what Russell must be thinking. Blue was right. He probably was scared and confused and on top of that, the fact that he had been shot and was bleeding had to be upsetting.

Blue's voice filtered down through the trees, "All right, come ahead. I picked up his trail and he's still bleeding. He's still climbing straight up. Looks like he's headed for the top. Let's get moving. Remember, ten yards apart. Stay behind the trees as much as you can." As they moved forward Grant could hear the constant beating of the blades as the machine passed over. He couldn't see the copter, but he knew it was nearby.

An hour later, Blue signaled for the foursome to stop as he turned back and addressed the group. "Looks like about fifteen yards and we'll be at the summit."

"Great," said Gephart, out of breath. "We'll rest up for a few minutes."

The forest floor of the summit was covered with brown pine needles and pinecones. William sat with his back against a tall pine as he opened his canteen and took a drink.

Gephart refused the canteen and spoke into the two-way radio. "Gephart to copter. Gephart to copter, come in."

A response came back immediately, "This is Chopper One, come in."

Looking up into the tall trees, Gephart spoke to those he could hear but not see. "We've reached the summit. Taking a short breather and will continue soon. What type of terrain is up ahead?"

Following some static the answer returned, "Summit continues for about fifty yards then it's down the other side of the mountain. We were contacted by the copters from Knoxville. ETA is approximately ten minutes. The men you requested are driving up and will gather in Newcomb at three o'clock. What are their orders?"

"Just tell them to sit tight until we contact them. On second thought, it would be better to drop the men at the clearing below rather than have them come all the way up the mountain. Then we need to determine the direction the suspect is now taking since arriving at the summit."

"When the other copters arrive we'll start bringing the Newcomb crew up. We'll be in touch."

Turnbull lit up a cigarette and pointed it across the summit. "I've been up here twice years ago when I was with the boy scouts. The first time I was up here, we hiked up to the summit and then down the other side. At the bottom, the Cumberland River Gorge extends down from Kentucky. About a quarter mile down the mountain you have to go to the right or left. It's almost like God took a giant cheese slicer and severed the side of the mountain for about a mile or so. In the middle, which is where we seem to be heading, the cliffs on either side of the gorge are nearly two hundred feet high then they slowly level off to the right and left where they meet the river basin. We stayed the night up here on the summit then in the morning hiked down to the edge of the gorge. There are gravel bars that you can camp on, if you're brave enough to stay that close to the water. I remember looking down over the side. It was one of my scarier moments. The cliff walls are covered with vines and stone outcroppings. There are also trees growing right out of the side of the mountain down to the river. The river is full of rocks and the rapids are pretty fierce around this area. Years ago, whitewater-rafting companies from Williamsburg and Corbin, Kentucky ran rafting trips down through the gorge, but the state of Tennessee put a stop to that about four years back when, on two different rafting accidents, six people were killed. The water is treacherous with shifting currents and undertows that will suck you to the bottom in a heartbeat."

William jumped in on the conversation. "I'm sure you didn't bring this topic up as mere conversation. There has to be a reason for this explanation of the gorge and river."

"Exactly," answered Turnbull. "If Pearl keeps heading in a straight direction he'll come to the cliffs at their highest point. He then has no choice. He has to go to the left or right. If he gets down to the river, he has a real chance at getting away from us. We might as well throw the towel in at least as far as it goes for catching him anytime soon. If he makes it to the river he could float for miles downstream and get out at a thousand different locations and escape. I'd guess if that's his plan, he'll go to the left...south. If he goes north, then he'd have to float by us, but by going south he can float away from our location, however we won't know which direction he's taking until we come to the gorge..."

Turnbull's voice was drowned out as the two copters from Knoxville flew directly over top of them. Gephart's two-way radio crackled followed by a voice, "Agent Gephart...this is Agent Burke...come in."

Gephart responded as he looked up at the tree tops that were being blown this way and that from the power of the rotating blades. "Gephart here. Listen, Agent Burke, you need to act quickly on this. How many men do we have?"

"Four agents, two per copter. On the ground we have seventeen agents and twelve state police arriving in Newcomb within minutes."

"Here's what I want done," ordered Gephart. "The Cumberland River Gorge is not far from where you are now. If you head due west you should be over it in less than a minute. We need all three copters to transport the twelve state police to the north and south ends of the gorge on the east side of the river. The remaining seventeen agents are to be dropped at a clearing east of where we are presently located. When everyone is in position start the state boys up the mountain next to the gorge from both the north and south ends. The remaining agents will spread out and start up the mountain behind us forming a three-sided box effect, the forth side being the cliffs of the gorge. This will cut down on the area the suspect has to operate in. As the three sides close in he'll eventually be trapped at the edge of the gorge. After the men are all dropped in, the three copters need to keep circling the entire area. We only have about three hours of daylight and then he could slip by us. Any questions?"

"Clear as a bell...we're on it."

Within seconds, all three copters flew away to the east toward Newcomb and a minute later the forest returned to a place of solitude. Grant stood and stretched as he asked, "Now what, William?"

"You just stay put for now. I'll see if I can pick up his trail and then we'll continue across the top of the summit and wherever his blood trail leads."

Confident that with the assistance of three copters and a total of twenty-nine additional men on the ground they would soon have Russell Pearl in custody, Gephart stood and walked a few feet across the summit, placing his foot on a moss-covered rock. Turning back to Grant and Turnbull he smiled. "Well, it won't be long now before we get our suspect. He's boxed in." Three shots rang out in rapid succession.

The first penetrated Gephart's upper right arm, the second sent a spray of bark off the tree that Grant was leaning on, the third nicking Grant's earlobe. Turnbull dove to the ground as he watched Gephart grab his arm and fall over. Grant raised his hand to his left ear and quickly ducked behind the tree. A forth shot rang out followed by someone yelling in pain.

"Damn it!" yelled Grant. "Sounds like Chief Blue got hit." Following what seemed like a period of prolonged eerie silence; William appeared at Grant's side. He looked at Turnbull and Gephart. "Is anybody hit?"

Grant, displaying a small amount of blood on his hand motioned toward his ear. "I think I got hit on my ear."

Blue turned Grant's head slightly as he looked at the side of his head. "Just a flesh wound. You're lucky. Another inch or so and you'd be joining Devers."

Staying low, Turnbull knelt behind a tree. "We better take a look at Gephart. I think he took a bullet."

William quickly moved to Gephart who was still on the ground. Holding his blood-soaked arm, Gephart spoke through the pain. "Got me in my right arm. Hurts like hell."

"Let me take a look," William said as he gently moved Gephart's left hand from the wound. "Yeah, he nailed you in your upper arm. Looks like the shot passed right through."

"When I fell I landed on my arm. I think it might be broken," added Gephart.

Grant and Turnbull were now at Gephart's side as Grant asked William, "I thought you got hit by the fourth shot. We heard you yell out."

"That was Russell," remarked William. "I think I got him in the right shoulder, but I still didn't bring him down. He's still on the run."

Turnbull looked off into the trees across the summit. "What happened up there?"

William sat against a tree and explained, "I had just located the blood trail when I heard a noise. I laid down in some

underbrush and not even twenty yards in front of me up pops
Russell. I guess he didn't see me. Before I could get my gun in
position, he fired three times and then turned to run down the
other side of the summit. I only had time to get one quick shot off.
As I said, I think I got him in his shoulder as he was running off.
He yelled and limped off into the trees. I came back down to see
what the situation was."

Gephart grimaced as he spoke, "Then he's no more than five
minutes or so ahead of us. We're closing in on him."

"That's right," said William, "But, unfortunately, you're not
going with us. We have to move quick and cut him off before he
gets down to the river. We can't leave you here alone. He might
double back. Here's what we're going to do. Sheriff Turnbull, you
need to get one of those copters here so they can haul Gephart out
of here. He needs medical attention. Grant and I are going after
Pearl. He can't be moving all that fast. Listen, Turnbull, after they
pick Gephart up you need to stay put until those men coming up
from the clearing arrive. By that time, Russell will probably be in
the gorge area. He's not stupid. Even though we've got him on the
run, he still might hide and double back after we pass by. We're
still not out of this yet." Looking at Gephart, Blue asked, "You
okay with that, Agent?" Nodding, Gephart agreed.

Blue tapped Grant on his arm. "Come on, let's get across the
summit then I'll explain our plan for going down the other side to
the gorge."

Grant didn't have time to think. Things were happening way
too fast for him. Looking at the blood on his hand, he followed
William up through the thick trees as he constantly looked to the
right and left, his previous confidence somewhat shattered.

At the edge of the summit, William stopped and waited for
Grant to catch up. Crouching behind a fallen tree, Grant looked
down into the trees below as he commented, "God, look how
much the ground drops off. Are you sure he went down over the
side?"

William pointed at some pine needles that were covered with
blood. "Right around here is where I shot Russell." Walking down
over the side of the summit a few yards, William pointed at
another blood covered area. "He went down this way. I'm sure he's
heading for the gorge and then the river." Pointing at another spot
he spoke again, "He's really dragging his left foot and his steps are
closer together. That means he's getting tired. We need to keep the
pressure on. Turnbull said it was about a quarter of a mile down to

the gorge. We need to move quickly, but carefully. Stay behind the trees whenever possible and keep a watchful eye ahead and to the side. He might lay up again and try to pick us off or wait for us to pass. Personally, I think he'll just keep moving and try to get to the river. Let's go."

For the next twenty-five minutes Grant, trying his best to stay low followed William's instructions as he trailed behind him down the steep mountainside. It was difficult to keep his footing in the loose pine needles and he found himself slipping with every other step, often sliding down the mountainside on his backside. Looking to his right, he saw William signal for him to stop.

"Hear that? Water...rushing water. Must be the river. We must be near the gorge."

Chancing a quick glance around the side of a tree, Grant saw the red hat just as Russell ducked behind a large boulder.

"William, I saw him! He's about thirty yards down, hiding behind a boulder."

"We've got him right where we want him," said William. "He can't go down the cliff gorge or go to the right or left. We'll just wait him out."

Grant heard a copter fly over and move off to the south. "I guess they're moving the men down to the river. Even if he somehow gets away from us, the men coming up both sides of the gorge will cut him off."

William agreed. "Let's not forget all the men coming up behind us. There's no way he'll escape. He's gone as far as he can go. It's the end of the line for ol' Russell Pearl."

"Do you think Russell realizes that," asked Grant.

"Let's find out," said William.

William cupped his hands around his mouth and shouted, "Russell Pearl! This is Chief William Blue, I've got another man out here with me and a couple dozen men coming up here to help out. You can't make it to the river. We have State Police coming up both ends of the gorge. There is nowhere for you to go now." Another copter flew over heading north. William continued to shout, "Russell, did you see that copter. We've got three in the area. You are completely out-manned and out-gunned. I know you've been shot. Just give yourself up and we'll make sure you get to a hospital."

William looked over at Grant and shrugged, thinking that all of his yelling was accomplishing nothing, but then Russell's voice answered back, "Go away...leave me alone. I want to go back to my cabin. Conrad told me I would be safe there. Go away. I want to be left alone."

"As long as you stay out here, you won't be safe," yelled William. "We don't have to bring you in alive. It's your choice. If you want to be safe, then give yourself up."

"No! Go away. That man I shot wanted to hurt me. He kicked me and called me a freak. You have no right to come to my land and my cabin. You have upset all of the birds and animals. I have to protect them from mean people. Go away!"

Grant signaled to William, "Mind if I give it a go?"

William shrugged, "Have at it."

Turning his head, Grant shouted, "Russell, this is Grant Denlinger. Conrad was my father-in-law. I'm married to Dana Beth, your niece. Remember, you were recently at our house. You talked with her at the grocery store. She had a baby with her. Her name is Crystal Ann. She's your great niece. You still have family. You're not alone. We can help you, but you have to give yourself up. Not everyone is mean. There are people who can help you. You can be safe again, but only if this stops now."

"No! If you were nice, Conrad would have told me about you. He told me to stay away from people. He was right. You're all mean. Go away!" Two shots echoed through the forest as Russell fired into the trees. Grant and William ducked their heads.

Grant shook his head in disbelief, thinking that if Russell realized that he had a family then he'd give in, but his response of firing at them squashed any hope of bringing him in alive. "It's no use, William. He's not going to give up."

William scooted over next to Grant. "Look, it's gonna be getting dark in a couple of hours. We have to bring this to an end before that happens. Russell is not as stupid as we think he is. He's already cut our group of nine down to just you and me. I figure he's lost quite a bit of blood. He's got to be getting weak. If we don't nail him before darkness sets in he might be able to crawl off. Here's what we'll do. I'm going to go out on his flank about twenty yards to the right and you do the same on the left. Wait for a few minutes until we're both in position. I'll get his attention by shouting at him. This way his back will be to you. I'll stand up and pull off a quick shot at him so he can see me. Before he fires back I'll hit the ground. You should have a few seconds to get a clear shot. Take him out."

Grant nodded, but reluctantly. "So, you're saying this is it. I should shoot him in the back?"

William gave Grant a look of concern as he stated, "Look, Grant, don't go getting soft on me. If you'd rather, you can do the shout out and get his attention and I'll do the deed."

Grant shook his head, "I'm okay with it, Blue. Let's get this over with." In less than two minutes, Grant was in position just three feet from the edge of the gorge. Down below he could hear the rushing water. Taking a deep breath he hid behind a tree and listened to the sound of the distant copters.

Grant drew a deep breath as William called out, "Russell Pearl, this is Chief William Blue. You're not going to get back down off this mountain alive." A shot rang out at which point Grant stepped out from the tree. He saw Russell bring his rifle up, aim and shoot in the direction from where William had fired.

Rather than shooting Russell in the back, Grant yelled, "Russell, drop the rifle. Give yourself up. You don't have a chance. I've got orders to take you out, but you don't have to die. Please...give up."

Russell slowly turned and looked directly at Grant. He lowered his rifle, but did not drop it to the ground. "I haven't done anything wrong." Raising the rifle, he spoke again, "Why do you want to hurt me...I don't want to hurt you." Grant looked at Russell's eyes, the same eyes that had stared at him at Conrad's funeral. He looked so pitiful. His left boot and lower left leg were soaked with blood as he struggled to remain standing. His right shoulder was drooping and covered with blood. Russell raised the rifle even higher. His eyes were full of fear and confusion. Grant realized that he needed to squeeze a shot off before Russell got his rifle into a firing position.

Just as Grant was about to squeeze the trigger, a shot rang out. Russell froze, with a look of disbelief on his face. He slowly lowered the rifle, dropped to his knees then toppled sideways over the side of the gorge.

Grant hesitated, and then stepped out onto a dirt trail that ran right on the edge of the cliff. Walking slowly toward the spot where Russell had fallen over, he looked down over the edge. Blue was all ready at the spot where Russell had fallen. Peering over the side, William commented, "Did you see him go over?"

Grant, now at Blue's side, apologized, "Yes, I was just getting ready to squeeze off a shot, but you beat me to the punch."

Blue patted Grant on his shoulder. "It doesn't make any difference who shot him. We finally got our killer."

Grant looked over the side of the gorge, "I can't believe it's finally over. Russell Pearl is dead."

William looked down over the side of the steep cliff. "It's not quite over...just yet. We can't say for sure that Russell Pearl is dead until we locate his body."

"Do you see him down there anywhere?" Grant asked as he looked over the side down into the bottom of the gorge.

"No, I don't see his body." Pointing to some flat jagged rocks, just a few feet from the rapidly moving water, Blue spoke, "Look, there on that rock. A bloody boot and then a little father to the left, his rifle broken in half...but no body...no Russell Pearl."

"Now wait a sec," said Grant. "You're not trying to say that he survived a fall like that...are you?"

William, surveying the cliff walls through binoculars, commented, "No one could survive a fall like that. He either fell in between some of those large boulders or, depending on how he landed, he might have gone into the water and got swept downstream. I don't think that even a strong man could survive that fall. Russell was shot three times, he's lost a lot of blood and was weakened to where he could barely move. No, he's dead, but all that being said, the powers that be will want a body. There is one more thing we need to settle before everyone shows up. We've got to decide how we want to close this whole thing out. It's up to you and me how this ends. Remember, we said that if Russell was captured and interrogated he might confess to four of the eight murders. We also said that if Russell was killed he'd take the fall for all eight. We need to make sure that happens. So, when the others get up here, we can get the ball rolling by simply telling them that Russell admitted to killing all those people. We don't have to mention what people. Believe me, the media will take it from there. Everyone will be so glad this is finally at an end they'll accept what they're told as the truth. Now, try to relax and get some rest. The next few days could be hectic. The authorities up here are going to have to go down into that gorge and search for Russell's body."

CHAPTER TWENTY-THREE

NEARLY TWENTY FOUR HOURS had passed since Russell Pearl tumbled over the side of the Cumberland River Gorge. It was a foggy, rain swept morning, but the low visibility and wet weather did little to deter the throng of media people from attending the news conference being held at the convention center in the Holiday Inn in Knoxville. Everyone who had taken part in the investigation for the past year and a half was present: Grant, Chief Brody, Chief Blue, Sheriff Grimes, Agents Gephart and Green, and more recently Sheriff Turnbull and Chief Drake. The room was filled to capacity with every available chair occupied. The perimeter of the room was lined with television cameras and sound equipment from all four major networks, along with local stations from Tennessee, North Carolina, and Kentucky. The buzzing of numerous conversations made it almost impossible to hear.

In an adjacent room, closed circuit TV had been set up to accommodate the overflow of interested parties. There was a sense of excitement in the air. The killer had finally been caught or killed depending on how those who attended looked at it. The fact that there were two officers present who had been wounded in the chase and eventual stand-off made for a dramatic ending to a long and frustrating search for the Smoky Mountain Killer.

Agent Green stepped up to the podium and tapped on the mic. "Ladies and gentlemen, may I have your attention please? The news conference will begin in fifteen minutes. If everyone would please take their seats, I have some important announcements to make due to the complexity of this case. There are a number of agents in the room who will now pass out a folder to each of you. In this folder you will find pertinent information for you to review. In this manner, I hope that we can answer many of the questions you may have before we begin." Holding up a folder of his own, he removed some stapled copies as he explained, "The first sheet in the folder will supply you with the name, rank and organization of all the officers who have worked on the case along with their email address and office telephone number. The second sheet is a complete analysis of the killer, Russell Pearl, from the time of his youth when he lived in the Iron Mountains and was known as Russell Pender, to the present time. The third sheet contains a chronological description of each of the nine murders committed by Pearl. Please read them over." Nodding at the sea of faces looking up at him, he stepped away from the podium causing the room to be filled with the rustling of paper as the reporters delved into the information.

Fifteen minutes later, right on schedule, Agent Gephart, his right arm supported by a blue medical sling, spoke into the microphone as he introduced himself, "Good morning, ladies and gentlemen, my name is Agent Gephart with the Federal Bureau of Investigation. As we get things underway, I'd like to suggest that you hold any questions or comments until we are finished. If we can do this it will make for a smoother and more informative session. You have all been given the facts on this case that led to the final confrontation with Russell Pearl. We now know he is the Smoky Mountain Killer. Please refrain from asking me questions regarding the information folder unless you are asking for additional details."

Looking down at a sheet of paper on the podium, he began to read his prepared speech: "On Saturday, July 11 of this year, at approximately one o'clock in the afternoon, a raid was conducted at the home of Russell Pearl in the Jellico Mountain region a few miles from the town of Newcomb, Tennessee. William Blue of the Cherokee Police and Officer Grant Denlinger from Townsend, who had been doing extensive research on the killer, informed the FBI and the authorities in the Jellico area that Russell Pearl was a suspect and was thought to be at his cabin on Lamb Mountain.

"The evidence they had gathered in the murders of at least four victims in the Smoky Mountain area established that it was necessary to take Mr. Pearl into custody. Along with the support of the Campbell County Sheriff's office and the Jellico Police Department, we surrounded Mr. Pearl's home. Despite our efforts to give Mr. Pearl ample warning, we discovered that he was not in the cabin. Officer Lamont Devers of the Campbell County Sheriff's Department was the first officer on the scene to encounter Mr. Pearl. During a scuffle, the suspect was wounded in his left lower leg. Unfortunately, Officer Devers was shot by the suspect and later on expired from the wound he received.

"At that point, a manhunt began as Pearl fled into the mountains. We called in backup, which included three helicopters and a number of men from Knoxville to assist in the search. The part of the mountains Pearl escaped in is heavily wooded and quite rugged. Hours later, there was a second confrontation when the officers in pursuit were fired upon by Mr. Pearl. Officer Denlinger was shot in the right ear and," holding up his arm, "I was also wounded. We are almost positive that the suspect was wounded when Chief Blue returned fire. It was only when the suspect reached the top of a ridge at the Cumberland Gap Gorge and suffering from fatigue and a loss of blood, he could go no farther. Chief Blue and Officer Denlinger tracked Pearl to the ridge. Numerous attempts to talk Pearl into giving himself up were futile. Pearl eventually appeared and after taking aim at Officer Denlinger, Chief Blue, having no other option, shot the suspect causing him to fall over the precipice."

Hesitating for a moment, Gephart cleared his throat, and then continued, "By the time we were able to get men and equipment down into the gorge, darkness set in so an extensive search for the body was postponed until the next morning. We did leave four officers on the riverbank below the area where Mr. Pearl went over the cliff. Two helicopters patrolled the area all night. At daybreak, three of our agents repelled down the side of the mountain, where Mr. Pearl had fallen. They were unable to locate any evidence of his body. Following an extensive search of the riverbank, the side of the mountain and the river, we have, so far, been unable to recover the suspect's body. However, the steep, jagged rock formations, not to mention the huge boulders and crevices at the base of the river ravine dictate that Pearl could not have survived the fall of over two hundred feet. Officer Blue indicated that he shot Pearl in the upper area of his body. The suspect could have been dead before he hit bottom. We located traces of blood on the side of the cliff walls in four different locations. In addition to this, we also found shreds of his shirt, his bloody left boot and his rifle which was broken in half. We also located a cap that he was reported as wearing snagged on some branches in the river. We will continue to search both upstream and down for the body. We are not giving up hope, but there is a strong possibility that the body may never be retrieved due to the swiftness of the river current. The body may have been sucked down beneath one of the boulders and forced into the mud at the bottom.

"All of the surrounding area is still being searched and will continue to be until we have exhausted every effort to locate the body. The FBI and the local law authorities have conducted an extensive investigation. We feel that Russell Pearl is responsible for all eight murders, including Officer Lamont Devers, which brings the total to nine. We, at this time, cannot close the case on Russell Pearl since we have not located the body. So for now, the case will remain an open-ended murder case." Hesitating, Gephart looked out across the crowd. "Now, I will take your questions."

An array of hands waved in the audience, many of the reporters calling out. Gephart pointed to a reporter from the Knoxville Times. "Yes, what is your question?"

The reporter stood. "How did you come to the conclusion that Russell Pearl killed all eight people over the past year and a half when the first four murders were committed without so much as a single fingerprint and the last four murders left clues seemingly everywhere?"

"To begin with," answered Gephart, "Russell Pearl was not of sound mind. Past medical records show that he had a psychological problem that affected his thinking process. In his earlier years, he was diagnosed as being a psychopath. We believe that he actually took the time to plan the first four murders. It took him a long time, but he was able to carry them off without leaving any clues, at least that would implicate him. The fifth victim was Bobby Mackinaw, but from what we have discovered it is thought that Pearl was accosted by Mackinaw and a Joseph Winfield, an altercation ensued and Pearl killed Mackinaw in order to protect himself. Next came Daniel Bock, which we feel was an unfortunate and unplanned meeting between Bock and Pearl. Evidence points to the fact that Bock was poaching turtles. Pearl disapproved and killed him. As far as J.J. Pickler is concerned, we believe that Pearl planned to kill him. If you will recall, there was a note left at the third murder scene from last year when Butch Miller was killed that read: Pickler...you're next! This may be the reason he returned to the area. Pearl, probably did not initially know that Pickler had a captive bear. When he found out, that compounded his annoyance with Pickler, causing him to steal and release the bear. I'm sure that Pickler at some point went after Pearl and Mr. Pearl killed him. Then Pickler was put in his car and was shoved over the side of the mountain where his body was later discovered. At a later date, Hawk Caine, a well-known bounty hunter, hired to track down Russell Pearl was shot and killed by Pearl in Mountain City, while Caine tried to apprehend him."

The same reporter continued with another question, "Isn't most of what you're saying speculation? There are really no concrete facts to support your suppositions."

Gephart replied, "I agree with you to a point, but you have to view each murder from every possible angle then come to a conclusion. The fact remains that even without a shred of evidence tying Russell Pearl to the first four murders, the evidence that we do have in regard to the last four, five when you factor in the death of Officer Devers implicates Pearl without question."

Looking the reporter directly in the eye, Gephart emphasized, "I have one more thing to say that helped us to come to the conclusion that Russell was responsible for the first four murders and that's this: Chief Blue and Officer Denlinger were the last two men to see Russell Pearl alive. They have stated that just before Pearl was shot he admitted to killing all those men. I think that says it all."

Another reporter toward the middle of the room raised his hand and Gephart gave him a nod. "Do you think Pearl was staying in the area so that he could kill others and is it true that he is in fact the brother of Conrad Pearl who lived in Townsend? Do you think that Conrad had any idea what his brother was up to?"

Gephart, trying to control the meeting, answered in a stern tone, "That's three questions. Please keep your questions to one per person. First, I have no idea what Russell Pearl was up to, but since he lived so close to the area there is a possibility that there could have been more murders down the line. Second and third, he was the brother of Conrad Pearl and knowing the quality person that Professor Pearl was, I'm sure he had no idea what Russell was doing or he would have turned him in to the authorities. Conrad Pearl was an upstanding citizen of Townsend and a noted professor at the University of Tennessee right here in Knoxville."

A young, blonde woman in the first row stood. She seemed nervous as she asked, "It states in your report that Russell and Conrad were the sons of the Penders who were murdered over forty years ago. Do you think that was Russell's motive for killing all those people and why do you think he waited so long?"

Gephart reacted in a frustrating manner at another multiple question, but went ahead and answered, "Young lady, I have no idea what Russell Pearl was thinking all those years, but I will say this: the trauma those two young boys suffered could have triggered all kinds of irrational behavior. Once again, like we have already established. Anything I could say on that subject at this time would be pure speculation on my part."

Grant sat quietly as he listened to the number of exchanges between Gephart and the reporters, occasionally glancing over at Chief Blue who was sitting across the front of the room from him.

He was pleased with the way Conrad's involvement had been squashed and for the moment it appeared that the secret of Conrad would not surface. He could tell from the way William looked back at him that the process of keeping Conrad out of the line of fire was going well.

After an hour of questions, Gephart held up his hand. "I think we have answered all of the pertinent questions. My staff and I will be available to answer any more questions by e-mail. We still have a few loose ends to tie up, but as far as the FBI is concerned Russell Pearl is the Smoky Mountain Killer. Now, I would like to commend all of the departments that have helped in this investigation and the excellent work of both Officer Denlinger and Chief Blue."

Someone began to clap toward the back of the room and soon the room was filled with applause. Axel, who was sitting next to Grant, tapped him on the shoulder and whispered, "Well, ain't you some kind of hero! By the way, what did the little wife say when she found out that it was her uncle who was the killer?"

Grant turned and glared at Axel. "Don't even go there, Brody! Not unless you want your face rearranged right here on the stage."

Axel slapped his knee as he waved off Grant's threat. "Aw, go on, Wonder Boy! I was just tryin' to get your goat." Folding his arms across his chest, he continued to laugh.

Grant angrily shoved his chair back as he stood and walked toward the door.

Blue caught up with him just as he was about to step outside. "Grant...let's talk. You got time for a cup of coffee...maybe a bite?"

Grant, still angry, answered. "Yeah, I am hungry, but right now I'm really pissed at Brody. Where does that son of a bitch get off talking about my wife like that? I'd like to punch that fat bastard right in the mouth."

William joked, as he punched Grant lightly on his shoulder. "Take it easy. He's just jealous because you're the one in Townsend that's going to receive all the credit for taking Pearl down. He's getting his five minutes of fame in the spotlight right now. After all, he had to convince everyone that he knew all about the investigation you were conducting. He would have looked like an idiot if the press and the FBI thought he had no idea what was going on. I saw him grab a microphone from one of the reporters. He's trying to make himself look good by expounding on your fine character and the wonderful job you did on the case."

Looking at Brody who was now surrounded by a number of interested reporters, Grant commented, "He's still a complete and utter asshole and I'm looking forward to the day when I don't have to work for him any longer."

Once outside, Grant and Blue circled the hotel to the parking area. Reaching for his keys, Grant spoke, "I'll drive. Pulling out of the parking lot onto Cedar Bluff, he made a quick left onto West Peters Road. A few minutes later they pulled into the parking lot of the Soups and Scoops Grill. "That was quick," said William as he climbed out of the car.

Taking a booth at the rear of the restaurant, Blue slid across the seat to a window. "You didn't have much to say on the way over here."

"My head is swimming right now," remarked Grant. "I'm not sure what I think. I feel Gephart did a bang up job on the summary, but I'm not sure how many of the news people bought into it. In the next couple of days the media might pick the bones clean on this case. As far as it goes for us protecting Conrad from being implicated, I'm not sure that we're out of the woods yet."

Blue disagreed, "I think you're worrying way too much. Look at it this way. The media doesn't have any better idea about the first four murders than the Feds do. By the time this story hits the circuit of all the rag papers and every exploitive program on television, they will have Russell responsible for every murder this side of the Ohio River. They'll milk it for every last drop they can squeeze out of it. The Feds are not going to spend any more time looking for another killer. As far as they are concerned—they got their man. It's over!"

Their server came to the table, took their order and then returned with a pot of coffee. Stirring a pack of sweetener in his coffee, William took on a solemn look. "Grant, do you have any idea how close you came to letting Russell Pearl shoot you up there on the ridge? When were you going to pull the trigger?"

"I thought I was ready, William. I thought I had things under control. I had my finger on the trigger. I thought just maybe I could talk him into giving himself up. The truth is you saved my ass. If you wouldn't have fired when you did, I might have joined Lamont Devers in the great beyond." Staring into his own cup of coffee, Grant shook his head in doubt. "What kind of an officer am I, William? I stand right in front of a killer, looking down the barrel of his rifle and I had to think about whether I should shoot or not. Maybe I'm not cut out for this."

"It's not easy to pull the trigger...to kill another human being. Not even someone like Russell. He was a human being...true, and once you make the decision to shoot, you have to come to terms with it. There was no way I was going to allow him to kill you."

Grant smiled. "Does that mean I owe you now, like some sort of Indian custom or something?"

William chuckled. "You might just be right, but I'd rather see you go home to your wife and baby girl than be obligated to me. By the way, how did that go...when you told Ruth and Dana Beth who the killer was?"

The server interrupted the conversation as she returned with two bowls of steaming vegetable soup and two egg salad sandwiches. After everything was placed on the table and the server left, Grant answered Blue's previous question. "I was dreading telling Dana Beth that an uncle she never even knew was the killer. When I called her last night and told her all that had happened, she remained quiet for a moment, trying to digest what I had said. That's the way Dana Beth handles things. She mulls them over in her mind before she makes any decisions. She didn't cry, but did say she was sad that her father felt it necessary to keep Russell a secret from the family. She feels that maybe we could have helped Russell. Ruth really took it hard. She cried and I didn't know what to say. I'm sure, that between the two of them, after I hung up they had a lot to talk about. It's going to take some time to get all this straightened out in their minds, especially since it's going to be headline news for at least a week or two. I don't think either of them know how to deal with this one. It's going to be tough."

William picked up his sandwich. "So, what's your next move?"

"Well, first I'm going to drive down to Chattanooga and get my family. I think I deserve a couple of days off with pay. After all, I was shot in the line of duty." He pointed at the Band-Aid on his ear. "I doubt if Ruth will want to come back with us to Townsend right now, but I'll at least ask her. When I go back to work I'm going to talk with Brody. He and I need to get a few things straight. I'll wait a couple of weeks then I'll turn in my resignation. After that, who knows?"

Blue leaned forward. "Listen, Grant. I know that things seem pretty sour for you right now, but don't get down on yourself. Learn from your mistakes and then let them go. I think you're a hell of a lawman and it would be a great loss if you were to give up now."

"Thanks," said Grant. "It's tough to think about changing careers. Being part of the law was all I ever wanted. I remember when I was just a kid and Dalton would bring his patrol car home. He would always pin his badge on my shirt and let me sit in the front seat. I couldn't wait to grow up and be an officer. But, the thing is, now that I am one, I think about all the mistakes I've made, especially recently."

William grinned. "I knew you wouldn't let this slip by, but since you mentioned it. First of all, you should never have gone back to the Pender farm by yourself. You're lucky you got out of there alive. Secondly, you took time to travel up to Minnesota when all of that business could have been handled with a few phone calls. And, of course, you took a chance not shooting Russell when the opportunity presented itself. Other than that, I think you did a great job on this case. In my opinion, you're responsible for this whole mess finally coming to an end. For what it's worth, you have a job with me anytime you want it."

"Thanks, you don't know how much that means to me. I have a great deal of respect for you and I owe you a debt of gratitude for saving my ass up there on that ridge."

When lunch was over, Blue stood as he reached for Grant's hand. "I guess you best be getting down to Chattanooga. Your wife is probably anxious to see you."

Grant objected. "I've got to drop you off in Townsend first so you can pick up your car."

"That won't be necessary. A friend of ours is driving my wife over to the Hearth and Kettle and then she will drive my car up here to Knoxville. I have a cousin who lives here in town. We're going to spend two or three days visiting them. Besides that, I want to hang around and see what, if anything, they pull out of the river. Russell Pearl's body might just show up yet. You can drop me back at the hotel and then you can be on your way."

Grant no sooner dropped Blue off in the parking lot at the hotel, when Agents Gephart and Green approached. Looking in the Jeep, Gephart smiled. "Well, I think the news conference went about as well as we could expect. Of course, this is just step one. We've still got to find the body. How did you manage to get away so quickly? There were several news people who wanted to interview you. Your boss, Axel, as usual, made an ass of himself. If you get time, watch it on the news tonight. I know you're in a hurry to get home, but I want to ask you a question."

Being polite, Grant turned off the motor and stepped out as he leaned up against the side of the Jeep. "Is there something else you need to know?"

"Actually, it's not about the case," said Gephart. "You told me once that you were taking classes in criminal law. Did you ever finish?"

"No, I still have about six months of study left before I get my degree."

"Then let me ask you this. What do you plan to do now? Are you going to remain on the Townsend Police Force?"

"Probably not, but then again I might stay on until I finish up my schooling. Then, I guess I'll decide what direction I'm going to take."

Handing Grant his card, Gephart smiled, "When you get that degree I'd be interested in talking with you about considering a career with the FBI. You've got what it takes. It's been a pleasure working with you. Keep in touch."

Grant watched as the two men walked across the lot back to the hotel. *Damn*, he thought, *didn't turn out to be too bad of a day. I was offered two job positions in the last hour.*

Six days passed since Russell Pearl disappeared over the mountainside. Grant pulled into the lot of the Cherokee Police Department, hoping that Chief Blue had returned from Knoxville.

Entering the office, he was greeted by the receptionist. "Officer Denlinger. What a pleasant surprise. What can the Cherokee Police Department do for the man who tracked down the Smoky Mountain Killer?"

Grant smiled as he had grown accustomed over the past few days to all of the accolades that were coming his way. "Thank you, but I did have some help, namely your boss, Chief Blue. I hope he's back from Knoxville."

"Just got back yesterday. He's been catching up on paperwork. You just missed him. He left not ten minutes ago. Said he was going uptown to the general store for a sandwich and a root beer. If you hurry you might be able to catch him."

Grant looked at his watch. "Well, I guess it is just about lunchtime. Might just join him. Where is this general store?"

"Can't miss it. Sits on the main drag. Right next to the post office. Sort of a log cabin type building. There'll be five or six rockers on the front porch. More than likely he'll be sitting there. Goes there about twice a week."

It wasn't even five minutes before Grant parked in front of the general store. Just like the receptionist said, there were a number of old rocking chairs on the porch, the one nearest the door occupied by none other than Chief William Blue. Stepping up onto the porch, Grant sat in the chair next to Blue as he spoke, "Didn't mean to interrupt your lunch. Thought I'd just drop by and see how things wound up in Jellico."

Taking the last bite of a sandwich, Blue tossed the wrapping into a nearby cardboard box, then placed two quarters in a jar on the windowsill, reached down and took a root beer from a bucket of ice and tossed the bottle to Grant. "Here, have a drink on me."

Grant made himself comfortable in the rocker, unscrewed the top, and took a long swig. Looking at the strange label on the bottle he stated, "Never heard of this brand before."

"Homemade," said Blue as he took a drink. "Owner makes it down in his basement. Best I've ever had. What brings you across the mountain? Thought you were taking some time off."

"I am taking some time off. I've had the entire week off and tomorrow will be my first day back."

Placing the bottle on the floor next to his chair, Blue asked, "How'd everything go with your wife and mother-in-law?"

"My wife was quite upset that I got shot and even though I explained to her that it was just a minor flesh wound, she wasn't having any of it. She was worried about infection setting in and if I'll have a scar for life. You know how concerned women can be over those sort of things. Ruth decided to drive back with us to Townsend for a few days. Then, about halfway through the week, she up and says she'd like to come live with us permanently if it was okay. Dana Beth was ecstatic, to say the least."

Changing the subject, Grant asked, "How did things pan out up at the gorge?"

"I left after four full days of searching every inch of that river basin and the side of that mountain. Gephart said they would continue the search for another week and then if nothing turned up they'd throw in the towel. I'm still guessing that with that heavy coat Russell was wearing, he got sucked under the water and probably is under a rock somewhere."

Grant took another drink. "So, you don't think they'll ever locate the body?"

"There's always a chance, but at this point, I'd venture to say Russell is going to stay put in his watery grave or if it ever gets dislodged it may wash up somewhere downstream. Hell, if that's the case, it could be years from now that someone stumbles onto a pile of bones which would be all that's left of the body. I'm ninety-nine percent sure that Russell Pearl is dead."

Grant gave Blue a strange look. "Ninety-nine percent! Why not one hundred percent?"

"Because without a body, we can never say for sure. You know, Grant, Russell was a strong man. If anyone could figure out how to stay alive, it would be him. However, when next spring rolls around if we haven't had a murder like we've had the last two years then I'll concede the other one percent. The bottom line is that I'm okay with the way things turned out. How about you? Have you started to put all this behind you?"

"It's strange you should ask me that. That's the main reason I drove over to see you. I don't know if I'll ever be able to put this behind me. All my life, so far, I've been a God fearing man. I've always tried to do the right thing in whatever situation I was faced with in life. When I first became a police officer, my grandfather, told me that being a Christian and a police officer, at times, could make for some tough decisions and that there might come a time as an officer of the law that my faith would be tested. The last year and a half my faith has indeed been tested, and in a way I feel that I have failed the test. I kept the truth about Conrad from everyone in Townsend. Then, on top of that, what we did up there on that ridge, telling everyone that before we shot Russell he admitted to killing all those people. We framed Russell for the first four murders, and by doing that, Conrad will always be remembered as an upstanding citizen."

Blue finished off his root beer as he remarked, "Yeah, we did frame Russell. But what choice did we have? We knew that if Russell was captured and interrogated he would only admit to the murders of this year, leaving last year's murders still unsolved. We also knew that if he was killed we could blame him for all the murders. Your wife and mother-in-law will never be exposed to the fact that Conrad was just as bad as Russell."

"Conrad told me whatever decision I made that I was going to have to live with it. I'll probably take the fact that I withheld evidence with me to the grave and I'll have to answer for the life I've lived."

William smiled. "I think you're splitting hairs, Grant. Sure, you lied. We both have lied about certain things in regards to this case, but the means justified the ends. Let's face it, both of the brothers were killers. Does it really make any difference if one gets blamed. They're both dead. I think God is going to give you more slack than you think."

Looking at his watch, Blue stood and threw his empty bottle in the trash box. "I've got to get back to the office. It's gonna take me a few days to catch up." Walking to his cruiser, he turned and waved at Grant. "Don't forget about that job I offered you. Just think about it."

Grant waved good bye. Once in his Jeep he made the turn for Route 441 that would lead him back over the mountain into Tennessee and eventually to Townsend. His week off with pay had come to an end and tomorrow he would have to report back to work. He had a lot of time during the past week to think about his career and what he wanted to do. Rather than giving Chief Brody his resignation, he had decided to first finish up his six months of schooling via the internet. Then, when he finally had his degree in hand he'd end his relationship not only with the Townsend Police Department, but with Axel Brody as well.

He thought about what Chief Blue said about thinking about the job that he'd offered him, but he was leaning toward Gephart's offer of possibly working for the FBI. The pay was probably better and the opportunity for advancement far outweighed what he could accomplish working for William over in Cherokee.

Stopping at a red light at the Route 321 intersection in Townsend, Grant checked his gas. He was down to a quarter of a tank. Rather than turning right and heading for home, he made a left toward the Parkway Grocery where he'd fill up.

When the tank was full, he thought a cup of coffee sounded good. Filling the insulated cup with the dark steaming brew, Grant watched as Luke Pardee walked in the front door and joined Zeb

Gilling and Buddie Knapp at their regular table by the front window. Glancing up at the large clock behind the sales counter, Grant noticed the time at 1:15 in the afternoon. Far too late for the old cronies to still be hanging around the Parkway. They normally showed up around six in the morning and were finished with their daily gossip by eleven. They were never sitting at their table this time of the day. Paying for his coffee, Grant didn't give it another thought. *What else did the old fellas have to do but sit around and talk?*

"Wasn't that Grant Denlinger over there by the coffee when you came in?" asked Buddie.

Luke pulled out a chair and sat. "Don't know, really wasn't paying all that much attention."

Zeb took a drink of coffee as he looked across the table at his friend. "Me and Buddie missed you this morning."

"Yeah," said Buddie. "You've been avoiding us like the plague. You haven't joined us for coffee for days now. When Zeb called me and told me you wanted to meet us here this afternoon I thought it was kind of strange. What's up?"

Zeb folded the newspaper that was laying in front of him in half. "What could be so important that it couldn't be discussed in the morning?"

Luke pointed to the newspaper, then looked over his shoulder as if everyone in the building were listening. "That's what's so important! All the news coverage of the killing of Russell Pearl... the Smoky Mountain Killer. Did you read all the gory details? Despite what the paper says, we know the real truth, now *don't we?* Russell Pearl, my ass! That was Russell Pender who they shot up there on that ridge. Do either of you feel better knowing that he was not right in the head...that he was some sort of a nut case? It doesn't change anything for me," Luke growled. "Forty some years of wondering what happened to those two boys and here all along one was living right here under our nose in Townsend, the other, just a stone's throw away."

"Keep your voice down!" ordered Zeb. "That's over and done with. That was over four decades ago and there's nothing we can do about what happened back then."

"I agree," said Buddie. "Both of those boys are dead now. We don't have anything to worry about."

Luke glared at Buddie. "Yeah, you're right...those two boys are dead and so are nine other people and whether you want to admit it or not the three of us are responsible for their deaths. He sneered at Zeb as he continued, "We got our friend, Charley killed...and he wasn't even with us that day in case you forgot."

Zeb leaned forward, his hands forming into fists. "What the hell are you talking about? We're not responsible for the people Russell killed. We didn't kill them...he did!"

"We might just as well have killed them," snapped Luke. "It's our fault that Russell went all nuts after what happened that day up in the Iron Mountains. How'd you feel if you saw your parents shot down in front of your eyes and then watched as all of your animals were killed?" Sitting back in his chair, Luke raised his hands. "He must have had a hell of a life!"

Buddie, trying to calm Luke down, reached out and touched his arm. "Take it easy Luke. Hell, we all know that it was all Asa's fault. He's the one who brought the hard liquor along and got us all drunk."

Pushing Buddie's hand away, Luke emphasized, "I don't remember him pouring it down our throats. We're all responsible for what happened."

"Buddie's right," said Zeb. "It was Asa who first shot at the bus. As I recall, it was also Asa who shot old man Pender first."

Luke rubbed his hand across his forehead. "God, I get sick just thinking about what we did."

Buddie tapped the top of the table with his finger. "Well, then don't think about it! There is nothing any of us can do to change what happened forty years ago."

Luke, getting more upset, ran his fingers through his grey hair. "We should have gone to the police that day. We should have turned ourselves in. That would have made it right. It was self defense. Pender fired on us first. He shot you, Zeb, in the arm and he got me in the leg. We could have proved self defense. Sure, we might have received a fine for shooting all those animals, but we would have gotten off."

"What's the matter with you?" asked Zeb as he looked around to make sure no one had noticed their conversation. "We did get off! No one knows that we were even up there that day. You think they would have just given us a slap on the hand when they saw Pender's wife and all those animals dead. I don't think so. Those two boys, sure they saw us, but they could never identify us. Now, you just better calm down, Luke, and stop talking crazy. If we would have turned ourselves in, hell we still might be in jail or have died staring out at the rest of the world from behind bars. We made a pact that day...remember? We said we'd never tell anyone what happened that day and after forty years we've stuck to what we promised each other."

"But, that was before all those people got killed," argued Luke. "I can't live with myself anymore. That day in the Iron Mountains ruined my life. I've never had a decent relationship with a woman. All I have to keep me company is a cat. Sometimes, when I look at my cat I start thinking about all those dead animals we left laying up there. It makes me sick to my stomach. All these past years I've been constantly afraid that I'd break down and tell someone so I remained a loner. You two, Asa and Charley were the only friends I've really had over the last forty years."

Buddie leaned back in his chair, as he stared at Luke in amazement.

"Don't give me that look, Buddie," said Luke. "You and Zeb are just as guilty as me. I've made a decision. I'm going to turn myself in. I'm going to go see Brody and tell him the whole sordid story. I already went to see him once, but I backed out. I never said anything to you fellas, but I only fired at the bus. I never shot at the Penders or any of those animals. I'll be damned if I'm going to suffer any longer for what the rest of you did."

Zeb was livid. "Luke...you can't do that! Giving yourself up means that me and Buddie will be picked up and questioned. We'll all go to jail and it doesn't make any difference that we're a bunch of old men. There is no statute of limitations on murder. Dammit, Luke! I've got a family. I've got a wife, and three sons that are married who live here in town. I've got seven grandkids. I'm a deacon in the church. I've been an upstanding citizen in this community for decades. We've gone this long without saying anything. Just let it be."

Buddie rubbed his hands across his face. "Zeb's right, Luke. You can't turn yourself in. You'll ruin not only what's left of your life, but ours as well. I've lived here in Townsend all my life. I'm well liked. I've got my fruit business, my employees to think about...my family. What will happen to them?"

Luke shook his head in disgust. "You self-righteous bastards! It's like you don't even remember what we did that day forty years ago. It's like you've cut it out of your minds and just continued with your lives as if nothing were wrong. Well, I haven't forgotten that day. I think about it every day and it still makes me crazy. My mind is made up. I'm going to go home and think about how I'm going to explain all this to Brody. Tomorrow morning I'm going to go see him."

Before Zeb or Buddie could react, Luke got up from the table and stormed out the door, climbed in his truck and sped out of the lot.

Buddie stood and looked out the window as Luke's truck disappeared up the Parkway. Turning back to Zeb he returned to his chair and slumped forward as he buried his face in his hands. "Dear God...what are we going to do, Zeb?"

"Take it easy," Zeb said. "Do you really think he's gonna turn himself in? Do you really think he'd do that to us? We've known ol' Luke since we was little kids. That's over sixty years. He's just blowing smoke. By tomorrow, he'll feel different. Why hell, he might be having a good laugh at our expense right now. He had me going for a couple of minutes there, but I don't think we have anything to worry about. Look, if it'll make you feel any better I'll stop by his place later tonight and see if he feels the same way. Maybe I can talk some sense into him. Come on, let's get out of here."

At six-o'clock the next morning, Grant rolled over in bed and stared into the face of his sleeping wife. He wanted to reach over and kiss her, but was afraid he would wake her. Getting out of bed, he checked on Crystal Ann, who was curled up in the corner of her crib, her blankets kicked off sometime during the night.

Covering his daughter, he then walked across the carpeted floor to the bathroom. From behind him he heard Dana Beth's voice, "I expect you back in this house by four this afternoon. My mother is making some of her famous pork chops tonight for dinner."

Grant looked out the bathroom door and smiled, displaying a mouthful of toothpaste. "You betcha!"

After dressing, he tiptoed back across the room and looked down at his sleeping daughter once again. He was amazed at how much she had changed in just the past few weeks. Giving his wife a peck on the cheek, he went downstairs, made coffee and went out to his Jeep, prepared to make the familiar trip into Townsend. He dreaded the upcoming conversation with Chief Brody. He wondered how he would accept the fact that he was only going to be with the department for maybe another six months, then it was either off to the FBI or over the mountain to Cherokee to work for William Blue. On the way in he passed Kenny Jacks who was still on patrol. Grant flashed his lights and gave him a wave.

In the next minute, he was in the thick of the early morning tourist traffic, but for some reason it didn't bother him. Besides that, he wasn't in any hurry to confront Axel. Pulling into the police department lot, he dumped the rest of his tepid coffee on the grass and headed for the office.

As he opened the door, he heard Brody's booming voice fill the building. "Son of a bitch! Got dammit all to hell! I can't believe this crap! That's it...I'm done! Come November election, I'm not gonna run. I'm gonna quit. Somebody else can have this crummy job!"

The onslaught of profanity caused Grant to hesitate just inside the door.

Grant looked at Brody who was standing across the desk from Marge who at the moment wore a look of disbelief. Axel's face was beet red, his hands clenched in tight fists.

Grant stared at Marge for a moment then asked, "What in the hell is going on now?"

Axel answered the question before Marge could respond. "You want to know what's goin' on? I'll tell you what's goin' on! I just got a call from Harlan Worley. He's out on his mail route and he walks up to Luke Pardee's place. While he's puttin' mail in the slot, Luke's cat is meowin' and scratchin' at the front door. Harlan, knowin' the cat is never supposed to be outdoors, knocks on the door and calls out to Luke...but, no answer. So Harlan tries the door and it opens. So, he lets the cat in and what does he discover? Luke, layin' face down in a pool of blood in the front hallway, with the back of his head practically blown off."

Brody grabbed his hat from the coat rack in the corner and headed for the door. "Come on, Wonder Boy. We've got another murder to investigate. Peaceful side of the Smokies...my ass!"

"Not so fast, Axel." said Marge. "We just got another call. The assistant manager from over at the IGA just called and said that Ambrose Stroud and his brood of kids are over there stealing everything in sight. When the manager approached Ambrose and politely asked them to leave the premises, Ambrose told the manager to go to hell and shoved him into a wall. One of the stock boys jumped in to help the manager and wound up being punched in the mouth. Now, Ambrose is knocking over displays left and right, demanding that he should get his groceries for free. You need to get over there. You know how the Strouds are. Nothing but trouble!"

Axel hit his hat on the side of his leg. "If the Strouds want trouble, I'll give them trouble, but not today. Send Kenny. Looks like we've got another murder on our hands."

About the Authors

Originally from St. Louis, Marlene makes her home in Louisville, Kentucky. A wife, mother, grandmother and great grandmother. Marlene has a wide range of interests including watercolor and oil painting, yet writing has always been her passion. That comes through loud and clear in her wonderful novels!

These novels reflect a genuine sincerity with very strong characters to which her readers can relate. To quote Marlene: "It took me a long time to start writing, but now I can't stop. The stories just keep on coming."

Gary Yeagle was born and raised in Williamsport, PA, the birthplace of Little League Baseball. He grew up living just down the street from the site of the very first Little League game, played in 1939. He currently resides in St. Louis, Missouri, with his wife and four cats. He is the proud grandparent of three and is an active member of the New Hope United Methodist Church.

Gary is a Civil War buff, and enjoys swimming, spending time at the beach, model railroading, reading, and writing.

Excerpt from Shadows of Death:

Stepping close to the car he peered in the rear window. What he saw not only took him completely by surprise but caused him to back away from the window in amazement. Moving back to the window, he looked inside again hoping that what he had previously seen was nothing more than his imagination. It wasn't his imagination, it was real! *A baby wrapped in an old blanket laying on the backseat.* Checking the front and backseats there was no one else in the car. Next, he checked the parking lot to see if anyone was close by—no one!

Looking back in the window it appeared the baby was sleeping. Then, he had a horrible thought. *What if the baby is dead!* He had heard the news on numerous occasions where people had left a child in a car while they were shopping and the child had died from lack of air or heat exhaustion. Thank God it wasn't that hot out. He tried the door but it was locked. The front passenger door was missing its handle so he couldn't open that door either. He tried both doors on the opposite side. Same thing—locked! Looking around the parking lot once again he wasn't quite sure what he should do. This was one of those things you heard about, but never experienced. But, *this was real!* It was actually happening right before his eyes. He had to do something—but what?

Running around to the side the baby was on, he tried to calm himself as he thought, *Calm down...use your head...do the right thing...call the police. No! That might be too late. Check and see if the baby is alive first, then call the police.* He shoved the car, but the baby remained perfectly still. Shoving the car more violently he spoke to himself, "Please let the baby be alive."

Also from BlackWyrm...

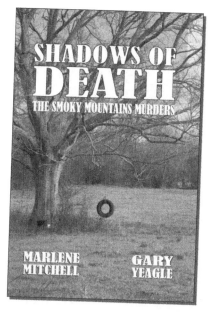

SHADOWS OF DEATH
THE SMOKY MOUNTAINS MURDERS
by Marlene Mitchell, Gary Yeagle

After nearly two years and ten murders, the people of Townsend, Tennessee are still plagued by unanswered questions and hidden secrets. Who killed Luke Pardee? What happened to Russell Pearl's body? Where is Ruby Jean Stroud? Why is Dana Beth so unnerved? When will peace return to Blount County?
[Murder Mystery, ages 14+]

IRON FIST VELVET GLOVE
by Gary Yeagle

Two young Irish boys, one Catholic, one Protestant, both fourteen years of age meet and form a friendship; a bond they agree will never separate them. Little do they realize how their friendship will be tested as they become involved in the seething activities of the terrorists on both sides of the ongoing conflict.
[Political Thriller, ages 14+]

PAST LIVES

by Christopher Kokoski

Secrets, Mystery, Destiny

Plunged into the center of a high-profile murder investigation, Eric Shooter discovers under hypnosis that he is a reincarnated serial killer. The only way to clear his name is to track down the most elusive and cunning predator in history, a methodical assassin with whom he shares a shocking connection.

[Paranormal Mystery, ages 14+]

CIRCLE OF PREY

by Marlene Mitchell

Ambition. Wealth. Greed. Power. Truths turning to lies, father against son, friends becoming enemies, predator turning into prey and the circle continues.

Pitting man against the largest and one of the smartest animals on the planet makes for an interesting turn of events as you follow the journey of Jakuta, a bull elephant who is the ultimate prey.

[Modern Thriller, ages 14+]

CPSIA information can be obtained at www.ICGtesting.com
Printed in the USA
LVOW05s0304071114

411804LV00003BB/4/P